PRAISE FO

"*The Professor* is that rare combination of thrills, chills, and heart. Gripping from the first page to the last."

—Winston Groom, author of *Forrest Gump*

"Legal thrillers shouldn't be this much fun and a new writer shouldn't be this good at crafting a great twisty story. If you enjoy Grisham as much as I do, you're going to love Bob Bailey."

—Brian Haig, author of *The Night Crew* and the Sean Drummond series

"Robert Bailey is a thriller writer to reckon with. His debut novel has a tight and twisty plot, vivid characters, and a pleasantly down-home sensibility that will remind some readers of adventures in Grisham-land. Luckily, Robert Bailey is an original, and his skill as a writer makes the Alabama setting all his own. *The Professor* marks the beginning of a very promising career."

—Mark Childress, author of *Georgia Bottoms* and *Crazy in Alabama*

"Taut, page turning, and smart, *The Professor* is a legal thriller that will keep readers up late as the twists and turns keep coming. Set in Alabama, it also includes that state's greatest icon, one Coach Bear Bryant. In fact, the Bear gets things going with the energy of an Alabama kickoff to Auburn. Robert Bailey knows his state and he knows his law. He also knows how to write characters that are real, sympathetic, and surprising. If he keeps writing novels this good, he's got quite a literary career before him."

—Homer Hickam, author of *Rocket Boys/October Sky*, a *New York Times* number-one bestseller

"Robert Bailey is a Southern writer in the great Southern tradition, with a vivid sense of his environment, and characters that pop and crackle on the page. This book kept me hooked all the way through."

—William Bernhardt, author of the Ben Kincaid series

"Bailey's solid second McMurtrie and Drake legal thriller (after 2014's *The Professor*) . . . provides enough twists and surprises to keep readers turning the pages."

—*Publishers Weekly*

"A gripping legal suspense thriller of the first order, *Between Black and White* clearly displays author Robert Bailey's impressive talents as a novelist. An absorbing and riveting read from beginning to end."

—*Midwest Book Reviews*

"Take a murder, a damaged woman, and a desperate daughter and you have the recipe for *The Last Trial*, a complex and fast-paced legal thriller. Highly recommended."

—DP Lyle, award-winning author

THE FINAL RECKONING

ALSO BY ROBERT BAILEY

McMurtrie and Drake Legal Thrillers

The Last Trial

Between Black and White

The Professor

THE FINAL RECKONING

ROBERT BAILEY

This is a work of fiction. Names, characters, organizations, places, events, and incidents are either products of the author's imagination or are used fictitiously. Any resemblance to actual persons, living or dead, or actual events is purely coincidental.

Published by Thomas & Mercer, Seattle

www.apub.com

ISBN-13: 9781503902268
ISBN-10: 1503902269

Cover design by Brian Zimmerman

Printed in the United States of America

In loving memory of my father, Randall Robert
"Randy" Bailey

We can do this.

—Randy Bailey

PROLOGUE

Riverbend Maximum Security Institution Nashville, Tennessee, May 15, 2012

"Come here."

The killer's icy voice caused the hairs on Tom's neck to stand up. The interview was over and Corporal Jacquetta Stone, who had escorted Tom and Helen to death row, had been in the process of unlocking the door to the cell so that they could leave. Tom glanced at Helen, and the prosecutor's pale face gave away nothing. Then, as if subconsciously agreeing to proceed at the same time, they both turned and started to approach the metal desk where the killer sat. His hands were chained to a bar running down the middle of the table, and his feet were shackled. But even when he was restrained, James Robert "JimBone" Wheeler's flat eyes, ruddy complexion, and cold voice gave off the vibe of a dangerous animal.

"Just you, McMurtrie," JimBone said, lowering his sights. "The other two can stand by the door."

Helen shook her head. *"Let's go,"* she whispered, but Tom held out his hands and made eye contact with both Helen and the corporal.

"It's fine," he whispered. "I want to hear what he has to say."

Tom took two steps toward the table and returned to his seat, while Helen and Stone waited by the door. "OK," Tom said.

JimBone leaned forward and rested his chin on his shackled hands. Then he raised his eyes and spoke just above a whisper. "Do you know what the word 'reckoning' means, McMurtrie?"

Tom felt the gooseflesh that had sprung up on his neck spread down his arms. "Revenge," Tom said. "Another word for revenge."

"It's more than that," JimBone said. "It's a balancing of the scales. A making of things right. A day . . . *of reckoning*."

"So what?" Tom asked, beginning to tire of the games.

"Your day is coming, old man." He paused. "And if you mess with Bully Calhoun, it may come sooner rather than later. I hope that isn't the case."

"Why?"

"Because when I get out of here I intend to give you your day." He paused and his voice became so low that Tom strained to hear it. "I'm going to kill you, McMurtrie, and everyone you hold dear. Your son the doctor and his wife. That grandson of yours and his baby sister. Your whole family." He paused again. "I'm also going to kill your partner, Drake, and his family. Your friend Haynes and his wife and kids. Conrad and that crazy detective. I'm going to bring a day of reckoning on you and everyone you hold dear, McMurtrie."

Tom's skin went cold as visions of this psychopath attacking his grandchildren, Jackson and Jenny, flooded his brain. He swallowed, and when he spoke, he was surprised that the words came out calm and deliberate, reminding Tom of the way he had once advised his son to hold steady before bringing the head of a shovel down on a snake that had gotten into the garage. "Let me remind you that you are on death row, Mr. Wheeler. You're going to be put to death by lethal injection." Tom hesitated before adding, "Your threats mean nothing."

"Really?" JimBone asked. "How is your partner's daddy doing?"

Tom leaned forward, sure he had heard him wrong. "*What?*"

"How is Billy Drake doing these days? I seem to recall hearing something about him having an accident." JimBone smiled.

Tom felt light-headed. "How could you—?"

"Who have we spent most of this meeting talking about?"

"Bully . . . Calhoun?" Tom asked, his voice distant, his body numb with fear.

JimBone squinted at Tom with eyes that danced with delight. Then he slowly nodded. "After I left Bully's employ, he eventually found need for a person with . . . similar talents. I knew someone that would fit the bill very nicely." JimBone paused and patted the desk with his fingertips. "Let's just say that my replacement was grateful for the job, and over the years we've helped each other out from time to time."

Tom leaned over the desk and forced his voice to be calm. "Are you saying that Bully Calhoun has a hit man who killed Billy Drake as a favor to you?"

JimBone grinned. "You must be hearing things, old man."

"I hear just fine," Tom said, his legs wobbly. "Why Rick's father? Why not me or Bo or even Rick himself?"

"I'm saving the rest of you for me," JimBone said, his voice just above a whisper. "But while I'm stuck in here, I thought I'd have a little bite. An appetizer before the main course."

Tom glared down at the psychopath, anger finally replacing shock. "You're a crazy son of a bitch. When I do investigate Bully Calhoun, I'm going to tell him that *you* led me to him. That his old employee James Robert Wheeler is the one who flashed the light on him." Tom paused. "How'd that be?"

The grin widened on JimBone's face. "Bully is too smart to ever mess with me. I'm that stray dog you're not quite sure of. That dog that never barks. That you see sneaking around your back porch at night and in the morning. After a while, your own dog turns up pregnant or dead, depending on whether I want to fuck or kill it, and your garden don't have any food left." He paused. "I'm a dog that only bites, Professor. A man like Bully Calhoun knows to leave me well enough alone."

Tom stood to leave. When he looked at Helen, her eyes were wide with worry, but Corporal Stone's face was bored. Just another day on death row.

When Tom reached the door, JimBone spoke in a clear, brittle voice from behind him. "Remember what I said, old man. Your day of reckoning is coming."

Tom didn't look back at him, but as the corporal opened the locked door, the killer's words, an octave higher and with more menace, rang out above the jangle of keys.

"Courtesy of the Bone."

PART ONE

1

There's a stink that a prison gives off. A stale smell, like the body odor of someone who has failed to bathe for a few days but who hasn't been active enough to work up any kind of sweat. It permeates the cinder-block walls and concrete floors and seeps into the skin of everyone present. The inmates, the guards, the warden, the medical personnel. Even the spouses in for their monthly conjugal.

Like the ever-present smell of excrement in a nursing home even after the facility's been doused with disinfectant, the stale aroma of a prison just won't go away.

On the morning of December 4, 2013, JimBone Wheeler lay in the fetal position on the floor of his cell, trying to inhale the stale fumes coming off the concrete and not the vomit that had just spewed from his mouth. But after a few seconds had passed, he forced his index finger back down his throat, and another wave of nausea hit him. He projectile puked across the five-foot-by-seven-foot enclosure, clipping the edge of the small metal footboard of his cot. Then he wailed, "Help!"

After a minute had passed and there was no sign of a guard, JimBone again plunged his finger deep into his throat, and the gag reflex this time produced five to ten seconds of dry heaving. Breathing deep and spitting, JimBone again called out. "Someone please help me. I . . . I can't breathe!" He closed his eyes and forced his mind to work. Had he miscalculated? He didn't have a timepiece. Watches weren't allowed in the cells, and there was no clock on the wall. He was doing everything by feel and instinct.

No, he thought. *I'm right on time.* It had been eight hours since lights out. He could feel the accuracy of his assessment in the same way he could always sense the presence of enemy forces during reconnaissance missions as an Army Ranger.

When he heard the jangle of keys, mixed in with the sliding of soft-soled shoes on concrete, he had to remind himself not to smile.

"Wheeler, you OK?" A gruff voice from outside the cell.

"No." He croaked the word out and then coughed. Raising his head, with his arms and legs still sprawled on the concrete, JimBone looked into the dull eyes of the night shift supervisor. The name on the officer's uniform lapel read "Davies."

"I . . . can't . . . breathe." JimBone spoke the words through clenched teeth. Then he doubled over and gripped his stomach with both arms. He gagged again and spat before wheezing up at the officer, "Please . . . help me."

The guard blinked, and JimBone saw him lower his gaze to the cell, no doubt seeing and then smelling the vomit that covered the floor. He unclipped a device from his belt and spoke into it. "This is Sergeant Davies. Got a medical emergency in cell five on the row. Request assistance ASAP." He paused before adding, "Has Charlotte arrived?"

There were a few seconds of muffled silence and then JimBone heard another voice come through the device. "I'm here, and I'm on my way, Glenn."

"Ten-four." He returned the speaking device to his belt clip and fumbled through his key chain for the one he wanted before placing it in the lock. "Just hold tight now, boy," he said, opening the door. "The nurse is on her way."

JimBone Wheeler nodded and turned his head to the far wall. He coughed and, knowing that Officer Glenn Davies couldn't see him, allowed himself a tiny smile.

Right on time . . .

2

Charlotte Thompson's heart pounded in her chest as she gathered the supplies she would need.

Oxygen saturation kit. Check.

Blood pressure cuff. Check.

Thermometer. Check.

She closed her eyes and sucked in a deep breath. She needed a smoke, but it would have to wait. Instead, she snatched a piece of gum from a pack of Extra sugar-free that lay on her desk and flung it in her mouth, chewing furiously and trying to calm her mind. One step at a time, and this next one was the biggest and most important. She had to be convincing, and to do that, all she had to do was be herself.

As the sweet, minty taste of the gum filled her mouth, she slung her supply bag over her shoulder and strode to the door of the medical unit. She grabbed the knob and looked back at the tiny office where she had slaved for the past twenty-seven years.

When she'd first taken the job, she hadn't planned on making a career out of correctional nursing. No, like so many long-term gigs that end up consuming a person's life, her position as the medical team administrator of the Riverbend Maximum Security Institution had started as a short-term, six-month interim contract. The prison had wanted someone with more institutional experience. Not some greenhorn who had worked four months in the emergency room and another eight for a pediatrician. But beggars can't be choosers, and prisons were at the bottom of the health-care food chain. The "interim" tag was taken off after Charlotte had finished her second six-month term. The year had been 1986. Ronald Reagan was president, and America was grieving the deaths of the astronauts who had blown up in the *Challenger* space shuttle.

Twenty-seven years, Charlotte thought, sucking in another breath. She let her eyes drop to the metal desk that she had utilized for her entire career. She had worked hard. Been the loyal employee. For almost three decades, she'd had a steady revolving door of staff nurses who worked under her and who, inevitably, would leave when something better came along or when they realized that providing nursing care to murderers, rapists, and other hardened criminals was not for everyone.

But Charlotte had stayed. She was now the longest-tenured employee of the prison, which, if she were honest with herself, was probably why Wheeler had sought her out.

He wasn't the first.

Seven years earlier, an inmate named Samuel Helstowski asked if she would assist him in breaking out of the prison. Helstowski had been a small Jewish man with an abnormally large penis. He'd gotten a wart on one of his testicles and, while Charlotte applied Silvadene to the affected area, the inmate, who was serving fifteen years for possession of child pornography and soliciting a minor, became fully erect. As she discussed the daily travails of prison life with Samuel—what fried meat would be the dinner meal, whether he'd been able to acquire any cigarettes, the heat in the group pod—Charlotte had felt an undeniable and irresistible impulse to act. To break the rules and shatter her mundane existence. It had been decades since she'd done anything that contained even the slightest hint of risk, much less danger.

With as much subtlety as she could manage, she had moved her hand from his balls to his cock, slowly stroking it at first and then increasing her pace until Samuel Helstowski shot a wad across the concrete floor of the unit.

"I think you're good to go now, Sammy," she had said. "But be sure to come see me for a follow-up these next few weeks."

He had and, after several similar encounters, had suggested that all he would need to break out would be to get to the hospital. Could she manufacture a reason for him to be sent out in an ambulance?

Charlotte had never seriously considered the proposition. Samuel was soft and stupid. He talked a big game, but, once out, he would be caught and everything would track back to her. She couldn't take that kind of risk without better odds.

And, most importantly, without something in it for her. Something *big*.

Charlotte's gaze caught on the framed photograph next to her computer. She'd put it up about a year and a half into her employment. In the picture, she held a baby girl in her arms. She was sitting in one of the wooden rocking chairs on the porch at Cracker Barrel. Behind her and the child was a man with swept-back blond hair, green eyes, and a crooked smile. He was leaning over Charlotte's chair, with his hand draped over her shoulder. His fingers touched the baby's head. The year had been 1988, and she was married to Aubrey Michael Thompson. Their daughter's name was Gillian, whom they both had called "Gilly" since she had come out of the womb. Aubrey was a professor of music at Belmont College. He was also a songwriter, and Charlotte knew that eventually he'd break into the country music scene. Her husband had talent and, more than that, he was driven. He was going to make it. He would have made it.

Only he didn't. On Sunday morning, January 24, 1989, Aubrey had taken one-year-old Gilly to church while Charlotte stayed behind with a stomach bug. A few weeks later, she would learn that it wasn't a virus but rather morning sickness. She was pregnant, her second child due in September.

But by the time her ob-gyn informed her of this news, she had already tended to her husband's and first child's funerals.

Charlotte hadn't wanted them to go that morning, but Aubrey was the pianist for the eleven o'clock service and it was bad form for him to back out so late. Gilly adored her father and wouldn't stop crying until Charlotte relented and let her go with him. She played in the church nursery while her father handled his duties. On the way home, Aubrey had stopped at the grocery store and picked up some chicken noodle soup and Sprite for Charlotte. A block after exiting the store, their car was T-boned by a drunk driver. Gilly had died on the scene after her unrestrained body—Aubrey always forgot to buckle her—had been propelled into the glass windshield. She broke her neck instantly.

Aubrey had clung to life for two days. He was paralyzed from the waist down. During Charlotte's visits to the ICU, he kept asking if Gilly was OK. Finally, toward the end of the second day, she had told him.

He died the following morning of a blood clot.

The fetus that Charlotte was carrying in her womb joined his or her—Charlotte never learned the sex—sister and father a few months later. Dr. Rushing said that she had lost the baby due to the stress of burying her husband and daughter.

Charlotte Thompson didn't know whether that was true or not. She had begun to believe that some folks in this world were just blessed with good fortune and others, like her, were cursed with bad.

Her body might die today, but her soul had expired on January 24, 1989. She had been a mother and a young nurse. She had been thin and attractive. On the night of January 23, 1989, she and Aubrey had made love on the kitchen table of their apartment—they had eaten takeout Chinese, and after she put Gilly down for bed, Charlotte had returned to the dining room completely naked. She removed Aubrey's dirty plate and sat her bare buttocks on the cool glass surface, informing him that she was dessert. When they were through, they lay on the couch and watched *Cheers* reruns, both of their sweaty bodies naked underneath a black-and-gold Vanderbilt Commodores blanket. The room smelled liked Kung Pao chicken, cheap beer, and sex. They were happy. They were so *fucking* happy.

The plan had been for Charlotte to finish out the decade working for the prison and then get a job at Vanderbilt Hospital. She and Aubrey could have driven to work together. Eventually, after he published his first songs, she would have quit working and been a stay-at-home mom. They had it all mapped out.

Then the twenty-two-year-old driver of a Ford Mustang, who had been drinking in Nashville's Broadway District since the wee hours of the morning and had continued to imbibe once he got back to his fraternity house, failed to see a stop sign at one in the afternoon on a perfect sunny day. The Mustang hit her husband's station wagon going ninety-two miles per hour.

The driver never even hit the brakes.

His name was Jeffrey Gullan. He was charged with vehicular homicide but pled guilty to manslaughter on the eve of his trial. He served eighteen months before being paroled. He got out of prison in October 1990. By the summer of 1994, when Al Cowlings was driving O. J. Simpson all around Los Angeles in the back of a white Bronco, Gullan had graduated law school from the University of Tennessee, in Knoxville.

In one of life's cruelest ironies, the murdering son of a bitch had become an attorney. A criminal defense lawyer, no less.

Meanwhile, Charlotte Thompson had stayed at the prison. She had gained fifteen pounds in the first twelve months after her husband's and daughter's deaths and had never lost the weight. Because everyone else at the institution smoked, she did too. First, a pack a day. Then two. Now she was up to three. When you've buried the only things you care about in the world six feet underground, the risk of lung cancer, or anything else, becomes pretty minute in the grand scheme.

Lost hope is a terrible thing. A cancer in its own right. A sickness that eats at a person. At the Riverbend Maximum Security Institution, lost hope was served with mashed potatoes and gravy in the chow line. And truth be known, there wasn't a whole lot of difference between the employees and the inmates. Nobody tells their third-grade teacher that they want to grow up and be a prison nurse or a security guard on death row. No, that sort of occupation just kind of happens to a person. *Like shit,* Charlotte thought.

I didn't mean to end up here. I was supposed to be an empty nester by now, and the kids would have been in college. Aubrey would have taken me to the Ryman every couple of weeks to see a new artist playing one of his songs. That was supposed to be my life.

But it hadn't been. Instead, after walking around in a numb sort of daze for two decades, being the good employee and slowly building the trust of every law enforcement officer at the facility as the toughest, most reliable worker at the prison, Charlotte Thompson had gone rogue. Like the chemistry professor in *Breaking Bad*, but without the redeeming qualities of trying to provide for her family.

Charlotte had no family left. When she had seen Samuel Helstowski's cock rise to full attention while she applied ointment to his stank testicles, something inside her broke. She had grabbed hold of his penis like it had been some kind of gateway to another life. A better life? *No.*

A more interesting existence than the soul-crushing experience of her day-to-day? Charlotte nodded as she allowed her eyes one last sweep around the medical unit that had become her own personal prison these last twenty-seven years.

Unlike Samuel Helstowski, James Robert Wheeler had offered her a return for the investment she was about to make. And "big" wasn't a strong enough adjective to describe the nugget that the convict had dangled in front of her.

"Priceless" was probably the more apt term.

And he's already delivered.

Sucking in a deep breath, Charlotte Thompson forced her legs to move down the hall toward the corridor that would take her to death row.

3

By the time Charlotte arrived at the cell, JimBone was dry heaving again.

"Anything I can get you, Ms. Charlotte?" Sergeant Davies asked, his voice deferential, the relief in his tone palpable. There were two other officers hovering over JimBone's contorted body, and Charlotte shooed them off with a wave of her hand.

"Space, boys. Give an old woman some space." Then she turned to Davies, the oldest and more experienced of the three men. "I need a cup of water and a warm washcloth. Can you grab that for me, hon?"

But Davies didn't budge, sending a piercing glare at one of the younger guards. "You heard the lady, Benny. Warm washcloth and some water. Hop to it."

"Yes, sir," the guard responded.

Charlotte knelt over JimBone's body and barked her first question. "Mr. Wheeler, what's going on?"

With his face wrinkled in agony, the inmate peered up at her with bloodshot eyes. His face was even paler than the white cinder-block walls that adorned the cell. The effect was vampire-like. *Perfect,* Charlotte thought, setting her bag on the floor and unzipping it. First, she took out the portable oxygen saturation kit and placed the tubing along Wheeler's index finger. Knowing this was the most important part, she turned and scowled up at Davies. "Where's that washcloth, Glenn? Goddamnit, this man is in bad shape."

The officer raised his eyebrows, but Charlotte didn't see anger in his pupils. Fear was the only emotion that she felt in the room. James Robert "JimBone" Wheeler was supposed to be lethally injected in three weeks. His sentencing for murdering a Pulaski attorney named Raymond Pickalew on the Giles County Courthouse Square had garnered national attention, and his execution was expected to also attract the media. Nobody wanted to screw it up by letting the killer die before he rode the needle.

What a country, Charlotte had thought to herself more than once as she and Wheeler had concocted a plan. An inmate on death row who was sentenced to die was still entitled to health care under the Constitution and laws of the United States.

Sergeant Davies took a step back and gazed down the hallway before grabbing the other deputy by the forearm. "Go see what the hell is taking Benny so long."

While the men were distracted, Charlotte took the reading off the oxygen saturation machine. The digits on the screen read 94. Low but not an emergency.

"Oh God," she said.

"What?" Davies yelled from behind her.

"Oxygen sat is 88. We're gonna have to get him to the ER." She put the kit back in her bag, placed the thermometer in the inmate's mouth, and ran it over his cheek. This time she didn't have to lie. "Temp is 101. Glenn, did those two guards take a vacation, or are they going to bring me a washcloth and some water?"

As Charlotte slid the blood pressure cuff up JimBone's arm and tightened it until the inmate yelped, Davies tramped down the hallway, snapping into his receiver. "Benny! Taggert! What the hell is taking so long?"

Charlotte pumped the cuff twice and checked the gauge. His blood pressure was 130 over 85, which was just above normal. Glancing behind her, she saw Davies shaking his head in the hall. Blinking, she sucked in a breath through clenched teeth. "60 over 40, Glenn!" she yelled, stepping back and looking at the supervisor. "He'll be dead in twenty minutes unless we get him out."

"Jesus H. Christ," Davies said, fumbling in his pocket until he had retrieved his phone. But Charlotte had beaten him to it, gripping her cell phone in her right hand. "You take care of the paperwork on our end. I'll get the ambulance." She dialed the number and yelled into the microphone when the call was answered, "Got an inmate whose pressure has bottomed out, and his sat is 88. Need assistance immediately." She nodded and clicked off her phone. When she spoke to Davies again, her voice was calm and cool. "Let's get him on a gurney and have him waiting in the sally port when the EMTs arrive."

"Are you sure we should move him?" Davies asked, his voice high and panicky.

"Do you want him to live, or do you want to be on the front page of the *Tennessean* tomorrow explaining how we let him die?"

Before he could respond, the two deputies finally arrived with the washcloth and water. Charlotte grabbed the items from them and turned to the one named Benny. "Go down to medical and get one of the gurneys in the supply closet and be up here on the double. Ambulance should arrive in less than five minutes." When Benny glanced at Davies for approval, Charlotte snapped, "Move, gentlemen! I haven't had a death on my watch in twenty-seven years, and I don't want to start tonight."

"You heard the lady," Davies finally chimed in, following the two officers down the hall.

Charlotte took the water and brought the glass to JimBone Wheeler's mouth, rubbing her thumb over his lips.

"Very good, Charlotte," he whispered, gently pressing his teeth against her thumbnail. "*Very good.*"

4

Five minutes later, an ambulance, sirens blaring, pulled into the sally port of the Riverbend Maximum Security Institution. Before the emergency vehicle had come to a complete stop, a paramedic hopped out of the passenger-side door. She had yellowish-brown skin and wore green scrubs with "Nashville Emergency Medical Transport" across the front of her shirt. Her hat, also green, had the shortened "NEMT" adorned in white on the crown. "Tell me," she said, looking at Charlotte.

"Pressure is 60 over 40, and sat is 88. Fading fast." Charlotte's voice was clipped, but it did not waver, and Sergeant Glenn Davies felt a reassuring warmth when he heard the weight of experience in Charlotte's tone.

"We'll check again on the way," the paramedic said. Then she turned and helped the driver, a compact, barrel-chested Mexican man, slide the ambulance stretcher out of the vehicle. Seconds later, they had moved Wheeler from the gurney onto the stretcher and placed him in the back of the ambulance.

"I'm coming with you," Charlotte said, grabbing the door handle and beginning to climb inside. The paramedic caught her by the forearm and pulled her backward. "I'm afraid I can't allow that," she said.

"The hell you can't," Charlotte snapped, poking the woman with her index finger. "That's my patient in there, and I'm not leaving his side."

The paramedic gazed past Charlotte to Sergeant Davies, who stepped forward. "Mr. Wheeler is a death row inmate, and we will need at least one guard in the ambulance with you. I'll have a cruiser following behind you and one out front leading the way." He paused, glancing down at Charlotte. "We'd also like Nurse Thompson to stay with him."

"Let's move!" Charlotte yelled, again grabbing the handle.

This time, the paramedic relented and held the door open while Charlotte and Officer Benny Cruz climbed inside. Once they were in, she entered behind them and turned back to Davies before closing the doors. "The hospital will call once we've arrived."

"Ten-four," he said, nodding at her and grabbing his voice unit. "Ambulance with inmate pulling out. Benny's inside. Follow close and report back as soon as he's in the emergency room."

Davies clicked off and watched as the ambulance moved away from the curb. His heart was pounding, and despite the cool of the morning, he had perspired so much that the fabric of his uniform stuck to his back. If JimBone Wheeler croaked on his watch, he could kiss any chance of a promotion goodbye.

C'mon Charlotte, he thought, saying a silent prayer. *Don't let the son of a bitch die.*

5

Seven minutes after leaving the prison, the ambulance pulled to a stop outside the emergency room of Nashville General Hospital. Charlotte and the female paramedic jumped out of the back and lowered the stretcher out of the vehicle. When two emergency room technicians arrived to help, Charlotte began dishing out instructions. "His blood pressure was 60 over 40 at the prison, but we intubated him on the trip over and it's up to 80 over 50 now. Oxygen sat has increased to 89, but still not good. Need to get him to the back immediately."

"Yes, ma'am," one of the techs said, pushing the stretcher through the entrance to the ER with the other tech on his heels.

"I'll be right in. I just need to notify the prison we're here."

But the techs ignored her and moved through the lobby with effortless precision. Charlotte watched as the doors that led to the patient care wing in the back opened and the stretcher disappeared behind them. Adrenaline surged through every blood vessel in her body. *Almost there,* she thought, turning and heading back to the ambulance. The female paramedic was gone, and though she couldn't see the front of the vehicle, she knew the driver was waiting for her signal before he departed too. To her left, she saw the four uniformed officers who had escorted them from the prison to the hospital approaching her.

"Where's Benny?" the one named Taggert asked. "I didn't see him get out of the van."

"He's gone to the ER," Charlotte said. "With the inmate. Everything is cool. We're here and there's not a damn thing we can do now. You guys need to get back to the prison."

Taggert started to protest, but Charlotte grabbed his forearm and gave him a nudge. "Since you were on Wheeler's hall, you probably need to help Glenn with the write-up. Take your partner with you, and the other two guys can stay here for additional security. I'll call Glenn and get him up to speed." Not waiting for a response, she turned and took out her cell phone, clicking the number for the prison.

Behind her, she heard Taggert say, "You heard the lady. Seeley, you and J. P. stay close and check in with Benny. Me and Dexter will head back."

"Ten-four."

Taggert and his partner jogged back to their cruiser while the other two uniforms strode toward the entrance to the emergency room. Meanwhile, Charlotte listened to the ringtone, heart pounding in her chest. When the dispatcher finally answered, Charlotte barked, "Get me Sergeant Davies."

Seconds later, she heard Glenn's voice. "He there?"

"Yes, and he's still alive."

Charlotte heard a sigh on the other end of the line. "Thank God."

"I wouldn't thank him just yet," Charlotte said, walking past the ambulance at a normal pace. As she did, she nodded at the driver, who returned the gesture. Seconds later, the van moved forward and approached Albion Street, which ran adjacent to the hospital. "With that pressure and sat rate, we aren't out of the woods. I'd say it's fifty-fifty he survives, and even if he does, his brain may end up scrambled. How long was he up there vomiting, Glenn?" She inserted the slightest hint of challenge into her voice. Up ahead, she saw the ambulance turn right onto Albion.

"We responded as soon as we were aware of it."

"Better make damn sure the guards on that wing will back you up." Before he could respond, Charlotte added, "And get an incident report started with witness statements. If he does die, you can bet your ass that inmates' rights lawyer will be circling for his next payday."

"Shirah?" The fear in Glenn's voice was palpable. Perry Shirah was an attorney in Davidson County who specialized in filing Section 1983 cases against prisons and jails based on the deprivation of prisoners' constitutional rights. If James Robert Wheeler met his maker tonight and there was even a trace of evidence that the corrections officers on duty weren't paying the proper amount of attention, Shirah would be on the trail like bees to honey, and Glenn knew it. He had been in his fair share of depositions with the bulldog lawyer, and Charlotte knew he'd just as soon undergo a root canal.

"Damn right," she said. "I've already sent Taggert back, so you can get his write-up." She continued to walk until she reached Albion.

"OK, I'll circle the wagons and get as many statements as I can. I'll need yours. When are you coming back?"

Charlotte squinted as a gunmetal-gray Toyota Camry approached from the north. "Not for a while. Gonna hang around and see if the poor bastard makes it. I tend to think he will. He's a tough cuss."

"I hope to hell you're right," Glenn said. "Keep me posted."

"Will do," Charlotte said, clicking off the phone as the Camry pulled to a stop beside her. She opened the passenger-side door and climbed inside. Once the car was moving, she stole a glance at the driver. It was the female paramedic.

"You did very well, Charlotte," she said. *"Muy bueno."*

"Where is he?" Charlotte asked.

"Trunk."

Charlotte Thompson sucked in a breath and closed her eyes. They had done it. They had really done it. "Where are we going?"

The driver gave her a reassuring pat on the knee. "You'll see."

6

The emergency room physician stepped back from the bed, gazing curiously at the patient, who had been rushed inside a few minutes earlier. The man had a fresh bruise above his left temple, and though he had yet to fully regain consciousness, he was beginning to stir.

The doctor glanced at the monitor above the bed. "Oxygen sat is 98 and blood pressure is 122 over 78," he said, hearing the distance in his voice. Something was wrong. "What were his vitals at the prison?"

"Eighty-eight sat and 60-over-40 pressure," a nurse to his left said.

"Other symptoms?"

"Vomiting, with complaints of trouble breathing."

The doctor took another step back. "Anything about a bruise on his forehead?"

When there was no answer, he gazed into the nurse's eyes. She shook her head, and her face was ashen in the harsh glow of the fluorescent light above.

"Shit," he said, grabbing the doorknob and exiting the room. In the hallway, he saw two men in uniforms.

"Everything OK, Doc?" one of them asked.

The physician glanced down at the name tag on the guard's lapel and spoke in a firm tone. "Officer Seeley, there is nothing wrong with the inmate who was transported here other than a fairly significant and very fresh bruise over his left eye. He has a concussion but is waking up now."

"*What?*" Seeley asked, brushing past the doctor and walking toward the room.

"Wait!" the physician yelled, but the officer ignored him. He pushed through the door and came to an immediate halt when he saw the patient lying in the bed. The man's eyes were now open, and he was blinking them in confusion.

"Oh my God," Seeley said, his voice weak. "*Benny?*"

Officer Benny Cruz lay on the bed with an IV hooked to his right forearm. His shirt was off, and monitors beeped all around him. Seeley quickly scanned the room, seeing a pile of clothes that had been discarded on a chair in the corner. He walked toward them and picked up the green cotton jumpsuit of a death row inmate. "Is this what he had on when he was brought in?" Seeley snapped, knowing the answer but seeking confirmation.

"Yes," one of the nurses said. "Per protocol we cut off his clothes for better access."

Seeley closed his eyes for a half second and then opened them. He turned to the door and saw his partner, J. P. Sanchez, gaping at the bed.

"Where's Wheeler?" J. P. asked, his eyes wide.

Not replying, Seeley ran past him. In the hallway, he turned and yelled over his shoulder. "Secure the unit! No one other than patients can come and go." Then he sprinted through the lobby and out toward the drop-off station, where the ambulance had been less than five minutes earlier.

It was gone. "*Damnit,*" he said as he ran to his cruiser and flung open the door. He grabbed his car radio and clicked the number for dispatch.

"Go ahead," a female voice scratched over the line.

Seeley let out a deep breath and closed his eyes. "James Robert Wheeler has escaped custody at Nashville General Hospital. Request backup and roadblocks in all directions within five miles of NGH." He sucked in a quick breath. "I repeat, we have a fugitive situation and I need backup and roadblocks."

"Ten-four," the dispatcher said.

Seeley was about to click off when he heard Sergeant Glenn Davies come through, his voice high and panicked. "Graham, please tell me you are joking."

"I wish I was, Sarge, but he's gone. He must have gotten the jump on Benny in the ambulance, because the paramedics didn't take Wheeler into the hospital. They took Benny in Wheeler's prison fatigues."

"Son of a . . . *bitch*!" Davies yelled. "Where the hell is Charlotte?"

Seeley licked his lips. "I don't know."

For three whole seconds there was nothing but static over the line. Then Davies, the authority in his tone somewhat restored, said, "The cavalry is on the way. Start interviewing staff and I'll be there in five."

"Ten-four," Seeley said, and clicked off. He stepped out of his cruiser and trotted back toward the entrance to the emergency room. In the distance, he heard the wail of police sirens, but Corporal Graham Seeley knew in his bones that they were too late.

"The horse is out of the barn," he whispered.

7

As the Camry cruised north along Highway 31A, and the small towns of Nolensville and Triune passed by her windshield, Charlotte Thompson felt numb, still not quite believing that the plan had worked. It had been more than an hour since they had left the hospital, and she had yet to hear anything on the radio about Wheeler's escape. *That will come in good time,* she thought, trying to imagine the shock on Glenn Davies's face when he learned the news.

They'll block off every road within a five- to ten-mile radius of NGH. They'll interview the emergency room nurses and technicians. They'll search for the ambulance and have a fleet of police sedans blanket the city. She scoffed and shook her head.

All in vain.

JimBone Wheeler was gone. Like dust in the wind.

"Charlotte, are you alright?" the driver asked. The woman spoke with an exotic accent that Charlotte couldn't quite place.

"Fine," she managed.

When JimBone had gone over the plan during his last sick call visit with her, he had referred to his person on the outside only as

"Manny," or "she." He had written a telephone number to call on a yellow sticky note. Though he had told Charlotte to memorize the digits, she had deviated slightly from this direction by creating a contact in her mobile phone identified as "Manny." She didn't want to risk fiddling with trying to dial the number and have one of the guards click 911 before she could make her call.

Once they were out of the prison and moving in the ambulance, everything had hinged on Charlotte's knowledge of the staff at Nashville General. She had called the emergency room's direct number from the back of the ambulance and spoken with the night shift house supervisor—a woman named Stephanie Stagner. She had told Steph that she was on her way with a death row inmate trying to cheat the needle and would need a couple of techs to meet the ambulance at the drop-off in front of the ER. Steph had muttered something under her breath about not getting any notice from the paramedic service of a dispatch but didn't protest further. "I'll have two transport techs waiting, Charlotte."

"Thank you," Charlotte had said, clicking off her cell phone and watching as JimBone Wheeler put on the uniform of Benny Cruz. Within ninety seconds of the ambulance pulling out, Manny had hit Benny between the eyes with a steel pipe. The officer had blinked once, gasped, and fallen over. Manny had unbuckled JimBone from the stretcher, and the fugitive had chuckled softly to himself, saying several times "Ms. Charlotte, you are as good as gold" as he removed the officer's uniform and put it on and Manny dressed Benny in JimBone's prison clothes.

Charlotte had felt no pride in playing her part in this opera. She knew she was the key to its ultimate success. Of course, they also had to be lucky. They couldn't have one of the guards jump the gun and call 911 before she arrived at the cell. Glenn Davies had to relent and let her ride in the ambulance. Finally, upon arrival at the ER, they had to get Benny into the building before the officers in the escort cruiser got a good look at him.

The diciest piece to the puzzle was the eight-mile transport from Riverbend to Nashville General. Traffic in Nashville, even that early in the morning, was always hit or miss. They could have an accident or blow a tire. The battery of the van might die. There was also the off chance that the guard who rode with them would prove to be tougher than JimBone presumed. A myriad of possible pitfalls, any one of which would doom the chances of success.

But JimBone had never seemed worried about the prospect that dumb luck could ruin the plan. "I've always been lucky when it comes to this kind of stuff, Ms. Charlotte," he'd said in another of his "sick calls" in the weeks prior to the escape attempt. After she'd written her nursing note—most of his fake visits to medical revolved around complaints of nausea and stomach pain—she let him massage her tired feet.

"Why is that?" Charlotte asked, enjoying the feel of his rough hands between her toes.

"Because the Bone doesn't give a shit," he fired back with no humor in his voice. "When I was a Ranger and there was a kill to be made, I could do it without thinking of the consequences. As a hired gun, same thing. I focus on my job and don't worry about anything else. Our thoughts are real things, Charlotte, did you know that? Microscopic force fields of energy. If you have stressful thoughts, you'll bring stress into your life." He paused. "I don't stress. We have a good plan, and I believe in your ability to bring it home. I'm not going to sweat details that I can't control. That stuff will work itself out."

And it has, Charlotte thought as the Camry began to slow down. Up ahead, she saw a gas station on the right. She glanced at Manny, who spoke without looking at her.

"Bathroom break OK with you?"

Charlotte didn't say anything. It had been hours since she had last peed, and she hadn't thought a second about it. Truth be known, if she saw a toilet right now, she'd probably puke in the bowl before she'd squat to urinate. She still couldn't believe they had pulled the plan off.

Subconsciously, she reached inside the pocket of her scrubs and clutched the torn-out piece of newspaper she had received in the mail last week and which she'd kept on her person in the days leading up to the escape for motivation and inspiration. She didn't have to pull out the article to read it, because by now she knew the content by heart. It was from the *Knoxville News Sentinel*, the Sunday edition from two weeks ago. The article was one of the small stories on the second page of the Local section.

"Attorney Gunned Down in Parking Lot" was the title. Underneath were just two short sentences. "Early Saturday morning, local criminal defense attorney Jeffrey Gullan was shot and killed walking to his car in the parking lot outside his office on West Main. No suspects have been arrested."

As the Camry eased into the entrance to the gas station, Charlotte sucked in a deep breath and removed her hand from her pocket. She had thought that the news of Gullan's murder would make her happy. Worst case, she had figured she would feel some satisfaction knowing that she, through JimBone Wheeler's person on the outside, had ended that worthless piece of shit's life just as Gullan had ended her husband's and daughter's futures.

But she had felt neither of those emotions. The only feeling that had come to her that Monday evening was fear. There was no going back now. JimBone had complied with his part of the bargain, and now she would have to carry out hers.

Manny parked the car along the side of the building, and Charlotte noticed that there were two outside bathrooms. "Be right back," she said, hopping out of the car and gliding around the front of the building.

Charlotte leaned her head against the glass of the windshield and closed her eyes as regret permeated her bones. She had tried to get out of it. On the Tuesday after she had received the article, during JimBone's feigned blood pressure check, she had thanked him but then said there was no way his plan would work. Too many variables. Too much risk for so little chance of success.

But JimBone had just gazed back at her. As she had wrapped the cuff around his arm, he had whispered, "*We are going forward on December fourth. It has to be then, and you will do your part.*"

"And what if I don't?" she had challenged, her voice shaking with trepidation.

"Then the authorities in Knoxville are going to be tipped off that Jeffrey Gullan was murdered in a killing orchestrated by one Charlotte Thompson. How'd that be?"

"There's no way they would believe that."

"They will when they find your DNA in his car and office." He paused. "Then when they find the sniper rifle that killed him in a dumpster a few blocks from his office with only your fingerprints on the handle, they'll arrest you in a heartbeat. After they learn about your history with Gullan and what he did to your husband and daughter . . ." He didn't finish the rest, letting her ponder the repercussions.

Charlotte had just stared at him, mouth hung open.

"You don't think I could pull that off?" He had grinned then. "The Bone is very resourceful. If I was able to murder Gullan from inside here, don't you think I could find a way to plant evidence?"

Charlotte hadn't said anything because there was no point in further argument. The die had been cast.

Three loud knocks on the passenger-side windshield mercifully broke her from the torturous memories. She looked through the glass and saw Manny dangling a key hooked to a piece of plywood.

Charlotte opened the door to the car and stepped out into the cool morning air. To the east, she saw the orange sun beginning its ascent over miles of hilly farmland. She gazed at Manny, who patted her shoulder and stuffed the key in her hand.

"Better to go now," she said. "Not sure how long it will be before we stop again."

Charlotte pointed behind her toward the trunk with her thumb. "What about—?"

"Don't worry about him. Still too much risk for him to show his face yet."

Charlotte sighed but didn't argue. She placed the ancient key in the slot to the door that said LADIES over the front, and once she heard the latch give, she pushed through the opening. The smell of stale piss wafted toward her like a sour breeze, but Charlotte paid no mind. When you've spent twenty-seven years working in a prison, old, dried-up urine is one of the more lukewarm scents the world has to offer.

There were two stalls, and she walked through the open door to the far one, not bothering to lock it. She put her hands on her knees and tried to vomit, but all that happened was a gag reflex followed by several spits. She sighed and wiped saliva from her lips. Then she pulled down her scrub pants. She started to turn around, but then his voice, colder than the morning air, froze her in place.

"Hold steady, Charlotte," JimBone said, stepping into the close confines of the stall and placing an open palm between her legs.

"Manny said—"

"*Shut up,*" JimBone said, his voice a harsh whisper. She heard the rustling of his own pants hitting the floor, and then hot breath in her ear. "You done good, Charlotte," he said, grabbing a fistful of her hair and yanking her neck back so that she had to look into his hazel, almost-copper eyes. His left hand slapped the inside of her left and right thighs, and she involuntarily spread her legs. She grimaced as he entered her.

"Relax, darling. It won't hurt for long." He let go of her hair, and Charlotte leaned forward, placing her hands on the dirty tile wall.

"Couldn't we have waited until—?"

This time his interruption came in the form of an open-handed slap that caught the right side of her face. She felt his rough hands under her shirt, unclicking her bra and then grabbing her breasts. Seconds later, he pulled her top and brassiere up over her neck, and they dropped to the floor in a pile.

"Step out of your pants," JimBone said, backing away from her. "You're too tight."

Charlotte glanced down at the damp, nasty floor. Her lip had started to tremble and she tasted blood from where he had slapped her. "Not here. Please . . ."

"Do it."

She relented, removing her shoes and slowly stepping out of each pant leg until she was naked but for the now-filthy cotton socks that adorned her feet. Then, before she could say anything else, he was back inside her, forcing her legs wider with the palms of his hands. Her feet slid out on the damp floor, and JimBone increased his pace. Thirty seconds later, he groaned and she felt his release. She also felt a sharp pain rip through her neck.

Slowly, she brought both hands to her neck, and when she gazed at her palms, she saw that blood covered every inch of them. She turned and saw his copper eyes peering at her with intense satisfaction. In his right hand, he held a pearl-handled knife.

"You were golden, Charlotte," JimBone said. "Just like I knew you would be."

As her consciousness began to slowly fade, Charlotte slurred. "Wh-wh-why? I . . . I did everything y-y-you asked."

She saw him nod. "Just putting a loyal dog out of its misery."

"You c-c-can't win, y-y-you know," Charlotte said, collapsing onto the commode as her slit neck continued to bleed out.

He pulled up his pants and clipped his belt. Then, leaning forward until he was just a few inches from her face, he whispered, "This ain't about winning, Charlotte."

"A r-r-reckoning," Charlotte managed, remembering the word she had heard him say over and over again.

"That's right, darling."

Charlotte Thompson sucked in one last gasp before her shoulders sagged against the back of the toilet. Her last thoughts before death took her were not of her late husband and daughter. Nor were they of her parents, who had both died years earlier.

She didn't think of God or Jesus or the Holy Spirit either. She had stopped believing in such things long ago.

Instead, she saw the shadow of a man she had never met before. A man she had only seen through the words of the killer who had just raped and murdered her.

Feeling the blood flowing out of her neck and the oxygen escaping her lungs, she met JimBone's glare. "You're sc-scared of him, a-a-aren't you?"

The killer cocked his head in confusion. "Who?" JimBone asked. To Charlotte, his voice sounded like it was a hundred miles away.

"Mc-Mc-McMurtrie," she gasped.

She saw his teeth grit and his nostrils flare. "Die, you dumb bitch," JimBone said, folding his arms.

Just before she followed his final order, Charlotte Thompson smiled. "McMurtrie," she repeated without any waver in her voice.

8

Thirty minutes later, Manny pulled the Camry into a used-car lot just outside of Eagleville and parked in between a relatively new-looking Ford Fusion and a dilapidated Honda Accord. She clicked off the ignition and slung the keys into the passenger seat. Then she walked toward the double-wide trailer that served as the business office. Inside, she paid for the Camry's replacement with cash.

Five minutes later, she was leaving the lot behind the wheel of a 2007 silver double-cab Toyota Tundra.

"You like our new wheels?" she asked, speaking without looking behind her.

In the back seat, lying with a blanket covering his body, JimBone Wheeler chuckled. "Perfect, Manny. Absolutely perfect. Did you find the cabin?"

"*Sí,*" Manny said. "We are all set."

"And the ammunition?"

"On the way," Manny said.

"And the money?"

"Half will be delivered tonight. Our benefactor says the other half will be wired to an account in the Caymans when we complete the job."

Underneath the wool blanket, JimBone smiled. "What about the ambulance driver? The Mexican? Any chance he could spoil anything?"

Manny laughed. "None. Pasco was one of Bully's illegals. He would just as soon put a bullet into his own head than rat us out. I paid him in cash to drive the ambulance, and he completed the task. He's gone . . . until we need him again."

JimBone took a deep breath and slowly exhaled, enjoying the taste of freedom after two years on death row. "Good 'ol Bully," he said. "Can I ask you something, señorita?"

"*Sí*, but I may not answer."

"Was it you who killed Bully last Christmas?"

When she didn't respond, JimBone added a few details. "Gunned down with a sniper rifle from at least a hundred yards out at the Jasper Country Club. No witnesses. No sign or trace of anything." He paused. "Sure sounds like my girl Manny."

She caught his eye in the rearview mirror. "But it wasn't. I did not kill Mr. Bully Calhoun. I could never have killed him. He was good to me."

JimBone scratched his chin. "Huh," he finally said. "Strange. I always figured you did."

For several seconds, neither spoke. Finally, Manny fired her own question. "Can I ask you something, *señor*?"

He grinned. "*Sí*, but I may not answer," he mimicked.

"Wouldn't it be easier to kill McMurtrie, Drake, and Haynes without all the others?"

JimBone's grin widened. "Easier? Yes. Satisfying? No. I want to see them suffer. I . . . especially want to see the old man reap the whirlwind of his actions."

"You know he is very sick," Manny said. "Cancer. What if he dies before we can kill him?"

"He won't," JimBone said, his voice stone cold and the grin gone. Gritting his teeth as he pondered the possibility of cancer cheating him out of balancing the scales, he repeated himself. *"He won't."*

For over an hour, silence filled the truck as it rumbled through the southern Tennessee towns of Lewisburg, Cornersville and, finally, Pulaski. *I'll see you soon,* JimBone thought, peeking over the blanket and through the windshield at the Giles County Courthouse in downtown Pulaski, wondering if General Helen Lewis was inside.

Twenty minutes later, after crossing the Elk River, JimBone leaned his hands against the driver's seat until he felt Manny's back pressing against him. As the Tundra passed a green-and-white sign saying "Welcome to Alabama the Beautiful," JimBone whispered, "Are you ready for this, Manny?"

"Sí," she said without hesitation. "Everything is in place."

"Good," JimBone said, pulling the blanket back over him. "We'll rest and prepare tonight." He paused and licked his lips. "But given the old man's health, there's no time to waste. In less than twenty-four hours, we're gonna declare war."

9

At 9:30 a.m. on the morning of December 4, 2013, four hours after JimBone Wheeler escaped custody at Nashville General Hospital, Steve Cook and Cindy Minkhos pulled off Highway 31A at a nondescript gas station on the outskirts of Triune, Tennessee. Steve and Cindy were high school sweethearts from Lewisburg who were in their first semester at Vanderbilt. Before the car had even come to a complete stop, Cindy opened the passenger-side door and hopped out. Frantically, she ran inside the store and asked for the key to the ladies' bathroom.

The clerk turned behind him and saw an empty hook where the key typically rested. He had a vague memory of a woman coming inside a few hours earlier for the key. *Bitch must not have brought it back,* he thought, looking over his shoulder at the teenager. "Should be open," he said, pointing at the empty hook. "The last person didn't return the key."

Hustling out of the store, Cindy ran back around to the bathroom. She was battling a horrific case of diarrhea and was about to bust. Otherwise, there was no way she would have insisted that Steve stop at such a rathole. She grabbed the knob and sighed with relief as it gave and she entered the restroom. She shut the door but was too anxious that she was going to soil herself to lock it. She ran to the first stall and almost slipped on the blood that had leaked into it from the adjacent enclosure. “Oh my . . .”

Her chest constricted when she noticed the blood, and she forgot about her need to use the toilet. Slowly, she opened the door to the far stall.

When she saw the woman, a scream caught in her throat for half a second. Then two heartbeats later, as her lungs filled with air and her bowels released, she screamed until her vocal cords finally couldn’t take the pressure.

“What is it?” Steve asked, barreling into the bathroom. “Are you—holy Christ!”

The woman in the stall was naked and had been propped against the commode. There was a reddish-purple gash all the way around her neck where she had been slit with a sharp-edged knife. But the woman’s ruined neck and nudity were not what made Steve Cook’s mouth hang open or Cindy Minkhos defecate in her pants.

Along the dead woman’s abdomen were nine letters that had been written into her skin with the tip of a blade.

“*M . . . C . . . M . . . U . . . R . . . T . . . R . . . I . . . E.*” Steve said each letter out loud before doing the honors of reading what they formed.

“McMurtrie,” he whispered as Cindy let out another bloodcurdling scream.

PART TWO

10

On the northern tip of Alabama, just a few miles south of the Tennessee state line, sits a tiny hamlet called Hazel Green. There are conflicting stories about how the town got its name. Some say that the early settlers were impressed with the green hazelnut trees in the area. Another report indicates that the town was named after the wife of its first store owner and postmaster. There's even a rumor that General Andrew Jackson, on his way to fight the Creek Indians at the Battle of Horseshoe Bend, described the region as hazel and green in color, and that's how the name came to be.

Though he thought the story about Old Hickory was likely a tall tale spread by his father, it was the one that Thomas Jackson McMurtrie enjoyed the most. Sitting on the back porch of the red-brick house that he and his dad had built with their bare hands, Tom took a sip of Coca-Cola from a straw and gazed out at the one hundred acres of land that had been in his family since just before World War II. At the edge of the yard, where grass turned to barren rows of farmland—this year's cotton had already been harvested and next year's crop wouldn't be planted until spring—Tom noticed that his

English bulldog, Lee Roy, was chasing a butterfly and becoming frustrated with the endeavor. The dog, whose coat was a mixture of brown and white, turned in a circle and occasionally snapped at the air, flapping his huge jowls. But he was too slow to catch the insect. Now weighing in at close to seventy pounds, Lee Roy Jordan McMurtrie was not as agile and fast as his legendary namesake. Tom couldn't help but smile as he watched the scene play out.

"Which version of how the town was named do you believe, Papa?" Jackson asked, also taking a sip of Coke, though he was drinking his straight from the can. The boy was thirteen years old and had a mop of light-brown hair on his head that was covered by a New York Yankees baseball cap. He peered at Tom with eyes that burned with curiosity. Tom had told the different stories of how his birthplace got its name on many occasions, and he was grateful that his grandson hadn't grown tired of them. *Or maybe he's just being nice and placating an old fool.* Either way, Tom was thankful for the company and loved this time that he was able to spend with Jackson. If there was a silver lining to being diagnosed with stage four lung cancer, it was that he got to see his grandchildren a lot.

"Probably the one about the storekeeper's wife, Forty-Nine." Tom ruffled the boy's hair. Jackson's jersey number in baseball was forty-nine, and Tom enjoyed calling him by it. Tom had worn that same number when he played defensive end on Alabama's 1961 National Championship football team. "But your great-grandpa really believed that General Jackson had marched his troops through here and proclaimed the place 'Hazel Green.' I wish that version was true." Tom paused and felt heat behind his eyes. It was funny how your emotions changed over time. For the first seventy years of his life, Tom had always thought of himself as being rather stoic. He cried when his wife, Julie, had died of breast cancer six years ago. And he had cried when his parents died. And he'd had to pull his car off the interstate on January 26, 1983, when a news reporter had interrupted the song that was playing and announced that Coach Paul William "Bear" Bryant had died at Druid City Hospital, in Tuscaloosa, of a heart attack at the age of sixty-nine. He had laid his head against the steering wheel and cried for his mentor, who had taught him so much about the game of football and life. But those were all big events. Now, at seventy-three years old and almost fourteen months into a terminal cancer diagnosis, he could barely get through any story without feeling his eyes beginning to moisten.

"Me too," Jackson said. Then, smiling wide, he asked, "Papa, can you tell me the story about how Darwin Holt broke that player for Georgia Tech's jaw again?"

Tom laughed. "Will do, but I need to take a break, OK? Why don't you go inside and finish up that math homework you were telling me about and let Papa rest his eyes?"

The boy sighed and reluctantly stood from his chair. "Yes, sir."

He began to walk away, and Tom grabbed him by the arm. "You're really growing, you know it? Flex that bicep for me."

Jackson did, and Tom felt the muscle. "Strong as a bull. Has basketball started yet?"

"We've been practicing for a couple weeks, and my first game is tomorrow night." Jackson's eyes widened. "Do you think . . . ? I mean, if you feel up to it—"

"I'll try," Tom said. "I have my scans tomorrow and that's an all-day thing, but . . . I'll sure give it a try."

Jackson hugged Tom's neck. "Happy birthday, Papa. Love you."

"Love you too, Forty-Nine." As the boy started to run off, Tom implored, "Finish that homework now. That's the most important thing."

"Yes, sir," Jackson said as he walked inside.

Tom turned his eyes back to the farm and noticed that Lee Roy was now lying flat on his stomach on the grass, a defeated look on his face as the butterfly fluttered above him. Chuckling, Tom reached for the blanket that lay in a clump at his feet. He set his Coke on a table beside him and then pulled the warm fabric over his bony shoulders. The wind had begun to blow, and though it felt fresh and pleasant on his face, it came with a chill. Nowadays, Tom noticed the cold a lot more often. He figured it was due to the weight loss. Before the diagnosis, he had weighed approximately 220 pounds. At six feet three inches tall, that was a proportionate number for him. But since Dr. Bill Davis had told him he had lung cancer in October of last year, he had lost almost 50 pounds and was now barely hovering over 170. None of his old clothes fit, so his daughter-in-law had bought him several pairs of light sweatpants and pullovers. He'd never worn a medium anything in his life, but all of the clothes had "M" on the tag, and even they were a bit loose.

Tom heard the sound of a car pulling up the driveway and saw Lee Roy bolt to his feet. The dog grunted and then took off toward the front of the house, barking to announce his presence. Figuring that visitors were beginning to show up for the party his son and daughter-in-law were throwing for him, Tom closed his eyes. Truth be known, though he appreciated the effort, he was dreading this get-together. He never felt hungry anymore, and he knew there would be hurt feelings when he barely touched the cake Nancy had made for him. Tom sighed and tried to adjust his back in the chair to lessen the pain. *Happy birthday to me.*

"Papa."

Tom opened his eyes and turned his head toward the familiar voice. His daughter-in-law stood in the doorway to the house, holding a baby on her hip.

"Yes?" Tom asked.

Before Nancy could respond, a six-year-old girl with blond hair pushed in front of her. The girl twirled a set of beads in her hand and had a mischievous smile on her face. "Your girlfriend's here, Papa," she said, speaking in a singsong voice before giggling.

"Jenny, get back in the house," Nancy scolded, and the girl scurried away, waving at Tom as she went. "I'm sorry," Nancy said, shaking her head. "General Lewis is here. Do you want me to send her out, or did you want to come in? The others should be here soon."

Tom, conscious of the blanket over his shoulders, said, "Send her out."

"Are you sure?" Nancy asked. "You look cold. Do you need—?"

"I'm fine, Nancy. Just have Helen come out here."

Tom could tell by his daughter-in-law's thin smile that she wanted to protest, but she held her tongue. "OK."

A few seconds later, Tom saw Helen emerge from the door wearing her customary black suit and heels. She smiled and Tom waved her forward. As the points of her shoes clicked on the wooden deck, Tom noticed the worry lines on her forehead.

She hovered over him for a second and planted a kiss on his forehead. "Happy birthday."

"Thank you," Tom said. "Wasn't sure I'd live to see this one. I guess seventy-three is better than dead, right?"

Ignoring his weak attempt at humor, Helen ran her fingers over the stubble on top of his head. "Your hair is growing," she said, and her voice sounded wan and far off, as if she were observing him on a television screen instead of in person.

"They say it comes back curly after chemo," Tom said, subconsciously swatting a hand over the stubble. "That'll take some getting used to. I've always liked my hair cut the same way I drink Kentucky bourbon." He smirked. "Neat and straight."

Helen laughed, but it sounded forced. She took the seat that Jackson had just vacated and leaned forward, holding her hands in her lap. It had been a while since Tom had seen Helen in her full courtroom garb. When she visited the farm, she typically wore jeans and a blouse, and he would have expected her to dress casual for the birthday party. It struck him as odd that she hadn't changed before coming. "So, General, have you been dishing out ass whippings today?"

In the state of Tennessee, the head prosecutor of a county was typically addressed as "General," and Tom had always thought the military designation to be the perfect fit for Helen Evangeline Lewis, who commanded respect with every word from her mouth and movement of her body.

Helen gave a tight smile but didn't look at him. She peered at the deck and spoke in a quiet voice. "I need to tell you something."

Tom felt a chill on his arms that had nothing to do with the temperature and squeezed the blanket tight against his chest. He had never seen Helen exhibit even the slightest hint of fear, but he could hear the trepidation in her voice. *She's scared to death,* he thought, scooting forward in his chair. "OK," he said.

"I just got off the phone with the warden of the Riverbend Maximum Security Institution in Nashville."

Tom felt gooseflesh break out on his arm. "And?"

When she spoke again, Helen's voice was just above a whisper. "Early this morning, with the help of a prison nurse, James Robert Wheeler escaped from death row."

"*What?*" Tom said, not believing it.

"JimBone Wheeler broke out of prison this morning. He's a fugitive and is believed to be armed and dangerous. The investigation is still in its infancy, but the Nashville police think he has an accomplice. A brown-skinned woman, also thought to be armed and dangerous."

Tom felt his chest tighten. "Bully Calhoun's Filipino enforcer."

Helen didn't answer, keeping her eyes locked on to Tom's. "Her identity has not been confirmed, but . . . that's a reasonable and logical conclusion."

Tom gripped the blanket tightly between his fingers and tried to remain calm as his thoughts drifted to his last encounter with JimBone Wheeler at the Riverbend Maximum Security Institution.

I'm going to bring a day of reckoning on you and everyone you hold dear, McMurtrie.

Tom narrowed his gaze and forced himself to concentrate. From the front of the house, he could hear Lee Roy begin to bark again. Another car must be coming up the driveway. "Do they have any leads?" Tom asked.

Helen nodded and pulled her cell phone out of her purse. She clicked a few digits and then handed the device to Tom. When she did, Tom noticed her hand was shaking.

From the driveway, Lee Roy's barking grew louder, with a few growls thrown in. Then there was the brief sound of a siren, followed by the shrill voice of a dispatcher from a police radio: "Have you reached the destination?"

"Affirmative," an officer blared back. "General Lewis is inside with the target."

Tom raised his eyebrows at Helen.

"Backup," she said, nodding at the phone in Tom's hand. "Go ahead and look."

Tom blinked his eyes to focus and then gazed at the photograph on the screen. His breath caught in his throat as he saw a naked woman propped against a bathroom toilet.

"That's the nurse," Helen said. "Her body was found this morning in the bathroom stall of a roadside gas station between Triune and Eagleville." Standing up and leaning over him, she took the telephone and enlarged the photograph so that the image focused on the dead woman's stomach.

Just as eighteen-year-old Steve Cook had done approximately seven hours earlier, Tom read the letters out loud. "*M . . . C . . . M . . . U . . . R . . . T . . . R . . . I . . . E*." Then he gazed at Helen, whose normally pale face was almost ghostly. "So . . . I'm the lead?"

Again, Helen nodded. "Based on this photograph, the history of how he ended up on death row, and what you told me about your last communication with him, the logical conclusion is that Wheeler has a score to settle with you." She paused and sucked in a quick breath. "And based on where this gas station is in relation to the prison . . . he's heading this way."

"And if that nurse was murdered this morning . . ." Tom paused as the gooseflesh that had initially sprung up on his arms ran down his legs all the way to his feet.

"He may already be here," Helen said, completing the thought.

11

Tom kept his guns in a locked case that hung on the bedroom wall. As he fumbled for the key hidden in the bottom drawer of his dresser, he heard Helen's impatient voice behind him.

"Mind telling me what you're doing?"

Tom tried to suppress his frustration as Lee Roy's barking continued to fill the air outside, along with the occasional police gibberish from the dispatcher that resounded from the radio of one of the squad cars. Tom's fingers finally closed around the teeth of the key, which had found a home between two pairs of boxer shorts. Sighing with relief, he pulled it out and undid the latch.

His heartbeat, which had begun to race as he listened to Helen's summary of JimBone Wheeler's escape and viewed the gruesome photographs of the dead nurse on the General's phone, steadied as he clasped the stock of a twelve-gauge shotgun. Tom removed the weapon and set it on the bed. *Where did I put the shells?* he wondered, turning back to the case and seeing Helen blocking his path. Her arms were folded, and her fierce green eyes, which had always reminded Tom of the emerald waters of the Gulf of Mexico, glowed with intensity.

"Tom, I know you're upset, but you need to calm down. There are two police cruisers in the driveway, and the house is being guarded by officers. Look." Holding her position, she extended a hand to the window and opened the blinds.

Through the opening, Tom saw an armed guard wearing a dark-blue uniform. The man held a walkie-talkie to his mouth and spoke into it. Seeming to sense eyes on him, the officer turned toward the window and nodded at Helen, who returned the gesture. "There are four deputies from the Giles County Sheriff's Department covering each side of the house, and I've dispatched four more to do a sweep of the farm." She paused and forced a smile. "There's also a very agitated English bulldog out there backing up those guys."

Tom didn't smile. Instead, his eyes locked on to Helen's and he spoke in a measured tone. "Thank you. Now . . . please get out of my way."

She glared at him but after a second's hesitation stepped to the side. Peering into the case, Tom removed another shotgun. He handed it to Helen, who reluctantly placed the weapon beside its counterpart on the bed. Tom then took out a nine-millimeter pistol and a .44 Magnum revolver and lay them both on the mattress. He gazed at the firearms on the bed and then back at the case. The only guns he had yet to remove were a .38-caliber revolver and a Remington deer rifle. In his lifetime, Tom McMurtrie had only killed one human being, and he had used the rifle to do it. He stepped toward the case, but Helen beat him to it. She pulled out the brown-and-black Remington and peered at the weapon with admiration. "I seem to remember you saving my life with this one a couple years ago."

"Let's hope I don't have to do it again," Tom said, taking the gun from her and adding it to the arsenal on the bed.

"You won't," Helen snapped, placing her hands on her hips. "Tom, you are going to have to trust the law to do its job. We will get him. *I promise.*"

"Can you arrange security for my son's house in Huntsville?"

"I already have. I contacted the Madison County Sheriff's Office and the Huntsville Police Department on the way here, and there are officers posted outside your son's house now." She paused. "If Tommy and Nancy decide to go home with the kids tonight after the party, they'll have a police escort."

Tom began to pace back and forth across the room, oblivious to the pain in his back. "Good," he said. Then, stopping on a dime, he peered at her. "We need to tell Bo. And Rick, Powell, and Wade." He reached into his pocket for his cell phone. "JimBone threatened all of them too."

As he searched his contacts list, Helen placed both of her hands over Tom's and gently removed the phone from his fingers. "I know, Tom, and I'm working on it," she said. "I've already notified Powell Conrad, and he said he would warn Detective Richey. They're going to try to make it up here tomorrow and join the search." She paused and licked her lips. "I haven't been able to reach your partner yet—all my calls go straight to voice mail—but Powell said that Rick was in the middle of a trial."

Tom closed his eyes. *The Simpson case.* In the chaos of learning about JimBone Wheeler's escape, he'd forgotten about the trial. Rick had been calling him at the close of each day's session with a summary. "I'm sure Powell will tell Rick," Tom said, opening his eyes and peering at Helen.

"He told me he would," Helen agreed.

"And Bo?"

"I haven't gotten him on the phone either—same thing, all calls go to voice mail—but the dispatcher with HPD said she would send a patrol car to his and Jazz's house. Besides, Bo's coming to the party tonight, isn't he?"

"Yes."

"Good. Then we can tell him then." Helen slid the phone back inside Tom's pocket and pinched his thigh through the fabric. "You are going to have to calm down and let me do my job." She paused. "And for the love of God, don't do anything crazy with these guns. After you've gathered yourself, please put them back in the case."

Tom sighed and sat on the edge of the bed. Helen took a seat next to him and wrapped an arm around his waist. After a couple of seconds, Tom placed his own arm around Helen and pulled her close to him. When he heard her chuckle, he looked into her green eyes. "What could you possibly find funny in all this?" he asked.

"Nothing really," she said, and her tone was sad with a hint of bitterness. "Just . . . this is the first time I've ever been on your bed."

Tom blinked his eyes, not knowing what to say. His and Helen's relationship had evolved from adversarial to friendly to intimate over the course of the past two and a half years. But there was one boundary they had never crossed. Tom hugged Helen's neck and looked past her to the dresser adjacent to the gun case. On it, he saw the framed photograph of his beloved wife, Julie, who had died six years ago. Though he had eventually stopped wearing his wedding ring, there were some bonds he had been unwilling to break. Perhaps if he hadn't been diagnosed with terminal cancer and could have imagined a life with Helen, things might have been different.

But a future had never been in the cards.

"I'm sorry," Tom finally managed.

"Don't be," Helen whispered. When she removed her head from his shoulder, he saw a lone tear on her cheek. She swiped at it and abruptly stood. "We need to brief Tommy and Nancy," she said, her voice sharp and matter-of-fact. "I'm sure they're wondering what in the world is going on." She stepped toward the door. When she grabbed the knob, she turned toward him. "We also need to discuss something else."

"What?" Tom asked, rising from the bed and gritting his teeth as a dagger of pain clipped his lower back.

Helen narrowed her gaze. "I'm worried about your partner."

Fifteen minutes later, after a tense conversation with Tom's son and daughter-in-law, where Helen covered the facts she knew about JimBone Wheeler's escape and the security measures taken both at the farm and at Tommy and Nancy's home in Huntsville, Tom walked the prosecutor out to the driveway. The General's government-issued Crown Victoria was black like her suit, which Tom thought was a perfect match. After he opened the door for her, she turned and gave him a kiss on the cheek. For a moment, they held each other as the sun made its final descent over the Hazel Green farm.

"Are they OK?" Helen asked, pulling back and nodding toward the house, where Tommy and Nancy were talking in the kitchen.

"Just shell-shocked," Tom said. "It's not every day you find out that an escaped convict might be on a mission to kill your family." He paused and clasped her hand. "I wish you could stay . . ." He glanced over his shoulder to the house. "Though I doubt it's going to be much of a party now."

Helen gazed at him, squeezed his hand, and then let go. "Me too, but there's too much going on. I just got a text from someone in the state troopers' office that an abandoned ambulance was discovered at a private airfield in Murfreesboro. A forensics team is investigating, but they think it must be the van Wheeler took to the hospital."

"How close is the airfield to the gas station where the nurse was murdered?"

"Forty-five minutes maybe?"

"Could Wheeler have gotten on a plane?"

Helen held out her palms. "I don't know, but I want to get over there and ask some questions."

"Shouldn't you leave that to the detectives?"

Helen smirked. "Perhaps. But I'm the one who convicted Wheeler and sent him to death row. He's my responsibility. Now I've got to run." She climbed inside the car and shut the door. After starting the vehicle, she rolled down the window and looked up at Tom. "Any word from Bo?"

Tom felt his stomach tighten. He shook his head.

"Shouldn't he be here by now?" Helen asked, and Tom could hear the anxiety in her voice.

"Probably just hit some traffic," he said, but the words sounded hollow. Bocephus Haynes wasn't one to be late and always called if he was running behind. *Something is wrong,* he thought.

Helen pursed her lips. "If you don't hear from him in the next thirty minutes, call me," she said, putting the car in gear.

"Wait," Tom said, leaning down and placing his hands on the window seal of the Crown Vic to steady himself. "You said you were concerned about Rick earlier. Why?"

Helen sighed and gazed over the wheel. "Because he's obsessed with avenging his father's murder." She slammed the gear shift back in park and gazed up at Tom. "He's burned my phone lines up for months asking for leads on Manny Reyes, and I know he's done the same in Jasper, Henshaw, and Orange Beach. He's also filed wrongful death lawsuits against the estate of Bully Calhoun in Walker, Henshaw, and Baldwin Counties in Alabama and named Manny individually in each of them. I'm sure you know about that."

Tom nodded. "I do, and . . ." He stopped and rubbed his back, which now throbbed with pain. Then he moved his eyes around the driveway and to the farmland beyond. It was now pitch dark, and Tom felt his pulse quicken at the thought of JimBone and Manny in the field to the north. Both were good with a rifle. He remembered the officers that Helen had assigned to the house and the farm, and he took a deep breath. *Trust the law to do its job,* he thought, echoing Helen's words from the bedroom.

"Helen, those lawsuits needed to be filed," he continued, peering down at her. "I know I'm retired now, but I'm behind Rick a hundred percent. The victims and their families deserve justice."

"I'm all for justice," Helen fired back. "I've been a prosecutor for over twenty years, and before that, I was a police officer. But I don't agree with unnecessarily making yourself a target. Kathryn Calhoun Willistone has become a powerful woman since her father's assassination. She's also the personal representative of Bully's estate. My sources tell me that she is beyond pissed at being sued all over the state of Alabama."

Tom looked down at the asphalt driveway, pondering Helen's comments. Then, meeting her eye, he asked, "Do you think it's possible that Kat could have had something to do with Wheeler's escape? The case filed in Walker County . . . *Jennings* . . . is set for trial on Monday."

Helen blinked but held Tom's gaze. He could tell that the impending trial was news to her. "All reports coming out of Riverbend are of an inside job orchestrated by a rogue nurse," she finally said, slapping the steering wheel with the palm of her right hand. "But even if Kat were somehow involved, *we can't prove it.* Just like the lawsuits your partner has filed. *He can't win.* The murders that he seeks justice for were clean hits. There's no direct evidence linking Manny or Bully Calhoun to any of those killings. Smoke? OK, there's a good bit, I agree. But fire? None. Not even a spark. And the crimes have been unsolved for over a year. They are dead ends."

"You seem to know a lot about those murders," Tom said, softening his tone.

Helen sighed and gazed up at the roof of the Crown Vic. "I'm trying to help him, OK? And I think he's right. I believe that the killings of his father, Greg Zorn, and Alvin Jennings were conspiracy-style mob hits. But you just can't go after these people swinging haymakers. You have to be patient and *you must have evidence.*"

"Rick has a better chance than you think, Helen," Tom said. "Don't forget that the cases he's filed are *civil* lawsuits, not criminal prosecutions. He doesn't have the prosecutor's burden of proof that you always bear. He's not tagged with proving the elements of murder beyond a reasonable doubt. In a wrongful death case, all he has to show is that it is more probable than not that Manny killed his father, Zorn, and Jennings while working under the direction of Bully Calhoun. That's a huge difference." Tom stopped and leaned his hands back on the window seal. "Remember what happened with O. J.? The State of California lost the criminal prosecution, but the victims' families won the wrongful death suit for millions. Take off your prosecutor hat for a second and see these cases through Rick's eyes. He has a fighting chance, and history proves out the strategy. He just needs to get to the jury on one of them, and he's four days away."

Helen peered up at Tom with a grim smile. "Spoken like the law professor you once were. Look, right now my main concern is putting JimBone Wheeler back where he belongs, and I'm very worried about your partner. Rick Drake's been on a vendetta since learning his father's death wasn't an accident. I'm concerned that Wheeler's escape and Manny's suspected involvement could send him off the rails, and so is Powell. It was the first thing Powell said to me after I told him. 'I'm worried what this is going to do to Rick.'" She licked her lips. "The kid's volatile, Tom. This could be the match that ignites the gasoline."

Tom took a ragged breath and coughed. Then he cleared his throat and pierced Helen's gaze with his own. "If JimBone Wheeler is coming to fulfill his promise to bring a reckoning on me and everyone I love"—he paused and looked down at the asphalt—"then I want my partner, volatile or not, in my corner."

"Why?" Helen asked.

"Because he's got skin in the game." Tom coughed again and met Helen's eye. "And he's no kid anymore. He's a man."

12

Rick Drake stood in the well of the courtroom. He studied the eyes of the jurors, trying to hold each of their gazes for half a second before settling on the young woman in the front row. Nicole Beasley was a registered nurse on the pediatric floor at Druid City Hospital. Late twenties, short brown hair, brown eyes, and a kind smile. Since the moment jury selection began eight days ago, Rick had found himself looking at her when talking to the group. It was like that with trials. There always seemed to be one or two jurors who were into the case more than the others. He thought of his first trial in Henshaw three years ago. Judy Heacock, a retired schoolteacher at Henshaw High, had been his ideal juror. Then a year later, in Pulaski, during Bo's trial, there was another teacher, named Millie Sanderson. He couldn't believe he still remembered their names, but he could. He would never forget any details of those cases, his first two trials.

Time to bring it home, Rick thought. He had already given his closing argument, and the defense had just finished theirs. Now it was time for rebuttal—his last chance to make an impression with the jury before they would make their decision.

"By this point, you've heard and seen all the evidence, and you're probably tired of hearing me and Mr. Tyler argue about it." Nicole Beasley smiled, and Rick returned the gesture, moving his eyes down the line of faces as his own smile gradually faded. Then, slowly and deliberately, he walked to the plaintiff's table and stood by his client. "This is normally the time in the trial when I would ask my client to stand." Rick's voice carried to every corner of the courtroom, and he felt adrenaline flood his veins. This was why he loved trying cases. There was no feeling like it in the world. "I'd ask her to stand and I'd tell you her name one last time and request that you go back in that jury room and do what you think is fair. I'd ask you to use your common sense and render a fair decision." Rick paused and looked down at the young woman sitting in the wheelchair. He put his hand on her shoulder and she clasped it with her own for a brief second. Then, letting go, Rick looked at the jury. "I'm not going to do that today. I'm not going to do that, because I *can't* do that. Grace Simpson *can't* stand. She *can't* walk. She *can't* feel her legs at all. Grace Simpson is paralyzed from the waist down."

The courtroom was silent as a morgue as Rick strode back toward the jury box, stopping at the defense table and pointing. "Grace Simpson can't walk anymore because JPS Van Lines didn't care enough to do even the most basic of background checks on one of their drivers. When JPS hired Mack Boone, they were putting a man with four speeding tickets and two DUIs back on the highway. Now"—Rick's voice dripped with sarcasm—"Mr. Tyler here wants to argue that those offenses were in the past. He wants to say that this was all just a terrible accident. That the light had just turned red, and that if Ms. Simpson had glanced in both directions before proceeding forward she would have seen Mr. Boone's speeding van before it plowed into her Honda Civic at fifteen miles over the speed limit. Mr. Tyler argues that Mr. Boone wasn't legally intoxicated at the time of the crash, but my question to you is this: Why would a person whose sole job is to safely drive a van have any alcohol in his system at three thirty in the afternoon on a Tuesday?"

Rick paused, glaring again at Brock Smith, the president of JPS, before approaching the jury for the final time. Noticing that most of them, even Beasley, were looking at the floor, perhaps unnerved by Rick's intensity, he spoke in a calm voice.

"Grace Simpson was on her way to lacrosse practice."

Then he paused and waited. After several seconds, he saw the desired effect. Every person on the jury had raised their head, and all eyes had returned to him. Rick forced back a smile, because he could almost hear Professor McMurtrie's gravelly voice in his head. *Sometimes the most effective tool in a closing argument is to stop talking.*

Rick continued in the same measured tone. "Grace had a lacrosse scholarship to the University of Alabama. She'd loved the game since she was nine years old and had realized her dream of getting a chance to play for the Crimson Tide. She could run like a deer." He stopped and pointed at his client. "Now she can't run at all."

Rick Drake counted a thousand one, a thousand two, and then a thousand three. Then he looked back at the jury. "I'm not asking for fairness today, ladies and gentlemen. I'm demanding justice for that young woman over there. JPS Van Lines negligently and recklessly allowed Mack Boone to drive for them, and Boone ran a red light while speeding and under the influence of alcohol and left Grace Simpson a paraplegic. You can't give Grace her legs back. But you can punish those who took them away." Rick peered at the defense table one last time and then turned back to the jury. "Don't let them get away with this."

Three hours later, at 7:30 p.m., Rick was jostled from sleep in the hallway of the courthouse with the words that make the hair on every trial lawyer's arms stand on end: "They've reached a verdict."

Rick made a quick dash for the restroom and splashed water on his face, trying to wake up. Normally, a trial will adjourn at five. But when Judge Poe had tendered the case to the jury at four thirty, Nicole Beasley and her eleven companions asked to stay late to see if they could reach a decision. After almost two full weeks of trial, the judge had not hesitated in his response. "You can stay as long as you like," he had said.

So, while all the courthouse staff, parties, and lawyers involved in other cases had left the building, everyone associated with *Simpson v. JPS Van Lines*, including the ample press corps following the case, had stayed. During the wait, Rick had found a quiet alcove, kept his cell phone turned off, and tried to get some rest. He was due in court in Jasper the following morning at ten, but he forced himself not to think about the obstacles that awaited him there or what he might do if the jury here was still deliberating. *They wouldn't have asked to stay late if they didn't think they could reach a verdict,* he had thought, and his instincts had turned out to be correct.

Now, feeling his heart pounding in his chest, he wiped his face with a towel and hustled into the courtroom to take a seat between Grace and her mother at the counsel table. As the jury filed back into their box to the left of the judge's bench, mother and daughter held hands and Rick said a silent prayer. *God, please give this family peace.* He had learned the most valuable lesson of his career in his first jury trial in Henshaw. The case was never about him, the lawyer. It was always about the client. This case was about Grace Simpson and her family. The pain and agony that they had been put through. The broken dreams. She would never play lacrosse again. She would never walk again. She would never bear children.

Feeling heat behind his eyes, Rick steeled himself to be calm and cool. *Never let them see you sweat,* the Professor had always instructed. *Win, lose, or draw, you're a professional first and foremost.*

God, I wish he was here, Rick thought. Then, as Judge Braxton Poe entered the courtroom, Rick stood and tried to breathe.

"Has the jury reached its verdict?" Judge Poe asked, his voice even raspier than normal from the effects of a bad cold.

"Yes, Your Honor." Nicole Beasley rose from her seat in the box, and Rick felt a warm and fuzzy feeling in his chest. *She's the foreman.*

"What says the jury?" the judge asked.

Turning to face the counsel tables, Beasley spoke in a loud, clear voice. "We the jury for the circuit court of Tuscaloosa County, Alabama, find for the plaintiff."

Rick felt Grace Simpson's hand squeeze his own. *Yes,* he thought, but that was only part one.

Beasley continued. "The jury awards compensatory damages to the plaintiff in the amount of two million five hundred thousand dollars." Beasley paused and gave Rick the slightest of nods. "And punitive damages in the amount of twenty million dollars."

Rick Drake closed his eyes and felt arms wrap around him. To his right, Barbara Simpson was hugging him and whispering into his ear over and over again, "Thank you, thank you, thank you." With this money, Barbara would be able to take care of her daughter for the rest of her life. There was joy but also an overpowering sense of relief in her voice. Then, opening his eyes, Rick looked to his left, where Grace Simpson cried softly in her wheelchair. What was she thinking about right now? The kids she would never birth? The lacrosse games she would never play? Or was she thinking about the last thing that Jameson Tyler, the attorney for JPS, told the jury? "If she had only looked both ways before entering the intersection, she could have prevented this tragedy." Or maybe it was the piece of evidence the jury didn't hear. That she had tried a synthetic marijuana cigarette a week before the accident to help her relax for two exams and that a minuscule trace of it was found in her system. Rick's board-certified toxicologist opined that the nominal amount of cannabis found in Grace's urine would have had no impairment whatsoever on her ability drive a vehicle and, on the eve of trial, Judge Poe had finally granted Rick's motion to exclude the evidence. The jury had never heard about the pot, but that didn't mean Grace Simpson wasn't thinking about it now.

There was never any peace for the victims. No jury verdict would give them that.

As he was packing up his briefcase, long after Barbara and Grace Simpson had said their goodbyes and left the courtroom, Rick felt a strong hand pat his shoulder.

"Great job, Rick."

Rick looked up and managed a tired smile. "Thanks, Jameson."

Jameson Tyler was a senior partner with Jones & Butler, the largest law firm in Birmingham. Tyler was widely considered to be the best defense lawyer in the state. He and Rick had a history, and most of it was bad. When he was in law school, Rick had clerked for two summers at Jones & Butler, and Tyler had been his mentor. An offer had been made, but then it was withdrawn after Rick got into a well-publicized altercation with the Professor after a trial team competition. When Rick and the Professor had teamed up to take on Willistone Trucking Company in a truck accident case in Henshaw, Alabama, three and a half years ago, Tyler had been on the other side. The verdict had been huge—ninety million dollars—and had started Rick on his path as a plaintiff's lawyer.

But it was still hard to look at Jameson Tyler and feel anything but bitterness and resentment. With his perfectly tailored charcoal-gray suit, heavily starched white shirt, light-blue tie, and carefully parted hair, which had turned from dark brown to salt and pepper in the last few years, Tyler was the walking embodiment of the big-firm lawyer. He was everything that Rick Drake had wanted to be when he was in law school.

Even now, after having been torched for twenty-two point five million dollars, Tyler had a toothy grin on his face, the picture of confidence. "You know we'll appeal."

"I do," Rick said.

"Judge Poe screwed the pooch when he denied my motion to bifurcate the negligence and negligent hiring and supervision portions of the trial. He also should've let the evidence of marijuana in your client's system come in." Jameson shook his head and scoffed. "It's almost like Braxton felt bad for all the grief he'd given the Professor over the years before Tom got sick and was trying to make up for it by throwing y'all some bones on these rulings." He paused, and his grin faded away. "It doesn't matter. The bottom line is that this case isn't over. Not by a long shot."

Rick didn't immediately respond. He was too tired to argue the law anymore after an eight-day trial and didn't have the first clue about Judge Braxton Poe's motivations, though he was aware of the bad blood between the Professor and Poe and had seen it firsthand in the trial of Wilma Newton the year before. Finally, licking his lips, he gazed at his nemesis and spoke in a voice hoarse from fatigue. "You know what my bottom line is, Jameson?"

The defense lawyer cocked his head to the side, waiting.

"A win is a win. Good luck with your appeal."

Jameson smirked and headed for the exit, grabbing his own briefcase on the defense table as he left. At the double doors, he stopped and looked over his shoulder at Rick. "Why in the world didn't we settle this case?"

Rick gazed across the gallery at him, realizing that they were the only two people left in the courtroom. "Because you're an asshole," Rick said.

Jameson guffawed. "And then some, kid. And then some." He shook his head. "Remind me again how we left it at the mediation."

Rick smirked, knowing damn well that Jameson didn't need a reminder. "You only offered two hundred and fifty thousand, and the insurance policy limits were three million. JPS is a two-hundred-million-dollar company."

Jameson rubbed his chin. "Well, this little development"—Jameson pointed to the now-empty jury box—"has changed the landscape. We'll forgo the appeal if your client will accept the limits. I suspect the Supremes will, at worst case, knock the verdict in half, if not more, and I'm betting on them overturning it altogether."

Rick wasn't sure what the Alabama Supreme Court would do, but he knew that an appeal would last at least two years, and Barbara Simpson had almost gone broke paying for all the extra medical supplies Grace needed that insurance wouldn't cover. "I'll get back to you," Rick said, figuring there was some water in Jameson's offer and JPS would probably go past the limits to five or even ten million, either of which Barbara Simpson would probably accept in lieu of the two-year wait and the possibility of having to try the case all over again.

"You do that," Jameson said, grabbing the door handle. Then, for several seconds, Jameson paused without moving.

"Something else on your mind?" Rick finally asked.

Without looking at him, Jameson spoke. "You kicked my ass, Rick. We tried this case because I convinced my client that you couldn't carry the ball without the Professor there to recover your fumbles. I . . . didn't think you could pull it off." Jameson turned and looked Rick in the eye. "My hat's off to you."

"Thank you," Rick managed, still not quite believing what he'd just heard.

"If you're ever interested in crossing back over to the dark side, let me know. Our firm would love to have you."

Rick smiled. They both knew that would never happen. "I'll keep it in mind."

13

Twenty minutes later, Rick trudged down the steps of the Tuscaloosa County Courthouse after granting a couple of interviews to the reporters who had waited. Most of the questions asked for his reaction to the jury verdict and whether he thought the result would stand up on appeal. Rick thanked the jury for its "fair and just award" and said he was relieved for Grace and Barbara Simpson that this ordeal was finally over.

When he reached the parking lot, he saw a green Channel 19 news van parked next to his car. A young woman stood by the van twirling a microphone. Next to her was an extremely tall and skinny man setting up a video camera on a tripod.

"Great," he whispered, sighing as he unlocked the trunk of his 1998 rusted gold Saturn and placed his briefcase inside.

"Got time for one last interview, counselor?" the woman asked, winking at him. Georgi Perry was a petite woman with short blond hair reminiscent of the way the actress Gwyneth Paltrow had worn her locks in several movies that Rick had watched as a kid. She had fair skin, green eyes, and a well-earned reputation as an incredibly hard worker not afraid to elbow her way into sticky situations and ask tough questions. Two years earlier, after the tornado hit in April, Georgi had spent weeks on the front lines interviewing survivors of the tragedy. She had also managed to obtain a rare death row exclusive with Foster Arrington, the middle school teacher convicted of abducting, raping, and murdering one of his students.

"Anything for you, Georgi," Rick said, managing a tired smile and beginning to adjust his tie for the camera.

"Keep it undone," she said, and he looked at her with a question in his eyes.

She walked over and undid the top button of his shirt and reloosened the tie he had just tightened. "I'm serious. It looks better this way. Gives you that battle-weary-lawyer look."

"Whatever you say," Rick said. He had gotten to know the reporter in the months after his return from Pulaski two years earlier. She had done a special on the social and racial implications of the trial of Bocephus Haynes, which had gone over well with her viewership and been a nice platform for the firm.

"OK, we good to go, Paul?" Georgi glanced at the beanpole of a cameraman, who gave a thumbs-up. Rick felt Georgi's hand grip his forearm and pull him closer to her. He could smell the pleasant scent of coconut coming from her hair. Then she let go as Paul counted down with his fingers: *Three, two, one* . . .

"We are standing here with attorney Rick Drake, the lawyer for Grace Simpson, the Tuscaloosa High lacrosse player who was left a paraplegic after a tragic accident with a vehicle on the JPS Van Line almost two years ago. Today, a Tuscaloosa County jury awarded Ms. Simpson twenty-two point five million dollars, the largest verdict that this county has seen in over a decade. Mr. Drake, would you care to comment on the jury's result?"

Without hesitation or conscious thought, Rick gazed into the camera and gave the same spiel he had said to the reporters on the courthouse steps. When he finished, he started to walk away, assuming the interview was over. Georgi's voice stopped him.

"Mr. Drake, one last question. Your firm has been involved in several high-profile trials over the last three years: The case against Willistone Trucking Company over three years ago in Henshaw, Alabama, that resulted in the largest jury verdict in west Alabama history. Your televised defense of Bocephus Haynes in Pulaski, Tennessee, on charges of capital murder, which we profiled on this news station. And last year, the defense of Wilma Christine Newton, who was charged with the murder of local trucking tycoon Jack Willistone. In all those cases, your partner, Professor Tom McMurtrie, was lead counsel, but it is our understanding that he was not present for the Simpson trial this past week due to health problems. Has Professor McMurtrie officially retired, and if so, what does the future hold for Rick Drake?"

Rick paused before responding. This was the kind of question that could make him look like a prick if he gave the wrong answer. But it also gave him a platform to say something meaningful. He gazed at the reporter and spoke in a soft tone. "The Professor has retired. He . . ." Rick paused, not wanting to elaborate on his partner's health, and Georgi raised her eyebrows. "He's earned it," Rick finished, gazing down at the asphalt.

Georgi started to wave at Paul to click off the camera, but Rick's voice, stronger and more forceful, broke through. The tape kept rolling. "As for me, now that justice has been obtained for Grace Simpson, I have only one goal." He took a step closer to the camera, not fully conscious of his movement, and looked directly into the lens. "I am representing the families of Alvin Jennings, Gregory Zorn, and William Drake in wrongful death lawsuits filed in Walker, Baldwin, and Henshaw Counties. Mr. Jennings, a middle school basketball coach, was killed in a lawn mower explosion at his home in Jasper. Mr. Zorn, a local bankruptcy attorney, was gunned down by three sniper bullets while walking on the sand a half mile from the Flora-Bama Lounge in Orange Beach. Mr. Drake, my father"—Rick forced the crack out of his voice—"was forced off Highway 82 in Henshaw by a hit-and-run driver, and his truck collided with a tree. He died on impact."

Rick paused, and despite the exhaustion he felt from the eight-day trial, his body trembled with adrenaline. When he spoke again, he could hear the intensity in his voice. "Our complaint alleges that a woman named Mahalia Reyes wrongfully caused these deaths at the bequest of her employer, the late Marcellus 'Bully' Calhoun. If you know of the whereabouts of Ms. Reyes, who is avoiding service of process and goes by the nickname Manny, please call my office. A cash reward will be given to any person who provides information that helps me find her." Rick paused and glared into the camera. "It is my mission in life to obtain justice for the victims and their families. Thank you."

When Rick stopped talking, the lights of the camera went out. "Alright . . . that's a wrap," Georgi said.

Rick opened the door to his car and climbed inside. After he started the vehicle, he heard knocking on the Saturn's window and he rolled it down. Georgi was standing there, smiling at him. She was still holding the microphone, but Paul had already loaded up the rest of the equipment. "Two more questions, counselor?" she asked. "Off the record."

Rick sighed. "Shoot."

"You're a multimillionaire trial lawyer and you're what, thirty years old?"

"Twenty-nine," Rick said.

"So why are you driving this piece of junk?"

Rick patted the steering wheel and smiled. He had fielded that same question at least ten times from the Professor. *And even more from Dawn.*

"What did Crash Davis say in *Bull Durham*? You don't mess with a winning streak." He shrugged, knowing that was only part of the reason. He also didn't like the idea of jurors seeing him arriving at court in a fancy sports car. If someone on the jury saw him, he wanted them to see a normal guy just trying to make it. "I've got to go, Georgi. I'll see you around."

"Wait, I said I had *two* questions." She held up the index and middle fingers of her right hand.

"And you've already asked them. My age and why I drive this piece of crap. So—"

"Three then," Georgi interrupted, holding up one additional finger, her lips curving into a shy grin. "Want to buy me a drink?"

Rick smiled up at her. He couldn't deny the attraction. He had felt it the first time they were around each other. "Not tonight," he said. "I have some things I have to do."

She creased her eyebrows. "Really? You just finished an eight-day jury trial. One drink. Don't you want to celebrate the victory?"

Rick rubbed his bloodshot eyes.

"You *are* single now, aren't you?" Georgi pressed. "You've been single for over a year, right?"

Rick sighed and squinted at her. "You're up to five questions, Georgi."

"Just one drink?" she asked, poking her lip out. "You don't want to hurt my feelings, do you?"

"I can't," Rick repeated. "I have to be in Jasper at ten in the morning for a pretrial conference, and it's going to take me all night to get ready for it."

The reporter blinked her eyes, and Rick could instantly tell that curiosity had replaced disappointment. "Is that the Jennings case you just mentioned?"

Rick nodded. "Pretrial tomorrow morning, and jury selection is supposed to begin Monday."

"*Supposed?*"

"Calhoun's estate has a pending summary judgment motion that will be heard in the morning. If it's granted, then the case is over." Rick paused and felt a cold chill on the back of his neck as he pondered the stakes in play at tomorrow's hearing. Prior to any civil jury trial, a defendant can move the court for a summary judgment if they can show that there is no issue of material fact and that the plaintiff has failed to present substantial evidence supporting the elements of their claim. Though the court is supposed to view all facts in a light most favorable to the plaintiff, Rick knew his evidence against Jennings was thin. Still, *We should win tomorrow,* Rick told himself. "But if the judge denies that motion like he should, then we're teeing it up next week."

Georgi frowned. "How can you try the case if you haven't served the killer with the complaint yet?"

"I've got the estate of Bully Calhoun served, and Bully was Manny Reyes's employer."

"So you say."

Rick glared up at her. "I have a witness who will testify that she worked for Bully, and I have an eyewitness that puts her near Jennings's house the day of the explosion."

"That sounds weak. I'm not surprised that Bully's estate has moved for a summary judgment."

Under normal circumstances, Rick might have been angry at the reporter's comment, but fatigue had settled in. Besides, he was impressed with her knowledge of the legal system. "Thanks for the vote of confidence," Rick said, leaning back in his seat and gazing over the steering wheel.

"How are the other cases going?" Georgi asked. "Zorn's and . . . your dad's."

Rick coughed and continued to peer through the windshield. "A lot depends on tomorrow. If the Walker County judge kicks us to the curb, then it's only a matter of time before the courts in Baldwin and Henshaw do the same." He paused. "Our best chance is in Jasper. As you accurately concluded, our evidence is thin, but I think we have enough to avoid summary judgment and get to the jury." He looked up at her. "And it's anyone's ball game in front of the jury. Jameson Tyler and JPS Van Lines found that out the hard way today. Kathryn Calhoun Willistone will too. I just can't lose tomorrow."

Georgi smiled down at him. Then, without prompting, she leaned her head through the open window and planted a kiss on his cheek. "Good luck, counselor," she whispered in his ear. Before Rick could respond, the reporter turned her back and started to walk away. When she reached the television van, she peered at him over her shoulder. "I'll let you buy me that drink some other time." Frowning, she added, "And winning streak or not, you really need to get a new car, Rick. The most eligible bachelor in Tuscaloosa shouldn't be driving that piece of crap."

Then, flipping her hair with mock bravado, she opened the passenger-side door to the van and it peeled away, leaving Rick alone in the empty parking lot.

Shaking his head, Rick Drake put his Saturn in gear but kept his foot on the brake. He had just won the biggest victory of his young legal career, but he felt hollow inside as his thoughts turned to Manny Reyes and the hearing in Jasper in the morning.

Rick sighed and pressed the accelerator. A long night was ahead.

14

The law office of McMurtrie & Drake, LLC, was located on a side street off of Greensboro Avenue, a couple blocks from the courthouse. Due to the close proximity, Rick normally walked to court, but he'd chosen to drive for the Simpson trial because of the media coverage the case had garnered. He had figured that driving would allow for a quicker exit.

I figured wrong, Rick thought, pulling his car to a stop on the curb in front of the building and looking down at his watch. It was 8:30 p.m., and it seemed that the only illumination in downtown Tuscaloosa came from the traffic and streetlights. The office buildings were dark, the business of the day done.

Rick grabbed his briefcase and climbed out of the car, taking a moment to breathe in the cold winter air. He was exhausted and knew that there would be no rest tonight. But as he took in a gulp of oxygen, he remembered the look on the face of Barbara Simpson after the verdict was read and smiled. Like many cases in the Alabama court system, the Simpson matter had dragged on for over two years before it reached a conclusion. *And if Jameson Tyler has his way, it could last two more.* Rick drew in another deep gust of air and slowly blew it out. *A win is a win,* he thought, repeating in his mind what he had told Jameson Tyler.

Then another phrase popped into his head. *Appeals are for losers,* the Professor had jokingly told their trial team during the first practice each year. And in a way he was right. A party can't appeal unless he or she has lost the case at trial. *I'm going to teach you how to win in front of the jury so that you can spend your time in appellate courts defending victories instead of trying to overcome defeat.*

Rick smiled at the memory as he trudged toward the breezeway that led to the stairwell. But as he thought about the Professor, the good vibes left him almost as soon as they had come. He missed his partner. As gratifying as winning the Simpson case was, especially with Jameson Tyler on the other side, the triumph was bittersweet without the Professor here to share it with him.

And today is his birthday, for Christ's sake, Rick remembered, snapping his fingers and resolving to call his partner as soon as he was upstairs. News of the Simpson win would make for a nice present, and he could also go over his plan for the Jennings hearing.

Rick picked up his pace as he passed the display window of Larry and Barry's Interior Design, the ground-floor business that had produced Rick's first few clients when he'd hung his shingle four years earlier. The two owners, Larry Horowitz and Barry Bostheimer, were gay lovers from Missouri who'd made a killing helping the ladies of the Junior League of Tuscaloosa decorate their lavish homes. They had become friends of Rick's over the time they had shared this building, and during the dark times of the past year, as Rick had dealt with the breakup with Dawn, his father's murder, and the Professor's illness, they had been kind souls who had offered support and encouragement. And the occasional unsolicited dating advice.

Rick managed another tired smile as he began to ascend the stairs that led to the firm's office on the second floor. An elevator had been discussed for years but had yet to happen. In truth, Rick didn't mind the climb. It was about the only exercise he got anymore.

"You always walk up these steps in the dark?" a loud voice rang out above him, and Rick blinked as the overhead bulb of the stairwell clicked on. When he was able to focus his eyes again, he saw a familiar and welcome sight. A heavyset man with sandy-blond hair sat on the top step clad in khaki pants, a white button-down, and a fire-engine-red jacket. A toothpick dangled out of his mouth. Ambrose Powell Conrad, the district attorney of Tuscaloosa County, broke into a grin. "I hear that Grace Simpson is twenty-two point five million dollars richer."

"Not exactly," Rick said. "Jameson's going to appeal."

"Appeals are for losers," Powell said, standing as Rick continued to ascend the stairs. "At least that's what my trial team coach always said."

"Mine too," Rick said. Powell had been Rick's partner on the Professor's last team. The sandy-haired prosecutor was also Rick Drake's best friend in the world and the loudest human being he had ever been around in person.

"You come to buy me a beer and tell me how great I am?" Rick said, extending his hand.

Powell's grin faded. "I wish."

"What then?" Rick asked, feeling his stomach tighten as he noticed the look of fear in his friend's eyes.

"JimBone Wheeler escaped from Riverbend this morning."

Rick felt his heart constrict and his breath catch in his throat. He opened his mouth, but no words came out.

"The cops in Nashville think he has an accomplice," Powell added, putting a firm hand on Rick's shoulder. "The only description they gave is of a tan-skinned woman."

Rick swallowed and his mouth felt as dry as sandpaper. "*Manny?*" he whispered.

In the dull glow of the overhead light, Powell Conrad's eyes blazed with fury. Finally, the prosecutor nodded his head.

15

Tom sat at the head of a long cherrywood table, listening to his grandchildren serenade him with a stirring rendition of "Happy Birthday."

His granddaughter, Jenny, yelled "Cha, cha, cha" after every line of the song, which caused her older brother to roll his eyes. Tom noticed that Nancy, who sat between Jenny and Jackson, was staring at the cake with a blank look on her face. Meanwhile, at the far end of the table, Tommy worked his jaw and gazed down at the table.

Though both of them had insisted that the "party must go on," the news of JimBone Wheeler's escape had cast a pall over everything.

Tom peered down at the cake that lay on the place mat before him. It was German chocolate, his favorite. Julie used to make him one every year for his birthday and Christmas. In the middle of the cake was one lone candle, and Tom smirked. If they had wanted to put seventy-three on the damn thing, the cake would have needed to be three times its current size. Of course, given his diminished lung capacity and overall weakness, he doubted he'd be able to blow out just this one. When the singing stopped, they all looked at him with expectation and perhaps a little worry.

Tom leaned forward and cocked his head at Jackson, who sat to his right. "How about a little help, Forty-Nine?" he asked, winking at the boy. Together, Tom and his grandson blew out the one candle.

"Did you make a wish, Papa?" Jenny asked, and Tom felt his stomach tighten. He had, in fact, made a wish, but he was not going to burden the six-year-old with what he had requested.

"All my wishes have come true, Jenny girl," he said, winking at her too.

Dutifully, Tom took a bite of the cake and a small sip from the glass of sweet tea that Nancy had poured him. He was conscious of the phone in his pocket, which still had not beeped or rang. He looked at Nancy. "Did Bo ever call?"

Her face fell. "No. I'm sure . . . he would be here if he could."

Tom nodded and felt a flutter in his stomach. At the prison nineteen months earlier, JimBone had not just promised to bring Tom a reckoning. He had also threatened to kill Bo and his family. *And Rick . . . and Powell . . . and Wade . . .*

. . . Everyone I hold dear.

Moving his gaze from Jackson, who had already cleaned his plate, to Jenny, whose lips and chin were now covered with a film of chocolate icing, to Nancy, peering at him with palpable fear in her eyes, to his son, who was staring at his coffee cup, looking, as he often did, lost in thought, and finally, behind them, to the baby's playpen, where one-year-old Julie, her grandmother's namesake, sucked on a pacifier, Tom felt his chest swell with equal parts love and terror. He dropped his fork, and the utensil clanged off his plate and onto the floor.

"I'll get it," Jackson said, leaning his head under the table and placing the fork back on the place mat.

"Go get Papa another one, son," Nancy instructed, and the boy hopped off his seat and strode toward the kitchen.

"You OK, Dad?" Tommy asked, his eyebrows creased with worry.

Tom tried to drink a sip of tea, but his throat clenched before he could swallow, producing a fit of coughing. He closed his eyes and tried to push through it. These episodes had become more and more frequent over the past few weeks, which Tom figured was not a good omen for his scans in the morning. *The mass has grown.* Tom knew it in his bones. After several minutes, the coughing finally subsided and Tom brought his fist to his mouth. He cleared his throat and opened his eyes. He saw that Nancy had removed everyone's plate at the table but his own, and that only he and Tommy remained. His son had taken Jackson's seat and was patting Tom on the back.

"Better now?" Tommy asked.

Tom nodded, hating the shell of a man he had become. *What have I brought on my family?* he thought, picturing JimBone Wheeler's copper eyes in his mind.

"Dad, what—?"

"Do you know where my shotgun shells are?" Tom interrupted, his voice a low wheeze.

Tommy again creased his eyebrows. "Of course. There's a lockbox in one of the cubbyholes in the utility room. Since the kids were born, you've always kept the shells and bullets separated from the guns."

Tom closed his eyes, nodding as he remembered. "The key is in a cabinet above the washer. Go get the whole box." He paused and let out a ragged breath. "I've laid out most of my guns on the bed in my room. Bring them too."

Tommy's eyes twitched. "Dad, General Lewis said she had lined up security here and at our house. I haven't been home yet, but this place is crawling with officers. Are you sure—?"

"Yes," Tom said, opening his eyes and peering at his son. "I trust Helen and I'm sure the deputies she's enlisted to protect us are good.

But all the same, JimBone Wheeler is a former Army Ranger, and he managed to break out of a maximum security prison. He's a trained killer and so is Manny Reyes." He paused. "Get the guns, OK?"

Tommy opened his mouth as if to argue some more but then thought better of it. He gave a swift nod and stood from the table. "Yes, sir."

16

Thirty minutes later, Tom and Tommy escorted Nancy and the kids to their car. Three Giles County Sheriff's Office sedans were parked side by side where the asphalt driveway abutted the farm, and beyond them Tom saw the headlights of two more government SUVs, one on the north end of the land and the other the south. But despite this police blanket, both father and son held twelve-gauge shotguns in their hands, and Nancy's voice shook with dread when she told Tom goodbye.

"It's OK," Tom said, patting her arm while moving his eyes around the driveway and the farm to the north. Like with the General an hour earlier, regardless of the security she had arranged, he had the same feeling of being sitting ducks for a sniper. *If someone wanted to pick us off with a rifle right now . . .*

He cut off the thought and shooed Nancy into the passenger seat of his son's SUV while Tommy put his shotgun in the back hatch. Once they were all inside the vehicle, Tom handed his son the nine-millimeter handgun, and Tommy stuck the weapon in the side of his jeans. Tom spoke softly through the open window.

"You'll be escorted home by Officer Satterfeal." Tom pointed to the closest sedan. "And there are deputies from the Huntsville Police Department and Madison County Sheriff's Office stationed outside your home."

Tommy nodded his understanding.

"No school tomorrow for the kids, OK?"

"OK, Dad. We've already discussed—"

"I know we have," Tom snapped. "But I want to say it again. No school for the kids. You handle your morning surgery—one of the officers will drive you to and from the hospital. Once you're back home, you stay put. And outside of the operating room, you keep that pistol on you at all times." He pointed at the gun and coughed. "Nancy stays in the house, and you promise me that you'll show her how to use the shotgun."

Tommy smirked. "Dad, Nancy grew up in Cullman. She's a better shot than me."

At this revelation, Tom managed a laugh. All the rounds of chemo and radiation over the past year had fried his brain, and he had a hard time remembering details like his daughter-in-law's background. "That's good," he said. "I hope she doesn't have to prove it."

"Me too," Tommy said, reaching for his father's hand and giving it a squeeze. "What about you, Dad? Who's going to take you to your scans tomorrow?"

"Bill Davis has that covered, but I'll have a police escort to CCI."

"And tonight? Are you going to be OK by yourself?"

Tom scoffed and held up the shotgun. "I still know how to use one of these. Besides, I won't be alone. I've got the General's cavalry canvassing the yard and farm." He smiled. "And Lee Roy will be here to back them up. Ain't that right, boy?"

Tom gazed behind him, where his bulldog stood guard in the carport. The animal's ears were up, and at the sound of his name, he let out a low, guttural, throat-clearing sound. Lee Roy had finally gotten used to the presence of the sheriff's deputies, but the dog remained hyperalert.

"If you say so," Tommy said, forcing his own smile. For a second, he blinked his eyes and gazed over the steering wheel. Then he peered at his father again. "You really think JimBone Wheeler is going to come after us?"

Tom squinted back at his son, seeing not the thirty-eight-year-old surgeon in his blue eyes but rather the ten-year-old boy who used to ask him whether the Crimson Tide was going to beat Auburn that year. *What have I brought on my family?* Tom pondered again, feeling a wave of fear and guilt wash over him. Gritting his teeth, he shook off the torturous thoughts and told his son the truth.

"Yes, I do."

17

For the next fifteen minutes, Tom sat in his recliner in the den, with Lee Roy lying at his feet. He held his twelve-gauge in one hand and his cell phone in the other. While saying his goodbyes to his family, he had received a cryptic *You OK?* text from Helen, to which Tom had responded, *Yes,* though that was a bald-faced lie. Tom was far from OK. He was tired. He was worried.

Most of all, he was scared.

Tom McMurtrie could count on one hand the times in his life when he had truly been engulfed by fear: As a first-year law student in October 1962 driving home through the night to be with his parents as they waited out the Cuban Missile Crisis while the whole country braced for a nuclear holocaust. Six and a half years ago, in the oncologist's office on McFarland, waiting for the results of Julie's PET scan and knowing in his gut that the verdict wouldn't be good. And two years ago in Pulaski, driving to Walton Farm after the trial—after he had figured it all out—and praying that he wasn't too late. Praying that his best friend in the world, Bocephus Haynes, was still alive.

Bo.

As the thought entered his mind, his phone dinged and there was another text from Helen. *Have you heard from Bo yet?*

As he rocked back and forth in the recliner, he peered at the message, not wanting to answer it. Not wanting to admit that something was wrong.

But something is wrong, he thought.

Bo should have called by now. He should've answered his phone. Tom had also called Bo's wife, Jasmine, and son, T. J., and neither one of them had answered or returned the voice messages he had left. He glared at the phone, trying to will his friend to respond. When his cell actually did ring, his body jerked and his gun fell to the hardwood floor. Fortunately, he had the safety on, or the weapon might have gone off. He propped the gun against the couch next to his chair and looked at the screen on his phone. The caller ID said "Tommy."

He tapped the "Answer" button and held his breath.

"We're home," his son said. "There's a deputy stationed in the backyard and two more in a sheriff's cruiser parked on the curb in front of the house. Doors are locked. Alarm is on. I've got the pistol, and Nancy has the shotgun. I even let the dogs out of their kennels."

"The toy poodles?" Tom asked, unable to suppress a grin.

"Oscar and Meyer have some fight to them," Tommy fired back, but there was a tease in his voice and the two men laughed.

"Thanks for calling," Tom said. "Give me an update in the morning, OK?"

"Ten-four," Tommy said. "You do the same."

They said their goodbyes, and despite his fatigue and the persistent pain in his back, Tom began to pace the house, every so often gazing forlornly at his phone. After one walk-through, he plopped on the couch and leaned his elbows on his knees.

He clicked on Bo's number, and his call again went straight to voice mail. Had his friend turned his cell off? Was the battery dead?

Tom shivered as he considered other alternatives for why the phone hadn't rung. *Could JimBone have gotten to him?*

Shaken but undeterred, Tom again pulled up the number for Jasmine Haynes, whom Bo had always called Jazz. He was about to click it when the phone began to ring in his hand. The caller ID said "Helen."

Tom sighed and answered the call. "I haven't heard from him," he said.

"I know."

Tom felt his stomach constrict as he stood from the couch. "What?"

"I just got off the phone with Jasmine Haynes."

"And? Is everything OK?"

"Jazz and the kids are fine. She was . . . a little perturbed at the whole situation. Especially the officers parked in front of the house. She's worried what her neighbors will think. She also has a speech she has to give tomorrow morning at the civic center."

"She'll have to skip it."

Helen snorted. "I'll let you try to win that argument. I failed miserably."

Tom rubbed the back of his neck. "Is there any way to arrange security for that?"

"The facility has guards on hand, and I'll alert the Madison County Sheriff's Office and the HPD. But . . ."

"But what?"

"Tom, I'm out of my jurisdiction and they have already cooperated a great deal. Both forces have deputies stationed at your son's house and Jazz's."

"Good grief, Helen. An escaped death row convict is on the loose and Jasmine Haynes could be a target."

"The convict could also be in the friendly skies heading toward Bermuda," Helen chimed in. "I'm at this airfield in Murfreesboro.

There doesn't seem to be much doubt that the ambulance abandoned here was the one that transported Wheeler from the prison to the emergency room."

"Did anyone see him get on a plane?"

"No, but that doesn't mean he didn't. Private airfields don't have the same surveillance and security that the international airports do. There have been thirty flights today, and the Feds are tracking them, but it's possible he could have slipped through the cracks."

"You don't believe that, do you?"

"No, I don't. All I'm saying is that there's now another lead, which my office, the police in Nashville, and the FBI are all investigating. We have security in place for your family and friends, but we can't guarantee their safety if they're going to step out in the open."

Tom closed his eyes, knowing she was right. "Surely Bo can talk some sense into Jazz. Where is he, for God's sake?"

Silence on the other end of the line.

"Helen, where is Bo?"

More silence, followed by a sigh.

"Helen, what's going on? Is Bo OK?"

"He's alive and safe, Tom, and I think I know where he is, but . . ."

"Helen?"

"He's not OK."

18

Old Town Beer Exchange is a beer and wine store in downtown Huntsville. Located on the ground floor of an upscale apartment complex on Holmes Avenue, OTBX had ridden the tide of a craft beer explosion throughout the state of Alabama. Since 2005, breweries had opened in Florence, Gadsden, Birmingham, and Fairhope. The epicenter of this movement was Huntsville, where Straight To Ale and Yellowhammer were mainstays, and it seemed like a new competitor emerged every few months.

OTBX carried most of the local brews, along with a healthy selection of lagers, pilsners, ales, and porters from all over the world. It also had a taproom, where kegs, growlers, and crowlers of over thirty different types of draft beer were available for purchase. Customers were welcome to a free sample, and if the mood struck them, they could sit at the bar and drink a pint or two.

One of the officers guarding the house—a deputy named Shames—had driven Tom to the bar. The officer hadn't been crazy about having Lee Roy in his cruiser, but Tom hadn't had time to argue. *If my dog can't ride along, then I'll drive my damn self.* He knew he was probably being foolish, but he wasn't keen on leaving the dog by himself after all the commotion of the evening. After making sure that Shames had cracked the window for Lee Roy, Tom climbed out of the sedan and trudged toward the front door, using a cane for balance and darting his eyes in all directions. The town was dead quiet, but that was what you would expect at 9:00 p.m. on a Wednesday night. With the hand that wasn't carrying his cane, Tom felt in the pocket of his jacket for the cold steel of the .44 Magnum. Shames had tried to convince him not to carry the weapon, but Tom had refused. Tom knew that the security arranged by Helen wouldn't stop JimBone Wheeler. The man had killed Ray Ray Pickalew in broad daylight in front of the Giles County Courthouse, which had been surrounded by cops. If anything, Tom figured that the crazy killer would relish the challenge.

Tom would have felt safer with his shotgun—he doubted if he could hit a bull in the ass with the revolver—but he knew his twelve-gauge was too big to take in the store and would arouse suspicion. He tapped his thumb on the handle of the handgun, feeling restless and a bit ridiculous. *I'm an attorney and a professor. Not Dirty Harry.*

When he reached the entrance, Tom leaned a hand against the door, which was adorned with a green Christmas wreath, and tried to catch his breath. He'd taken two oxycodone that morning, but despite the pain, he'd missed his evening dose in the chaos of learning about Wheeler's escape. His back was throbbing.

Tom opened the door, and his nostrils filled with the pleasing scents of malt and barley. The sound of Elvis Presley's melodic voice belting out "Blue Christmas" played softly on speakers somewhere in the taproom, and Tom remembered that the song was one of Julie's favorite holiday tunes. He smiled despite his pain and, with the assistance of the cane, began to move toward a long wooden bar to the right, where he'd already spotted his friend.

Tom took a seat on the adjacent stool and cleared his throat. "Excuse me, sir, but I'm looking for a man named Bocephus Haynes.

Big, tall black fella. Played football for Bear Bryant in the '70s. Used to be a successful lawyer in Pulaski, but he's fallen off the grid for a while. Have you seen him?" Tom wanted to add more to the spiel but gave up, waiting for any sign of acknowledgment from his friend.

The man sitting next to Tom slowly turned his head. Both of his elbows were on the table, and he held an almost-empty pint glass in his right hand. His eyes were bloodshot and he had at least a week's worth of beard on his face. The top of his head, which was typically shaved smooth, bore the same amount of stubble. But otherwise he was just as Tom had described him a few seconds earlier. Even slouched on a stool and half-drunk, Bocephus Aurulius Haynes looked every bit of his six feet four inches and 240 pounds.

"Professor?" Bo managed, his speech slurred but his mouth curving into a lazy grin. "What . . . ?" He looked behind Tom and then, despite his drunkenness, straightened himself on the stool. "How did you get here?"

"That doesn't matter," Tom said.

Bo raised his eyebrows. "Is everything alright?"

"No," Tom said. "How many of those have you had?" Tom pointed at the glass.

"Four . . . I think," Bo said "Maybe five. Was about to order another. What's going on?"

"Why haven't you been answering your phone?" Tom knew he should cut to the chase, but seeing his friend in this sorry state angered him.

Bo wrapped his hands around the pint glass and gazed at the long row of taps that lined the back of the bar. He didn't say anything. Finally, he took a long sip, draining the last of the amber-colored fluid.

"Another, Mr. Haynes?" A bartender had approached from the back. He had a scruffy beard and black hair tied up in a ponytail.

Bo nodded and scooted his empty glass across the bar. A few seconds later, a full pint of beer was placed in front of him. "How'd you know I'd be here, Professor?"

"Helen talked with Jazz."

Bo's arms tensed. He turned and glared at Tom. "What's the General doing calling my wife?"

"She called when you didn't show for my birthday party and weren't answering anyone's calls. Eventually she got Jazz, who provided your new address and said if you weren't at home you'd probably be here." Tom paused. "Bo, why didn't you tell me that Jazz had filed for divorce?"

Bo turned back to his glass and raised his eyes to the digital menu above the taps, which showed all the different flavors of beer. On the bar's speakers, Mariah Carey broke into a stirring rendition of "Santa Claus Is Coming to Town." Finally, he sighed and closed his eyes. "I'm sorry I missed your birthday party, Professor. I just . . . didn't want to bring everyone down."

"Why didn't you tell me, Bo? You come out to the farm every week. You take me to most of my appointments at CCI. We shoot the bull, and you never once even mentioned that y'all were having problems again. Why?"

"I didn't want to bother you with my issues, Professor." He opened his eyes, finally meeting Tom's harsh glare. "You've got enough on your plate."

"I'm dying," Tom said, speaking through clenched teeth. "*I'm not dead.*"

"I'm sorry," Bo said, sighing and rubbing his bleary eyes. "I would have gotten around to it eventually."

For several seconds, there was silence, and the bartender approached them again. "Last call, gentlemen. Can I get you anything?" He looked at Tom.

"Water," Tom said, his voice hoarse with fatigue.

The barkeep nodded and turned to Bo. "How about you, Mr. Haynes. Crowler for the road?"

Bo glanced at Tom and then squinted at the bartender. "I better not."

A minute later, Tom stirred his bottle of water with a straw and watched his friend, who took a long pull off his pint glass. One of the things Tom missed most about being healthy was the ability to chug water when he was thirsty. Now, if he took in too much liquid, it led to a coughing fit, so he'd begun drinking everything through a straw.

"Any chance at reconciliation?" Tom asked. "Y'all seemed to be doing so well last year after the Newton case."

Bo shook his head. "Not this time."

Tom couldn't think of the right thing to say, and even if he could, he was losing energy. He coughed and took a sip of water through the straw.

"Why are you here, dog?" Bo finally asked, turning in his stool to face Tom. "I doubt the General was calling Jazz trying to find me just because I missed your party, and I know you didn't come all the way into town with stage four lung cancer to console me while I cry into my beer. What's the deal?"

Tom started to speak, but then the coughing fit he was trying to avoid overtook him. He doubled over on the stool and pressed his fist firmly against his lips to fight back the ripples of pain that each cough caused.

"He OK?" Tom heard the bartender's faint voice from above. He didn't hear Bo say anything, but when he opened his eyes, his friend was holding a bottle of water in front of him.

Tom shook his head and waved Bo off. After at least two full minutes, he felt his throat and chest finally relax and he took in several ragged breaths.

"Fits getting worse?" Bo asked.

Tom nodded. His body now throbbed with pain.

"Next scans are tomorrow, right? Dr. Davis still taking you?"

Again, Tom nodded.

For a moment, neither of them spoke, and Bo took a sip from his glass. Finally, Bo began to talk, and Tom knew his friend was just trying to make the situation less awkward until he gathered himself. "You ever try these India pale ales, Professor?" Not waiting for an answer, Bo continued. "I swear they should have to sell this stuff by prescription. My favorite is Bell's Two Hearted. It's from a brewery up in Michigan. Smooth with plenty of hop—"

"JimBone Wheeler escaped from prison today," Tom finally managed. He looked at Bo, who had stopped dead still with the pint of beer pressed to his lips.

For a long moment, they just looked at each other, neither man moving a muscle. Tom saw the veins at Bo's temples stick out and the muscles in his forearms and biceps tense. Finally, he set the glass down without drinking from it.

"*When?*" Bo asked, and his voice was no longer slurred.

"Early this morning. JimBone feigned a life-threatening medical condition, and a rogue nurse helped him escape on the ambulance ride to the hospital." Tom paused. "Helen told me about it right before the party, and that's when we started trying to reach you."

Bo rubbed his chin and blinked down at the bar. Then he peered at Tom with eyes that blazed with intensity. "Any leads?"

Tom's eyes narrowed. "Yeah . . . Me."

"What do you mean?"

"The nurse was found dead at a roadside gas station outside Triune, Tennessee." Tom paused and took a tiny sip of water. "*My name* had been carved into her abdomen with a knife."

Bo shook his head. Then he peered down at the concrete floor that had been stained a dark brown. When he spoke, his voice was just above a whisper. "He promised a reckoning."

"Yes, he did," Tom said.

Bo hopped off the stool and placed two twenty-dollar bills on the counter. Then he peered at Tom. "Triune is a little less than two hours from here. When did he kill the nurse?"

"She was discovered around nine thirty this morning."

Bo ran both hands over the stubble on his head. "Damnit," he said. "We need to arrange security."

"Helen has been working with the Giles and Madison County Sheriff's Departments and the Huntsville PD. There are two officers stationed at your house and more deputies at my son's home and a damn army at the farm."

Bo let out a sigh of relief. Then he squinted at Tom. "My house being where Jazz and the kids are, right?"

"Right. We didn't know about the divorce until tonight."

Bo nodded. "I understand, and that's good. I don't need any protection, but I want a thick blanket around Jazz, T. J., and Lila."

"We're going to make sure an officer is with you too, Bo," Tom said, grabbing his friend's massive shoulders. "But I need you to be engaged. You've got to get back in the world, turn your cell phone on, and stop feeling sorry for yourself. JimBone Wheeler was in the Special Forces, and it looks like Manny Reyes assisted him and the nurse in the breakout. You remember Manny?"

Bo nodded and gritted his teeth. Any trace of drunkenness had been drained from his body by the adrenaline that Tom knew was burning through the man's veins. Tom, who should be asleep, felt it too. It was the only thing keeping him going.

"They're both trained assassins," Tom continued. "And if they're coming to bring the reckoning JimBone promised, they aren't going to let a bunch of police deputies stop them. You know that better than me. You remember what happened to Ray Ray?"

Again, Bo nodded.

"We have to be ready for anything and everything, and even that may not be enough," Tom said, hearing the dread in his voice and fixing his jaw. "Do you understand?"

"I do."

Tom glanced at the money that Bo had laid on the bar and then back at his friend. "Are you ready?"

Bocephus Haynes glared at Tom with bloodred eyes. "Wide ass open."

19

Following Bo's directions, Deputy Shames parked in the driveway of a single-story cottage a quarter mile from the beer store.

While Shames waited in the car and surveilled the house and surrounding area, Tom and Bo went inside. This time Tom brought Lee Roy with him, and the bulldog now lay under the kitchen table, snoring and occasionally clearing his throat. *Past his bedtime,* Tom thought. *And way the hell past mine.*

As Bo brewed them both mugs of coffee in his Keurig machine, Tom was saddened by the emptiness he felt in the house. The breakfast nook was bare of photographs, and the adjacent den contained only an old leather chair. No pictures or paintings hung from the walls, and there were no Christmas decorations, not even a tree. The place looked like it was being rented by a college kid or an elderly widower.

"Bo, what are you doing living in a place like this?"

Bo shrugged as he placed a steaming cup of coffee on the place mat in front of Tom. "It's close to Jazz and the kids. Lease was only for six months. And it's walking distance to my favorite bar." Bo faked a smile. "What's not to like? Now, tell me everything you know about JimBone Wheeler's escape."

Tom took a sip of coffee and felt the liquid burn his tongue. He rarely felt good enough for a cup of java anymore. The chemo had made everything taste bland, and ever since his last round had finished, he had not regained his love of coffee, which he used to drink every morning. Still, he was in survival mode and a jolt of caffeine would probably be good for him. He forced another sip down and peered at his friend across the table. Then, clearing his throat, he told Bo everything he knew.

Twenty minutes later, Tom leaned his elbows on the table while Bo paced back and forth across the tile floor. "So, Rick, Wade, and Powell all know?" Bo asked.

Tom nodded. "Yes, and they've promised to take every precaution necessary." He paused. "What I'm most worried about right now is my family and yours, but I think, with Helen's help, we've done everything we can to protect them." He cleared his throat and took a sip of coffee. "Bo, I understand that Jazz is giving a speech at the Von Braun Center in the morning. Is there any way you can convince her not to go?"

Bo finally turned and gazed down at Tom. "How did you know about that?"

"Helen's already quizzed Jazz about it and strongly advised her to cancel."

"Any luck?"

Tom shook his head.

"And you think she'll listen to me?"

"You have to try, Bo. Helen's doing all she can do, but the civic center is a huge, open place. It's going to be damn near impossible to guarantee Jazz's safety."

"Didn't you say the ambulance was found at an airfield and that JimBone may have flown the coop?"

Tom gritted his teeth as a wave of pain rolled up his back. He was losing steam at a rapid pace. "My gut tells me that the ambulance is one of JimBone's games. Shuck and jive. Trying to throw the authorities off the scent and burn resources chasing a dead end." He let out a ragged breath. "Will you at least talk to Jazz? You know what JimBone and Manny are capable of."

Bo rubbed his chin. "The General really believes that Manny Reyes is running with Wheeler?"

"Yes, and it makes sense. JimBone told me at the prison last year that he had helped Bully Calhoun hire a new hit man. We know from the Wilma Newton case that Manny was Bully's enforcer. You've seen her up close, Bo. She's Filipino with light-brown skin, right?"

Bo nodded.

"Well, that matches the description the police have for the woman believed to be Wheeler's accomplice."

When Bo didn't answer, Tom added in a low voice, "You remember what happened to Greg Zorn, don't you? And Alvie Jennings? Manny is an assassin. And I don't have to tell you how dangerous JimBone is. You've seen him up close too. You'd be dead if it wasn't for—"

"Ray Ray," Bo interrupted, his voice sounding distant, as if his mind were traveling back through time and the events of the past few years. "Ray Ray Pickalew took the bullets meant for me." He took his cell phone out of his pocket and pulled up Jazz's number. He waited a few seconds and then shook his head. "A phone call ain't going to do it, Professor. She'll just hang up on me." He sighed. "I'm going to have to go over there and talk to her in person."

"Want me to come with you?"

Bo shook his head. "No, you get back to the farm. You have a big day tomorrow."

Tom nodded and rose from his seat. When he did, Lee Roy jostled awake and began to shake his small tail as he moved out from the under the table.

"Don't forget this," Bo said, snatching the revolver Tom had set on the kitchen counter and handing it over.

Tom returned the .44 to his jacket pocket. He hadn't even bothered to remove his coat when he'd come inside because it was too much work and he always seemed to be cold. He tapped the handle of the weapon and then walked toward the front door, with Lee Roy on his heels, Bo following behind.

"Professor, can I tell you something?" Bo asked once they'd reached the door.

"Of course," Tom said, gazing into his friend's dark eyes.

"This doesn't seem right to me," Bo said, kneeling down and rubbing Lee Roy behind the ears.

"What do you mean?"

"I mean that JimBone Wheeler and Manny Reyes are both contract killers. They kill for money."

"Bo, JimBone told me—"

"I know what he told you. Threatened to bring a reckoning on you and everyone you love. I know all that. But . . . it still doesn't seem right to me."

"Why?"

"Because I don't think a cold-blooded assassin like JimBone Wheeler would commit a revenge crime. Much less a rampage of them."

"You think he's gone then?" Tom asked, his voice weak. He needed to get home to his bed. "Took that plane in Murfreesboro and went to Mexico? The Caymans? Canada?" He paused. "Gone and not coming back?"

"I don't know," Bo said. "I just don't believe JimBone or Manny would come after us if there wasn't a pot of gold at the end of the rainbow."

Tom leaned his forehead against the hardwood door. He closed his eyes, thinking it through for several seconds. Finally, he remembered something he and Helen had discussed before she had left the farm. "Maybe there is," Tom said.

20

The cabin was made of logs and sat on a bluff above the Flint River. JimBone guessed that in the summertime the foliage and trees surrounding the dwelling would make it impossible to see the house from the road or the water. In early December, however, with the limbs on the trees bare and the vegetation dead, the cabin was probably visible, but only if you were looking for it. Twelve hours out from a prison break, JimBone knew he couldn't ask for much better cover.

Of course, the best protection was that the owner of the place wore a badge.

JimBone gazed at the gold emblem now, not looking at the man who wore it. Stenciled into the badge in lighter gold letters was the word SHERIFF.

"There's enough food for a week," the man said, his voice jittery. They were sitting in the front parlor of the cabin in two rocking chairs facing a large picture window. JimBone had cracked the blinds so that they had a view of the road a quarter mile down the dirt driveway. At 10:00 p.m., it was pitch dark outside and he could see nothing except the faint shadow of the lawman's government-issued Chevy Tahoe parked out front. *Perfect,* he thought for at least the tenth time since he and Manny had arrived several hours earlier.

"There's also plenty of bottled water and coffee." The man paused and smoothed out his mustache. "And I got the fifth of bourbon you wanted."

JimBone smiled. "Blanton's."

The man nodded and stood. "I best bring in the rest of it."

"DeWayne?" JimBone remained seated and rocked deliberately back and forth in the chair.

"Yeah?"

"You can give me the briefcase now."

The sheriff had set the bag on the floor below his chair when the two men began to talk. He grabbed the handle and extended the case to JimBone.

JimBone took it and clasped both of his rough hands around the smaller ones of the sheriff. He squeezed until he heard the lawman grunt in pain. "I'll count all of it later. If there's a single missing bill, I'll cut off your cock and balls with a butter knife and force you to eat them."

JimBone released his grasp, and the sheriff stumbled backward a few steps, wringing his hands and rubbing them on his khaki pants. "The money's all there," DeWayne said. "The down payment, I mean."

JimBone undid the latches on the briefcase and peeked inside. He did a quick inventory in his mind, nodded, and closed the case. "Alright then. Bring in the rest."

DeWayne Patterson walked to the truck with his hands stuck deep in his pockets. They had begun to shake during his interaction with JimBone, and he could still feel his fingers twitching inside his khaki uniform pants. When the killer had grabbed hold of him, he had leaked a little piss in his pants, and he could feel the damp strand of urine in his boxer shorts. *What in God's name have I gotten myself into?* he thought, peering into the darkness, knowing there was another killer, perhaps even more dangerous than JimBone, watching his every move.

"Everything OK, Sheriff?" Her voice was alluring and had the power to arouse both fear and lust.

"Fine," DeWayne said, fumbling for his keys and clicking the button for the back hatch. It opened, and he gazed for a few seconds at the firepower requested by JimBone. Two sniper rifles, four handguns, and a sawed-off twelve-gauge that was illegal in most states, including Alabama.

As he leaned over to retrieve the first of the rifles, he heard soft footsteps behind him and then felt warm breath in his ear. "You aren't having second thoughts, are you?" she whispered. She reached between his legs and ran her fingers down his zipper until she reached his bulge. "Are you?"

"No, ma'am," DeWayne said, and despite how hard he tried to control his bladder, he felt another dribble of urine seep out. "I'm in way too deep to turn back."

"*Sí,*" Manny said, removing her hand from his scrotum. "You are."

DeWayne let out a shallow breath and slid the first rifle out of the back. He began to walk to the house but stopped at the sound of her voice.

"I presume that the hearing in Jasper is still on for the morning?"

He glanced behind his shoulder at her and nodded. "Ten a.m. They should finish by eleven or eleven thirty."

"And . . . barring some tragedy, the case remains set for trial on Monday?"

There was a tease in her voice, and DeWayne felt a chill run over him that had nothing to do with the temperature. "Kat's lawyers have filed a motion for summary judgment that will be heard tomorrow. If that motion is denied, then yes. The case would presumably proceed to trial on Monday." The sheriff paused and squinted at her. "Barring some tragedy."

Manny smiled in the moonlight. "And what about the criminal investigation?"

DeWayne forced a chuckle. "That crazy prosecutor from Tuscaloosa calls twice a week asking whether we've found any leads as to your whereabouts."

"And what do you say?"

"I say no. I also remind him that there's no evidence linking you to the murder in Jasper. I can't speak for the car accident in Henshaw or the shooting in Orange Beach, but the lawn mower incident in Jasper is an unsolved crime." He paused. "And as long as I'm the sheriff of Walker County, it's going to remain that way."

Manny Reyes approached the sheriff. She appeared to almost glide as she walked. Her gait reminded DeWayne of a coral snake slithering on sand. As she got closer, he felt another dribble of urine drip into his underwear.

"Do you think I killed Jennings?"

DeWayne blinked and gazed down at the red clay road. "I don't know, ma'am. All's I know is that there was no direct evidence linking you or Bully Calhoun to Alvin Jennings's murder." He gave his head a quick jerk. "If you did kill him, you sure covered your tracks well."

For several seconds, neither of them spoke. The woods surrounding the cabin were dead quiet, and the sheriff could hear the labored sound of his own breathing. Finally, DeWayne slowly raised his eyes. "Can I ask you a question, ma'am?"

"Sí."

"Did you kill Bully Calhoun?"

She smiled and took a step closer. "What do you think, Sheriff?"

DeWayne slowly exhaled. He knew he was treading on dangerous ground. Hell, this whole thing was like walking across an ice-covered river. One false step could cause a fissure that would lead to his and his family's immediate doom. But still . . . the murder of Marcellus "Bully" Calhoun also remained unsolved. If he was to survive the chaos of the next few days, he'd eventually have to close the Calhoun case. The populace would demand it. When the richest man in town is assassinated playing a round of golf on Christmas Eve morning, people want answers. "I don't think you killed him," he said, speaking the God's honest truth.

"Why?"

"Because if Kat thought you did, she'd be coming after you."

"You think that much of Bully's *chica*?"

DeWayne smirked. "Kathryn Calhoun Willistone isn't stupid. She's a survivor. Her husband and father were both murdered in a span of six months, she's been investigated by the FBI and the Tuscaloosa County Sheriff's Department, and she's been sued all over the state of Alabama, both individually and as personal representative of her father's estate. And somehow she's walked away from it all as a multimillionaire." He ran his thumb over his lips and bit down until the pain made him pull back. He wiped the thumb on his shirt and squinted at the killer. "Kat doesn't think you killed Bully, so neither do I."

"So that leaves the question open," Manny said, taking another step closer to the sheriff and tapping her index finger on his chest. "Who did kill him?"

DeWayne took a step backward and swept his eyes around the woods. "I don't know, ma'am. I figure that Kat blames the folks we're about to declare war on for her father's and husband's murders, and Mr. Wheeler has his own reasons for wanting them dead. But . . ."

"But what, Sheriff?"

"I wouldn't underestimate them. I haven't been around McMurtrie, but I've seen Drake up close, and that rascal scares me."

"And why is that?"

"Because whether you killed his father or not, Drake believes you did."

"Belief will only take a person so far," Manny said, gliding forward and running her smooth fingers up the handle of the sniper rifle that the sheriff had clasped over his shoulder. "Action will be required to defeat us. And I don't mean filing frivolous lawsuits and begging the law to investigate." She snickered. "A bunch of lawyers and detectives are no match for me and the man in that cabin."

DeWayne nodded. "I'm sure you're right, ma'am. But think about this." He paused and ran a boot over the dirt. "We still haven't answered the question."

"What are you talking about?"

"Who killed Bully Calhoun?"

Manny snickered. "Surely you don't think Drake pulled the trigger."

DeWayne Patterson rubbed his chin and peered down at the killer. "I don't know, OK? But I see the same look in that man's eye that I do in you and Mr. Wheeler's."

"And what is that, Sheriff? Is he a fearless *chico*?"

DeWayne shook his head. "It's more than a lack of fear," the sheriff said. "Drake doesn't care anymore. He's playing for blood . . . and he doesn't give a shit who gets in the way."

Manny Reyes gripped the sheriff's forearm and gave it a firm squeeze. Then she smiled. "We'll see how he feels about it after tomorrow."

21

By 10:00 p.m., Rick's eyes burned from fatigue, but the rest of his body hummed with equal parts adrenaline and frustration.

"So that's it?" Powell asked him, bringing a bottle of beer to his lips and draining what remained in one gulp. "You're still gonna go?" They were seated on opposite sides of Rick's conference room table at the office. Between them was a half-eaten bag of Golden Flake vinegar-and-salt potato chips and a six-pack of Miller High Life with only one beer left in the carton. Though Powell had brought the "refreshments" under the guise of celebrating Rick's victory in the Simpson case, the room held no laughter or smiles. The tension was palpable. When Rick didn't respond or break eye contact, Powell finally sighed and turned to the other man in the room. "Wade, please remind our friend of what he could be stepping in tomorrow."

Wade Richey, who was seated at the end of the table, pulled on his salt-and-pepper mustache and ran a hand through his similarly colored hair, thick and unwieldy. Combined with the black T-shirt and black jeans that he typically wore when he wasn't in court, it gave the detective a striking resemblance to the Sam Elliott character in the movie *Road House*. He took a sip of beer and then pushed the bottle to the side. He placed both elbows on the table and formed a steeple with his hands, gazing at Rick with blue eyes that had investigated hundreds of homicide cases during thirty-some-odd years in the Tuscaloosa County Sheriff's Office. "In a word . . . ," Wade began, smirking, "shit. A huge pile of it. I can probably arrange for a deputy escort, but there's only so much one officer can do. You're in the open when you walk into the courthouse and when you leave. And even though there's a metal detector at the entrance, those things can be untrustworthy." Wade paused. "You need to postpone the hearing tomorrow, and you should probably ask for a continuance of the trial until JimBone and Manny are in police custody."

"Just file a motion to continue first thing in the morning," Powell cut in, standing from his chair and beginning to pace back and forth. "You can say that you've been warned by law enforcement personnel that Manny Reyes is believed to be involved in JimBone Wheeler's escape from death row and that you could be a target. Then call the judge's judicial assistant and let her know the deal. Hell, I'll call too. I doubt Judge Conner wants to bring that kind of threat into his courtroom. I'm sure he'll grant the motion under the circumstances."

Rick shook his head. "You're wrong. Conner's already continued the hearing and the trial twice. He's also transferred venue of the trial to Florence and has an agreement with Lauderdale County to let us try the case next week in front of other cases pending in that jurisdiction. I don't think he'll postpone everything because of the remote possibility that an escaped convict is going to come after me." Rick paused. "I have to be in Jasper tomorrow morning."

"No, you don't!" Powell pleaded, his voice booming so loud that Rick involuntarily placed his hands over his ears.

Rick gave a weak smile, looking past his partner to the far wall. "Yes, I do. Same as how you and Wade have to go to Pulaski."

"That's different," Powell snapped. "Wade and I apprehended Wheeler the first time. We're both in law enforcement. It's our job to go."

"And it's my job to represent the family of Alvin Jennings," Rick said, slapping the table with both hands and standing. "It's late, fellas, and I have to be in court by ten. It's a good hour on Highway 69 to Jasper."

Powell again sighed, shooting another glance at Wade. "That's another thing. They could take him out on the trip. 69's not exactly the safest road in the state."

"You're being ridiculous," Rick said.

"Really?" Powell glared at him, his eyes on fire with intensity. In law school, Rick and Powell had studied for exams together, and when this side of Powell came out, Rick liked to call him "Ultra Intense Guy." Under normal circumstances, Rick probably would have smiled or maybe even laughed at how red his friend's face had turned. But not now.

Powell slowly walked around the table and stood in front of Rick. "Remember how they got your dad?" he asked.

Rick crossed his arms and pressed them tight to his chest. He said nothing.

"Manny ran him off the road and left him for dead, right?" Powell squinted. "Not so ridiculous then, is it, to think she might do the same thing tomorrow with you on Highway 69?"

Rick licked his lips, trying to stay calm. He'd always had a hot temper, and the inability to control his emotions had caused him a lot of problems early in his career. Oddly, though, he didn't feel all that mad at the moment. Something else was going on with him.

I'm glad he's out. Rick heard the thought in his mind and was unable to squelch it. The feeling had been festering through Powell's entire summation of what had taken place at the prison in Nashville. JimBone's escape with the help of nurse Charlotte Thompson . . .

The woman seen in the ambulance who resembled Manny Reyes . . . The murder of Thompson at the gas station outside of Triune, Tennessee . . . and even the message left for those who found her.

M . . . C . . . M . . . U . . . R . . . T . . . R . . . I . . . E.

I'm glad.

Rick felt a strong hand grasp his shoulder, mercifully interrupting his thoughts. He looked up into Powell's concerned gaze. "Sit this one out, brother. At least until we know more."

Rick looked past the prosecutor to Wade, who remained seated at the table. The detective was gazing at him intently, his hands still steepled together. "There's no percentage in tempting the devil, son," Wade croaked. "Powell's right. Sit this one out."

Rick moved his eyes back and forth between Wade and Powell. Then he sighed and crossed his arms. "I'm sorry, fellas, but I can't. I have a hearing tomorrow morning in Jasper, and I'm going to be there."

On the street outside the office, Wade and Powell leaned against the passenger side of Powell's black Dodge Charger and split the last bottle of beer. Both men gazed up at the second-floor office of McMurtrie & Drake. Finally, after taking a long sip, Wade handed the bottle to Powell and growled, "We did all we could do."

The prosecutor's only response was a grunt.

"You think he's right about Conner?" Wade asked. "That he wouldn't continue the trial?"

Powell took a sip and grunted again. "Maybe." Then, with the sound of defeat creeping into his tone, he added, "Probably. I forgot about the transfer of venue to Florence." He turned the beer up and drank the last of it. When he finished, he hurled the empty bottle toward a green trash can on the sidewalk and it clanged against the inside of the dispenser.

"Nice shot," Wade said.

Powell ignored him and walked around the front of the car to the driver's side. "Can you get him an escort in the morning?"

Wade grabbed the handle to the passenger-side door and pulled it open. "I think so."

"Then do it," Powell said, opening his own door. "It's probably a waste of time, but I want to at least try."

Once they were both inside the Charger, Powell cranked the ignition, and the haunting voice of Merle Haggard singing "Mama Tried" seeped from the speakers.

"I love this song," Wade said. "Is this on the greatest hits CD?"

Powell smiled and nodded. "Track one."

For a moment, the two men gazed out the front windshield, listening to Merle and lost in their own thoughts. The shadow of the Tuscaloosa County Courthouse and the attached sheriff's office loomed in the distance. Finally, Wade cleared his throat and spoke in a low drawl. "You think JimBone and Manny are really going to make a play?"

Powell continued to peer through the glass. When he spoke, the intensity was back in his voice. "I don't know, but I have that same feeling I did that night in Lawrenceburg when we were chasing Wheeler the first go-round."

"And what's that?"

Powell turned and looked at the detective. "That something's about to go down."

PART THREE

22

At 3:59 a.m. on Thursday, December 5, 2013, JimBone Wheeler opened his eyes and sat up in bed. He reached over and grabbed the alarm clock, which he'd set to ring at 4:00, and turned it off. Smiling, he wondered when was the last time he'd heard the shrill sound of an alarm buzzer. He'd always seemed to have an internal system that woke him at precisely the time he needed to get up—in the prison yesterday morning . . . during contract kills . . . and on reconnaissance missions as an Army Ranger. It didn't matter the job, JimBone Wheeler's body knew when it was time to go.

He slid his legs off the bed and looked over his shoulder. Manny Reyes lay naked with her back facing him. She had yet to stir, but JimBone knew that his partner was awake too. As if to confirm his suspicion, he heard her voice—soft—whisper, "It is time."

JimBone smiled and rose from the bed, stretching his arms to the sky. He was also nude, and as he watched Manny glide to the restroom, he felt another tingle in his loins. It had been several years since JimBone had been thoroughly laid—he didn't count his rape of Charlotte Thompson yesterday, because that was business. Not since his sessions with Martha Booher in the Amish country of Ethridge, Tennessee—in the weeks before he tried to kill Bocephus Haynes on the Giles County Courthouse Square and ended up sending Ray Ray Pickalew to his grave instead—had he felt so satisfied. If he was honest with himself, which he always was—the Bone didn't lie to the Bone—he would agree that last night's sex might have been the best of his life.

He walked around the bed, peeked his head into the bathroom, and watched Manny apply soap to her breasts and legs in the glass-covered shower. *Might have, hell,* he thought, shaking his head. It wasn't even close.

JimBone slipped on some underwear and a pair of jeans that Sheriff Patterson had gotten him on his supply run and walked, shirtless, out of the bedroom toward the kitchen. The smell of fresh coffee drifted down the hallway and JimBone breathed it in.

"Glad to see you up and at 'em, DeWayne," he said as he plopped down in a chair at a table in the breakfast nook. A large bay window looked out on the Flint River, which, at this time of the morning, was nothing but shadow through the cracked blinds.

DeWayne Patterson stood in front of the kitchen sink, sipping from a steaming mug. The sheriff of Walker County was dressed in his full uniform and even had his gun belt attached to his waist. Every few seconds, he shifted his weight from his right to his left foot and then back.

"Coffee?" DeWayne asked.

"Please," JimBone said, placing a foot on one of the empty chairs and stretching his leg out.

As the sheriff placed the cup on the table, JimBone grabbed him by the forearm. "You need to relax, DeWayne. You're making me nervous."

When DeWayne tried to pull out of his grasp, JimBone let go, and the sheriff sprawled backward. But for the island in the middle of the kitchen, he would have fallen down. "Damnit," DeWayne said. "Aren't you even the least bit anxious about today? I mean . . . what we're trying to pull off is . . ." DeWayne trailed off, and JimBone began to rub the sandy-blond hair on his chest.

"I don't get anxious, DeWayne. It's not in my DNA. Anxious men have a hard time getting their dick up. They can't complete a task because they're worried they won't be able to perform. Whether it's pleasing a woman or shooting a rifle, they're too busy worrying to get the job done." He paused and moved his hand up to the stubble on his face. "Let me guess. You need Viagra to get a boner, don't you?"

DeWayne ignored the question. "We need to leave in thirty minutes if we're going to get there in time."

JimBone took a sip from his mug and squinted up at the sheriff. "I trust you have my outfit for today's events ready?"

DeWayne grimaced. "It's on the couch in the living area. Ironed, pressed, and ready to go."

"And the hat?"

"On top of the shirt and pants."

JimBone rubbed his chin. "Excellent." Then, after taking another sip of coffee, he stood and walked over to the sheriff. "Do you believe in God, DeWayne?"

The sheriff looked down at the floor in defeat.

"I do," JimBone said, his voice just above a whisper. "But not the God of Israel or Jesus or any of those foolish stories in the Bible. Those are just old wives' tales written down by a bunch of pansies to try to keep men from realizing their own godlike power." He paused. "Do you know what that power is, Sheriff?"

DeWayne Patterson continued to gaze down at the floor.

"*Free will*," JimBone said. "The exercise of free will to change the course of history. That's what we're going to do in these next few hours. We're going to make history." He smiled and leaned closer to the sheriff's ear. "Embrace the moment, DeWayne," he whispered. "We get to be God today."

JimBone slapped the sheriff on the back and strode down the hallway. "Now, make us some breakfast, boy. God can't work on an empty stomach."

DeWayne Patterson took no notice of the fact that he had slightly wet himself again while the psychopath was talking. He felt his heartbeat pounding in his chest, and he figured that at any moment the organ might burst. In truth, he wished that would happen. A quick and clean death was probably his best endgame at this juncture.

We get to be God today.

The sheriff had hoped without hope that the crazy bastard might change his plans. That a good night's sleep might bring on some hesitation. *No dice,* DeWayne thought. If anything, Wheeler seemed even more determined. He wondered if the madman meant anything that he had just said or if he was just trying to scare DeWayne.

DeWayne unclipped the badge from his shirt and gazed at the word chiseled into the gold. SHERIFF. He was supposed to be the protector of innocent people in his county. The long arm of the law. Seeker of truth and justice. DeWayne chuckled bitterly. In a few short hours, he wouldn't be upholding the law. He'd be unleashing hell.

We get to be God today.

DeWayne shivered and rubbed his thumb over the badge. He hadn't always been dirty. There was a time when he was just a deputy trying to make his way up the ranks in the department. Then, about seven years ago, he arrested Marcellus "Bully" Calhoun driving home from the Jasper Country Club going a hundred miles per hour in a forty-five-mile zone. The woman in the passenger seat was completely naked and didn't even stop giving Bully a blow job when DeWayne approached the car. "What seems to be the trouble, Officer?" Bully growled, dangling ten one-hundred-dollar bills out the window.

DeWayne had at least hesitated. He asked Bully for his license and registration and politely requested that he step out of his Cadillac Escalade.

"I'm busy, son," Bully said, pointing at the woman's head bobbing up and down in his lap. Then he reached across the cab of the SUV and undid the glove compartment. When he took a wallet out of the hatch, DeWayne thought Bully was abiding by his request. But instead of his driver's license, Bully pulled out five more Benjamin Franklins and stuffed them into DeWayne's outstretched hand along with the original ten. By that time, Bully's passenger had removed her head from his lap and lit up a cigarette.

"Are we good now, Officer . . ." Bully hesitated as he read the name on DeWayne's lapel. "Patterson?"

Again, DeWayne hesitated. Selling your soul, at least for the first time, was a hard thing.

"I assume that you know who I am, son?" Bully asked, raising his eyebrows.

DeWayne nodded but was unable to speak. His boss, Sheriff Lawson Snow, had told him all about Marcellus "Bully" Calhoun. Owner of half the land in Walker County and at least a dozen different businesses. *And also the methamphetamine king of Alabama,* Law, as everyone in the sheriff's office called him, said with a twinkle in his eyes, before adding, *not that we could ever prove it or would even want to.* DeWayne hadn't understood why the department would knowingly allow a drug operation on the scale of Bully's, but he didn't question Sheriff Snow.

"Well, then, I'm going to go now," Bully had said, jarring DeWayne from his thoughts. "Layla here"—he pointed over his shoulder—"needs to finish what she started, and you need to get back on patrol." He smiled. "A lot of dangerous criminals out there." Then he laughed, but before rolling up his window, he added, "I remember the folks who are good to me, Officer Patterson. Are you my friend?"

Before DeWayne could answer, the Escalade pulled away, leaving him standing alone on Highway 78 holding fifteen hundred dollars in cash.

The next morning, DeWayne received an envelope at the station with five more hundred-dollar bills and the same question written in blue ink on a napkin. "Are you my friend?"

DeWayne Roderick Patterson, who had grown up in Winston County and married his high school sweetheart, a bucktooth country girl named Annie, going on to have two bucktooth daughters before moving to Jasper in 2004, had spent his life up to that point grinding out any money that he made eight hours at a time, nine to five, Monday through Friday. He had never seen a thousand dollars in cash, much less two thousand. And all he had to do to keep it was look the other way. At that moment, as he remembered the naked woman in Bully Calhoun's Escalade and the look of absolute uninhibitedness in the rich man's eyes, DeWayne had made his decision.

The answer was yes. He was Bully Calhoun's friend.

That choice would have consequences that DeWayne could not possibly have foreseen. Initially, the return was all positive. He had advanced to lead deputy in the department within a year. And once Bully began to involve him in the meth trade, making deliveries in his squad car, it didn't take long for DeWayne to amass quite a war chest. When Law had decided not to run for reelection in 2010, DeWayne became his handpicked successor. With Bully's financial backing, he won in a landslide.

Once DeWayne had risen to the office of sheriff, everything had been hunky-dory until Bully's son-in-law, Jack Willistone, a trucking tycoon in Tuscaloosa, was murdered on the banks of the Black Warrior River in May 2012. The subsequent investigation by the Tuscaloosa County Sheriff's Department shone a bright light on

Bully and, in turn, everyone on Bully's payroll, including DeWayne. The murder of Alvin Jennings in his front yard in August 2012 only intensified the scrutiny of the sheriff's department. But when Bully himself was assassinated last Christmas Eve, the pressure actually let up, and DeWayne thought everything might go back to normal. Bully had been in the crosshairs of the Tuscaloosa County Sheriff's Office and the FBI, but his death seemed to take the wind out of the two agencies' sails. Even better, Kathryn Calhoun Willistone, Bully's daughter, had made sure the gravy train DeWayne was riding kept chugging along.

Then Rick Drake filed wrongful death suits against Bully's estate all over Alabama, putting the ten-million-dollar life insurance proceeds that Kat received at her father's death in jeopardy.

At first, the lawsuits appeared groundless and without merit in law or fact, especially the cases filed in Orange Beach and Henshaw.

But the case in Jasper filed on behalf of Alvin Jennings's family had grown some teeth, and Kat was terrified that Drake might be able to sway a jury into ripping away her fortune and giving it to Jennings's family. Based on reports from Tuscaloosa that Drake had obtained a jury verdict against JPS Van Lines for twenty-two point five million dollars last evening, DeWayne couldn't say that Kat's concerns were unwarranted. Anything could happen in front of a jury.

If Drake were able to get past Kat's motion for summary judgment—which would be decided in approximately six hours—he would have a chance in front of a jury.

Kathryn Calhoun Willistone was determined not to let that happen. And like her dead father, she was used to getting her way.

When Kat had proposed the plan involving JimBone Wheeler and Manny Reyes during lunch at Black Rock Bistro, in downtown Jasper, DeWayne refused. Of course, he would help in any way he could, but he couldn't just aid and abet two known fugitives in committing multiple murders. There was a line there somewhere, and DeWayne couldn't cross it.

Undeterred and acting as if she wasn't surprised, Kat had slid a package across the table. "Think about it and call me in the morning." When DeWayne got back to his office, he locked the door and opened the large manila envelope. Inside, there was a thumb drive. He slipped the disc into the USB port on his computer, and the only thing on it was a folder entitled "Sheriff Patterson." He clicked on the folder, and there were seven images and one video. After looking at the first photograph, DeWayne didn't bother viewing the rest. Instead of calling her, he drove out to the Calhoun mansion on the edge of the Sipsey Wilderness. A security guard led him into the fitness room, where Kat was running at a steady pace on a treadmill.

"Change your mind already, DeWayne?"

He met her eye in the wall-length mirror that hung opposite her and simply nodded.

Staring at the badge he'd worn for the last four years at his cabin on the Flint River in Maysville, Alabama, DeWayne Patterson again considered his options. If he backed out now, odds were that JimBone would kill him before he made it out of the house, much less to his Tahoe parked in the driveway. If in some pipe dream he could escape the cabin—which he might have pulled off while the two killers were screwing each other's brains out last night—he knew they would still go through with the plan, his involvement would most certainly be leaked, and no one would believe him when he said he had backed out at the last minute. Aborting the mission would accomplish nothing, and Kat would no doubt release the photographs and video on the thumb drive she'd given DeWayne at Black Rock. It didn't matter that the girl in these shots looked twenty-five then and actually was nineteen years old now. She had been fifteen at the time DeWayne

Patterson had his thirty-day tryst with her. He had committed statutory rape, and the charge and conviction would ruin his career and his life.

I'm trapped, DeWayne thought for at least the hundredth time in the last eight hours. His hand shook as he reattached the badge to his shirt and pulled three cereal bowls out of a cabinet. In a few short hours, he would help two contract killers exact bloodshed all over the state of Alabama.

And there's not a damn thing I can do about it. DeWayne opened a box of cornflakes and poured the cereal into the bowls. Then he filled them with milk and set them at the kitchen table. As he took three spoons out of the silverware drawer, he cleared his throat and yelled, "Breakfast is served."

Then, taking a seat and bringing a spoonful of flakes to his mouth, he said a silent prayer. *God forgive me.*

After a quick shower, JimBone took the outfit that DeWayne had arranged for him to wear and dressed in front of the bathroom mirror. Manny watched him with her arms folded. A smile played on her lips. "How was the high sheriff?"

"Scared. He looks like he's doing all he can do not to piss himself every second."

"Will he follow through with his end of the bargain?"

JimBone fastened the last button on his shirt and straightened it in the mirror. "He doesn't have a choice. Not unless he wants all of Walker County to know about his attraction to underage girls." JimBone moved his eyes from his reflection to Manny. "A desperate man is a dangerous one. The sheriff is a first-rate pussy, but he's also desperate to save his ass." JimBone paused and began to comb his hair. "He'll follow through."

"Can I ask you a question?"

JimBone caught her gaze in the reflection. "Shoot."

"Why not send me to Jasper? If stopping the trial is our number one goal, then shouldn't killing Drake be our top priority?"

"That's two questions, my dear," JimBone said, turning to face her. "But I'll oblige. First off, Jasper may be a no-go. If the summary judgment motion filed by Bully's estate is granted by Judge Conner and the case is thrown out, then killing Drake—at least right away—is unnecessary. So sending you to Jasper would be a waste, and we can't afford to have you sitting on the sidelines today. Second, if Conner denies the motion and action must be taken, all we need is an incident to get the trial postponed. Even if your Mexican friend fails to kill Drake, the shooting"—he paused and smiled—"and everything else that happens in the next few hours will delay the trial."

For a moment, silence filled the bedroom. Then JimBone felt her hands on his shoulders and her voice in his ear. "Why do you hate him so bad?"

JimBone wrinkled his face. "Who?"

"Professor McMurtrie."

"He's cost me a half a million dollars, and he and his cronies sent me to death row. No one's ever gotten the jump on me before."

"So this is all about payback? Sorry, but I don't believe that."

JimBone stepped away from the mirror and sat on the edge of the bed. As he began to slip on his boots, he chuckled. "Well, it's also about a payday. A million dollars split two ways will give us a nice start back in your homeland."

She walked over to the bed and knelt beside him. "That's still not all of it."

JimBone finished lacing up his boots and glared down at her. "No."

"What then?"

"There are people in this world who never have a chance to live out their dreams. That grow up without a father and watch their mother get tag teamed by rednecks all day long, every day, so that they can eat. People that only know survival." He paused. "People like me."

"And McMurtrie?"

"He grew up in Hazel Green on a farm about ten miles from this cabin. Had a momma and daddy who loved him. Was good at football and got a scholarship to play for the God Almighty Bear. Won a national championship. Was a lawyer. Then a professor. Then a lawyer again. Along the way, he married a woman, had a kid, who grew up to be an orthopedic surgeon, a couple of grandkids, and made friends that stood by him." JimBone paused and spoke through clenched teeth. "Two of those friends took me down on the square in Pulaski a couple years ago."

"So life isn't fair and you got the short end of the stick. Is that what you're saying, *señor*?"

"No, darling. That's not it. The Bone has known that life wasn't fair since he was three years old. I never had a dream in this world. I live to survive, and that attitude got me through childhood, the Army Rangers, and working for Jack Willistone and Bully Calhoun. I don't pity myself and I'm not envious of the folks like McMurtrie who have had every advantage and who have lived the American dream. But"—he stopped and moved his eyes to the window—"that son of a bitch got the jump on me. I had a chance to kill him once in downtown Pulaski, but under orders from my employer all I did was wound him. Most men would have quit after the beating I gave him, but McMurtrie didn't. He came back, won the case, and managed to keep me from killing his nigger friend Haynes." He licked his lips and turned to Manny. "And I ended up on death row in Nashville. Not killing Bocephus Haynes and getting myself arrested was the first time I ever failed at anything I tried to do."

"But you didn't quit either."

JimBone felt a heat wave of anger roll down his chest and legs. "No. That sandy-haired prosecutor and his detective friend had their chance to kill me, and they put their faith in the law to put me down." He snorted. "They'll find out today what a mistake they made."

"So this really is all about payback."

"It's more than that, honey," JimBone said as he attached the last part of his costume—a gun belt just like the one the sheriff was wearing in the kitchen. "This is a reckoning." He glanced at his watch and nodded. "And it begins now."

23

The hallucinations had started a couple weeks earlier, but Tom hadn't told anyone about them. Perhaps "hallucination" was too strong a word, but Tom didn't know what else to call them. He was seeing things—or rather, a person—who simply couldn't be there.

Normally, they came on when he was dozing in his recliner in the den. To his knowledge, the only person to witness one of these episodes was Bo. When Tom had snapped out of it, Bo had asked him if he knew he had been talking in his sleep. Tom had lied and said no. He didn't want his best friend to think he was losing his marbles.

Now, as the last vestiges of a restless sleep began to leave him, Tom saw a figure in the corner of his bedroom. The man wore a plain gray T-shirt, khaki shorts, and a crimson visor with a script *A* threaded in white across the front. He was leaning against the wall with his arms folded. He looked at least fifteen years younger than the last time Tom had seen him. His skin was tanned a golden brown, and flip-flops adorned his feet. A hell of an outfit to wear in December, but, of course, the man wasn't real.

"You gonna answer the door, Tommy, old boy?" the man asked. When he smiled, his lips seemed to curl up past his cheekbones. Coach Bryant had always called Raymond James Pickalew "Joker" because of the grin. The rest of the man's family and friends, including Tom, had called him "Ray Ray."

"You look better as a ghost than you did in real life, Ray Ray," Tom said, hearing a muffled sound that he couldn't make out in the background.

"You look like a pile of warmed-over dog shit that's been pissed and vomited on," Ray Ray said. The sound in the distance was growing louder. More clear. Was someone hammering a nail?

"You need to get up, Tommy boy. Big day." The sound was now louder. "Come on, big 'un. Next play."

Tom blinked his eyes and rose in the bed. He recognized the sound now. Someone was knocking on the door. He swung his legs off the bed and stepped on Lee Roy's hind legs as he stood up, causing the dog to yelp. "I'm sorry, boy," he said. Tom leaned his hand against the same wall where he had seen the ghost of Ray Ray Pickalew just a few seconds earlier. *Of all the dead people to see in a recurring hallucination, why in the hell does it have to be Ray Ray? Why not Julie. Or Mom or Dad? Or Coach Bryant?* When Tom did finally die of cancer, he had a growing list of grievances that he needed to discuss with the Almighty.

"Coming!" Tom yelled after he had caught his breath and adjusted to the pain and soreness in his bones brought on by his ride to Huntsville and back last night. *That was crazy,* Tom thought as he walked down the hallway of his house, through the den, and into the kitchen. He cracked the door and peeked through the opening between the lock chain.

"Expecting someone else?" Dr. Bill Davis said, holding up a white McDonald's sack and giving Tom a sheepish grin. In his younger years, Bill had been a redhead, but his once-fire-colored hair had been reduced to two white patches on the side and a bald top. He had a ruddy complexion, and a pair of glasses covered his face. At seventy-five years old, Bill was older than Tom but looked a decade younger. He was semiretired from his urology practice, working one weekend and one "call" a month, and wouldn't do that if it weren't for the money, which he said was too good and easy to pass up. When he wasn't working, he spent most of his time entertaining his eight grandkids at his house on Lake Tuscaloosa, shooting his collection of handguns at a target range in Northport that he co-owned, and taking Tom to the occasional doctor's appointment. Bill and Tom had met in the late 1960s after Tom had gone to see him for groin pain that turned out to be a long-undetected hernia, which Bill repaired. Over forty years of friendship, they had been through a lot together. Bill had three daughters, all grown now, and Tom had attended each of their weddings. Likewise, Bill and his first wife, Trish, had hosted a party for Tommy and Nancy when they got married. When Trish succumbed to ALS ten years ago, Tom had been a pallbearer at the funeral. And Bill, along with Bocephus Haynes and seven members of the 1961 National Championship team, had carried the casket at Julie's burial.

It was Bill Davis who had delivered Tom's bladder cancer diagnosis three years ago after Tom had seen blood in his urine. And in late October 2012, it had been Bill who informed Tom he had stage four lung cancer in front of Coach Bryant's statue on the Walk of Champions.

Tom smiled and undid the latch on the lock.

"Don't dress up for me or anything," Bill said as he stepped through the opening, and Tom realized that he was only wearing a T-shirt and boxer shorts.

"Sorry. Overslept," Tom said as Bill set the sack of food on the kitchen table.

"You weren't kidding about an army of squad cars," Bill said, pointing through the picture window. On the way into Huntsville last night, Tom had called Bill and filled him in on everything that was going on. Tom had suggested that his old friend sit this one out and let an officer take him to CCI, but Bill had refused, and Tom hadn't pressed the issue.

Tom squinted through the glass and saw the three police cruisers parked on the edge of the driveway just as they had been yesterday evening. Then, shaking his head, he grimaced and eased into one of the chairs. While Tom appreciated the protection being offered him, he had hoped they would assign more officers to his son's house and to Bo and Jazz today. When he had told the deputy such, he just shrugged and said he had his orders. "You're the target, sir."

I'm the target, Tom had thought. A broken-down, just-turned-seventy-three, stage-four-cancer-fighting dead man walking. He didn't like it, but there was no use arguing.

"Did you find Bo last night?" Bill asked, still standing by the door. "He OK?"

"Yes and no," Tom said, sighing and trying to rub the sleep out of his eyes. "It's a long story, and I'll fill you in on the drive to CCI."

"Well, hop to it," Bill said. "Your first test is at eight thirty and"—Bill took off his glasses and gazed at his watch—"it's seven fifteen."

Tom gave a mock salute and trudged out of the kitchen. As he passed into his bedroom, he tapped the wall where he'd seen the image of Ray Ray Pickalew.

"Next play, Joker," he whispered, feeling a cold chill of trepidation as he thought about the three scans he would receive today. CT of the chest at eight thirty. MRI of the brain at nine thirty. PET scan at ten thirty. Then he would see Dr. Maples at one for a verdict that, based on his increase in back pain, more frequent headaches, and now the occasional hallucination, he knew wouldn't be good. He grabbed his cell phone from the bedside table and clicked on the screen, hoping he might have received a call or a text from Rick, Bo, Powell, or Helen while he was asleep.

He hadn't. The screen showed no missed calls or text messages. Tom set the phone down and sighed. JimBone Wheeler was still out there, which meant his friends and his family were still in danger.

Tom closed his eyes and said a silent prayer asking God to watch after the people he loved. After he whispered "Amen," he opened his lids and forced his legs to move toward the shower.

"*Next play,*" he said again.

24

Bocephus Haynes watched the house from inside the cab of the Sequoia. Glancing at the clock on the dashboard—it was 7:20 a.m.—he knew that the lights in the kitchen would be turned on any . . .

"There," Bo said, smiling and rubbing his unshaven face as the overhead bulb in the breakfast nook flickered on. Then, as was her habit, Jazz opened the blinds in the kitchen and living room so that the sun could shoot its morning rays through them. He watched his soon-to-be ex-wife glide through the home, wearing the pink robe he'd given her as a birthday gift during their first year of marriage. Seeing the ritual from outside the house made his heart ache for another chance that he knew wouldn't be coming.

I'm out of mulligans, Bo thought, grabbing the door handle and forcing himself to exit the vehicle. He trudged toward the two-story brownstone that he'd bought for Jazz last year hoping that a fresh start in Huntsville would erase the turmoil they'd experienced during their two decades plus of living in Pulaski.

It hadn't. If anything, the new home had only shined a brighter spotlight on their long-festering problems. Bo gritted his teeth as he made his way down the walkway.

The house was on Adams Street in the area of downtown Huntsville known as Twickenham. Jazz, who had grown up in a middle-class home in north Huntsville, had always dreamed of owning one of the mansions in the oldest neighborhood in town, and now she did.

Bo hated the house, thinking it looked and felt like a Southern plantation with its exterior columns, high ceilings, and drafty, old-money scent. He didn't care for the neighbors either, many of whom looked at them like they were aliens from outer space. Occasionally, he asked Jazz out of spite if she noticed any other black families in the area, and she just rolled her eyes and reminded him that they hadn't had any African American neighbors in Pulaski either. *Didn't stop us then; won't stop us now* was her rallying cry, but Bo didn't feel like fighting that battle again. Though his past in Pulaski had been traumatic and tragic, Bo found himself longing for the hilly landscape and small-town feel of Giles County, Tennessee. It was home, and despite his history there, he missed it.

When he reached the front stoop, Bo paused and gazed at the mahogany door. After his conversation with the Professor last night, he had driven over here in a cold sweat, hoping he would arrive before Jazz had gone to sleep. No such luck. When he rang the doorbell, it woke up not just his estranged wife but also both kids. The look on Jazz's face when she saw him would have melted ice. He hadn't even been able to get the question out before she told him she was giving the speech in the morning and nothing was going to stop her. Not the cop guarding the house. Not Bo. "*Not any damn body.*" She ushered him out the door before he could even take his jacket off.

Bo hadn't fought with her but hadn't left either. He stayed in the front seat of his Sequoia and kept it parked in the driveway. When it was obvious what he was doing, he got a call on his cell phone from Jazz. She said if he didn't drive away in five minutes, she was going to ask the officer, whose cruiser was stationed on the curb, to advise Bo to leave.

"Go for it," Bo said. "I own the house. I haven't hit you and I'm not doing anything but annoying you. It's been a while since I practiced any criminal law, but I don't think those are grounds for an arrest."

She hung up the phone, and Bo spent the rest of the night in his vehicle.

Now, eight hours later, Bo didn't bother with the doorbell. He stuck his key in the lock and opened the door. "Honey, I'm home," he said as he walked through the front parlor of the museum of a house. He stopped for a moment at the huge Christmas tree by the staircase and ran his fingers over the familiar ornaments. One was a cardboard-cutout nativity scene that T. J. had colored in preschool. The boy had drawn a crimson number twelve on Joseph's robe, which had gotten him a playful rebuke from his teacher. Bo smiled at the memory as he touched the cardboard. His favorite ornament was a crystal ball with a painted beach, the words "Saint Lucia, 2005" written in the sand. He'd taken Jazz to the Caribbean island for their twentieth wedding anniversary, and they'd spent four nights and three days swimming, snorkeling, drinking Piton beer, and making love.

There should be more of these, Bo thought, rubbing his thumb over the beach and gazing up at the angel at the top of the tree. Placing the final ornament had always been his job. *But not this year—not ever again.*

He let his hand drop to his side as guilt and sadness enveloped him. Finally, knowing he was stalling, he forced his legs to move toward the kitchen.

As he approached, he smelled the pleasing aroma of eggs and coffee and felt another pang of sadness. For as long as he'd known her, Jazz had always eaten scrambled eggs for breakfast. As he entered the kitchen, he saw her sitting on one of the three stools in front of the island in the middle of the massive room. Once, not too long ago, there had been four stools. Another razor wire of regret slashed at Bo's heart, but he shook it off.

Jazz was eating and reading something on her iPhone. She didn't look up or acknowledge his existence as he approached her.

"What's the good word on Facebook?" Bo asked. "Are any of our new neighbors skiing in Vail? Scuba diving in the Caymans? Hiking the Appalachian Trail?" Bo didn't bother trying to hide the sarcasm in his voice. He had tried Facebook for a while but got annoyed by the combination of political posts, vague pray-for-me updates, and people trying to outdo each other with their pictures from exotic trips.

Jazz didn't respond or look up. Instead, she ate a forkful of eggs and sipped her coffee. Even wearing the old robe, with nothing on her face but a scowl, the former Jasmine Henderson was still a beautiful woman, with her milk-chocolate skin, wavy brown hair cut to just below her neck, and toned figure that, despite her forty-nine years of age, retained the long, sinewy muscles that had made her a track star at the University of Alabama.

"Jazz—"

"I'm going, so please don't waste your breath," she said, continuing to run her thumb across the phone and still not looking at him.

Bo snatched the device off the counter and held it high above his head. Jazz shot off the stool like she'd been launched from a pad at Cape Canaveral. "You give me that back right now, Bocephus Haynes, or I will call the police. You can't just walk in here and take my phone away. That would qualify as an assault—I watch enough Investigation Discovery to know that—so they would come. You know they would."

Bo smirked. "I thought you only watched The History Channel."

"What I view on television and what I do with my spare time is none of your business anymore. *Now give me back my phone.*"

Bo sighed and began to hand her the device, but Jazz had already started to lunge for it. When she did, her index finger poked him solidly in the left eye.

Bo yelped in pain as the phone dropped from his grasp. He covered his eye with his hand and walked away from her, trying to squelch the anger growing inside him. When he pulled his hand away, he saw a couple of droplets of blood on his fingers. He gazed across the kitchen at Jazz, who was staring at him with both hands covering her mouth.

"Are you OK?" she asked.

"I'll live," Bo said, walking toward the sink and grabbing a paper towel from the rack. He ran some cold water over the towel and dabbed at his eye, which stung like hell. When he blinked, though, he could still see out of it.

"I'm sorry, Bo," Jazz said. Then she began to cry.

"I guess I should call the police," Bo said, but there was a tease in his voice. "I know damn well that poking someone's eye out qualifies for assault."

Jazz smirked at him, her eyes no longer shooting rays of anger.

"But I won't if you'll just forgo the speech today and stay home with the kids until I know more about JimBone Wheeler's status." He smiled, but Jazz didn't return the gesture. Instead, she gazed down at the tile floor.

"All these years I've sacrificed for you, Bo. Twenty-eight trips around the sun while you pursued the men that murdered your father. You spent the rest of your time practicing law. I gave up my career to handle the kids while you chased your obsession."

"All I'm asking for is today, Jazz. One more day. Please."

"No. This event has been a year in the works. We're trying to raise money for the art history program so the college can build a new facility. All of the prior donors will be there as well as a lot of influential alumni and town leaders." She paused and walked toward the sink, where Bo continued to dab at his eye with the wet towel. "I'm the chair of this fund-raiser. This is my rodeo, the invitations have been sent out, and there's no turning back. I can't just not show up because of some crazy hunch that you have."

"When have my hunches been wrong?" Bo asked, feeling another bubble of anger float up his chest.

Jazz's lips curled into a tired smile. "Bo, baby, your whole life is based on a wrong hunch. You lived your whole existence to bring the men who lynched your father to justice only to learn that the man who was murdered wasn't your daddy at all, and the man who led the lynch mob was."

"That wasn't a hunch, Jazz. My momma told me that Roosevelt Haynes was my father, and he never said any different right up until the time the rope stretched the life out of him. I saw him snatched from our shack, and I saw the men in the white hoods and robes who hung him." He paused to catch his breath. "What did you expect me to believe? What was I to do?"

Tears began to form in Jazz's eyes, and she wiped them with her hand. "It was an impossible situation, OK? You did the best you could, and I don't blame you, Bo. I don't blame you for what you did. For seeking justice for Roosevelt. You earned the right to be obsessed with that, and two years ago, you succeeded. All the men who murdered Roosevelt are now either dead or rotting away in prison. You *won*. The only problem is your victory shattered everything you ever believed about yourself."

"I didn't come over here to rehash history. I just—"

"Shut up and let me finish!" Jazz yelled. Her hands were now balled into fists. "I know it crushed you to learn that Roosevelt wasn't your real daddy. I can't even imagine how you felt when that crazy witch told you that Andy Walton, the Imperial by damn Wizard, was your father. I know it's been tough to deal with. I'm sure that's why you've had a hard time practicing law again. I thought last year when you helped Professor McMurtrie as his investigator on that murder case in Tuscaloosa that you would snap out of it and move on." She paused and placed her hands on his shoulders. "But you haven't, Bo. Your suspension's been lifted, and you can start practicing again at any time. Here in Huntsville like I had hoped you would. Or even back in Pulaski. It's only a forty-minute drive. But you've done nothing."

"Not true," Bo said, shaking his head and gazing down at the floor. "I'm helping Rick Drake with the Alvin Jennings wrongful death case. Trial is supposed to start on Monday in Florence." He raised his eyes to Jazz's, and her mouth hung open, but she didn't immediately speak.

Finally, after giving herself several seconds to process what she'd just heard, Jazz squinted at him. "How can Alvie's case be tried in Florence? I thought he was murdered in Jasper."

"He was, but the judge transferred the venue to the Shoals because there's no way that Alvie's family or Bully Calhoun's estate could get an impartial jury in Walker County. Half the county hated Bully, and the other half worked for him." Bo gave a weak smile. "But I am practicing again, hon."

"Well . . . that's good. I'm glad." Her face hardened. "But it doesn't change anything. I'm still giving my speech today."

"And you're still going through with the divorce."

Fresh tears formed in Jazz's eyes. "I'm tired of sacrificing my life for you, Bo. All those years of you working until me and the kids were already asleep and then being gone in the morning before we even got up. When was the last time we took a family vacation? Or a couples' trip? Hell, before I filed my petition for divorce, when was the last time we'd even been on a date? We got all this money that you've worked so hard to earn, and you can't relax enough to enjoy it. Our whole life you've lived 'wide ass open,' as you like to say. Every second has to be ninety-to-nothing wide ass open or you're a restless, frustrated, and miserable person to be around. I thought the suspension last year might mellow you out and that learning about your true family origin would change how you were with me and the kids, but it's only made things worse. Now you hate yourself worse than you ever hated Andy Walton, and you've got no outlet for your frustration." She paused and put her hands on his shoulders. "Bo, when was the last time we really even *talked* to each other? The truth is that we haven't talked in years, and sex is just something we do twice a month because we always have. It's a habit no different than me eating scrambled eggs in the morning."

"You're exaggerating," Bo said, pulling out of her grasp. "Remember Saint Lucia?"

"I do," Jazz said. "It was wonderful. *And it was more than eight years ago!*"

She cupped a hand over her mouth, which was something she always did after raising her voice. Then, grimacing, she folded her arms tight across her chest. "You only seem to thrive in a crisis, Bo. It's the only thing you know. Like now. This crazy psycho has busted out of prison, and Bocephus Haynes is going to rise up and rescue everyone. *I'm tired of it.* Tired of the way you are. There are things I want; can't you see that? Now that I've had a taste of teaching again, of living in Huntsville, where I've always wanted to be, I can't ever go back to the way it was." She paused. "And you hate the way it is now. I can read you like a book, and I know you hate this house. Hate the neighborhood. Hate my job and the people I work with. And hate the woman I've become."

"That's not true," Bo said, but the words sounded hollow coming out of his mouth.

"It is too, and you know it. You want me to follow your lead like I always have, but I'm not going to this time, Bo. I can't and I won't." She paused. "Look at me."

He obliged and saw that tears now streaked down both of her cheeks.

"The awful truth, Bo, is that a divorce would do us *both* a lot of good."

"But . . . I love you," Bo said.

"I love you too," Jazz said, her voice cracking. "I always will." She choked out a sob. "But I can't live with you anymore. I just . . . *can't*."

For almost a full minute, there was silence in the kitchen as Bo stared at the only woman he'd ever loved. Finally, dabbing his eye again with the wet towel, Bo began to walk away. He stopped at the place in the floor where the tile of the kitchen met the hardwood of the family room and gazed over his shoulder at her. "Will you at least let me or the officer outside take you to the speech?"

Jazz shook her head. "No. I'll drive myself."

Bo gritted his teeth. "I'm going to follow you, and there will be police surveillance of the civic center both inside and out."

Jazz crossed her arms over her chest. "It's a free country."

"Will you keep the kids home from school?"

When she didn't answer, Bo took a step forward. "Please, Jazz. Just today and tomorrow. By the weekend, I'm sure Wheeler will either be in custody or the cops will have a better idea of where he's going." He paused and saw that Jazz was now gazing at the floor.

"Please," Bo pleaded. "I'm their father, and—"

"OK," Jazz said. "But T. J.'s going to be ticked if he has to miss basketball practice too."

"He'll get over it," Bo said. "I'm sure Coach Thornton doesn't want anything to happen to his best player."

At this, Jazz finally broke into an uninhibited smile. "I'm sure he doesn't."

"Has the letter from Alabama come yet?" Bo asked. T. J. had received scholarship offers from Vanderbilt, Middle Tennessee State, and Auburn, but Alabama had yet to make an offer. It had always been their son's dream to follow in his parents' footsteps and play for the Crimson Tide.

"Not yet," Jazz said. "But it will."

"Damn right," Bo said. Then, nodding at her, he added, "Be careful today, Jasmine."

During their marriage, Bo had seldom addressed his wife by her proper name. Jazz nodded back, but for the first time since they began their argument last night, Bo saw something else in her eyes.

Fear, he thought, turning to walk away. He had finally scared her.

25

Highway 69 is a long, curvy two-lane road that runs from Tuscaloosa to Jasper. At 7:30 a.m., Rick turned his ancient Saturn onto this stretch of asphalt and gazed into his rearview mirror as a Tuscaloosa County Sheriff's Office cruiser continued to follow him. Wade had been able to obtain the police escort, and Rick was grateful for it. If JimBone Wheeler or Manny Reyes wanted to kill him in the same way Rick's father was murdered—by running him off the road—they couldn't pick a much better route than Highway 69. It was hard enough to stay on the road without someone trying to kill you.

But though seeing the cruiser waiting in the parking lot outside his apartment was comforting, he knew there was only so much the officer could do. Rick would be exposed going into the courthouse and leaving. *And if someone really wants to take me out on this highway, one police car probably won't be enough.*

Still, it was something, as he saw a green sign indicating "Jasper. 44 MILES."

Before leaving his apartment, Rick had called his mother in Henshaw. As a farmer's wife, she was always up with the sun, and that hadn't changed when Rick's father was killed. Allie Drake told her son that all the doors were locked and bolted, Keewin and the dogs were guarding the wraparound porch, and Sheriff Jimmy Ballard himself was sitting in his patrol car at the entrance to the farm. "They'd need the National Guard to get in this house," Allie said. "And if they somehow made it that far, I have your father's Remington and I know how to use it."

Rick had smiled at his mother's brazen toughness and also at the mention of his dad's twelve-gauge shotgun, which Rick had used last year to save Bocephus Haynes's life outside the Pink Pony Pub, in Gulf Shores. "Sounds good, Momma," he had said. "Keep me posted and don't let your guard down until I say."

"OK, but you promise me that you'll watch after yourself. I wish you would stay home. Powell called me and said he begged you not to go to Jasper today."

Rick had closed his eyes and gritted his teeth. "He shouldn't have done that."

"He loves you, son. More like a brother than a friend. He's just looking out for you."

"I know, but I have a job to do, and I'm not going to be scared off from doing it."

She had surprised him then. Instead of continuing to argue, she chuckled and said, "So much like your daddy. He was stubborn as a mule, and the apple didn't fall far. I swear."

Rick had forced back tears as he said goodbye and told his mother he loved her.

Now, as his fifteen-year-old car hurtled down Highway 69, he let his emotions go. Rick wouldn't allow himself to cry around his mother or his friends. But alone behind the wheel of the Saturn, he would occasionally drop his guard when he thought about his father. One of the things he missed most was their conversations in the car. As a trial lawyer, Rick traveled a lot, and to break up the monotony of the trips, he would often call his dad to shoot the bull. These conversations usually revolved around Alabama football or golf, which had become a passion of Billy Drake's. Sometimes they talked about the farm, and occasionally they asked each other for advice. *Hey, big boy* was how Billy always answered the phone when Rick called him. Same as when Rick had been eight years old. *Hey, big boy.*

"I miss you, Dad," Rick said out loud, tapping the dashboard with an open palm and then wiping his eyes. *"And I'm gonna make things right,"* he whispered through clenched teeth.

The ring of the cell phone from the passenger seat startled Rick out of his memories, and he glanced at the caller ID. The word "Professor" popped up on the screen. Rick groaned, realizing he had forgotten to call his partner last night after Powell had dropped the bombshell about JimBone Wheeler. He snatched the phone and clicked the "Answer" icon.

"Happy belated birthday," Rick said, looking in his rearview mirror to make sure the police car was still tailing him. It was.

"Where are you?" The Professor's voice was hoarse and weaker than Rick had ever heard it.

"On Highway 69. Headed to Jasper. Summary judgment hearing on Jennings is at ten."

"Did Powell arrange the police escort?"

"Yep. There's a deputy in hot pursuit right behind me."

"Good." There was a pause and then a cough on the other end of the line. "Congratulations on the Simpson verdict. I know Barbara and Grace had to be pleased."

Rick blinked his eyes as the road took another sharp turn. It seemed like a hundred years since the verdict in Simpson was read just twelve hours ago.

"Thanks," Rick said. "You laid the groundwork, Professor. I just finished things out."

"That's horse manure and you know it," Tom said. "You won that trial with very little input from me, and you carried the case from the discovery phase all the way to verdict. That victory is all yours, Rick, and you earned it. I'm proud of you."

Rick felt heat on his face, embarrassed at hearing accolades from his partner. "Jameson is going to appeal."

"Appeals are for losers," Tom said, and they both laughed.

"Don't you have your scans today?" Rick asked, feeling a nervous trickle in his stomach.

"Headed there now."

"Bo taking you?"

"No, Bill Davis. I'm hoping that Bo is at home watching after his family." Another pause and cough. "I had hoped that you might ask for a continuance of the hearing today and head to Henshaw. I trust you've told your mom about things."

Rick smiled. "The farm is being guarded by the sheriff of Henshaw County. Mom says it would take the National Guard to get inside the house. Besides . . ." He felt the smile fade. "I had to go today, Professor. The judge isn't going to continue the case after transferring venue, and he darn sure isn't going to postpone this hearing again. You know how odd it is to have a summary judgment hearing four days from trial."

"It's unusual, but I've seen it happen before. Some judges hate to rule on dispositive motions because they can't bear the thought of not allowing a plaintiff to have his or her day in court." He coughed again. "So they put it off until the last second."

"I hope that's what's going through Judge Conner's mind."

"The Cock says Conner is the best draw in Walker County. Tough, fair, and, best of all, smart."

Rick couldn't help but smile. "The Cock" was the Professor's friend, the Honorable Art Hancock, a now-retired circuit court judge in Birmingham who had judged mock trials for all of the Professor's trial teams when he was teaching at the law school, including Rick and Powell's. He had also been a leader among the judicial branch in Alabama and was familiar with most of the judges in other counties. "He would know," Rick said.

"Damn right he would. Conner transferred venue, which was the right thing to do but not an easy decision. I like our chances today."

Rick felt his heart warm when he heard the word "our." Even fourteen months into a stage four lung cancer diagnosis and a year into retirement, the Professor still talked like he was an active member of the firm. Rick prayed he always would. "I hope you're right." He paused. "Good luck with the scans."

"Thanks, son. Take care of yourself, OK? Keep your eyes and ears open."

"Will do. You heard from Powell?"

"Yeah. He called a little while ago from the Waysider."

Rick again smiled, thinking of all the times he'd eaten at the Tuscaloosa breakfast establishment with the prosecutor. "What's his status?" Rick asked.

There was a pause on the other end of the line, but no coughing this time.

"Professor?"

"Yeah, I'm still here."

"What's wrong?"

"Nothing. Just . . . Powell sounded weird on the phone. Grunted a lot and didn't say much other than he was heading to Pulaski today and would call when he got closer."

"When he gets focused on something, he can check out for a while," Rick said. "Everything disappears but what he's thinking about. It's what makes him such a damn good lawyer, but . . . it can be a little unsettling if you're not used to it."

"I guess," the Professor said, unconvinced.

"You can't worry about all of us," Rick said, his voice rising. "I know what Wheeler threatened at the prison, but you can only do so much. You take care of you—get through the scans and keep your own eyes and ears open. The rest of us can fend for ourselves."

For a long moment, there was more silence, and Rick knew his partner was continuing to worry and think it through. Finally, there was a cough, and the gravelly voice that had taught Rick everything he knew about being a lawyer came through, even weaker than when the conversation started. "I have every confidence in you, son." Then, coughing again, he added, "But if the only protection you have at this hearing is a police escort to the courthouse, then you're bringing a knife to a gunfight."

"That's not all I'm bringing," Rick said, squeezing the wheel as he saw another green sign: "Jasper. 28 MILES."

"What are you—?" the Professor started to ask, but Rick cut him off.

"I've got to go, Professor. You take care of yourself and I'll do the same. Call me when you have the results of the scans."

They said their goodbyes, and Rick felt a deep resolve come over him as the Saturn passed another sign. This one said "Entering Walker County." In a few minutes, he'd drive through the small town of Oakman, Alabama, home of the famous Bull Pen Steakhouse. Ten minutes after that, he'd be in Jasper. Rick set his phone back on the passenger seat and unclicked the glove compartment. His Glock pistol was inside, and he pulled it out, holding the steering wheel steady with his thighs while he took the handgun out of its case and placed it beside his phone. The weapon was loaded, and he was prepared to fire it if need be. Of course, once he parked on the Walker County downtown square and stepped out of the car, he wouldn't be able to take the gun with him. He didn't want to walk into the courthouse with a weapon and, even if he did, he'd have to relinquish it at the metal detector. No, he'd be flying naked once he was out of the friendly confines of the Saturn, his only protection being one uniformed deputy from Tuscaloosa, his instincts, and . . .

. . . *That's not all I'm bringing.* He repeated in his mind what he'd told his partner a few moments ago. He wondered if he was a fool to think there was actually someone else out there who might be watching his back today.

But there is, Rick told himself, nodding and gritting his teeth as he thought of the one stop he had to make before going to the courthouse. "*There is,*" he whispered out loud, pressing the accelerator down and feeling the wheels of his sedan tug the asphalt.

Another green sign came into view: "Jasper. 15 MILES."

26

The Clearview Cancer Institute is a fortress of a medical facility located behind the old Butler High School, off Fourteenth Street in west Huntsville. At 8:32 a.m., just a few minutes after checking in to the imaging area and taking a seat in the waiting room, Tom saw the wooden door to the back swing open and a technician step through.

"McMurtrie," she said, scanning the waiting room until her eyes met his. Though he didn't recognize every face at CCI, after fourteen months of treatment he knew a lot of the staff. This tech—a twentysomething light-skinned African American woman with a great smile—was named Keisha.

Tom stood and gazed down at Bill Davis, who was reading *USA Today*. "I'll see you in a few hours," Tom said, patting his friend's shoulder. Bill nodded up at him, knowing the drill, and then returned his focus to the headlines. As Tom walked gingerly toward Keisha, he moved his eyes around the waiting room, and the familiar depression began to set in. On a Thursday morning, he counted at least ten folks just in this small wing of the facility. When Tom and Bill had arrived in the parking lot a little while earlier, it had taken them several minutes to find a place. Tom was astounded and saddened by how many people from all walks of life came to CCI for treatment. Young and old. Rich and poor. Black, white, Asian, Mexican, and other ethnicities. He saw Alabama and Auburn shirts. Democrats and Republicans.

Unlike people, cancer didn't discriminate. And when you were touched by any form of the awful disease, you joined a club that wasn't marked by skin tone, political affiliation, or religious denomination. The uniform of the cancer patient and his or her family was always some combination of fear, desperation, and depression that Tom saw in everyone's eyes and which he knew he carried in his own gaze. As he passed by a middle-aged black couple, who a few moments earlier had kissed their teenage daughter on the cheek as she was taken to the back in a wheelchair, Tom nodded at them both. He recognized them from prior visits.

"How is she today?" Tom asked.

The father's eyes were bloodshot from either lack of sleep, crying, or both. He glanced at his wife, who peered up at Tom. "She's having more pain, so . . ." She trailed off, and Tom didn't need her to fill in the rest. *So they're doing more tests.* "How are you?" she managed.

Tom forced a smile. "I guess I'm about to find out."

The woman opened her mouth as if to say something else, but then she closed it and forced her own smile. Hard to know what to say to people whose life could be changed forever by the results of a test. Tom found himself reaching for words many times that wouldn't come. Instead, he would give a nod, or perhaps shake the person's hand or squeeze their shoulder. As a lawyer and a professor, Tom had learned that sometimes the most effective tool of communication wasn't found in words but in nonverbal cues. And though not all the patients and family members at CCI exhibited it in the same way, there was another vibe that permeated these walls.

Grim determination. He saw it in the woman's tight smile and in her husband's red-rimmed eyes.

The feeling reminded Tom of something his father, Sut, had told him a few years after returning from World War II. Sut had fought with General McAuliffe at the Battle of the Bulge and was part of the battalion that refused to surrender at Bastogne. He had been badly injured in combat but was lucky he wasn't killed, like many of his fellow brothers-in-arms. Sut said that as the army faced certain casualties, one of his commanders would softly utter four words over and over again: *We can do this.*

Sut had told young Tom that hearing the words and repeating them had helped in the moments when he thought his demise was certain and that, even years later, when he was worried about a crop or whether he could pay the mortgage, he'd whisper them to himself.

Though Tom had never seen combat, he'd been in many football games, trials, and crises in his life that had seemed like lost causes. Fighting a stage four lung cancer diagnosis was the ultimate uphill battle, and he found himself repeating the commander's words to his father for comfort and motivation, both to himself and others. Tom stooped and placed a hand on the father's shoulder, looking first at him and then the mother. "*We can do this*," he whispered.

The woman bit her lip and Tom saw her eyes glaze over. She nodded and her husband put his hand over Tom's and gave a squeeze.

Then, wiping his own eyes, Tom strode toward the imaging technician, who was patiently waiting to take him for a collection of tests that could mean more bad news. As he walked, he thought about JimBone Wheeler and Manny Reyes on the loose and presumed to be coming after him. When he reached the door, he took as deep a breath as he could manage and slowly exhaled.

"Hello, Keisha," he managed.

"Professor McMurtrie, how are you today?" Her voice was warm and cheerful.

Tom thought for a half second about telling her the God's honest truth—that he was scared to death and exhausted—but then he just smiled. "I'm great. Let's get this mess over with."

27

Once Rick had reached the Jasper city limits, the barren landscape of Highway 69 had transformed into a steady stream of strip malls and fast-food chains. Most of the businesses and restaurants were advertising Christmas specials, and the marquee at the Jasper Mall said that Santa was in the house. With everything that was going on, Rick had a hard time even contemplating Christmas.

As Rick had done on several occasions since filing the Jennings lawsuit, he passed the turn for downtown and, a mile or so later, pulled into a Waffle House. He locked the Saturn and ambled toward the front door. His stomach was queasy—he doubted he'd be able to eat anything—but food wasn't the reason for this stop.

Rick opened the door and breathed in the mingled scent of bacon and coffee. As was the case with every Waffle House he'd ever been in, he saw a long counter directly in front of him with about ten stools. On both sides of the counter and curving around to the back were a number of booths.

At 8:35 a.m. on Thursday morning, the place was crowded but not full, and Rick found a stool at the long counter. He ordered raisin toast and a cup of coffee. Then he waited.

Ten minutes later, after he'd taken a few uninspired bites of the meal, a waitress whose name tag said "Jill" handed him a napkin that he hadn't requested. Rick took the paper and made a show of wiping his mouth before unfolding it. The message on the inside was always the same, the only difference being the color ink pen Jill was using to write her tickets that day. Today, appropriately enough, the shade was dark red.

"*Now.*" Rick read the word silently. Then he crumpled the napkin and placed it on his plate.

"Need anything else, sugar?" Jill asked, glancing at him briefly over her shoulder before simultaneously pouring coffee from a steaming pot into a white mug and removing several slices of bacon with a spatula from a pan on a burner. Jill was a bone-thin woman, whom Rick guessed was in her late thirties or early forties. It seemed that every time he came in, her hair was colored a different hue of brown or blond. Today, her medium-length locks were lighter, which Rick thought was a better choice given her wan skin and yellowish-gray teeth.

"No, I'm good," he said, lifting himself off the stool and laying a five-dollar bill on top of the ticket that had been placed by his plate. "Keep the change."

"Thanks, sugar," Jill said, but Rick was already on the move.

Instead of heading for the exit, he walked to the bathroom in the back. He opened the door and stepped inside, locking the door behind him. As always, the lights were off, and when he turned around, the only thing Rick could make out was the shadow of a very large man in the corner of the small room.

"What color today?" the man asked.

"Blond," Rick said. "I think it's more becoming."

The man chuckled, but Rick could tell it was forced. "Brown is my favorite. If Jill would gain fifteen pounds, get a decent haircut, and invest in some teeth whitener, she'd have to beat the boys off with a stick."

"She doesn't seem to have any trouble keeping you interested," Rick teased. When the man didn't answer, Rick thought he might have gone too far.

"Beggars can't be choosers, boy. Besides, when you get to my age, there are certain qualities you value more than appearance. Loyalty for one . . ." He trailed off and took a few steps closer to Rick. Now they were only a foot apart, and Rick could make out the whites of his eyes. The faint scent of hair gel mixed with cinnamon gum filled the small space. "And persistence," he added, placing an enormous hand on Rick's shoulder and squeezing. "Thank you for getting us this far."

"Don't thank me yet," Rick said, hearing the tension in his voice. "In a little over an hour, Judge Conner may kick us out of court." He paused. "Besides, without your help we wouldn't have stood a snowball's chance in hell today."

For several seconds, neither man spoke. In the small confines of the dark restroom, Rick felt a tad dizzy and a lot scared. "You know about Wheeler?" Rick finally whispered.

The other man nodded. "Escaped Riverbend yesterday morning."

"My sources tell me that Manny is suspected to be helping him."

"Mine tell me the same thing."

Rick crossed his arms and gazed down at the tile floor. "You know what's crazy?" he asked. "When I heard that she might be involved, I"—he swallowed and felt the guilt envelop him—"I was glad," he forced himself to finish. "I know that's wrong."

"No, it's not." He put his large paws on Rick's shoulders. "What it is . . . is natural."

"How so?"

The man stepped away from Rick and began to pace around the bathroom. "She's been a ghost for over a year. By aiding and abetting Wheeler, she's showed her hand and is out in the open. She's exposed herself." Again, he paused and stepped back into Rick's view. "I'm glad too."

"It's wrong to be happy that a killer is on the loose," Rick said, hearing the guilt and frustration in his voice.

"Not when you've been through what we have," the man said. "Not when you've buried your blood. The only way we can bring justice to the ones we've lost is to find Manny Reyes. By helping Wheeler bust out, she's made that task easier."

Rick sighed and felt his heart beating hard in his chest. He took his phone out of his pocket and clicked on the screen. It was now 8:55 a.m., and he was supposed to meet his client in the courthouse at 9:30. "There's a Tuscaloosa cop in the parking lot who followed me here. He'll escort me to the courthouse and hang around outside until after the hearing."

"Piss in the wind," the man said. "I'd say it's better than nothing, but I'm not so sure that's true."

"What do you mean?"

"It means I don't trust the police."

"This guy is from Tuscaloosa, and Wade and Powell wouldn't have assigned him to me if they didn't trust him. And I know Sheriff Patterson hasn't been helpful to our case, but I wouldn't think he'd want a murder in the courthouse on his watch." Rick rubbed the back of his neck. "Especially not after Bully Calhoun's unsolved assassination last year."

The man scoffed and then began to pace again. "I guess not, but I don't trust DeWayne Patterson. He didn't seem very motivated to find Alvie's killer. He . . ." The man trailed off and stopped pacing. He hunched his shoulders and gazed at the floor.

"He what?"

"Doesn't matter. At least not today."

"Have you heard something from your guy in Auburn?"

"I'd rather not say, OK, kid? It may be nothing—I've had leads that didn't go anywhere before."

For several seconds, silence filled the restroom. Now that Rick had adjusted to the darkness, he could make out the other man's skinny six-foot-seven-inch frame. It wasn't hard to imagine him playing for the Philadelphia 76ers in another life. Rick cleared his throat. "Powell and Wade are worried that Wheeler and Manny might make a play against me today."

The man nodded but continued to peer down at the floor. "Because of what Wheeler told Professor McMurtrie in the prison last year." He paused. "JimBone gonna bring the reckoning he promised."

"Something like that," Rick said. "They wanted me to postpone the hearing and ask for a continuance of next week's trial."

The other man shook his head. "But you didn't."

"This case has gone on long enough. It's time to let it ride. With the affidavit you were able to acquire from Harm Twitty, we ought to survive today. Judge Conner should deny the motion. On Monday, we should be teeing this thing up in Florence."

The man continued to stare at the floor, now rubbing the stubble on his chin. Finally, he glanced at Rick, his giant shadow looming behind him on the far wall. "You're right about one thing, kid."

"What?"

"Today is about survival."

Rick felt a cold shudder run up his chest. "Are you going to be there?" When the man didn't immediately answer, Rick took a couple of tentative steps forward. "I know you've wanted to lay low, and up until now, I think that's been the proper play. Having you in the shadows tracking down leads and evidence has been a successful strategy. But"—Rick set his jaw—"if they kill me today, then everything we've worked toward in the last year will be lost. My other cases . . . my father's case . . . will be lost too. Everything." He gazed down at the other man's worn loafers. "Alvie will have died in vain."

For a long ten seconds, neither man spoke. Finally, Rick pressed on, his voice just above a whisper. "But if we survive today, I promise you that I'll win next week." He looked into the other man's eyes. "So, how 'bout it? Are you going to be there today, Rel?"

Santonio "Rel" Jennings chuckled and raised himself to his full six feet seven inches. "Bo was right about you, kid," he finally said. "You're a believer. My brother is lucky to have you representing his family." He paused and the smile faded from his face. "I'll be around."

28

Tom lay on the metal table with his arms stretched over his head. He peered at the clock that hung on the side wall of the compact exam room. It was 8:59 a.m. Focusing on the second hand as it slowly made its pass toward the top of the hour, he braced himself for the warm sensation that the injection of contrast always brought on.

"OK, Professor, here it comes," Keisha said. Immediately, Tom felt the heat in his groin and, as usual, wondered if he was peeing in his pants. He knew he wasn't, but that was what the shot felt like. A few seconds later, the table began to move forward through the cylinder-shaped CT machine. He'd already had fifteen minutes' worth of scans without contrast, and now they were taking the pictures with the radioactive agent. Tom knew that the contrast enhanced visibility and would make whatever was going on with the mass in his lung show up better to the radiologist who interpreted the scan.

With a lung cancer diagnosis, the CT of the chest was the most common diagnostic test, and Tom had lost count as to how many he'd undergone. But his familiarity with it didn't make the scan any more comfortable. The only cushion on the rock-hard surface was a thin white sheet covering the table and a wedge pillow up under his knees. Neither did much for the throbbing pain in his back. He had taken his morning dose of two oxycodone, but after twenty minutes of lying still on the metal table, the effects of the opioids had already faded. *And this is only the first test of three,* Tom thought, gritting his teeth and forcing himself to focus on the conversations he'd had on the drive from the farm.

He wasn't sure what Rick had meant when he said he was bringing something for protection other than just the police escort to the hearing in Jasper, but he was glad his partner had a backup plan. Rick Drake had proven both resourceful and tough as nails during their partnership. Tom felt better about Rick's situation after the call, and that was a relief.

But the conversation with Powell Conrad bothered him. The prosecutor and former student of Tom's had always seemed to have an innate sense of danger. His instincts were what had made him such a force in the courtroom. They had also served him well on the outside, especially in Pulaski two years earlier when Powell and Wade had apprehended JimBone Wheeler on the Giles County Courthouse Square. *I'm worried, Professor,* Powell had said during their short phone call. *I think we've done all we can do. Everybody that needs to be aware of Wheeler's escape has been notified and are taking precautions, but . . .* He had trailed off and then grunted.

But what? Tom had asked.

I'm not sure it's going to matter, the prosecutor had finished, and Tom had felt a chill in the cab of Bill Davis's pickup truck. Tom had almost asked Powell what he meant but had stopped with the words on the tip of his tongue.

I know what he meant, he thought as the table moved back and forth through the round CT contraption.

Tom sighed, imagining JimBone Wheeler as he'd seen him last. The killer's copper-colored eyes glaring at him with white-hot hate from across the desk in the Riverbend Maximum Security Institution. It had been over twenty-four hours since JimBone's escape, and according to the report Tom had received from Helen on the way over, the primary lead in the investigation was still the message that the psychopath had carved into the rogue nurse's abdomen.

Me, Tom thought. *Me and everyone I hold dear.*

Tom squeezed his hands into fists as the pictures in his subconscious returned to the killer who, up until yesterday morning, had been locked away on death row. Powell Conrad's last salvo on the telephone formed a question in his thoughts that he hated to even consider.

Is it going to matter?

29

Wade Richey lived in a one-story rental house on Eighth Avenue. The home was just a few blocks from Bryant-Denny Stadium, and Powell enjoyed parking at Wade's place on game days during the fall.

At just after 9:00 a.m., Powell pulled his Charger into the driveway and hopped out of the car. He was holding a steaming to-go bag from the Waysider with two buttermilk biscuits inside in his right hand and a brand-new compact disc in the left. As he strode up the cobblestone path to the front door, Powell hummed the tune to Robert Earl Keen's "Merry Christmas from the Family," which he'd been listening to on the drive over, and smiled to himself. He normally would honk his horn, but since he was carrying a present that the detective might not want to bring on this trip, he decided to knock on the door. As he walked, he caught movement out of his right eye and noticed a police car approaching from the north. It was a white SUV with the gold crest of the sheriff's office along the side. *Backup,* he thought, nodding his head at the vehicle and trotting up the three steps to the front stoop. Just before his knuckles touched the wooden frame, the door swung open.

Wade gazed back at him with bloodshot eyes. The detective appeared to be wearing the same black T-shirt and jeans he'd had on yesterday and was putting on a black leather jacket.

"You look like crap," Powell said, handing him the plain white sack of food.

"Thanks," Wade said, hovering his nostrils over the sack and breathing in the scent of the biscuits. He stepped out onto the stoop and shut the door, bringing a key to the knob.

"Before you lock it, you might want to put this inside," Powell said, grinning and handing him the compact disc. "Early Christmas present. I saw it at the Chevron on Hargrove. Five freakin' bucks. Bargain if you ask me."

Wade glanced at the disc but didn't take it. "Merle's greatest?" he asked, but his eyes were now looking past Powell to the road.

Powell nodded. "Come on. Take it. I've already got all these songs on my iPod in the car. You—"

"Get down!" Wade screamed, stepping in front of the prosecutor and pulling a pistol out of the front of his jeans. Before he could pull the trigger, the rapid patter of a semiautomatic rifle engulfed the morning air.

Powell ducked and turned, seeing Wade drop to his knees in front of him. The gun fell from the detective's outstretched hand, and the biscuits spilled out of the sack and down the steps.

"Wade!"

Powell lunged forward to cover his friend, but before he could get there, his left knee exploded in pain, followed by a shearing snap of his right shoulder. Instinctively, he brought his hands up for protection as another bullet pierced his rib cage. Then his face and eyes were covered in a shower of sharp plastic daggers as the CD case that he was holding in his left hand was blown apart by another round of gunfire.

Powell screamed in pain and staggered sideways. He fell off the stoop and landed on his stomach. He felt the breath go out of him and his head fill with stars.

The world went black.

30

JimBone Wheeler calmly placed the AK-47 back in its case. "You can roll up the window now, DeWayne."

In the front seat, Sheriff Patterson gripped the wheel with two shaking hands. Without looking back at the killer, he clicked the button inside the door and the back passenger-side window slowly ascended. "You g-g-get them?"

"The detective is dead as a doornail. I hit him with at least five, maybe seven, bullets in the chest."

"And the prosecutor? C-C-Conrad?"

"I got him in the knee, the stomach, and the shoulder. I had one tracking the bastard's head, but it must have ricocheted off something he was holding. I don't think it connected." JimBone paused and rubbed his chin, calculating the damage. "He may not be dead immediately, but there's no way he'll survive."

"M-m-mission ac-ac-accomplished, then," the sheriff managed, and JimBone caught a whiff of urine coming from the front seat.

"Yeah. We've done our part. It didn't go down exactly like I thought," he said, speaking more for his own enjoyment than DeWayne's listening pleasure as the sheriff turned left onto Fifteenth Street. "I figured Conrad would honk and we'd get the detective walking to the car. Then that would draw out the prosecutor, and we'd either shoot him getting out of the car or through the windshield." JimBone smiled. "Conrad made it easy pickings by walking to the door."

"Better to be lucky than good, I guess," DeWayne said, and JimBone noticed that the lawman's hands were still shaking.

"No," JimBone said. He leaned forward and slapped the sheriff on the side of the head with an open hand. "You guess wrong. I'm very good. And when you're good . . . *you get the breaks*. You hear me, shit for brains?"

DeWayne Patterson rubbed his head with his right hand while keeping his left on top of the wheel. "Yes. I'm sorry. I—"

"Just shut up and drive," JimBone said. "We need to be somewhere in an hour."

"You promised to let the Mexican handle Drake," DeWayne whined as he took another left onto McFarland Boulevard. "With my officer's help."

JimBone didn't respond. Instead, he saw the familiar sights of Tuscaloosa. When the SUV passed the old Ultron Gasoline plant, the Bone gave a mock salute to the new structure that had replaced the warehouse he'd burned down for Jack Willistone four years earlier. *Some of my best work,* he thought.

Five minutes later, at 9:15 a.m., the sheriff's vehicle passed a white-and-black sign indicating the junction for Highway 69. DeWayne turned on his right-turn blinker. "Mr. Wheeler, you're going to let my deputy and Pasco handle Drake, right? That was the plan."

JimBone held his eye through the rearview mirror as the Tahoe pulled onto Highway 69. "That's correct, DeWayne. But sometimes plans have to be adjusted." He paused. "Let's hope your guy doesn't get cold feet."

"He w-w-won't," DeWayne said, glancing at the road and then peering back at JimBone in the mirror.

Through the windshield, the killer saw a green sign. "Jasper. 48 MILES." Then he ran his hand along the case of the assault rifle. "We shall see."

31

It was the taste in his mouth that brought him back. Iron. *Blood . . . Wade . . .*

Powell opened his left eye. He tried to open his right, but the lid wouldn't budge. His face was pressed against something rough and his ears were ringing. "Wade." He tried to say the word, but he wasn't sure if it came out or not. He couldn't hear anything but a high-pitched tone. Like the alarm the television used to make when they interrupted normal programming and then a monotone female voice would say, *This is a test of the Emergency Broadcast System. This is only a test.* But here there wasn't a voice mercifully interrupting the alarm. Instead, the tone persisted, pounding Powell's eardrums with its steady intensity.

He blinked his open eye, and with all the effort he could muster, he raised his head a few inches off the ground. He was lying in a bed of mulch, and his right arm was twisted underneath him. He attempted to move it and cried out in pain. The limb wouldn't budge. *Broken,* he thought. He moved his left hand along the mulch, relieved that he still had one good arm, and felt for the concrete stoop. When he grasped it, he tried to pull himself up, but he wasn't strong enough. He couldn't bend his left leg. He gazed down, saw that his kneecap was covered in blood, and remembered the searing pain. Using his right leg and left arm, Powell pulled himself up on the stoop.

Wade Richey was lying on his side and gazing at him with blank eyes. *No,* Powell thought, gritting his teeth and beginning to crawl along the bloody concrete toward his friend. Out of his still-functioning eye, he saw three police cars pulling to a stop along the curb. Their blue and red lights were flashing. Powell knew the air had probably filled with the blaring of sirens, but all he could hear was the alarm tone. *This is only a test,* he thought. In front of the police vehicles, Powell saw an elderly woman waving her hands and pointing toward the house. Tears streamed down her cheeks. Next to her, there was an overweight man holding a leash while his dog thrashed below him, trying in vain to run toward the bodies on the porch.

Powell pulled himself along the stoop with his left arm until he was a foot from Wade. His friend was lying on his right shoulder with his right hand outstretched, grasping hold of something that Powell couldn't see. The detective's legs were extended straight out and his cheek was on the concrete. Underneath the detective's body was a puddle of blood that was slowly spreading out and away.

Biting his lip, which was trembling, Powell touched his friend's face.

Wade's eyes flickered and Powell saw his mouth move.

"What?" Powell said, crawling closer. The tone in his ears was growing fainter, but he still couldn't make out any other sounds.

Wade's mouth again moved, but Powell couldn't hear him. He pulled to within a couple of inches of the other man's mouth. "What?" he asked again.

Wade's eyes rolled back into his sockets, and Powell grabbed his cheek. "Wade?" Above them, Powell saw movement. People were approaching and the tone was fading. He thought he heard a voice.

It was a man's. Words came in and out like a radio that was losing its frequency. "Walking . . . machine gun . . . police car."

Powell squeezed his friend's cheek and felt his eyes burning with tears. "Don't die, brother."

Wade blinked and focused his gaze back on Powell. He removed his left hand from under his chest and placed a blood-streaked index finger on the pavement. He moved the finger shakily across the stoop until he had managed to form four letters.

W . . . C . . . S . . . O.

Powell squinted at the message with his good eye, not understanding. His head was spinning and he felt the adrenaline draining from his body. *I'm going to die,* he thought for the first time. *Too much blood. I'm going to—*

Movement interrupted his thoughts. Wade was motioning with his bloody finger for Powell to come close. When Powell was an inch from the detective's face, Wade kissed him on the cheek. Then he brought his right hand around, and Powell could tell what the detective had been holding. It was the CD that Powell had brought him as a gift. The case had been destroyed, but the disc had somehow remained intact.

"Mama . . . tried," Wade said, and Powell was barely able to make out the words. Then the disc slid from Wade Michael Richey's fingers.

And the life went out of his body.

32

The ringing in his ears was the worst part.

It didn't matter whether they used earplugs, headphones, or both, the constant blare of the machine—like a lawn mower's engine—was so loud that it easily made the MRI of the brain Tom's least-favorite test and the one he dreaded the most.

At 9:30 a.m., Tom was brought into the MRI room. He lay down on another hard table, cringing as the rough surface lurched toward a narrow, cylinder-shaped tunnel. Once his head had passed through the tubelike contraption, the table stopped. Though he knew it was coming, Tom still flinched when the engine-like sound blasted his eardrums, announcing that the procedure had begun. Tom's only job during the scan was to remain as still as possible; any movement could hurt the quality of the images taken.

Every so often, the roar of the machine eased momentarily with three sharp clicking sounds. *Click, click, click.* Then the loud banging of the engine was back. For the next forty-five minutes, this pattern was repeated more times than Tom could count, and as always, he found himself longing for the few precious seconds of *click, click, click*.

The other thing Tom hated about the MRI of the brain was the sense of entrapment. His face and head were completely covered, so all he could see were the four sides of the machine. Tom had never been that bothered by enclosed spaces. Claustrophobia was not even on his radar. He had no problem in elevators or airplanes. But for some reason, once his head was in the cylinder, he felt trapped and scared.

In these moments, he wondered if this was what death would be like. He had heard stories of people whose heart had stopped beating, and how they had seen a sharp twinge of light before doctors brought them back to life. Would he see the light when he died?

Or would it be like this? Would he feel trapped, unable to move, as his ears pounded with the piercing sound of death?

Thomas Jackson McMurtrie had been a Methodist his whole life, attending Hazel Green United as a child and teenager, and First United Methodist in Tuscaloosa all of his adult life. He believed in God, Jesus, and the Holy Spirit. He had read the Gospel. He had faith that there was a heaven as the Bible said.

But it was easier thinking of these things when other people were involved. He wanted desperately to believe there was a place where all of his departed loved ones were waiting on him. A beautiful place. A safe and peaceful place filled with light and love.

But if he were brutally honest with himself, he had his doubts. And they seemed to be increasing as he edged closer toward the afterlife. And now, with his friends and family threatened by an escaped killer, his brain seemed to be riddled with doubt.

Realizing he'd been holding his breath to stay still, Tom slowly exhaled. He closed his eyes and then opened them, but the image in his mind was the same.

JimBone Wheeler's copper eyes.

He flinched and then a voice rang out above the sound of the machine. "Stay still, Professor."

"OK," Tom said, knowing they couldn't hear him. He let out another ragged breath and felt his heartbeat picking up speed as the blaring noise mercifully softened for three short seconds.

Click, click, click.

33

The Von Braun Center is Huntsville's primary event location. In addition to a ten-thousand-seat arena, where hockey and basketball games take place, there's also a performing arts auditorium and two halls, where high school proms, wedding receptions, and speeches can be held. The VBC has a parking garage and also two lots adjacent to the North and South Halls.

At 10:05 a.m., Bocephus Haynes waited in the North Hall parking lot, on Clinton Street. As he had promised, he'd followed Jazz to the event, and despite her protests, he, along with two officers from the Huntsville Police Department dressed in street clothes, had walked beside her as she had entered the building an hour and a half earlier. One of the lawmen went inside to scope out the area. According to the deputy who stayed behind to watch the front entrance, there were four other officers inside the hall as well as the entire security detail for the VBC, which consisted of over ten guards.

Despite the battalion of officers, Bo had asked Jazz to text him when she was finished so he could escort her back to her car, but she had rolled her eyes at him.

The breakfast had started at 8:30, and Jazz had been slated to speak at nine. Adjournment was at ten.

Bo peered at the clock on the dash inside the Sequoia. 10:06 a.m. He glanced at his phone. No text yet from Jazz, and he wondered if she would follow his instructions.

I doubt it, he thought, shaking his head and grabbing the door handle. He climbed out of the vehicle and scanned the lot, which was packed to capacity. There had to be over fifty cars in this area alone, and Bo had noticed that the security guard at the gate had directed the overflow to an adjacent lot for the South Hall in the back. *She got what she wanted,* he thought, smiling and beginning to walk toward the entrance.

For December, the weather was balmy and warm. It couldn't be much less than sixty-five degrees. This was typical for North Alabama and South Tennessee, where you could have a winter day in the seventies as easily as you could have one in the thirties. Bo slid his sunglasses off the top of his head and over his eyes to shield himself from the light. He took out his phone and glanced at the screen. 10:08 a.m.

In front of him, people began to exit the building, and Bo breathed a sigh of relief. He noticed that the plainclothes officer at the door was holding a cell phone to his ear and talking into the microphone. Three other members of the civic center security crew had spanned out to cover the parking lot. Gazing over his shoulder and looking past the vehicles to Clinton Avenue, Bo wondered if maybe he was taking JimBone Wheeler's escape too seriously. *He's a cold-blooded killer. A revenge rampage doesn't fit the profile.*

Bo leaned against one of the concrete pillars on the landing in front of the building, nodding as the patrons left the event, almost all of whom were African American. Alabama A&M was a historically black university, and Bo had always had a lot of admiration for the school. One of his football heroes had been John Stallworth, the Hall of Fame wide receiver for the Pittsburgh Steelers and former Alabama

A&M graduate. Bo had met Stallworth, a Huntsville resident, a few times over the years and found him to be just as impressive in the business world as he had been on the football field. Wondering if his childhood hero was in attendance, Bo continued to scan the faces, finally seeing his soon-to-be ex-wife talking to a group of people in the lobby.

Bo sighed, glancing again at his phone. 10:10 a.m. He took several steps toward the parking lot and placed his right hand above his forehead, looking for anything that might be suspicious. Across Clinton Avenue, there were a couple of buildings catty-corner to the right, and Bo squinted at them, noting nothing out of the ordinary. Cars in lots. People walking inside. Christmas decorations. He glanced upward and saw that on top of the nearest building there appeared to be an officer looking back at him with binoculars. Bo took a deep breath, grateful for the police presence that had materialized on such short notice. Based on what the officers who had accompanied Jazz into the North Hall had said, there was a crew of Madison County deputies watching Clinton Avenue for anything abnormal.

Bo turned back to the exit and saw Jazz coming through the door, accompanied by a light-skinned black man wearing a perfectly tailored navy suit. The man stood just over six feet tall and had the lean build of a runner.

Bo knew the man. They had met once at a school function that Jazz had dragged him to. He was Dr. Todd Erwin, the dean of the art history department. Bo had instantly taken a disliking to Erwin, not appreciating the way the other man peered at his wife.

Erwin noticed Bo first. Bo saw him nudge Jazz with his elbow, and the gesture sent a razor wire of jealousy down Bo's spine. He glanced down at his own clothes. Bo was wearing the same jeans, boots, and white button-down in which he had slept in the car last night. For the first time since his arrival, he felt self-conscious and disheveled.

"Mr. Haynes," Erwin said, extending his hand, which Bo reluctantly grasped, gripping it a bit firmer than he normally would and piercing the other man with a look that eventually made Erwin avert his eyes.

"Why are you still here?" Jazz asked. She was dressed in an elegant cream dress, which Bo thought created a beautiful blend with her complexion. She crossed her arms and waited.

"You know why," he said. "I just want to make sure you get home safe."

"Is something wrong?" Erwin asked.

"This isn't your concern," Bo said, shooting him another glare.

Erwin's gaze narrowed, and Bo took a step toward him, invading his space. "I'm not messing around, OK? There's a dangerous situation involving an escaped convict in Tennessee who wants to hurt my family, and the best and safest thing for you to do would be to walk to your car and get the hell out of Dodge. Do you hear me?"

Erwin glanced at Jazz, and Bo saw out of the corner of his eye that she gave him a swift nod.

"Alright then," Erwin said. "You're scaring me, man."

"You should be scared," Bo said.

As the other man turned to go, Bo noticed that the police officer on the building across Clinton was now facing frontward and appeared to be peering over the edge, as if to look directly below him. *Does he see something?* Bo wondered, feeling his heartbeat pick up. A pain in his rib cage interrupted his focus, and he turned to see that Jazz was pinching him.

"What was *that* all about?" she whispered through clenched teeth.

"Just warning your friend that he could be in danger if he walks out with us," Bo said, forcing a smile. "It seemed like the neighborly thing to do."

"You acted like a horse's ass," she said.

Bo's face tightened. "The papers on the divorce won't be dry before that prissy bastard is going to be calling asking you out." He paused. "Unless he already has."

"So you're going to add jealous to overprotective and stubborn. That it, Bo? I *work* with Todd. He's my boss. I don't like him in that way."

Bo gazed back toward the parking lot, where Todd Erwin was sliding into a maroon Escalade. Past the vehicle, Bo again noticed the officer on top of the building across the street. Now he was standing up and appeared to be watching the cars pass by on Clinton Avenue below.

Bo turned back to her. "Well, *Doctor* Erwin sure likes you in that way, and it's obvious."

"You're an idiot," Jazz said, pushing past him toward the lot.

Bo reached out and grabbed her arm, pulling her back. "Jazz, I want you to wait inside. I'm going to bring my car around and get you, OK? Please, honey." He glanced over her shoulder and saw both plainclothes officers heading toward them and breathed a sigh of relief. He waved them forward with his other hand.

"Take your hands off me, Bo, or I'm going to scream bloody murder, you hear me?"

Bo tightened his grip. "Please, Jazz. Please just listen to me today. That's all I'm asking. There are officers here to protect you, but we can't be too cautious."

For a second, Jazz's eyes softened, and he thought he had reached her. Then she yelled loud and strong, "*Help!*"

Bo loosened his grip and Jazz pulled away from him. When she did, the sleeve on her dress tore.

She opened her mouth and gazed at her ripped clothing. Then she scowled at him and tears welled in her eyes. "I hate you," she said. Folding her arms, she walked out into the sunshine.

On the roof of the bank across the street, Manny Reyes reached behind her and grabbed the sniper rifle she had used to kill Greg Zorn in Orange Beach, Alabama, a little over a year earlier. She had hidden the gun in an equipment bag when she walked into the bank an hour earlier, telling the branch manager she was with Smith Roofing Company, which was the name she'd been given the week prior when she'd called and asked who installed the roof. She'd informed the manager that Mr. Smith had instructed her to come by and make some adjustments, and he had shown her the way.

Amazing how easy it is sometimes, she thought. Of course, this assignment had become more adventurous when the sheriff's deputy had surprised her on the roof ten minutes earlier. But fortunately for her he hadn't been as alert as he should have been. When he asked for her ID, she fumbled in her wallet and was able to knee the man in the groin when he looked away. Then she'd swiftly pulled out a pistol and shot him in the side of the head. Because of the silencer, the only sound was a muffled pop that was disguised by the traffic from the cars on Clinton Avenue below. She'd dragged the officer's body to the small electrical room on the roof and changed into his uniform. Because the man was thin and wiry, her new threads fit well enough to not arouse suspicion.

They were also the perfect disguise, provided that no one began to miss the fallen officer. Manny figured that when someone did notice his absence, she'd be long gone. *Dust in the wind.*

She had learned about the breakfast speech by doing a simple Facebook search for Jasmine Haynes. Manny was always amazed at how much you could learn about a person by perusing their Facebook page. During the year or so she'd been hiding since carrying out her duties for Bully Calhoun in the Wilma Newton case, she'd successfully robbed at least a dozen people by checking their Facebook pages and finding out where they lived and when they would be out of town.

For the past week, Jasmine Haynes had been sharing nonstop posts on her page, trying to bolster attendance at the breakfast, which was meant to raise money for the art history department of her university. Manny literally knew every detail about the event.

She lay flat on her stomach and looked through the scope of the rifle. The face of Bocephus Haynes appeared in the crosshairs. For a half second, Manny thought about pulling the trigger. They were going to kill the lawyer eventually. Why not take him out right now?

Those aren't my orders, she thought, hovering her right index finger over the trigger as she focused the scope on the woman Haynes was arguing with.

"Ah, a lover's spat," Manny whispered, seeing the woman pull away from the attorney's grip. Then seconds later, Jasmine Haynes broke into the open, walking briskly toward the parking lot.

Manny Reyes smiled. *Amazing how easy it is sometimes.*

As Jazz marched away, Bo sighed and waved at the plainclothes officers to follow her. Both deputies immediately changed direction and sprinted toward Jazz. They caught up to her within seconds and then walked on each side of her. Turning toward the entrance door, Bo saw a group of men and women looking at him, the disapproval palpable in their eyes. Down the sidewalk, one of the security guards was hustling toward him, guided by a woman who was pointing in his direction.

Great, he thought. He spun back toward the lot, seeing that Jazz and the two officers were now halfway to her car. Bo stepped out from under the covered landing and began to follow them.

"Wait right there, sir," he heard the guard say behind him, but Bo kept walking. He glanced across the street and saw that the officer on the roof . . .

Where is he?

Bo picked up his pace and focused as hard as he could on the top of the building. Moving his eyes back and forth, he finally saw him. The man was lying on his stomach on the roof and holding a—

"Jazz!" Bo screamed her name at the same time that he heard the crack of the rifle.

"No!"

He ran toward her and saw her wheel around to face him. For a moment, their eyes met. He saw that her cream dress with its ripped right sleeve had blood splattered across the front. Her hands had gone to her chest. Removing them, she gazed at her bloody fingers and then into her husband's eyes.

"Bo," she cried.

He was just a few feet away from her, running as fast as he could.

He reached out his hands just as the next rifle shot pierced the air.

34

The final test was the PET scan.

The PET, which stood for positron emission tomography, was by far the most comfortable of the three imaging studies. As opposed to a hard table, Tom lay in a recliner chair similar to the ones in the treatment area where he had received chemotherapy months earlier. His only instructions were to lie still.

Also different was the darkness. Prior to beginning the scan, the lights in the room were turned off.

Though physically comfortable, the PET was the most anxiety provoking of the tests. It was this scan that determined if the cancer had spread.

Though he had to be alone in the dark room, he was allowed one creature comfort while the scanner worked its magic. He was able to have his phone, which he now gripped in his right hand. Glancing at the screen, he noticed that it was 10:20 a.m. Since his first test had begun almost two hours earlier, Tom had received no messages or missed calls.

No news is good news, he thought, wondering if that were true in this instance.

Not willing to wait for the answer, he fired off texts to Powell, Wade, and Bo, trying to move as little as possible while his thumb tapped in the letters. He knew Rick was in court, so he chose to hold off on checking in with his partner. *I'll call him after the hearing.*

Tom closed his eyes, again imagining JimBone Wheeler sitting across from him at the Riverbend Maximum Security Institution. He immediately opened his lids, but the view was the same.

Pitch darkness. He once more thought of death. Would the view ever change when he breathed his last? Or would it be like it was in this small room?

Perpetual darkness, your thoughts tortured by the things you can't control.

If so, then perhaps that means I've gone to hell, Tom thought to himself, gazing at his phone and willing it to flash a message.

But it didn't. All the small screen showed was the time.

10:25 a.m.

35

Alvin Lamont Jennings, who had been called "Alvie" since he was two weeks old, had faithfully attended the Black Warrior Baptist Church in Jasper before his untimely death the previous August. He was the youth director for the church along with being the head basketball coach for Jasper Middle School. To make ends meet, when he wasn't coaching or teaching, Alvie also worked as a driver for C&G Security, a local outfit owned by a lifelong Walker County resident named Harm Twitty. In the spring of 2012, Twitty assigned Alvie the detail for Marcellus "Bully" Calhoun. A few months later, Alvie saw something he wasn't supposed to see, eventually paying the ultimate price for his misfortune.

On the afternoon of August 4, 2012, a week before the official start of school, Alvie had been about to mow his yard. He was having trouble getting his push mower started, and his six-year-old son, LaByron, had come outside to watch, even asking his father if he could have a turn. Alvie had said no but promised the boy that he could mow the backyard once Alvie had gotten it started.

On his fourth attempt to crank the machine, a bomb rigged to the ignition switch exploded. The blast killed Alvie instantly and spread his remains all over the yard. The boy, who had watched the horror from just a few feet away, had been covered in his father's blood and brain matter. The resulting blaze caused by the explosion spread to Alvie's house, and by the time the fire department arrived, the flames had destroyed the garage and kitchen. Though the home was saved and Alvie's wife, LaShell, and LaByron continued to live there until the end of the year, they eventually moved to Birmingham to be closer to LaShell's parents. LaShell had also been pregnant at the time of her husband's death, and the child, another boy, was born that November. She had named him Alvin Lamont Jennings Jr.

LaShell Jennings and LaByron, now seven, both sat at the counsel table next to Rick. Behind them, in the first row of the gallery, LaShell's eighty-year-old mother held the baby on her chest, gently stroking his back. A bottle was perched in the boy's mouth, and the only sound in the courtroom was the soft sucking of the thirteen-month-old's tongue on the rubber nipple. In the rows behind them were a sea of black and white faces, which included the Reverend Tyson Blackwell, from Black Warrior Baptist, a huge man who had played basketball himself for Walker County High in the early '90s. The rest of the spectators were a split between the church congregation and students and administrators of Jasper Middle.

The victim's popularity and the heinous nature of the crime that took his life were two things that Rick knew he had going for him in this case, and he had decided to pull no punches for the summary judgment hearing. Though he knew Judge Conner would decide the motion on the law, if the decision was as close as Rick thought it would be, he wanted His Honor to see the number of voters he would be disappointing. Circuit court judges were elected, not appointed, in the state of Alabama, and a decision like this could send a ripple of negativity toward Conner throughout the community—the kind of publicity most political candidates, even judges, would like to avoid.

For the umpteenth time since arriving at the courthouse forty-five minutes earlier, Rick pulled his phone out of his pocket. The device was on silent mode, and Rick quickly entered his security code. No messages. No calls. The time was 10:30 a.m. The hearing was supposed to start at 10:00, but Judge Conner had to take his mother to the hospital for cataract surgery and was running late.

Rick stifled a sigh and lay the phone on the table so he wouldn't have to keep reaching into his pocket. He glanced at his client, whose feet had continuously pattered on the floor since she'd sat down. "You OK?"

LaShell Jennings gave a swift nod but didn't say anything. She gripped LaByron's hand tight, and Rick moved his eyes to the young boy. "How about you, big man?"

LaByron smiled but he also didn't say anything. According to his mother, he'd barely said a word since the murder and was being seen by a counselor in Birmingham. Rick, whose own father was also murdered, though he mercifully hadn't had a front-row seat for it, felt a kinship with the kid. He reached across the table and held out his fist, which the boy bumped with his own.

Rick then gazed across the courtroom to the other counsel table. Since his arrival, Rick hadn't said a word to the defendant's attorneys, and they hadn't so much as acknowledged him. Rick decided he'd try to break the ice and perhaps fish for a little information. "Be right back," he whispered to LaShell.

Rick strode across the courtroom toward the defense table. There were three lawyers sitting side by side. Two of them were from the Ashe & Rowe law factory in Birmingham, second in size only to Jones & Butler. Joel Axon, an amiable middle-aged man of average size with salt-and-pepper hair, wore a charcoal suit and burgundy tie. Next to him, in the middle of the group, was Melody Tunnell, an attractive thirtysomething woman wearing a dark-blue suit. Both were gazing at their smartphones and working their thumbs over the devices like there was no tomorrow. They barely took notice of Rick, who was now standing in front of the table. The last of the group, seated at the edge closest to Rick, was a small, bone-thin man with wild white hair on both sides of his head and a bald streak right down the middle. He wore a plaid sports coat with patches on the sleeves, black slacks, and brown loafers that were dusty and scuffed. Unlike his two colleagues, he was not looking at his phone. Instead, he held a copy of the *Daily Mountain Eagle* in his hands, extending his arms as far out as they could go, presumably to allow him to see the small print better due to farsightedness. Sensing Rick's presence, he peered around the paper.

"Drake, I hear you had a nice pop yesterday."

"Virgil, how are you?"

Virgil Leonard Flood set the paper down and stood, squinting at Rick with blue eyes that always seemed to contain a hint of amusement. They shook hands, and Rick was struck as usual by the other man's papery skin. A little too firm on the grip, and Rick feared he might leave a bruise on the older lawyer.

"Twenty-two point five million dollars," Virgil said, licking his lips and cocking his head. "That how much you asked for?"

"I just asked them to deliver justice," Rick said, flashing a grin. "Same as I'll do next week in Florence in this case."

Virgil's head remained cocked. "Florence is a lovely town. Every time I'm there, I like to eat at that Italian joint a few blocks from the courthouse. Ricatoni's." He snorted. "It's too bad that Joel and Melody have done such a fine job on this motion for summary judgment." He looked behind his shoulder, where his counterparts continued to check their phones. "I would have enjoyed teeing it up next week against you. Been a while since I waited on a verdict."

Rick made a show of looking at a watch he wasn't wearing. "I suspect you'll be waiting on one this time next week."

"Dream on, kid. But I'll hand it to you. You put on a nice show." He nodded toward the gallery, which was standing room only in the back. "I've never had an audience for a summary judgment hearing, and we both know you aren't going to win today with sympathy. Lloyd Conner isn't my favorite judge over here by a long shot, but he calls balls and strikes based on the law. He won't let all this clutter, as Coach Saban likes to say, affect his decision."

"I hope you're right," Rick said.

Virgil scoffed. "About what?"

"About Conner following the law."

Virgil opened his mouth to respond, but the sound of the door to the judge's chambers squeaking open and slamming shut stopped him cold. They both turned as Judge Lloyd Conner walked briskly toward the bench. Next to them, Virgil's two partners set their phones down and scrambled to their feet.

"Sorry I'm late," His Honor said, plopping down in his chair and peering over the bench, holding a manila folder open in front of him. Rick felt his stomach tighten as he gazed up at the man who was about to make a decision that would either kill or keep alive the chances for Alvie Jennings's family to obtain justice.

The Honorable Lloyd Christian Conner was in his forties, with a head shaved bald to hide what was once a receding hairline. He had grown up in nearby Winston County and played football on scholarship at Samford University, in Birmingham. Conner was a stocky man who looked every bit the offensive guard he had once been. Wearing the black robe of the judiciary, with a white shirt and tie underneath, Conner appeared even more robust than normal. "*Case of LaShell Jennings, as personal representative of the Estate of Alvin Jennings, plaintiff, versus Kathryn Calhoun Willistone, personal representative of the Estate of Marcellus Calhoun, and Mahalia Blessica Reyes, defendants.*" Conner paused, glancing up at Rick and Virgil, who had both remained in place. "Before we get to the motion, have there been any developments in the attempts to serve Ms. Reyes with process?" Conner focused his gaze on Rick.

Surprised by the question, Rick cleared his throat and collected his thoughts. "Not exactly, Your Honor. We've learned that a death row inmate in Tennessee named James Robert Wheeler escaped custody yesterday, and it is believed that Ms. Reyes, a known colleague of Wheeler's, may have assisted him."

The judge ribbed his chin. "How about that television interview you gave in Tuscaloosa last night? Any response to that yet?" Conner's voice gave away nothing, but Rick could tell by the hard look in the man's eyes that he was annoyed Rick had gone to the press.

"No, Your Honor."

"Really? I would have thought with your 'mission in life' tirade, some noble citizen would have come forward, especially given the reward you promised."

Rick felt heat radiate up his legs all the way to his face. Judge Conner was a straight shooter, but he had a sarcastic streak. Rick also knew that judges universally hated it when their cases showed up in the media before a big hearing or trial. *Stay cool,* Rick thought to himself. When he spoke, his voice was clear, under control. "No such luck, Your Honor."

Conner gazed down at his folder. "Alright then, we're here on Ms. Willistone's motion for summary judgment, which has been postponed a number of times." Conner paused, looking first at Rick and then at Virgil. "Is everyone ready?"

"Yes, Your Honor," Virgil said.

"Yes, sir," Rick agreed.

"It's a Christmas miracle," Conner said, and the sarcasm in his tone was back and palpable. "Virgil, since this is your motion, I'll let you begin."

"Yes, Your Honor," the older lawyer said, snatching a yellow pad from the counsel table. "I think our motion speaks for itself, Judge.

In this case, the plaintiff has sued the estate of Marcellus Calhoun for wrongful death, claiming that Mr. Calhoun hired a contract killer named Mahalia Blessica Reyes to cause the wrongful death of Alvin Jennings and that Ms. Reyes did, in fact, cause the wrongful death of Mr. Jennings. Your Honor, the plaintiff has no direct evidence linking Mr. Calhoun or Ms. Reyes to this murder. If they did, Sheriff Patterson's office would be all over this case and they would have charged Ms. Reyes with murder. But there have been no criminal charges, Your Honor, and the civil case brought by Mr. Drake is a farce."

"What do you make of the evidence that Mr. Drake has recently filed in opposition to your motion, Virgil?" Conner's voice had a challenge in it that lifted Rick's spirits.

"Judge, all they've presented is evidence that Ms. Reyes worked for Mr. Calhoun and that Ms. Reyes was seen near Alvin Jennings's house. Your Honor, that simply isn't enough to get past a properly supported motion for summary judgment. They have to present substantial evidence showing a question of fact, and the circumstantial facts they've presented in the affidavits of Mr. Twitty, Mr. Corlew, and Ms. Purdy are beyond weak." Virgil hesitated. "This is a travesty, Your Honor, and Mr. Drake knows it. Why else would he have his client and her sons here today as well as half of Walker County? He knows his case is weak and is trying to apply pressure on the court to let this case go to the jury. I have practiced in this county since Lyndon Johnson was president, and I've never seen such a spectacle."

Judge Conner smiled at Virgil, no doubt having heard the LBJ reference before. Then he turned to Rick. "Response, Mr. Drake?"

"Yes, Your Honor," Rick said, strategically walking back over to his table so that Judge Conner would have to see LaShell Jennings and LaByron sitting behind him. "Your Honor, this is a summary judgment motion. As you know, any questions of fact should be resolved in favor of the nonmoving party, which is Ms. Jennings. We have presented the affidavit of Carmella Purdy, Mr. and Mrs. Jennings's neighbor, and Ms. Purdy testified that she saw a woman matching the description of Manny Reyes on the street by Mr. Jennings's house on the day of the explosion. She also testified to seeing the same woman walking down Mr. Jennings's driveway the week prior. Ms. Purdy identified the woman as Manny Reyes and further testified that, to her knowledge, she had never seen Ms. Reyes before. We've also submitted the affidavit of Ronald Corlew, a golfing buddy of Mr. Calhoun's, who testified that he witnessed Mr. Calhoun have multiple meetings with a woman Corlew identified as Manny Reyes behind the third green at the Jasper Country Club. Finally, and perhaps most importantly, we have offered the affidavit of Harm Twitty, the owner of C&G Security. Harm testified that Alvie Jennings was employed by C&G in the spring and summer of 2012 and drove almost exclusively for Mr. Calhoun. After May 8, 2012, which was the night that Jack Daniel Willistone was murdered in Tuscaloosa along the banks of the Black Warrior River, Mr. Calhoun advised Mr. Twitty to assign him another driver. Not trusting anyone else with the job due to the fact that Mr. Calhoun was C&G's biggest client, Mr. Twitty himself took over the detail. Mr. Twitty has testified that on at least three occasions in the weeks prior to Alvie Jennings's death, he drove Mr. Calhoun to the Jasper Farmer's Market out by the airport, and each time, he witnessed Mr. Calhoun have a lengthy conversation with a woman matching the description of Manny Reyes." Rick paused and looked out over the courtroom, hearing several amens from the gallery. "Harm Twitty saw Mr. Calhoun give Ms. Reyes a wad of money that would have bought the whole market, much less the pound of tomatoes he'd carried back to the car in a sack."

More amens from the gallery, this time louder and with more intensity.

Judge Conner banged his gavel and stood from the bench. "Ladies and gentlemen, this is a court of law, not a church. I'd ask you to remain silent, or I will have my bailiff escort you from the courthouse. Is that clear?"

No one said a word, but Rick saw several of the people in the audience, including Reverend Blackwell, nod at the judge.

"Mr. Drake, this is not a closing argument in trial, and the folks out there"—he waved his arms at the gallery—"are not the jury. I'd ask that you make your arguments to me and not the crowd. The decision maker today is me."

Rick gazed up at the judge. "Yes, Your Honor. The bottom line, sir, is that we have presented substantial evidence of a factual question on the claim we've brought in this case. As you see in the case law we've cited in our brief, circumstantial evidence can be considered just as much as direct evidence. There's even a jury instruction on circumstantial evidence that the jury in this case would no doubt be given. All of the pieces to this puzzle point toward Manny Reyes, at Bully Calhoun's direction, wrongfully killing Alvie Jennings." Rick paused and glanced behind him to LaShell and LaByron Jennings. He walked around the table and stood behind them. "Judge Conner, the other bottom line is that on August 4, 2012, this woman's husband and this little boy's father was murdered. Even the high sheriff of Walker County has classified his investigation as a *homicide* case. Sheriff Patterson and the district attorney apparently don't feel like prosecuting Ms. Reyes for murder because either they can't find her or don't want to—I can't figure out which. But we have presented substantial questions of fact on our claims for wrongful death in this case." Rick placed his hands on LaByron's shoulders. "Respectfully, Your Honor, the decisions of the Alabama Supreme Court mandate that you deny the defendant's motion and send this case to the jury. The law is clear, and this family deserves it."

Judge Conner gazed down at the bench. He had remained standing since his admonition of the gallery. He peered over at Virgil Flood. "You got anything else?"

"Judge, Mr. Drake puts on a nice show, but he hasn't met his burden at this stage. We'd ask that our motion be granted and . . . given the short amount of time between now and the trial setting on Monday, we'd further ask for a speedy ruling."

Conner turned back to Rick. "Drake, how about you?"

Rick still stood behind LaByron Jennings. "We'd also request a speedy ruling, Your Honor."

Judge Conner rubbed his chin and sat heavily down in his chair. For five seconds, the courtroom was silent again, except for little Alvin Jennings's sucking sounds as he continued to work on his bottle. Finally, the judge cleared his throat and looked at Virgil. "The defendant's motion is denied." He glanced at Rick and then again stood from the bench. "I'll expect to see the parties and their attorneys on Monday morning at 8:30 at the Lauderdale County Courthouse, in Florence. We'll cover motions in limine at that time. At 9:00 a.m. sharp, we'll start jury voir dire." Conner paused. "Everyone understand?"

"Yes, sir," Virgil said, and Rick relished the sound of defeat in the old man's voice. Virgil had been handpicked by the Ashe & Rowe lawyers as Jasper local counsel. He was their ace in the hole. The man who knew the judge and jury like the back of his hand. Now he had lost a motion for summary judgment, and the trial was moving out of his territory. A jury in Walker County might know and perhaps be swayed by the legendary legal career of Virgil Flood, but in the Shoals he'd have no advantage.

"Yes, Your Honor," Rick said, squeezing LaByron Jennings's shoulders and hearing a cacophony of sniffles from the gallery.

"Very well," Conner said, nodding at both men. "I'll see y'all on Monday."

36

“Denied,” Sheriff Patterson said from the front seat of the cruiser as he gazed down at his phone. Then, under his breath, he added, “*Damnit.*”

“Go time, then,” JimBone said, and, at least to the sheriff, the killer sounded giddy.

They were parked in the garage underneath the courthouse. It would take the sheriff all of three minutes to get upstairs. “OK, I’m on my way,” DeWayne said. “Is the Mexican ready?”

“Don’t worry about him. You just make sure that you and your deputy get Drake to walk through the exit in the basement.”

“What are you going to do?” DeWayne asked, grabbing the door handle with a shaky hand.

“I’m going to take a better look,” he said. “You got a car for me if I need it?”

“On Second Avenue. Right behind Pinnacle Bank.”

"Good. Now get on with it, Sheriff. I don't want Drake to miss the party we have waiting for him."

DeWayne Patterson sucked in a gulp of oxygen and hopped out of the cruiser. *God forgive me,* he thought as he ambled toward the elevator that would take him to Lloyd Conner's courtroom.

37

Rick was engulfed in a flurry of hugs and backslaps. LaShell Jennings cried unabashedly, and Rick had a hard time getting her to release her embrace. "Thank you, thank you, thank you," she said, and Rick could feel her heart pounding over her sobs.

"We haven't won anything yet, LaShell," he reminded her.

"But we haven't lost," she said. "And now we have a chance. A real chance. Not here in Bully World but in Florence." She stepped back and gazed at him with tear-streaked eyes. "All I've ever wanted was a fair shake for Alvie. *We've got that now.*"

Rick nodded and looked down at LaByron, who was holding out his fist. Rick bumped the young man's knuckles with his own and then turned to the other counsel table, noticing that Virgil Flood and his two Birmingham cohorts had made a quick getaway. He had hoped to ask Virgil what to order at Ricatoni's next week. Rick couldn't help but smile at the thought as his eyes swept over the gallery. He allowed himself a few seconds of satisfaction at having won the hearing.

But the good vibes evaporated when he saw Sheriff DeWayne Patterson enter the courtroom, followed by one of his deputies. Based on the speed with which the lawman was walking, Rick figured he wasn't coming in to offer his congratulations. Patterson pushed through the crowd of onlookers until he reached Rick.

"Mr. Drake," the sheriff said, his voice sharp and on edge.

"What is it, Sheriff?"

For a moment, the wiry man just pierced Rick with a look of what appeared to be concern. "There was a shooting in Tuscaloosa. About an hour and a half ago in the neighborhood by Bryant-Denny Stadium." He paused, and Rick felt his legs growing rubbery. "I don't have all the particulars yet, but my sources inside the TCSO say that there were two victims. I think you know them."

No, Rick thought.

"A detective named Wade Richey was shot multiple times. He was pronounced dead on the scene. The other guy was the district attorney. His name escapes me right now. Conrad, I think."

Rick opened his mouth, but no words came out. He tried again. "Is he dead too?"

"I don't know," the sheriff said.

"Is everything OK, Rick?" LaShell Jennings asked, and he felt her strong hand grip his forearm. Rick felt dizzy and tried to keep his composure. Hot tears formed in his eyes, and he brought a hand across his face to wipe them.

"Was it Wheeler?" he asked the lawman, and Sheriff Patterson's face was blank. "Was it?" Rick pressed, his voice rising.

"I've told you all that I know," the sheriff said. "But because Richey and Conrad were the two men who apprehended Wheeler, he is probably the prime suspect."

"You figure that out all by yourself, Sheriff?" Rick said, glaring at the man.

Patterson returned the look. "I came here to let you know and to make damn sure that the same thing doesn't happen to you. You also had a role in putting James Robert Wheeler in prison, and according to the all-points bulletin that came across the wire yesterday, you and Professor Tom McMurtrie could both be potential targets of a vendetta that Mr. Wheeler has against all of you."

"Not a vendetta," Rick said, gritting his teeth. "A reckoning. Wheeler promised that he'd come after us, and he's proving to be a man of his word."

"Rick?" LaShell Jennings squeezed his arm again, and Rick looked at her.

"It's OK, LaShell. You remember I told you when I got here about the man who escaped prison yesterday and how Manny Reyes might be helping him?"

She nodded at him, her eyes wide and scared.

"He just killed one of my friends in Tuscaloosa, and . . ." Rick paused, licking his lips and forcing the crack out of his voice. "And may have killed another one. Tuscaloosa is only forty-five minutes from Jasper."

"You think he could be coming here?" LaShell looked at Rick and then the sheriff.

"We don't know that yet, Ms. Jennings, but just in case, I've arranged for you, your children, and Mr. Drake to be escorted out of the courthouse through the basement," Patterson said, glancing at the other uniformed officer standing next to him. "Sergeant Morris and I will personally take you down to the basement. Mr. Drake, we've spoken with Deputy Wainright of the TCSO." He hooked a thumb toward the double doors leading out of the courtroom, and Rick remembered that the Tuscaloosa deputy who had escorted him here was waiting outside. "Wainright is going to bring his squad to the basement and pick you and the Jennings family up there. Then he'll either take you to your vehicles, or he can drive all of you home." Patterson paused. "Whatever you're most comfortable with given the circumstances."

Rick's entire body tingled with adrenaline as he tried to take it all in. Wade was dead. Powell might be dead. Sheriff Patterson was concerned enough about their safety that he was here in person, promising to make sure they got out safe.

I don't trust DeWayne Patterson. Rick heard the voice of Rel Jennings in his mind and looked into the lawman's eyes.

"Are you ready?" the sheriff asked.

Rick nodded.

"Alright then," Patterson said. "Follow me."

38

They took an elevator to the basement. Inside the stale-smelling box with Rick rode LaShell Jennings, LaByron Jennings, and LaShell's mother, Evelyn, whom everyone called "Mimi" and who continued to hold baby Alvin. Standing in front of them was Sheriff Patterson, Sergeant Morris, and Deputy Wainright. If anyone were to start firing when the elevator doors opened, the three officers would block the fire.

So far so good, Rick thought as the doors slid open. Instead of gunfire, the only sound Rick heard when he stepped out onto the basement landing was the whirring of two overhead fans. A long hallway greeted them, at the end of which was a door with an exit sign hanging over the top.

Rick and the Jennings family followed the officers as they strode down the narrow corridor. "The exit opens to a sally port, where delivery trucks make their drop-offs. Deputy Wainright is going to bring his cruiser around to pick you up." He paused and looked over his shoulder at Rick. "That sound OK?"

Rick forced a nod as he heard the words in his mind again. *Don't trust DeWayne Patterson.*

"Alright then," Sheriff Patterson said when they had reached the door. "Wainright, go ahead and get your car."

"Yes, sir," the Tuscaloosa deputy said. He opened the door and disappeared through it. The sheriff held it open and peered out into the sally port. When he did, Rick saw through the crack that the area was abandoned. No cars. No other people.

"Shouldn't you have some more officers down here?"

Patterson glared at him with impatience in his eyes. "More commotion makes it harder to protect you. I know what I'm doing."

Rick saw the sheriff pull his cell phone out of his pocket and gaze at it. Behind him, through the opening in the door, Rick saw Wainright's cruiser pull to a stop. The Tuscaloosa deputy hopped out of the vehicle and walked around to the passenger side, opening up both doors. Then he waved with his right hand.

"OK, everyone," the sheriff said. "Don't lollygag. I want all of you in the car as fast as you can go. Got it?"

"Yes, sir," LaShell Jennings said.

"Drake?" Patterson glared at Rick.

"You promise this is the safest way?" Rick asked.

"I'm the sheriff of this county," Patterson said. "I promise."

Rick thought of Powell Conrad. He needed to get back to Tuscaloosa. It was time to fish or cut bait. "Fine," he finally said. "Lead the way."

39

Pasco is ready and waiting, the text on Sheriff Patterson's new phone had read. It had come from a number he didn't recognize and from a phone that would be destroyed within the hour, along with the one the sheriff was holding.

God forgive me, the sheriff thought again as he made his promise to Rick Drake.

When the sheriff heard the lawyer utter the words "Lead the way," he hadn't hesitated. He swung the door open wide, hoping to pull the Band-Aid off as swiftly as possible and already thinking of the steps he'd take immediately after Drake was murdered. But as he attempted to step through the door, he saw a huge shadow, followed by an even bigger man, blocking his path.

The man had to be at least six feet seven inches tall, and DeWayne didn't recognize him at first. But a half second later it clicked. "Just what in the hell are you doing here?"

Santonio "Rel" Jennings took a long step forward, forcing the sheriff back into the hallway. Then, as the sound of gunfire crackled behind him, the huge man slammed the door and glared at the sheriff. "Making sure you don't hurt any more members of my family."

40

Rel Jennings stood in front of the exit door in the narrow hallway, blocking the passage out with his huge frame. He glanced past the sheriff and Sergeant Morris to Rick. "What did I tell you about this weasel?"

Rick said nothing. He wasn't sure if he was more shocked by Rel's appearance or the gunshots he'd just heard from outside the door in the sally port. There had been three quick cracks—*pow, pow, pow*—and they sounded to Rick like they'd come from a revolver.

"Mr. Jennings, you're under arrest," the sheriff said, bringing his hand to his holster.

"I just heard gunshots outside, DeWayne," Rel said, his voice calm. "Shouldn't you and your deputy deal with that first?"

DeWayne Patterson glanced at Sergeant Morris, whose eyes had gone wide. For a long second, silence filled the corridor.

"He's *right*, Sheriff," Morris finally said, peering hard at his boss and unholstering his gun before looking at Rel. "Get out of the way, sir."

"By all means," Rel said, pivoting his body to the side so that the two lawmen would have room to pass.

Morris moved for the door, but the sheriff didn't budge, still glaring at Rel.

"Sheriff," Morris whined, "let's go."

"Listen to your deputy," Rel said.

"I'm going to put you under the jail," Patterson finally said.

"I'm sure you will," Rel said. "Now go on."

Patterson shot a quick glance at Rick. "You're on your own," he snapped. Then, without further delay, he removed the pistol from his belt and barreled out of the door with Morris right behind him.

As he took in the bizarre scene, Rick was too shocked to say anything. *What the hell is going on?* From behind him, he heard baby Alvin crying. He glanced at LaShell, and her lips were trembling in fear, but LaByron didn't look scared. He had a curious expression on his face. He stepped forward. "Hey, Uncle Rel."

It was the first three words that Rick had ever heard the boy say.

Rel knelt and grabbed his nephew in a tight hug that LaByron returned.

"Where you been?" LaByron asked.

"I been around," Rel said, peering at Rick. "We've got to go."

"What about—?"

"No time to explain," Rel said. "Right now we've got to get out of here."

"How?" Rick asked as they shuffled down the hallway toward the stairs.

"The same way everyone else left," Rel said. "The front door."

JimBone Wheeler looked at his phone with only mild surprise. *We got a cluster. Drake didn't go out the basement and the Mexican fired anyway. He didn't hit anyone, but it's a mess. Abort.*

JimBone shook his head and stuck the phone inside his pocket. He was standing in an alley on Second Avenue a block from Pinnacle Bank and directly in front of the Walker County Courthouse. In his right hand, he was holding a guitar case, but a musical instrument was the last thing a person would find inside. JimBone had already located the unmarked police vehicle that would be his getaway, and contrary to the sheriff's instructions, he would not be aborting anything today. For that matter, he had already planned for this contingency. If he were being brutally honest, JimBone had almost expected the sheriff to fail.

Sometimes you just have to do things yourself.

41

Once they were up the stairs, the closest exit was the one that opened onto Second Avenue. Rel led the way, with Rick and the Jennings family right behind him. "When we get out of the doors, there should be a car waiting on us. Just get in and don't ask any questions."

"Rel—" LaShell was immediately cut off by her former brother-in-law.

"I'll explain everything when we are in a safe place, OK, LaShell? But we aren't out of the woods yet."

She nodded as they approached the double doors and walked past a security guard. When they reached the door, he looked through the glass. "On my signal," he said, glancing at Rick. "OK, counselor?"

"OK."

Ten seconds later, Rel spoke in a loud, clear voice. "Now."

42

When they had passed through the doors and were heading toward the steps, Rick saw a baby-blue minivan that had pulled to the curb waiting for them. He couldn't quite make out the driver, but he didn't ask questions. Based on the gunshots he'd heard in the basement, he figured Rel Jennings had already saved their lives once today.

When they were almost to the stairs, Rel stopped abruptly. "He's on the roof! Get down!" The big man turned, spread his legs, and held out his arms, while Rick ducked down, covering LaShell, LaByron, Mimi, and the baby. A half second passed and then came the rapid patter of a semiautomatic weapon. Rick heard a gasp and a groan from above him, but Rel remained on his feet. Rick looked up and saw the security guard who had been stationed at the metal detector run out of the courthouse with his gun drawn. Several other officers were now behind him, including Sheriff DeWayne Patterson. All had their guns out as the air continued to be peppered with the sound of the assault rifle.

"The roof!" Rick screamed, and he saw the officers who had come out of the courthouse all raise their heads. Two of them returned fire.

After a couple more seconds, the fireworks ended and the only noises were the screams of baby Alvin Jennings and the men and women who had been walking down the sidewalk when the shooting began. Rick turned and gazed upward at Rel.

The tall man's chest was a bloody mess and both ears were gushing blood. His arms remained stretched straight out from his sides. "Father, God!" he screamed, looking up into the sky. "Why have you forsaken me?" Then he dropped to his knees.

He was now eye to eye with Rick. "Finish it, son." He fell over on his back, and Rick crawled toward him. Sirens filled the air, and Rick saw an ambulance approaching from Second Avenue. He climbed on top of Rel and shook his arms.

"Rel!" Rick slapped the man's face, and the former private investigator's eyes opened.

Santonio "Rel" Jennings blinked and smiled up at Rick. In the seconds before he breathed his last, he managed to repeat his final order.

"Finish it."

43

JimBone Wheeler put the AK-47 back in the guitar case and quickly descended the fire escape. He threw the case into a dumpster, placed headphones over his ears, and walked briskly down the sidewalk. He was wearing a fleece sweat suit, baseball cap, and sunglasses, and he took out his phone and began to point at the steps of the courthouse, as if he were telling a friend what he'd just seen. Around him, he saw a handful of people running in all directions, their heads on a swivel, clearly wondering where the shooter had gone and fearing they would be the next target.

JimBone began to jog down the sidewalk. When he reached the bank, he hooked around to the back and climbed behind the wheel of a black Tahoe. The keys were already in the ignition. He put the siren on top of the vehicle, flipped it on, and cranked the engine of the SUV. Then he pressed the accelerator down, and the wheels squealed as he pulled away from the parking space.

Five minutes later, he was speeding north on Highway 69 toward Cullman, Alabama. By the time he reached the first turnoff for Smith Lake, he had cut the siren off.

I didn't kill him, JimBone thought, knowing that the bullets intended for Rick Drake had been absorbed by Alvie Jennings's brother. Finally, though, JimBone smiled at himself in the rearview mirror. *But I did enough.*

He imagined Professor Tom McMurtrie as he'd seen him last. The old man sitting smugly across from him in the interview room of the Riverbend Maximum Security Institution. Then, thinking of the carnage he and Manny had reaped today, JimBone couldn't help but chuckle.

"How do you like me now, old man?" he said out loud.

And I'm not done, JimBone thought. *Not by a long shot.*

44

At 11:45 a.m., Tom limped out of the imaging area and back into the waiting room. The scans were finally over, and now all that was left was to wait for the verdict, which would be given at 1:00 by Dr. Maples in the physician area on the other wing of CCI. Tom looked for Bill Davis and found his friend standing by the television, eyes glued to the screen. Tom gazed up at the tube and saw that a reporter was talking in front of what appeared to be Druid City Hospital, in Tuscaloosa.

"What's going on?" Tom asked, but Bill didn't say anything. Instead, he stepped forward and turned up the volume.

"Earlier today, on Eighth Avenue, two men were shot in an apparent drive-by. One of the men is believed to be a detective in the Tuscaloosa County Sheriff's Office, and our sources tell us that the other was the district attorney for Tuscaloosa County, Mr. Powell Conrad."

"Oh no," Tom whispered, grasping for a nearby chair and falling into it before his legs gave way. He took out his phone, which he had checked repeatedly during the PET scan. He had gotten no calls or texts during the test, and the screen remained blank. *No news is bad news,* he thought. *Awful news.* Tom closed his eyes and tried to calm his heartbeat.

"You OK, chief?" Bill asked from above him.

"No," Tom said, leaning forward and trying to catch his breath.

Bill squatted beside him. "Tom, it just says they were shot. We don't know anything else. Those two boys are tough. Let's not jump to any conclusions."

"Bill, we've got to get out of here," Tom said, rising to his feet and beginning to walk toward the door. Once he was in the hallway, he saw her. She was in the parking lot, approaching with a grim look on her pale face. When she entered the automatic doors, Tom could hear the clicking of her high heels on the tile floor. He found a bench against the wall and sat down, not trusting his legs. *Please let them be alive,* he prayed.

General Helen Lewis strode toward him and stopped a foot from the bench. She folded her arms across her chest and, for a couple of seconds, just gazed down at Tom.

"Are they alive?" Tom finally asked.

"You know?"

Tom cocked his head toward the imaging area. "We saw it on the TV. Helen . . . are they alive?"

She frowned and took a seat beside him, looking straight ahead. Across from them, Tom saw their reflections in the glass windows of the imaging waiting room. "Wade is dead. He was shot seven times and died at the scene. Powell . . . is still breathing. He was hit four times, and he's in the intensive care unit of Druid City Hospital. Two of the bullets were glancing blows, but the other two found their mark. He went through surgery to remove them and he's lost a lot of blood." She paused. "He hasn't regained consciousness . . . and his surgeon doesn't think he will. The prognosis is fair to poor."

Tom closed his eyes and placed his face in his hands. He felt Helen's hand on his back.

"That's not all, Tom."

Tom felt his whole body go stone cold. "What's not all?" he asked.

Helen again gazed at the glass window across from them. "There's been a shooting in Jasper too. On the courthouse steps."

"Is Rick—?"

"That's all I know."

Tom shot to his feet, and then his legs gave way, and he would have fallen if Bill Davis hadn't caught him underneath his arms and helped him back into his seat.

"Easy, fella," Bill said.

"Helen, is my family—?"

"They're all fine and safe at home."

Tom looked down at the floor and said a silent prayer of thanks, immediately feeling guilty for it. Then he heard something he had never heard before in his life. The General was crying.

He looked into her eyes. "What aren't you telling me?"

She gazed at him with her emerald eyes. "Jasmine Haynes gave that speech at the civic center this morning."

Tom felt a dagger of panic grip his heart.

"There were at least six deputies guarding the interior and exterior of the building, and over a dozen additional security guards providing backup," Helen continued, her voice trembling. "The HPD had canvassed Clinton Avenue as well, but it was impossible to secure the entire area."

Tom swallowed and his mouth felt dry. "Helen, what—?"

"Jazz was shot leaving the Von Braun Center an hour and a half ago. Three bullets from a sniper rifle." Helen bit her lip. "She died on the scene."

Tom's hands began to shake, as did his legs and arms. *No,* he thought. *No, no, no.*

He squinted up at Helen. "Is Bo—?"

"He's OK," Helen interrupted. "But, Tom . . . he saw it. He was right there. He's . . . inconsolable."

"Where?"

"The Madison County Jail."

"*What?*" Tom asked.

Helen sighed. "He went . . . ballistic after the shooting." She paused. "I've done all I can do, but I think they are going to hold him overnight and probably longer."

For several seconds, they just looked at each other. "Tom, I'm sorry," Helen finally managed, breaking eye contact and folding her arms across her chest once more. "I'm so sorry."

With all the effort he could muster, Tom again rose to his feet. Images of Wade, Powell, Jasmine "Jazz" Haynes, and Rick flashed in his mind. He was having a hard time breathing.

"He's doing exactly what he said he was going to do," Tom said, gazing at Helen, whose tears had streaked a line of mascara across her face.

"We told the police . . . got the law involved . . . but it didn't make any difference. Wade and Jazz . . ." Tom's lower lip trembled as he remembered the young detective he'd befriended in the early 1970s who'd devoted his life and career to investigating homicides. *Forty years we were friends.* And then he saw Bo's beautiful and charismatic wife in his mind, who had stoically stood by her husband during the trial in Pulaski two years ago. Jazz had been the mother of two children. She'd been in the prime of life.

"They're both dead." Tom's breathing had become shallow and his voice was ragged. *And Powell and Rick may be gone too. And Bo . . .* Tom thought of how broken his best friend had appeared last night at Old Town Beer Exchange. The defeat he'd seen in Bo's eyes because of the failure of his marriage. Tom knew that Bo had loved Jazz more than life itself. *He watched her die.*

A sob escaped Tom's mouth, and his throat tightened. He coughed, trying to hold off the coming fit, but it was no use. He coughed again, louder and longer. And then again.

"Tom, please sit back down," Helen advised, but Tom could barely hear her as he continued to cough. He turned to Bill, whose red-rimmed eyes were filled with concern.

"Easy," Bill said again, placing his hand on Tom's back and tapping it.

Behind the doctor, Tom saw someone else. He blinked, knowing the man leaning against the wall couldn't be there, but Tom still saw him. The figure was wearing the same outfit he'd had on that morning. Shorts, flip-flops, and visor.

"Ray Ray," Tom whimpered between coughs. "Why is this happening?"

Tom grasped his heart and the world went blurry.

"Tom!" Helen screamed, but her voice sounded like it was a mile away.

"Got us a knife fight in a ditch, Tommy." The voice of Ray Ray Pickalew seemed closer than Helen's. *"What's our play, old boy?"*

"Shut up," Tom managed.

"Tom!" Helen's face came in and out of focus. He heard nothing now, not even Ray Ray's voice. He looked into Helen's eyes, but they were no longer green.

They were copper.

Remember what I said, old man. Your day of reckoning is coming.

The killer's voice filled Tom's eardrums. Behind the voice was the sound of rushing water. Loud and getting louder.

"Tom!"

The roar became deafening. He couldn't feel his legs anymore. He couldn't feel anything.

Tom's eyes rolled into their sockets. He shouldn't have been able to see anything, but he could see.

He saw the maniacal grin of JimBone Wheeler, mocking him.

"*This is all my fault,*" Tom whispered. Then, mercifully, his field of vision went blank.

And there was nothing.

PART FOUR

45

On Sunday, December 15, 2013, ten days after he was murdered, Detective Wade Michael Richey was laid to rest at Memory Hill Gardens Cemetery, in Tuscaloosa. He was buried next to his deceased wife, Rita, and his mother, Lois. The funeral was attended by all members of the Tuscaloosa County Sheriff's Office and every employee of the district attorney's office save one.

The lone absentee, the district attorney himself, remained in critical condition in the intensive care unit at Druid City Hospital. After the graveside service was concluded, Rick Drake approached the tent where the family had gathered, wishing to pay his respects. He found Eleanor Richey, Wade's sister, standing by the casket. She was a tall woman with silver hair and appeared to be in her early seventies.

"Ms. Richey, my name is Rick Drake. I'm so sorry for your loss."

"Drake?"

Rick nodded.

"I've heard my brother mention you. Wade helped you and Professor McMurtrie in Pulaski a few years ago." She paused. "Is it true that the man Wade arrested in Pulaski is who killed him?"

Though JimBone Wheeler had been rumored for days to be Wade's killer, there had been no official statement made by the sheriff's office. *Just following protocol,* Rick thought, figuring that law enforcement didn't want to cause a panic by linking the shooting to Wheeler unless they were one hundred percent sure.

Rick was bound by no such restrictions and told Wade Richey's sister the truth. "Yes, ma'am. I'm sure of it. He also tried to kill me in Jasper."

"But he didn't."

"No, ma'am. A friend was struck by the bullets meant for me."

Eleanor smiled sadly. "Is your friend OK?"

Rick shook his head.

"Do you think it would be appropriate if I visited Mr. Conrad in the hospital?" Eleanor asked. "He and Wade were so close. I . . ." Her lip started to quiver and Rick felt a pang in his heart.

"I'm sure that would be fine, ma'am, but Powell is still unconscious in ICU. They will let family and friends visit, but only for a few minutes at a time." Rick paused and clenched his jaw. "He's not doing well."

"Is he going to make it?"

"I don't know," Rick said.

"What about Professor McMurtrie? I know Wade was very close with him over the years. Is he OK?"

Rick shook his head. "No, ma'am."

Now Eleanor Richey began to cry in earnest. "This is all so awful. My brother should have stayed retired."

"He loved his work, ma'am."

"And it killed him," Eleanor said, grasping Rick by the shoulder. "Don't let it kill you, son."

Rick nodded at her as another attendee pushed past him and embraced Eleanor. For a moment, he stood by the coffin, placing his hand on the hard mahogany surface.

Feeling tears well in his eyes and remembering a similar scene at the Drake farm when his father was buried the year before, Rick kissed his hand and placed it on the casket. "We'll get the SOB, Wade. As God is my witness, we will."

46

At the same time that Wade Richey was being buried in Tuscaloosa, the ushers at the Episcopal Church of Jasper were collecting offerings. When the plate stopped on the pew where Kathryn Calhoun Willistone sat, she placed an envelope with a check for one thousand dollars in it. Just as she had done one Sunday a month since moving back home. Just as her father, Marcellus "Bully" Calhoun, had done almost one Sunday of every month his whole life. *It's always nice to be in the good graces of the Church, darling, and twelve thousand bucks makes for a nice tax write-off.*

Kat nodded at the usher, who took the plate from her, but her thoughts weren't on God, the Church, or taxes. She was thinking about JimBone Wheeler and the deal she had struck a month earlier when it became clear that Rick Drake might actually get his crusade against her to a jury.

He who has the gold makes the rule, her father had always said.

There were few times in his life when Bully Calhoun's life philosophy had been wrong. *But this might turn out to be one of them,* Kat thought, standing with the congregation to sing the closing hymn.

Over the past ten days, she had endured lengthy interviews with the sheriff's offices of Walker, Tuscaloosa, and even Madison Counties. She had told each of them that she was at home during the times of the murders of Santonio Jennings, Wade Richey, and Jasmine Haynes. That she had not been in contact with James Robert Wheeler and, in fact, had never spoken to the man. Likewise, she had never talked with or even seen Mahalia Blessica Reyes. It was the truth, every bit of it, and she had no problem selling it.

Her contact was and always had been DeWayne Patterson. She'd leaned on DeWayne to make the deal with Manny and Wheeler, because she was afraid of losing the millions she'd inherited from her father. She'd already had to split half of her late husband's life insurance proceeds with his ex-wife and retarded son by virtue of a settlement of the case Barbara Willistone had filed against her last year. She wasn't going to lose any of her daddy's money, and she damn sure wasn't going to lose because of Tom McMurtrie and Rick Drake. She blamed the two lawyers for both her husband's and father's downfalls.

All they were supposed to do was kill Drake and Harm Twitty.

That would have ended the case. The lead attorney and the star witness both dead. The lawsuit would then be continued by Judge Conner, and no fool would be crazy enough to step in after Drake and Twitty were dead. Certainly not McMurtrie, who was battling terminal cancer and basically dead already.

But that was not how it had gone down. Wheeler had flown off the reservation. He had failed to kill Drake and, as far as she knew, hadn't even attempted to kill Twitty. Instead, he'd shot the prosecutor and detective who arrested him in Pulaski two years earlier, and apparently Manny Reyes had assassinated Bocephus Haynes's wife.

Leaving one gaping mess, Kat thought as she remained standing for the benediction.

Kat shook hands with a few of the men in the congregation and gave several hugs to women she knew as she left the church and stepped into a stretch limousine. During the ride to the Calhoun mansion, on the edge of the Sipsey Wilderness, she tried to let her mind rest, but it was impossible. All she could think about was how out of control the situation had become.

And the trial is still going forward, she thought, knowing that was the worst consequence of all. After the shooting, Judge Conner had set an emergency conference call the next morning, where he asked Rick Drake if he needed or wanted a continuance. Kat had been in Virgil Flood's law office, listening to the call, and she had heard Drake's crazy voice. "I want to go forward on Monday, Judge. My client wants to go forward. Santonio Jennings would have died in vain if this case doesn't proceed to trial." Kat had burned a hole into Virgil's eyes, holding out her hands for him to do something, and the old fossil had given it his best effort.

"Judge, the defendant would like a continuance, at least until this fugitive Wheeler is in police custody. Based on what I'm hearing, he managed to murder people in Tuscaloosa and Jasper yesterday and perhaps had something to do with the killing in Huntsville. If Mr. Drake is a target of this psychopath, then that makes us all a target, and between me and you, Judge, I'd kind of like to be at home on Christmas this year and not in a pine box."

Conner had taken a full minute to think about it. Then, finally, he let out a long sigh. "I already checked with the presiding judge in Lauderdale County, and he said they had set aside two weeks for us. So, if we don't go forward on Monday, we could push the trial back a week to December the sixteenth if y'all think you can be finished in five days. Otherwise, the earliest we could get the case reset would be June. That's how backed up they are." Conner paused. "Mr. Drake, given everything that's happened, I thought for sure you'd want to postpone until June."

"I don't, Your Honor," Drake had said without hesitation. "My client and I still want to tee it up. We're fine with starting the case on

Monday, but given everything that's happened, an extra week would be helpful. I can't imagine this case taking longer than four days to try, much less five. We don't want to wait another six months."

Again, Conner had taken his time before answering. When he spoke, there had been a stubborn resolve in his voice. "OK. Then we'll postpone the trial by a week and I'll see everyone in Florence on Monday morning, December the sixteenth."

As the limousine pulled to a stop in the driveway of the mansion that she'd lived in as a girl and which she now resided in alone, Kathryn Calhoun Willistone went over the reality of the situation in her mind, still not believing it.

I've spent a half a million dollars to avoid this trial. Three people are dead. Two more are in the hospital . . .

. . . and the trial is still on.

As she stepped out of the car, she saw a police sedan pulling up the long drive. Kat flicked her hand, and the limousine driver, a squat redheaded man named Anson, parked the stretch in the garage.

Kat crossed her arms and waited for the cruiser until it stopped right beside her. The window descended, and Sheriff DeWayne Patterson peered up at her. "We need to talk," he said.

"You're damn right we do."

He nodded toward the house. "In there, OK?"

Kat tramped toward the house, feeling the anger inside her bubbling over.

Once they were safely inside, Kat wheeled on the wiry lawman, swinging a closed right fist at the sheriff's face and connecting with bone. DeWayne's nose erupted in an explosion of blood.

"Just what in the *fuck* is going on, DeWayne?" she demanded. As the sheriff brought his hands to his face, Kat kicked him square in the balls, and the sheriff groaned in pain and dropped to his knees.

Kathryn Calhoun Willistone was a petite, lean woman, but her muscles were toned from daily workouts, and since moving back home, she had begun taking Tae Kwon Do again. Though she was tempted to continue her ass beating of the man, she needed information. "Talk, moron."

"Mr. Wheeler says that everything is fine and that he is going to fulfill his contract."

"He better." Kat spat the words out. "He was supposed to kill Drake and Twitty. Why did he go cowboy and start killing randoms?"

DeWayne coughed and spat a loogie of blood on the floor.

"If you spit on my hardwoods again, numb nuts, I'm going to kick you in the face so hard you're gonna shit these leather boots, you hear me, DeWayne?" Kat said, pointing at her feet, and the sheriff nodded his head.

"I'm sorry," he said. "Wheeler promised McMurtrie in the prison that he was going to bring a reckoning down on him and everyone he holds dear. He thinks these killings will be interpreted as revenge murders, which won't implicate you."

"If I'm not implicated, then why in the hell do all these police departments want to interview me?"

"Due diligence, Kat. That's all. You aren't on the radar, but we have to cross off our boxes. That's why my detectives interviewed you."

"It's all bullshit, DeWayne, and I'm tired of it. I've paid a half-million dollars and all I have to show for it are a bunch of dead bodies that I don't care about. Meanwhile, Rick Drake and Harm Twitty are still breathing."

"Harm's gone," DeWayne said. "He may be alive, but the shooting scared the crap out of him. He wants to live a little longer."

"Where'd he go?"

DeWayne shrugged. "I don't know, but his house is deserted, he's not answering his phone, and none of his friends know where he went. The manager at C&G said the last he heard from him was

Thursday after the shooting, when Harm called in and said he was taking a long vacation."

For several seconds, Kat peered down at the weak, bloody man below her. Finally, she managed a smile. "Did Drake subpoena him for trial?"

DeWayne nodded. "He did, but . . ." The sheriff stopped and actually began to laugh. Kat thought about kicking him again but resisted the urge.

"But what?"

"I think Harm is gone. I believe the only reason he signed that affidavit is he thought there wouldn't be any repercussions with Bully dead. Harm doesn't have family in Jasper anymore. Hell, I don't even think he has any family at all. He liked Alvie Jennings, but not enough to die for him." DeWayne smiled up at Kat. "Harm's flown the coop. He's got a nice nest egg from owning C&G all these years, and my money is on him being in the Cayman Islands or the Caribbean." He paused. "I'd bet both my testicles that he doesn't show up in Florence this week."

"I'm going to remember you said that," Kat said, but now she was smiling in earnest. Slowly, the sheriff climbed to his feet and dusted off his pants.

"So how is Mr. Wheeler going to fulfill the contract?" Kat asked.

DeWayne sighed. "Honestly, ma'am, I don't know. And to tell you the truth, I'm glad." He paused and wiped blood from his nose. "I don't think either of us wants to know."

47

As a golden sun set over the black waters of the Flint River, JimBone Wheeler lay naked in a hot tub bubbling with scalding water. The Jacuzzi was the centerpiece of the back deck of DeWayne Patterson's cabin, and JimBone was finally getting to enjoy it. Both of his arms were draped over the side behind him, and in his right hand he held an ice-cold beer. He brought the bottle to his lips and watched Manny Reyes walk toward him from across the wooden surface of the deck. She wore a silk robe but removed it when she was a couple feet from the tub. "Like what you see?" she asked, doing a mock twirl. Then she climbed into the tub until only the tops of her breasts peeked out of the water.

"Beer?" JimBone asked, reaching backward into a cooler and pulling out another bottle of Coors Light.

"No, thanks," Manny said.

"Suit yourself," JimBone said, popping the top off the new beer while he finished the one he was drinking. Once the first bottle was empty, he flung it out into the grass that led down to the river. Then he took a long swig off the new soldier.

"So, you gonna get drunk tonight, *señor*?"

JimBone shook his head. "Nah, just buzzed. I thought I'd finish this one and then we could have another go." He held his arms out wide. "Right here in front of God and everyone."

She smirked at him. "Aren't you tired of all the sex? That's about the only thing we've done for the past ten days."

"Manny, girl, that's about the only thing in this world that I don't get tired of." He winked at her, but then his eyes went cold. "Did you learn anything on your trip into town?"

"McMurtrie remains alive. He's on the fourth floor of Huntsville Hospital, and his room is heavily guarded."

"And Haynes?"

"Still in jail." She paused and wrinkled her nose. "But should be released tonight."

"When is his wife's funeral?"

"No arrangements have been made yet."

JimBone gazed at her with admiration. "Some of your finest work, darling. Not only did you manage to kill the poor bastard's bride, but you somehow got the police to put their focus on him."

"That was a stroke of luck. They were in the throes of a divorce, so our timing was good." She paused. "And he went crazy after I killed her."

JimBone grinned and took a long sip of beer. "And what about the prosecutor?"

"Still breathing, but he hasn't regained consciousness. Prognosis remains poor."

For a long minute, neither of them spoke, and JimBone nudged her foot with his own and then began stroking her leg with his toenails.

"What are we going to do about the trial?" Manny finally asked. "The sheriff called, and our benefactor is furious at how everything has gone down. What is the expression that you like to use? She . . . has her panties in a wad?"

JimBone laughed. "That's the one, darling. I hope you explained to DeWayne how the first phase of the war we've declared fits into the overall master plan."

She squinted at him. "I gave him the big picture, but he didn't want the details. All he said was that Mrs. Willistone had paid good money for the trial to be put off and for Drake to be dead, and neither had happened yet."

JimBone gazed up at the roof that covered the deck. "Ah, impatience. One of her father's and her husband's greatest virtues. She's also wrong. The trial was postponed a week."

"True," Manny said. "But Mrs. Willistone had hoped for a longer delay. It starts tomorrow."

"And we have a plan," JimBone said.

Again, silence filled the air. Finally, JimBone set his beer on the ground and scooted around the tub until he was next to his partner. He stroked her black hair and then lifted her onto him. He slid inside her like a key going into a lock, and the only sound was Manny's gasp when penetration occurred. "Did you do the other thing I asked you to do in town?"

She nodded and began to rock slowly back and forth on top of him. "McMurtrie had visitors at 10:00 a.m. and 4:00 p.m."

"Family?"

"And his doctor friend."

"What about Drake?"

Manny shook her head and picked up the pace of her movement. "He was in Tuscaloosa today." She groaned. "Burying the detective."

JimBone put his hand on her lips and she licked his fingers, now moving vigorously above him. "Any word from the Mexican? Was he able to put a tracking device on either of the sons' vehicles? Is he keeping tabs on them?"

She nodded and ran her hands through her hair, arching her back. "He placed the tracker on the wife's van when they were at the hospital visiting the old man Friday. Posed as a maintenance man scraping ice from the parking garage." She paused and moaned with pleasure. "According to Pasco, on Friday and Saturday the only place the family went was to the hospital and back."

"And today?"

Manny grimaced. "They went to the hospital in the morning, and . . ." Another gasp escaped her lips and a stream of saliva ran out of her mouth that JimBone wiped away with his thumb.

"And what?"

"And the son took the boy to a rec center in south Huntsville called Fern Bell to play basketball."

"Was it a team practice?"

"No." Manny's breaths were now coming shallow. She was close, JimBone knew. "Just the boy and his father."

"Security?"

"One officer came in the gym with them and another watched the parking lot. The other guard in their detail stayed at the house to watch the family."

"Does the kid still have a game tomorrow?"

With her eyes closed, Manny groaned a yes. "According to his travel team Facebook page, it's at 6:00 p.m." She paused. "At Optimist Park, off Oakwood Avenue."

"He's missed his last three games," JimBone said, placing his hands on Manny's perky breasts and thrusting hard. "And it sounds like the family is getting restless."

Manny opened her mouth but didn't say anything. Instead, she let out a barely audible scream as she reached climax.

A few minutes later, after she'd stopped shivering, JimBone whispered into her ear. "Are you ready to finish this war?"

She pulled back and gazed at him with her black eyes. "Yes, but . . ." She trailed off and JimBone stared hard at her.

"But what?"

"Do you think we are taking it too far? We could have already killed them. We could already be in my homeland, counting our money and having sex in a hot tub overlooking the Pacific Ocean instead of this snake hole." She pointed behind her to the dark waters of the Flint.

"Do you think I'm crazy?" JimBone asked.

She remained silent for several seconds. Finally, she said, "No. But I think your desire to make McMurtrie suffer has clouded your judgment. The doctor and his wife are not going to expose their children." She paused. "The boy will not play in his game tomorrow."

JimBone Wheeler reached behind him for the beer he'd set on the ground. He took a long swig and belched. "Maybe not," JimBone said. "But every instinct I have tells me that they're about to slip up. If not the game, then there'll be something else. It's the Christmas season after all, and those kids have been cooped up in that house for over ten days. The husband has already ventured out on his own with the son." He pressed his thumb into the indention between her chin and mouth. "The wife is due an outing, don't you think?"

Manny brushed off his thumb and folded her arms over her breasts. "Perhaps."

"When that happens, we'll be ready."

"What about their security?"

"Three officers can probably hold us off if they stay in the house." He took a long pull on the beer bottle. "At least until backup is called in." He ran his tongue along the edges of his teeth. "But not in the open."

She scooted closer to him. "Why does it have to be this way? Why not just kill Drake now? That would end the lawsuits against our benefactor, which is all Mrs. Willistone cares about. Then, once McMurtrie is released from the hospital—assuming he doesn't die there—we take him out. When Haynes gets out of jail, we kill him too. Why not piecemeal the murders?"

"Because this isn't just about a payday for me, sweetheart. McMurtrie put me in prison. He hasn't suffered near enough." He took another sip of beer and peered at her. "You knew the ultimate endgame when you signed up for this mission. It was *never* just about the money." He gazed up at the night sky. "We're going to draw them out. McMurtrie, Drake, Haynes." He counted them off with his fingers. "When we do, it'll be like shooting fish in a barrel."

For a long moment, the only sound on the deck of the cabin was the subtle breeze blowing through the barren tree limbs. Then Manny whispered in his ear, "What if your instincts are wrong? What if we can't bait the targets out?"

JimBone held the beer to his lips but didn't drink. He peered at his partner and finally gave a swift nod. "We'll watch them for two days. If they haven't given us an opportunity by Tuesday evening, then we'll go with your idea and take them out one by one, starting with Drake." He turned the bottle up and drank the last of the beer, tossing it in the grass with the other empties. "But, Manny girl, the Bone's instincts are never wrong."

She leaned forward and brought a hand beneath the surface of the water, running her fingers down his thigh. "Do you ever think that maybe you underestimate McMurtrie?"

JimBone again stared up at the sky, enjoying the feel of her touch. "I did before. But then, I was playing by other people's rules." He lowered his eyes to hers. "Now I'm playing by my own."

"Your turn?" she asked.

"*Sí,*" he said, admiring her bronze body as she climbed on top of him. Then, thinking of the twenty-six months he'd spent on death row, the hell he'd brought on Tom McMurtrie in the past ten days, and how he would turn the heat up even higher very soon, he grinned with satisfaction, whispering under his breath, "*My turn.*"

48

At 6:45 p.m. on Sunday evening, the iron doors of the cell clanged open. "Alright, time to go," a guard said.

Bocephus Haynes sat on the concrete floor with his back propped against the cinder-block wall. His eyes were open but he saw nothing. He wore the orange jumpsuit they'd given him after he was booked ten days earlier.

"Haynes, let's go!"

Bo looked up at the man with disdain, but using the wall for leverage, he climbed to his feet. "Who posted bond?" Bo asked.

The guard ignored the question and gestured for Bo to walk ahead of him down the long corridor of cells. As they made their way to the exit, Bo heard catcalls from the other inmates and breathed in the stale scent of the place, knowing he must reek himself.

He was brought inside a holding cell, and the guard tossed a laundry bag on the floor at Bo's feet. "These are the only clothes we have for you." He paused and put his hands on his hips. "Just knock when you're ready." The officer slammed the door shut.

Bo trudged toward the sack, feeling his heartbeat begin to pick up as snapshots from the morning at the civic center invaded his mind.

Jazz reaching her bloody fingers toward him, almost touching his own, crying his name before her head . . .

Bo reached inside the sack and pulled out the button-down and jeans. His wife's blood had caked into the front of the shirt and, over the course of the last week and a half, the fabric had turned a dark pink. He pressed the shirt to his nose and grimaced as the images overcame him.

Jazz flying backward as a rifle shot sliced through her forehead . . .

The sound of blood rushing to his ears and face as he shook his dead wife's arms, trying in vain to will her back to life . . .

Turning in a circle as an army of faceless officers converged on him . . .

Bumping into the nearest car—an SUV of some kind—and beginning to beat his fists into the windshield until the sound of shattered glass peppered the air.

Dropping to his knees as he ran his ruined knuckles through the stubble on his face and head, feeling the prickle of glass fragments dig into his skin . . .

Gazing forward at his wife's lifeless corpse as the faceless men put her body in a bag . . .

And then . . . nothing.

The next thing he could clearly remember was opening his eyes and sitting on the hard floor of a jail cell. According to the night shift guard, who had gotten his information from one of the deputies who had been standing next to Jazz at the time of the shooting, Bo had gone catatonic, not speaking and barely blinking as he was first taken to the hospital to have his injuries addressed and then brought to the jail. He was held overnight for observation and questioning related to his erratic behavior in the aftermath of the shooting. There were also reports from bystanders of an altercation with the victim just before she was murdered, where her dress was torn. The following morning, after he had failed to answer any questions, he was charged with criminal mischief and domestic violence.

Bo hadn't come out of his funk for seventy-two hours. The only thing he could decipher from those three days was the steady hum of Jazz's voice playing in his mind, repeating her last words to him.

"I hate you."

Over and over and over.

"I hate you."

"I hate you."

"I hate you."

When he had finally regained some sense of self, he'd used his one phone call to dial his father-in-law, Ezra Henderson. Their conversation had been tense and brief. Ezra blamed Bo for his daughter's death and said there was no way he was going to let the police drop the domestic violence charge, nor would he relinquish custody of T. J. and Lila. He also said that he had reported Bo to DHR. Finally, he said he didn't want Bo at Jazz's funeral, and that he'd have him arrested again if he tried to show up.

Bo hadn't argued as the old man ranted. When Ezra finished, Bo made his request. "Take care of my children, Ezra, and tell them I love them. Are there officers watching your house?"

Ezra had said there were.

"Good," Bo had said. "Be careful, and don't go anywhere without a police escort."

"You think I'm as foolish as you?" Ezra had asked. "T. J. and Lila will be just fine. As long as you stay the hell away." The old man then hung up the phone.

Bo put his arms through the sleeves of the ruined shirt. He slipped on his jeans and knocked on the holding cell door.

At the checkout window, he was given his wallet and car keys. His Sequoia had been impounded, and the clerk gave him a ticket with directions to the city lot.

A minute later, Bocephus Haynes was discharged from the Madison County Jail.

He saw the person who had posted his bond leaning against the driver's side of a rusty sedan in the parking lot. Bo trudged toward the man, feeling the fatigue of ten days with virtually no sleep. When he reached the hood of the car, he asked, "Why'd you post my bond?"

Rick Drake took a tentative step forward. "I didn't. It was General Lewis. She said you hadn't yet, so . . ."

"So she interfered."

Rick took another step closer. "Bo, I'm so sorry about your wife."

Bo glared at him. "Is Powell dead?"

Rick shook his head. "He's still in critical condition in ICU."

"What about the Professor?"

"Bo, can I take you home so you can get cleaned up?" Rick asked.

Bo kept his eyes on Rick as he walked around to the passenger side of the car. Finally, he looked at his reflection in the windshield. The sight of the bloodstained shirt made him wince. It was one thing to see the button-down in a laundry bag but another to visualize it on his body.

I hate you, he heard Jazz's taut voice whisper in his mind as he peered at himself. Then he gazed down at his hands, which were covered with scabs. The jail nurse had gotten the glass out of them, and the X-ray she'd taken revealed no fractures.

"Answer my question, dog," Bo said, peering over the top of the car at Rick. "How is the Professor?"

"He's in the hospital. After he found out what happened to Jazz and Wade, he passed out and was admitted for exhaustion and dehydration." Rick paused, and when he spoke again his voice cracked with emotion. "The cancer has also spread to the brain and he's having hallucinations." He looked down at the ground. "It doesn't look good."

Bo chuckled bitterly. "Ain't nothing good."

For a long minute, neither man said a word. "Bo, what can I do?" Rick finally asked.

Bo glared at him. "Nothing. Everything's already done."

49

Rick checked into the Muscle Shoals Marriott at 9:00 p.m. On the drive over, he'd spoken with Powell's mother, who said there had been no change. He also called Tommy McMurtrie, who said the Professor was in a holding pattern. "He's really weak. The fluids they are pumping into him may be helping, but he's just not himself." Finally, he called the General.

"How's Bo?" Helen asked.

"He's . . . not right," Rick said, shivering as he remembered Bo's haunted eyes when Rick dropped him off at the city lot. Rick had said goodbye, but Bo hadn't responded. He'd just looked at Rick for a second and then exited the vehicle.

"He's been through hell."

Rick had felt another shiver. "I think he's still there."

"Do you know where he was going?" Helen asked.

"No, but I didn't even mention the trial. He was supposed to help me with the case, but—"

"There's no way," Helen interrupted.

"I didn't think so."

They had said their goodbyes, with Helen promising to check up on Bo and wishing Rick luck on the trial.

We're due for some luck, Rick thought as he rode the elevator to his room. When he inserted the key, he immediately saw the blinking light on his hotel phone, indicating he had a message. His stomach tightened. *Please, no bad news tonight.*

Rick pushed the button on the phone and began to unpack as a shaky voice came out of the speaker. "Mr. Drake, this is Harm Twitty. I . . . I'm sorry, sir. I just can't do it. I know I told you I'd be there for you, but I can't testify. Not after the shooting last week and everything's that's happened. They'll kill me. I know it." There was a pause, and Rick heard another voice—female and monotone—in the background. *Did I hear that right?* Rick thought. Sounded like "All boarding for Dallas." More static. Then Harm again. "I'm sorry, son. I hope you win, but life's too short and I don't want to end up like Rel. Goodbye."

Rick sat on the edge of the bed and glared at the telephone. He listened to the message two more times. Harm Twitty was his ace in the hole. He was the witness who placed Manny Reyes in Bully Calhoun's employ. He checked off the box establishing an agency relationship. Ronnie Corlew would help with that argument, but all Corlew could testify about was a couple of instances of seeing Manny and Bully together on the golf course. Harm had seen more. Harm had watched a pile of money exchange hands between Manny and Bully Calhoun in the days before the murder of Alvie Jennings.

And now he's heading to Dallas. And beyond that, who knew? Rick had him under subpoena, but judging by his voice on the message, Harm Twitty didn't seem to care much about the consequences of violating a subpoena. *He's gone,* Rick thought.

And so is my case.

"Shit!" Rick screamed, punching his left hand with the fist of his right until his palm stung with pain. He ran his hands through his hair and thought about everything that had happened in the last few days. He could have continued the case until June during the conference call with Judge Conner last week, but he'd stubbornly forged ahead, not realizing what Rel's death might do to the witnesses the investigator had gathered.

But I spoke with Harm. I talked with him after the shooting. Hell, I spoke with him a couple hours after the conference call with the judge, and he said he would be here. That he would honor the subpoena. I spoke with him again three days ago and he said the same thing.

"He lied to me," Rick said out loud, pacing the carpeted floor of the hotel room. *Or did he? Maybe someone got to him. Maybe Kathryn Calhoun Willistone made him an offer he couldn't refuse.*

Rick stopped and gazed up at the ceiling, realizing he would never know. *All that matters now is he's gone.*

Rick took out his cell phone and dialed the number for Ronnie Corlew, who answered on the first ring. "Hey, Ronnie, it's Rick Drake."

"Hey, son, we still on for this week?"

Rick exhaled with relief. "Yeah, man. Won't need you until Tuesday morning. Got you a room reserved here at the Marriott."

"Sounds good. I'm going to come over tomorrow and get eighteen holes in on the Fighting Joe. Then I'm gonna eat at the revolving restaurant at the hotel. Want to meet there for a drink and go over everything again?"

Rick smiled. "Sounds good, Ronnie. Thank you."

"Have you heard from Harm?" Ronnie asked. "I tried to call him to see if he wanted to ride over together, but I couldn't get him."

Rick cringed at the thought of his two star witnesses sharing a ride together but then realized he wouldn't have to worry about that anymore. "Come alone, OK, Ronnie? I don't want the defense to be able to argue we are in collusion."

"Alright, man. Sorry about that."

"No worries."

"Tuesday morning then?"

"Yep," Rick said, and they exchanged goodbyes.

Thank God, Rick thought, pressing the "End" button and immediately dialing the number for Carmella Purdy, the neighbor who'd seen Manny Reyes walking along the Jennings's driveway. Ms. Purdy likewise answered the phone and said she would be there on Tuesday. Again, Rick sighed with relief. He'd pick the jury tomorrow, deliver opening statements, and if they got that far, he'd call LaShell Jennings as his first witness.

On Tuesday, he'd call Ronnie Corlew and Carmella Purdy. *Then I'll have to rest.*

Rick Drake closed his eyes, relieved that Purdy and Corlew were still on the team, but knowing that not even a handpicked jury would find Bully Calhoun guilty of Alvie Jennings's wrongful death with only that scintilla of evidence.

"Shit!" Rick screamed again, kicking the mattress and then howling in pain as his foot caught the metal edge of the box spring. As he tried to walk off the pain, four loud knocks on the door stopped him in his tracks.

Rick reached inside his pocket for his Glock and brought it out without hesitation. He tiptoed toward the door and spoke in the deepest voice he could muster. "Who is it?"

"A friend." The voice was female and vaguely familiar.

Rick cracked the door until the chain caught. He squinted at the redheaded woman standing outside. "Jill?" he asked. It was the waitress from the Waffle House in Jasper.

The woman nodded and gave a sheepish smile. "Didn't recognize me without my uniform."

Rick almost said, "And the new hair color," but stopped himself. "I'm sorry about Rel. I know . . ." Rick trailed off because he didn't know anything. He had only assumed there was a relationship between Jill and Rel.

Jill bit her lip. "Thank you."

"What do you want?" Rick asked.

She took a deep breath and slowly exhaled. "To help. If I can."

"How?"

"Did Rel ever mention to you an angle he was working in Auburn?"

Rick Drake felt a warm tickle in his chest. He undid the latch and the door swung open. "Yes, ma'am, he did."

50

Sandra Conrad sat in the rubber chair by her son's bed in the intensive care unit of Druid City Hospital. She had barely slept in the ten days since learning of her son's shooting. Her husband, John David, was out in the waiting area, not able to sit and watch their boy "hooked up to all these tubes anymore." She wiped a tear from her eye and repeated a phrase she must have said a thousand times since Powell's admission to the ICU.

"Wake up, son," she said, her voice cracking from the fatigue and the horror that perhaps her boy, her only child, wouldn't wake up. That he'd never open his eyes again.

As she'd done for the past three days, Sandra placed her son's iPod on his chest and played the songs she knew he loved.

She sang along with Willie Nelson as he crooned "Whiskey River" and "Always on My Mind" and kissed Powell on the cheek. As the music played, she heard the ding of two more text messages from her phone and she gritted her teeth with irritation. It seemed like everyone in Decatur wanted to know her son's condition by the hour. She knew she should be grateful for such caring friends, but she hated the obligation she felt to return every message.

Sandra rocked her body back and forth in the chair and tried not to cry. Thoughts of preparing for a funeral crept into her mind, and she blocked them. *No, no, no. My boy is going to live. He will live.*

When these torturous thoughts came, she turned the volume on the iPod up louder. Now a jazz number by the great Ella Fitzgerald came through the speakers and Sandra smiled. She loved her boy's taste in music, which consisted of outlaw country, Mississippi blues, and jazz. She continued to rock, whispering softly over and over again, "Wake up, sweet boy. Wake up. Wake up."

Finally, a nurse gently knocked on the door and came in. "Mrs. Conrad, visiting hours are over."

Sandra wiped fresh tears from her eyes as Merle Haggard's haunting voice rang out in the tiny room. It was a song Sandra had never liked that much, even if it was about a mother. Sandra leaned over the bed and grabbed the iPod.

When she did, her son's hand reached out and clasped her own.

Sandra Dale Conrad felt her heart constrict as she sensed the pressure in her fingers. She looked at her boy, whose eyes were still closed. "Powell! Son!" She felt him grip her hand again, and then her sandy-haired son, who had always talked too loud despite her admonitions to speak with an inside voice, croaked out the most beautiful word that God had ever created.

"Momma."

51

The only Waffle House in Lauderdale County was on Florence Boulevard about three-quarters of a mile from downtown. Rick and Jill sat in a booth, and Jill turned and stretched her right leg out on the portion of the seat she wasn't sitting in.

"Any reason why we couldn't just talk at the bar at the hotel?" Rick asked. "The one on the top floor revolves and gives you all different views of the Tennessee River."

"Sounds lovely, hon, but I feel more comfortable here."

Rick nodded, trying to remain patient. It was now past ten o'clock at night and he was due in court at eight thirty the following morning. He'd need to get up at four to prepare and practice his opening statement. They'd driven from the hotel to the diner in Jill's minivan, and Rick had immediately recognized it as the vehicle that was waiting on them outside the courthouse just before the bullets started firing. He hadn't said anything when he'd gotten into the van, but now that Jill was "comfortable" he thought he would wade in.

"You saw the shooting," he said. "It was your van that we were going to get in to leave."

She bobbed her head up and down and took a cigarette out of a pack in her purse. Lighting up, she held out her now-empty coffee cup to their waitress, who was passing by. "Can you top me off, sugar?" Jill asked, and the waitress smiled. Seconds later, cigarette smoke mixed with the steam rising off the fresh cup of java to create a cloud in front of Jill's face. She wiped a hand across the air and smiled at him. "Sorry." Then she sighed. "Yes, I was there. I saw the whole thing." She paused. "I saw Rel die to protect you."

Rick felt a lump in his throat and gazed down at his own untouched coffee mug. The last thing he wanted to do now was drink caffeine when he planned to go straight to bed once he got back to the hotel. He swirled the liquid around in the cup and finally met her eye. "I'm sorry."

"Rel felt so guilty about his brother's death. He . . . held himself responsible."

Rick shook his head. "But he wasn't. Alvie saw something he shouldn't have seen. He saw a deal being made that led to a powerful man's death. Bully Calhoun was never going to let Alvie live."

Jill peered down at the table. "I met Rel a month before Bully Calhoun was killed. He'd come in after working his job at the post office and have a cup of coffee. One night, I let him take me home and we . . ." She smiled and puffed on the cigarette. "Well, you know. After that, he started coming in more regular, and about twice a week he'd go home with me." She took another drag on her cancer stick and looked around the restaurant. "You want to hear something crazy?"

"What?" Rick asked, growing even more impatient.

"I think it was Rel who killed Bully Calhoun."

"Get out," Rick said, cocking his head at her.

"I'm serious. Rel told me that he worked as a manager at McDonald's before taking the postal job. Now why would someone making the kind of money a manager does quit and be a postman? And Rel was an investigator too. If he was going to quit, why not go back to doing what he had done before?" She shook her head. "But no, he goes and joins the post office and just happens to have a route that carried him right by the Jasper Country Club."

Rick felt a chill go down his spine. There was a ring of truth to what she was saying. He thought of one of his last meetings at the Waffle House in Jasper with Rel. Something the man had said. *I've chopped off the head of the snake, but we still got to get the tail.* Rick had asked him what he meant, and Rel had clammed up. But now . . . *It makes sense.*

"He quit the job with the post office a month after Bully's death. And then he starts working with you in the shadows on your case for Alvie's family."

"I never paid him," Rick said. "He said he didn't want any money for it."

Jill's eyes glistened. "Like I said, whether true or not, Rel felt guilty about Alvie's death and blamed himself."

Rick gazed down at his coffee cup, knowing that the liquid inside had probably gone cold by now. He still hadn't heard what he'd come here to hear. "Tell me about the Auburn angle, Jill. What was Rel up to in Lee County?"

Jill puffed on the cigarette and sipped her coffee. The waitress put down a plate of waffles, and Jill took her time applying butter and syrup. She crushed the Camel out in the ashtray and cut a bite of waffle off with her fork. As she chewed her food, she pointed her fork at Rick. "For a long time, I didn't figure it out. He'd be gone for the weekend, and I'd ask him where and he'd just say he was working Alvie's case. About a month ago, he slipped up and told me he was going to Auburn. I'd asked him why he was going to that godforsaken place, and he said there was a person there who might unlock the whole case. If he could just get the SOB to talk."

"Who?" Rick asked.

Jill took another bite of waffle and washed it down with a sip of coffee. Then she pulled something out of her purse. Appropriately enough, it was a napkin, and Jill pushed it across the table.

Rick grabbed it and read the words written in black ink on the paper. The handwriting wasn't Jill's. It was chicken scratch that had to be the late Rel Jennings's. Rick read the name and number written on the napkin and cocked his head. Then he looked at Jill.

"You recognize that name?" she asked, her eyes glowing with satisfaction.

"Lawson . . . Snow." Rick said the words slowly, trying to recall where he'd heard them before. He couldn't. "No, ma'am. I don't. Should I?"

Jill took her pack of Camels and lit another cigarette. After taking a quick puff, she said, "You would if you were from Jasper or Oakman or Carbon Hill." She took another drag. "Or Parrish."

"Why is that?"

"Because for thirty years, Lawson Snow was the sheriff of Walker County." She snorted and took another puff on the Camel. "You like irony, Mr. Drake?"

Rick raised his eyebrows, waiting for the punch line.

"Lawson Snow was the crookedest sheriff that ever lived, and he was so deep in Bully Calhoun's pocket that he could have told you Bully's exact change every day." She paused, milking the story. "But you wanna know what folks in town called him?"

Rick held out his palms.

"Law," Jill said. "Everybody called him Law."

52

At the sound of the beeping noise, Tom's eyes shot open and he sat up straight in the bed. He blinked and gazed around the hospital room, getting his bearings, as another beep rang out. He glanced to his left, where the IV pole stood, with its numerous bags of medicine and fluids. When he heard the beep again, Tom knew one of the bags was out. He sighed and rubbed the back of his neck.

How many days had he been here? He'd lost count. And what time was it? He looked at the window, but the blinds were closed. His cell phone lay on the bed beside him, right next to the remote control. He grabbed it and clicked his security code. No missed calls. No text messages. Since he'd been hospitalized, everyone was scared to tell him anything. He gritted his teeth with irritation. The time on the screen was 12:05, but the phone didn't tell him whether it was a.m. or p.m.

Tom wiped his forehead, which was covered in sweat. He was so thirsty. He grabbed the remote and pressed the red "Help" button.

"Yes, Mr. McMurtrie?" a woman's voice blared through the microphone on the remote.

"I think the IV with my pain meds is out," Tom said, gazing to his left at the pole and hearing another beep coming from it.

"OK, sir. Someone will be right there."

"Can they bring me some water too?" Tom asked.

"Yes, sir."

Five minutes later, a nurse named Michael came into the room. *Night shift, right?* Tom thought but didn't say. He brought a cup of water over, and Tom took it from his hand with both of his.

"Easy does it, Mr. McMurtrie," Michael said as he hung another bag of morphine on the IV pole, but the advice didn't take.

Tom took a big gulp of water and his throat immediately locked up. He spat half of the liquid over the edge of the bed and then began to cough. He felt the nurse's hand on his back, and Tom wanted to tell him not to slap him, but he couldn't speak.

Michael brought his hand down on Tom's back, and Tom cried out in pain. There was nothing that hurt so bad when you had lung cancer that had reached the bone than a hard slap on the back. Even bracing for it, the sting rippled through his muscles and joints. Tom continued to cough and held his hand up for Michael to stay away. Finally, the fit subsided, and Tom squinted at the nurse. "What time is it?"

"It's ten past midnight, sir. Do you want to try another sip? This time maybe a little slower."

Tom nodded and Michael pressed the cup to his lips.

"Thank you, son," Tom said.

"No problem. Do you need anything else?"

"Not now," Tom said.

"OK. Try to get some rest, sir," Michael said, beginning to walk away.

"Wait!" Tom yelled after him, and his lungs stung from the effort. When Michael turned, Tom leaned forward so that he wouldn't have to talk any louder than necessary. "When does Dr. Maples make his rounds?"

"The last three days it's been around six thirty."

"Are you here then?"

"I'm going off shift, but I should still be around."

"Will you make sure I'm up? I haven't had a chance to talk with him during his prior visits." That wasn't entirely true. Tom had a vague memory of talking to Dr. Maples at least once, but everything was hazy from all the pain medication they had been pumping through him. He'd also had more of the visions of Ray Ray Pickalew that had been dogging him these last few weeks, and the interactions were becoming longer. One thing he knew from talking with Tommy was that the cancer had spread to the brain. He'd asked Tommy how bad it was, but his son hadn't given him a direct answer. *I'll get it from the horse's mouth,* Tom had resolved.

Michael nodded. "Of course, sir."

"Thank you," Tom said, and Michael closed the door behind him.

Tom lay back on the bed and closed his eyes. The effort of the past three minutes had completely worn him out. He thought back to the day at CCI. The scans. And then Helen meeting him outside imaging. Helen Lewis, the General, crying and telling him Wade Richey was dead. Powell Conrad was shot and might be dead. Jasmine Haynes was dead. And there'd been a shooting in Jasper.

Tom sighed, knowing now that his partner, Rick Drake, had emerged unscathed from the ruckus at the Walker County Courthouse. He had spoken with Rick yesterday, and the trial in Florence was still going forward. It made Tom proud to think of Rick pressing on. Not quitting.

Never quit. It's the easiest cop-out in the world. Coach Bryant had said those words, and Tom could hear them now as if the gravelly voice were in the room with him.

"Never quit," Tom repeated, trying to will his body to work. But just as the thoughts were entering his mind, the morphine began to hit him. Tom forced his eyes open. His family needed him. So did his friends. "Never . . . quit," he mumbled again, but he was falling once more. He smelled salt in his nose and saw a vision of a crimson fifty-four rolling over him. Then he heard the gravelly voice again. Louder. Younger. Excited.

Bingo.

Tom closed his eyes as the morphine flooded his bloodstream. Five seconds later, with Coach Bryant's voice ringing in his ears along with the sounds of shoulder pads popping against each other, he was out.

53

At 8:55 a.m. on Monday, Judge Conner brought the jury panel in. Rick watched the forty-some-odd men and women of various ages and sexes stroll into the circuit courtroom of the Lauderdale County Courthouse, almost all of whom had that sheepish look on their faces that let you know they weren't entirely sure what they were doing. Rick had heard the Professor describe jury service as like attending someone else's church—you don't know when to stand, when to sit, when to pray, or whether it is OK to say "amen" out loud.

Rick had thought it was an apt analogy. Being a juror—especially if you were selected for a trial and had to hang out, against your will, all week with eleven other people you didn't know, only to have to come together with this group of strangers to reach a decision as to the guilt or innocence of a person, or whether a person or company was liable in money damages—had to be one of the most unusual and awkward experiences a human being could endure.

But it's what makes this country the greatest in the world, Rick thought, echoing words he'd heard the Professor say on the first day of trial team every year: *We are the last country in the world that decides civil and criminal disputes with a jury system.*

Rick smiled and looked down at his loafers. Then he turned to LaShell Jennings, who gave him a nervous nod. LaByron and little Alvin had stayed in Birmingham with Mimi this week, so LaShell was going it alone. She had a room on the same floor of the Muscle Shoals Marriott as Rick, and they had eaten a nervous breakfast together that morning. Rick hadn't told her about his meeting with Jill the night before. He didn't want to get her hopes up for something that probably wasn't going to happen. He'd left Lawson "Law" Snow two voice messages this morning on the number Rel had written on the napkin, and so far he'd gotten no response. Though he wasn't sure if the number was a mobile one or not, he'd also sent a text to the former sheriff of Walker County.

Rick nodded back at LaShell and looked out over the panel, trying to make eye contact with as many of the potential jurors as possible. When they were all seated, Judge Conner addressed them.

"Ladies and gentlemen, you are about to go through the part of the process called voir dire. The attorneys will ask you some questions in an effort to decide who will eventually sit on the jury in this case. If you are unsure of the answer to any of the questions asked, it is always better to speak up and let the attorneys decide. Does everyone understand?"

In response, as often was the case, no one said a word.

"Mr. Flood, is the defense ready?"

Virgil Flood sat with his one leg crossed over the other, his perpetually amused eyes lighting on Rick's before looking over his shoulder at His Honor. "Yes, sir," Virgil said. The wily attorney had turned his chair around to face the gallery and made a tent with his hands as he surveyed the crowd. Next to him, Kathryn Calhoun Willistone wore a black dress fit for a funeral. She, like Virgil, faced the panel, her expression appropriately grave. When they had arrived that morning, Rick had tried to introduce himself to the woman, but Kat turned her back on him as if he weren't there. At the end of the defense table were Axon and Tunnell, the two Birmingham attorneys, who had managed to put their smartphones away and were likewise peering at the crowd.

"Mr. Drake, are you ready to proceed?" Conner's loud voice punctured the air, and even though he was expecting the question, Rick felt a charge of adrenaline.

He calmly rose to his feet. "Yes, Your Honor."

54

Kat felt hate burning through her body as she watched Rick Drake address the jury panel. *You should be dead,* she thought, cursing JimBone Wheeler in her thoughts. *I should be at home planning my vacation to Bermuda. Not in this god-awful place.*

But here I am. She reminded herself to breathe and took in a gulp of air, remembering her conversation with DeWayne Patterson the day before. *Mr. Wheeler says that everything is fine and that he is going to fulfill his contract.*

Kat exhaled and tried to keep her heartbeat steady. She looked at Drake as he asked the jury if any of them had ever heard of Marcellus Calhoun. A few stray hands were raised, and the young attorney followed up with more questions.

Virgil had warned her when she arrived that the process of voir dire could drag on all morning. Kat ground her teeth, but when she saw one of the potential jurors looking at her—a middle-aged man in the front row—she smiled and he returned the gesture. The man blushed, and Kat knew she had found a winner. She looked down at the grid that Virgil had place in front of her and ran her index finger along the page until she found the name. Juror number seven. Pete Crigger.

She put a star by Crigger's name on her grid and then began to look more closely at the rest of the panel. She had never sat through a trial before, so she might as well try to participate.

At least until Mr. Wheeler makes good on his end of the deal, she thought, peering up at Rick. *And you're finally dead.*

55

While his partner started the process that would culminate in a jury verdict in Florence, Tom McMurtrie braced for another kind of verdict.

Trey Maples sat on a stool in front of Tom, rolling his hands over each other. Maples was a large, round man with dark-black hair and a clean-shaven face. During office visits at CCI, he was a constant whirl of motion as he turned from Tom to his computer and back, simultaneously documenting his visit, ordering tests, and delivering news to the patient.

Now, though, the doctor was fidgeting, with no computer to keep him busy. It was 9:30 a.m., and the oncologist was late in making his rounds. He'd had an emergency that morning, which put him three hours behind. Though Maples was normally almost annoyingly positive, today his big eyes were hound-dog sad.

"Well," Tom said, "just spit it out."

"You've got a tumor in your brain. It's about a centimeter and a half." Maples measured the distance with his index finger and thumb.

"Is that why I'm waking up in the middle of the night and talking to a friend who's been dead for two years?" Tom smiled, but Maples didn't. Instead, the doctor rubbed his chin.

"It's possible. Brain cancer patients sometimes report hallucinations." He paused. "The disease can also lead to some dementia."

Tom scoffed. "So you're telling me I'm crazy."

"No, sir," Maples said. "You have stage four lung cancer that had already spread to the bone. Now you have a brain lesion that we could treat with radiation, but . . ." He trailed off and held up his hands.

"But what's the point, right?" Tom asked.

Maples grimaced and folded his arms across his chest. "Let's just say I don't think radiating the brain would be beneficial at this juncture."

For a long moment, the doctor peered down at the floor. "Professor McMurtrie, most lung cancer patients at your stage are dead after six months." He paused and looked at him. "You've made it fourteen. With the regime of chemo and radiation we've put you through, you've more than doubled the average."

Tom smiled at him. "You've done good, Doc. I . . ." Tom felt heat behind his eyes as he reached for the doctor's hand. "I've cherished the time you've given me."

Maples chuckled. "I haven't done anything special, sir. You're just a very strong man." The doctor's voice cracked ever so slightly, and Tom squeezed his hand. In over a year, he'd never seen his oncologist show any emotion other than good-natured humor.

"I'm sorry I couldn't help you more," Maples said, rising to his feet.

"Hey, Doc."

The oncologist stopped at the door and turned to face him.

"How long?"

Maples shook his head. "I've stopped trying to predict with you."

"Doc?" Tom pressed, and hated the desperation in his voice.

"If we can get your labs a little more stable, you can probably go home by the end of the week."

"That's not what I meant."

"I know, Professor McMurtrie," he said, glancing up at the ceiling. "You know what I always say."

"Eat, walk, pray," Tom said, and Maples smiled.

"Keep doing that, and who knows? Another month? Maybe two or three months?"

Tom bit his lip, which had begun to shake. "Thank you, Doc."

Maples paused for a long moment in the doorway. "Thank you, Professor," he finally said.

56

Sandra Conrad paced the floor of her son's room on the ICU, cursing her honesty. The first thing her son had asked her after waking last night was "How is Wade?"

Why hadn't I just lied and said he was fine? Instead, she'd told him the truth. "He's dead, honey. I'm so sorry."

Powell's face had cringed and then he'd gone back to sleep. Since then, he had stirred a few times—good signs—but he hadn't said anything. For her part, Sandra had made the nurses keep the iPod playing his music.

Now, as visiting hours were about to conclude and she would once again have to go out to the waiting room and give her husband a discouraging summary, she saw one of her boy's eyes flutter open.

Ambrose Powell Conrad blinked and gazed up at the hospital room ceiling. Sandra tiptoed toward him, noticing that the song playing was the duet "Pancho and Lefty," from Merle Haggard and Willie Nelson.

"Powell, baby, are you OK?"

Her son continued to gape at the ceiling. His left eye was open, but his right was shut closed. The doctor had said that even if he lived he'd probably have permanent vision loss in his right eye, as several shards of plastic from the CD case he'd been holding had scratched his cornea.

Sandra placed her palm on his forehead. "Powell, baby, talk to me."

After several seconds, he slowly turned his head to her. He tried to speak, but the words wouldn't come. When she leaned in, she could tell he was using all the energy he had to try to speak.

"Rick," he said. "I need . . . to see . . . Rick."

Sandra nodded and kissed his cheek. "OK, honey. I think he's in a trial in Florence."

Powell grimaced.

"Why do you need to see Rick, honey?"

But her boy didn't answer. His eye had closed again, and all Sandra Conrad could hear now were his shallow breaths.

Sandra peered up at the same ceiling her son had just been staring at. *Please, Lord Jesus, don't let my boy die. Please.*

Then, kissing his cheek, she walked out of the hospital room and took her phone out of her purse. Seconds later, she dialed the number for Rick Drake.

57

At just after 5:00 p.m., Judge Conner adjourned the jury for the day. Voir dire had taken until 2:30 p.m., and all the parties were able to accomplish after striking the jury was opening statements. Slowing things down further, Conner said that they would be getting a late start on Tuesday because he had to handle an emergency request for a temporary restraining order in Jasper. "Be back at 1:00 p.m. tomorrow, and I promise there shouldn't be any further delays."

Once all twelve jurors had left the courtroom, Rick took his phone out of his pocket. He'd kept it on silent during the entire afternoon session, and he'd felt it vibrate several times, indicating new emails, texts, and phone calls.

His heart caught in his chest when he saw the missed call from Sandra Conrad. *Please don't be dead,* he thought, letting out a nervous breath. Though he had received numerous other emails and several check-in texts from his secretary, Frankie, there was nothing from Lawson Snow. No call. No text. No nothing.

Damnit, Rick thought as he dialed Sandra's number and felt his heart rate speed up.

"Hello, Rick?" Powell's mother answered.

"Yes, ma'am," Rick said, holding his breath and closing his eyes.

"He's awake," Sandra cried, the relief palpable in her voice.

Rick breathed in a lungful of oxygen. "That's wonderful, Mrs. Conrad."

"He's not out of the woods yet, but the doctors say that regaining consciousness was a huge step."

"I'm just glad he's alive," Rick said.

"Me too. Listen, how busy are you?"

"I'm in the middle of a trial, Mrs. Conrad, but what do you need?"

"Well . . . is there any way . . . ?" She trailed off, and Rick cocked his head to hear better.

"Mrs. Conrad, what is it?"

"Is there any way you could come? Powell drifts in and out of consciousness, but when he's awake he keeps saying the same thing."

"What?" Rick asked.

"That he needs to see you."

Rick Drake imagined his best friend as he'd last seen him. Hooked up to tubes and lying on a cot in the intensive care unit. Gazing around the almost-empty courtroom and now thankful that Judge Conner had a conflict in the morning, he spoke into the phone. "I'm on my way."

58

"I have to go to Tuscaloosa," Rick said as he and his client walked out of the courtroom.

LaShell gazed back at him with tired eyes. "What? Why?"

Rick took a seat on one of the wooden benches in the hallway and patted the spot next to him for LaShell to join him. "LaShell, on the day Rel was killed, there was another shooting in Tuscaloosa. Remember me telling you that my best friend was shot?"

She nodded.

"I just got off the phone with his mother, and my friend, Powell Conrad, is alive. He's awake and he needs to see me." Rick paused. "I have to go."

"I understand," LaShell said. "Will you be back tomorrow?"

"Yes." Rick started to add more, but his cell phone began to ring in his pocket. He pulled out the device and looked at the screen. He didn't recognize the number, from a (334) area code. For a second, Rick almost didn't answer, thinking it was probably a solicitor. But when the phone had rung five times without stopping, he clicked it.

"Hello," Rick said.

There was no response, but Rick thought he heard the sound of breathing on the line. "Hello," he repeated.

A voice came through, a high-pitched male whine. "Rick Drake?"

"Yes, who is this?"

"This is Lawson Snow," the voice answered, followed by several coughs. "I got your messages."

"Why didn't you call me back on your cell?" Rick asked.

"Because I didn't want to," the man snapped. "Do you want to talk with me or what?"

"Yes," Rick said.

"Can you be in Auburn tomorrow morning at 9:00 a.m.?"

"Mr. Snow, I'm in the middle of a trial, sir. I—"

"Fine, then, sorry to bother you. Have a nice—"

"I can't be there in the morning but I can tonight," Rick pleaded.

For several seconds, the airway was silent, and Rick pressed the phone hard to his ear to make sure he didn't miss anything.

Finally, Lawson Snow cleared his throat. "When's the earliest you can make it?"

Rick glanced at the time on his phone. It was 5:20 p.m. It would take all of four hours and maybe more to get to Auburn. *And I still need to see Powell.* "Ten o'clock," Rick said, praying that would be soon enough.

More silence, followed by a fit of coughing. Then, finally, Snow's voice chimed back in. "Ever hear of a place called Toomer's Corner?"

Rick managed a nervous smile. He'd never been to the famed spot that Auburn fans rolled with toilet paper after big victories, but he'd heard about it. "Yes, sir."

"Meet me there at ten sharp."

"Thank you, Mr. Snow."

"Don't thank me yet, boy," he said. "And you can call me Law."

Ten minutes later, Rick was in his Saturn and heading west on Highway 72. He crossed the bridge over the Tennessee River into Colbert County, and thirty minutes later he was on Highway 157 headed toward Cullman.

An hour later, at 6:45 p.m., he took the exit for I-65. *Two hours to Montgomery and then another hour to Auburn,* Rick thought, pushing the accelerator down on his ancient sedan. He'd called Sandra Conrad and told her that he'd had an emergency come up in his case and that he couldn't make it to the hospital until morning. She said she understood and that she would greet him whenever he arrived.

Now, as his car hurtled down the interstate, Rick felt adrenaline flooding his veins. He'd had no food yet and doubted he could eat anything if it was put in front of him. He had no idea what awaited him in Auburn, but he knew his whole case hinged on it.

The irony wasn't lost on him. Here he was, Rick Drake, an Alabama fan since the day he was born, whose partner, Tom McMurtrie, had been an Alabama football legend and played for Coach Paul "Bear" Bryant.

And the entire case, and perhaps even life or death, depended on a former lawman who called Auburn home.

"*War Eagle,*" Rick whispered as he pushed the accelerator past eighty.

59

The Galaxy of Lights is an animated holiday light show put on every year by the Huntsville Botanical Garden. Patrons can drive their vehicle through a winding path of illuminated Christmas displays, tuning their car radio to a station that plays a holiday song to go along with the scene they are passing. There are over a hundred exhibits to see in the two-and-a-half-mile circle through the gardens. The show opens on Thanksgiving and closes on New Year's Eve. Each year, thousands of people from all over the state of Alabama and beyond converge on Huntsville for this tradition.

For the past thirteen years, ever since Jackson was a baby, Nancy and Tommy McMurtrie had taken their young family through the Galaxy at least once during the holidays.

Nancy's heart pounded in her chest as she, following the lead of the cars in front of her, flicked her left-turn blinker on and waited to pull into the light show. It had been twelve full days since she'd driven her car. In their two visits to the hospital to see her father-in-law, Tommy had been behind the wheel. *He's going to be mad at me,* she thought. Then she gazed in her rearview mirror, where Jenny's legs were shaking with excitement. Their eyes met, and she gave Nancy the sweetest, most grateful smile. "Thank you, Mom."

"You're welcome, honey." Then Nancy moved her eyes to the seat next to her daughter, where Jackson gazed straight ahead with his arms crossed. He was still fuming over not being able to play in his basketball game. Nancy let out a sigh and returned her attention to the road.

"Are you OK, ma'am?"

Nancy glanced to her right, where Deputy Brad Onkey sat in the passenger seat. Brad was a lanky, bearded man in his midtwenties. After a few days of spending every second guarding the interior of the house, Brad had begun to eat meals with the family. Unlike Sawyer and Dawson, the two older and more stoic officers assigned to watch the outside of the house, Brad liked to cut up with the kids and seemed to enjoy his job.

"I'm fine," she said. "Just nervous. I haven't been out of the house in twelve days."

"Well, this is about as safe an activity as you could have chosen," Brad said. "There's security all through the Galaxy, and on a Monday night it shouldn't take us much longer than thirty minutes to get through it."

"You think the other two officers are OK back at the house with my mom and the baby?"

"They're good, ma'am," Brad said. "Dawson's inside with them and Sawyer's out on the curb. Your security system is armed, too, so if any door is opened or window is cracked the alarm will go off and the whole police department will be over there in less than five minutes."

Nancy took in a short breath.

"Mom, can you turn the radio to the station that plays the Christmas songs?" Jenny asked.

Nancy hit a button on her dash, and Bing Crosby's voice crooned through the van, singing his version of "Silent Night." From the back seat, her daughter joined in and, after a while, so did Nancy. *This is going to be OK,* she thought, flashing a smile at Brad, who had also begun to sing along. Only Jackson remained quiet, still sulking as he gazed out the window.

We needed this, Nancy told herself.

For most of the day, she had paced the floors of her home, feeling the walls beginning to close in around her. The kids were out of school for the next three weeks, which would have been a challenge in and of itself. They always got bored during the holidays, but not being able to leave the house made the monotony almost unbearable. Instead of going to the movies, or the indoor trampoline park, or the YMCA, or *anywhere*, they were stuck. In the first few days after Jasmine Haynes's murder, Nancy had been glad to stay home. She was scared to death and wanted nothing more than to be locked inside her house. But they were going on twelve days now. Almost two weeks. It was terrible what happened to Jazz, whom Nancy had met several times, but they couldn't stay holed up forever, could they? When, on a whim, Tommy had driven Jackson to Fern Bell for some basketball practice yesterday, Nancy felt the invisible chains begin to loosen. Then, this morning, her husband said he couldn't have other surgeons covering his patients any longer. He had to go to work.

Nancy was worried, but she was also glad to see Tommy move forward with his medical practice. *We can't stop living,* she had told her husband at breakfast, and he had agreed. But then in the next breath he had told Jackson that he couldn't go to his game tonight. "Baby steps," he'd said when Nancy had given him a disappointed look.

"What's the difference between a practice and a game?" she'd asked.

"A lot more people," Tommy had fired back, shaking his head. "We can't take that risk yet." Next to him at the table, Brad Onkey had agreed.

"Too unpredictable, ma'am. Not controlled enough."

Nancy had reluctantly conceded the argument.

But for the next eight hours she'd had Jackson in her ear, whining, *I'm going to miss the whole season, Mom. Please . . .* Like a continuous broken record. Over and over and over. *Please, Mom. Please . . . Please.*

To make matters worse, Jenny and Jackson seemed to be fighting every few minutes, and there were only so many times they could watch *A Christmas Story*.

At noon, Nancy's seventy-six-year-old mother came over and things got even worse. When Nancy had broached the subject of possibly taking the older kids to the Galaxy of Lights while Mom stayed with Julie, Mammie, as the kids called her, was stern in her rebuke. *There is no way you should leave this house. Not until those killers have been caught.*

"What if they aren't ever arrested, Mom? What then?"

Her mother had just blinked at her, and Nancy's resolve to do something—*anything*—only deepened.

When she wasn't pacing, she surfed Facebook and saw all of her friends' pictures of their kids sitting in Santa's lap at the mall. There would be no McMurtrie family photograph with Old Saint Nick this year. If a basketball game at a rec league park was too much exposure, then Parkway Place Mall was Exposure Palooza. Nancy had one of her neighbors do some Christmas shopping for her, and, luckily, most of the kids' Santa presents had been purchased before JimBone Wheeler broke out of prison. *But still . . . what is Christmas without a trip to the mall to see Santa?*

Am I that shallow? she had asked herself, finally signing off Facebook and vowing not to log back on.

No, she wasn't. But she was sick of being scared and stuck.

At 5:30 p.m., she made her decision and mentioned the idea to Brad, who, after talking with the other two officers, went along with it. He wanted to call Tommy and tell him, but Nancy begged him not to. "He's working late to catch up and I don't want to bother him with this. I'm sure he'd be fine with it if y'all were."

Now, Nancy felt a weird mixture of excitement, guilt, nausea, fear, and anxiety as she pulled the van up the drive and handed twenty-five dollars to the attendant. A minute later, the radio station began to play songs that correlated with the displays they were passing by. One of Nancy's favorites was the Twelve Days of Christmas, which had a different exhibit matching each of the verses to the song.

As Jenny and even, finally, Jackson began to sing the familiar tune, Nancy's heart calmed and warmth passed through her.

She felt alive for the first time in days.

Less than five minutes after getting Pasco's message that the wife was on the move, JimBone and Manny were in the Tundra and heading into town. They met Pasco at a church parking lot a half mile from the house. JimBone handed him a package.

"What's this?" Pasco asked, opening the box and pulling out a brown UPS uniform that Sheriff DeWayne Patterson had acquired weeks ago for this particular job.

"Put it on," JimBone said, removing his jacket to show Pasco that he was wearing the same outfit. "It'll give us some cover." Then he turned to Manny. "Are you ready?"

She had on leggings, a sweatshirt, and a baseball cap, looking like any of fifteen moms who liked to run in the neighborhood.

"I am," she said.

"Are you ever going to doubt my instincts again?"

She squinted at him. "No."

He turned to Pasco, who was changing inside the cab of the truck. "Are they still at the light show?"

"No. They're back on Bob Wallace Avenue."

"How far to the house?"

"Five miles," Pasco said.

"Alright then," JimBone said. "Everybody know their role?"

Manny and Pasco both nodded.

"Good," he said, patting Manny's backside. "Roll out, partner."

Without hesitation, she took off down the sidewalk at a brisk pace.

Officer Sawyer Davidson, whose police vehicle was parked on the curb outside Tommy and Nancy McMurtrie's home, glanced down at his phone, checking the score to *Monday Night Football*. The Patriots were playing the Dolphins, and Tom Brady was in his fantasy league. As he reviewed the quarterback's stats for the first quarter, he sensed movement. Reaching his hand to the gun clipped to his belt, he looked in the rearview mirror and noticed a woman approaching his police sedan from the west. She was dressed in jogging clothes, which hung tight to her body, and a baseball cap.

Hot, Sawyer thought, tapping his gun with his index finger. As she got closer, her pace slowed and she began to walk. Seconds later, she was knocking on his windshield.

Sawyer removed his weapon from the holster and held it in his lap. Then he pressed the automatic button for the window to roll down. He peered hard at the woman as the glass descended, thinking about the picture he had been shown of JimBone Wheeler's female accomplice. *Could this be her?*

It was possible but too difficult to tell at this time of night and especially with the woman wearing a cap. He had also seen several of Nancy McMurtrie's neighbors running at night wearing similar outfits. *Could this be one of them?*

"Can I help you?" he asked.

"Yes," the woman said. "I live at the top of the street and my husband and kids are out of town." With her left hand, she slowly pushed her top up.

Sawyer sucked in a breath as he gazed at the woman's bare breasts and brown nipples. "Ma'am, I—"

He didn't see the Glock pistol in the woman's other hand until it was too late.

Manny Reyes pressed the tip of the gun into the officer's temple and fired two shots, both muffled by the silencer attached to the weapon. She let her pullover fall back in place and returned the pistol to her pocket. Then she began to jog again.

Behind her, she heard the engine of the Tundra approaching.

60

At 7:05 p.m., exactly an hour after they had left the house, Nancy turned left into her driveway. On the radio, Bobby Helms wailed "Jingle Bell Rock," and Nancy tapped her fingers on the steering wheel.

"Mommy, Jackson farted," Jenny squealed from the back of the van.

"Jenny!" Nancy whirled her head and glared at her daughter. Then she shot an embarrassed glance at Deputy Onkey. "I'm sorry."

"No worries," Brad said. "I was a kid once."

Then, on her Bluetooth device a monotone voice announced through the speakers of the van that Nancy had received a new text from Jackson. Smirking, she pressed the "Read Message" icon on the dash, and the same monotone voice said, "I farted."

"Damnit, son!" She glared into the rearview mirror at her thirteen-year-old, who was laughing uncontrollably and looking down at his phone, and she couldn't help but laugh herself. Things were beginning to get back to normal.

She slowed the van as she approached the garage and moved her hand to the automatic door opener. When she pressed the button, the giggling in the car was drowned out by the roar of an explosion.

As Nancy and her children screamed in terror, orange flames engulfed the front of the house.

61

"I have to get inside!" Nancy shouted at Brad over the piercing sound of the security alarm as they both jumped out of the van. "My baby and momma are in there. Watch Jackson and Jenny!" she yelled behind her, and ran toward the back of the house.

Deputy Brad Onkey didn't try to stop her. He opened the sliding door for the children. Jenny was crying and her brother had his arm around her as they quickly exited the vehicle.

"Get in there and help Mom!" Jackson yelled at the guard, but Brad stayed in place, moving his eyes around the burning building.

Where the hell is Sawyer? Or Dawson? He glanced at the sedan parked at the curb and saw the other officer sitting in the driver's seat. *Why isn't he moving?*

Then he noticed a light-colored Toyota Tundra approaching from the east. Had it been there when they turned into the driveway a few minutes ago? Brad's brain was scrambled as he tried to think through what to do. "Come with me," he yelled at the kids as he ran toward the cruiser. When he opened the door, Sawyer Davidson's body fell out of the driver's seat.

"Oh God," Brad said, and turned just as Jenny McMurtrie noticed the dead man. Her squeal was almost as loud as the explosion and the resulting security siren. She ran toward her brother, who scooped her in his arms.

Behind the two kids, Brad saw Nancy McMurtrie emerge from behind the house. She had her mother's arm draped over her shoulder and the baby in her other hand.

"Mommy!" Jenny screamed, and she wiggled out of her brother's grasp and ran toward her mother.

Hearing the squeal of tires, Brad turned as the headlights of the Tundra passed over his face. He put a hand up to block the blinding light and saw a man in a uniform on the passenger side. The driver appeared to be wearing the same outfit.

Off-duty UPS drivers? Brad wondered, walking toward the truck. "Can you help . . . ?"

Brad stopped talking when he saw the passenger hop out of the van holding an AK-47 assault rifle.

"Run!" Brad yelled, wheeling toward Jackson.

"If you do, you die," JimBone Wheeler said, pointing the assault rifle at Tom McMurtrie's grandson. "And so does your momma, your grandmomma, and both of your baby sisters. You want that, boy?"

Jackson shook his head.

"I didn't think so. Now get in the truck."

"Jackson, don't—"

Brad's words were interrupted by the patter of the AK-47 as JimBone turned and fired at least five rounds into Brad Onkey's chest and shoulders. The deputy dropped to his knees. "Run," he gasped at Jackson, who had frozen dead still. As Brad fell over on his side, he saw the driver of the truck approach the boy and shoot him with what looked like a Taser. The boy dropped to the ground.

"*No,*" Brad whispered, seeing the driver sling the kid's limp body over his shoulder.

Then Brad felt the barrel of the rifle against his ear, and he closed his eyes.

62

"Jackson!" Nancy shrieked as she saw her son being thrown into the cab of a truck parked on the curb. She ran toward the vehicle, but it was already pulling away.

She started to shout his name again, but then the patter of an assault rifle filled the air. She ducked to the grass and rolled as the windows of her minivan shattered behind her. Finding it hard to breathe, she moved her eyes frantically around the yard. Her mother and two daughters were huddled together by a tree a safe distance from the burning house. They were OK. But just a few feet away from Nancy, Deputy Brad Onkey lay on his side, gazing at her with still eyes. Blood gushed from the back of the officer's head.

A scream caught in Nancy's throat, but she forced it back as she returned her eyes to the road.

The truck was gone. *Jackson* . . . was gone.

"No," she whimpered, bringing her hands to the side of her face. In the distance, she thought she heard the wail of police sirens. *Too late.*

Then, as fear and shock and anguish overcame her, Nancy McMurtrie's throat loosened.

And she screamed.

63

During football telecasts, Rick Drake had often heard the town of Auburn, Alabama, referred to as "the loveliest village on the plains." At 9:45 p.m., as he drove his Saturn down College Street, it wasn't hard to see why. Even in the darkness, with the orange-brick buildings lit only by the street and traffic lights, the place was beautiful. As he passed iconic Samford Hall on the left, with its historic clock, he heard his stomach growl. He'd had nothing to eat since scarfing down a burger at lunch, and he realized he was famished. *No time for food,* he thought as he blinked his eyes and tried to focus.

Seconds later, he saw the intersection with Magnolia Avenue and the green-and-white sign indicating "Toomer's Drugs."

Rick found a parking space in front of the store and pulled to a stop. He glanced at the time on his dashboard. 9:47 p.m. *Early,* he thought, taking a deep breath and rubbing his eyes. He climbed out of the vehicle and stretched his legs. For a second, his calf tightened and he thought he was about to have a cramp, but just as quickly the tension in his leg eased. Rick ambled toward the front door to the drugstore, seeing the CLOSED sign hanging over the door. Then he turned in a complete circle, taking in the scene.

He'd only seen Toomer's Corner on television after Auburn wins, when the streets were overflowing and the fans rolled the area with toilet paper. Up until last spring, there had been two iconic oak trees that usually bore the brunt of the party, but that all changed when a disgruntled Alabama fan named Harvey Updyke poisoned the trees in November 2010 and then bragged about doing so on the Paul Finebaum radio show.

The school had tried in vain for a couple of years to keep the trees alive, but they were finally removed in April 2013 and as of yet hadn't been replaced.

"It was prettier when the trees were still here," a scratchy voice rang out from behind Rick, and he turned to see a man leaning his head out the window of a Ford F-150 pickup truck. He wore a brown cowboy hat pulled low over his eyes, and a cigarette dangled out of the corner of his mouth. "But we still rolled the hell out of this place after the Kick Six."

Rick cringed at the mention of the play that had ended the Iron Bowl three weeks earlier. Alabama had tried a 57-yard field goal as time expired with the game tied. The kick missed, and Chris Davis, from Auburn, had caught the ball in the back of the end zone and run it back 109 yards for the winning touchdown. "That was a hell of a play," Rick said, forcing a smile. Then he approached the vehicle and stopped a foot from the man. "Mr. Snow."

"I told you to call me Law."

"Law," Rick corrected himself.

"Are you hungry?"

Rick smiled. "Kinda."

Law nodded. "Hop in then. I'm going to introduce you to a sandwich that ought to be illegal."

Two minutes later, they sat across from each other at a table at Momma Goldberg's Deli, on the corner of Magnolia and Donahue. Rick had let the former sheriff order for both of them, and Law ordered two Mama's Loves on wheat with regular chips and two draft Blue Moons.

Once the food had been brought to the table, Law waited while Rick took a bite.

"Good, huh?" he asked, coughing and then clamping down on his own.

Rick had to admit that the sandwich, which consisted of ham, smoked turkey, and roast beef along with lettuce, tomato, mayonnaise, and some other sauce that Rick couldn't identify, was fantastic. "Great," he said.

"The sauce is what makes it," Law said, then took a long swig of beer from the frosty mug.

Rick did the same and gazed at the man, who had removed his hat when they'd entered the restaurant. Law Snow had matted-down silver locks that were thinning at the temples. His eyes were gray, and they reminded Rick of the Professor's. "Thank you for dinner," Rick said. "I was starving."

"No problem," Law said. Then, wiping his mouth, he added, his voice low, "I was really sorry to hear about Rel."

Rick gazed at the golden liquid in his glass. "He saved my life."

For a minute, the two men ate in silence. Finally, after wolfing down the entire sandwich in about five bites, Rick eyed the other man. He had thought of all the ways he might open this conversation during the five-hour trek, and he knew there was no good or perfect way. *Just keep it simple.* "Law, why'd you ask me to come here tonight?"

The retired sheriff wiped his mouth with a napkin and crossed his right leg over his left knee. He gazed around the empty restaurant—the dinner hour had long since passed—and, by the impatient glances the waitress had given them when she'd set the food down, he figured they were about to close.

"Now that your stomach is full, are you up for a walk? I don't know about you, but I think better when I'm moving. The story I'm about to tell you is a long one, and I don't believe the folks here are going to like it if we stay much longer."

"Sure thing," Rick said, finishing the rest of his beer and standing up. "Lead the way."

A couple minutes later, they were walking down a lit path across the campus of Auburn University. Law had his cowboy hat back on and had put a chaw of Red Man in the side of his mouth. He spat a stream of tobacco and spoke while looking straight ahead. "I'm about to tell you something that might get us both killed. But, seeing as you may get killed anyway and I've just been diagnosed with lymphoma, I figure we should take our chances." He paused and spat more tobacco juice onto the grass adjacent to the walk. In the distance, Rick heard the clock on Samford Hall chime. It was 10:00 p.m.

"I was the sheriff of Walker County for thirty years. Because of me and my efforts, a lot of bad people went to jail. Ninety-nine percent of my work was honest and on the up and up." He sighed. "With one notable exception."

"Bully Calhoun," Rick chimed in.

Law snorted. "We all have our weaknesses, I guess." He sighed. "Mine was money. I knew I'd never make enough to keep my wife satisfied as a sheriff, so I started taking little hits from Bully every time he needed the law . . ." He paused. "No pun intended, to look the other way." He coughed and brought his hands to his jacket, running them up and down his sleeves as if he were cold. Rick, who was still wearing the suit he'd worn to court that morning, hadn't noticed the temperature, but he did now. He crossed his arms, thinking it couldn't be much above forty.

"So I looked the other way," Law said. "And I made a little money." He sighed. "But it wasn't until I bought the cabin that I started making big bank." The former sheriff came to an abrupt stop and arched his head. Squinting, Rick saw the shadow of Jordan-Hare Stadium. "You know what the happiest day of my life was, son?"

Rick gritted his teeth at the change of subject right when Lawson Snow's story was beginning to get good, but he indulged the old man. "What day was that?"

"December 2, 1989," he said, his voice wistful. "It was the first time Alabama ever came to Auburn to play the Iron Bowl. Before that, all the games were played at Legion Field, in Birmingham, which was supposed to be a neutral site but was really just a de facto home field for Alabama. It wasn't fair, and Coach Dye finally got the game moved here." He paused and continued to peer up at the concrete facade of Jordan-Hare. "I have never heard a stadium, nor will I ever hear a crowd again, roar like we did on that day. I swear, Alabama could have suited up the New York Giants that day and we'd a still have beat 'em. That's why Coach Dye will always be the greatest Auburn coach. He brought big brother to our house, and we lit that ass up." He spat tobacco on the ground and sighed. "Second-best day of my life was when I retired as sheriff. I moved down here a week later, and I haven't ever been back."

"You said you started making the big money when you bought the cabin."

Law nodded. "I've always loved fishing. Hell, even now I like to hightail it over to Lake Martin any chance I can get. Don't matter whether it's catfish, crappie, bass, trout." He guffawed. "Hell, I even like fishing in the afternoon off the dock for bream." He spat again. "I bought the cabin for myself, but when Bully began to get hot and heavy into meth, he started 'renting' it from me." Law made the quote symbol with the index and middle fingers of both hands. "My cabin was close to his primary distributor. It was a neutral location and, because of who I was, no one ever suspected anything. On big transactions, I'd come myself and park my police car out front." Law nodded, smiling up at the stadium. "Yeah, ole Law made himself some bank—yes, sir, I did." He sighed. "Course, by that time it didn't matter. My wife had divorced me and taken my two daughters to live in Cullman. I didn't need that kind of money anymore, but you might say I got . . . *addicted* to it."

"How long did this go on?"

"Oh, at least ten years. Maybe longer. I can't remember." He chuckled. "Funny, I can remember a football game in 1989 like it was yesterday, but the ten years I helped Bully Calhoun run meth blend together like one long dream."

"Did you ever do meth yourself?"

Law scoffed. "Me? Hell, naw. I've got two vices, son. One is Tennessee whiskey."

"And the other?"

Law turned and looked Rick in the eyes. "The other is why my wife left me." He paused. "And how I met Santonio Jennings."

Rick waited, sensing that everything was building to right now. Finally, when the retired lawman spoke again, his voice shook with emotion. "I never was much good with women, you see. I . . . Well, let's just say that my hardware operated more like software, you catch my drift?"

Rick thought he did, but he didn't dare speak. Instead, he sucked in a breath and tried to be patient.

"One night, about a year before my divorce, I got drunk at a police officer's banquet in Tuscaloosa." He laughed. "I mean, knee-walking drunk. Went out afterwards on the Strip and did shots at several places. Gallettes, the Booth before it closed down. The Hound's Tooth. After the guys I was with were gone, I stumbled downtown and ended up at this bar that I didn't recognize." He paused. "I went inside and ordered a glass of Jack Daniel's Black over ice. This fella sat down beside me and struck up a conversation. I don't remember much about it, other than my software started acting like hardware again." Law sighed. "I spent that night in Tuscaloosa and, after that, I began going to that same bar once a month. I could tell my wife knew something was up, but I couldn't stop." He spat on the ground and wiped his mouth with the back of his hand. "One night, as I was leaving a motel in Northport, I saw a huge black man leaning against my truck."

"Rel," Rick said.

"Right," Law said. "My wife had sicked him on me. He told me that he knew what I was doing, and that he figured it would be hard to hold the sheriff's spot if the county found out I was a homosexual and cheating on my wife with a man. I asked him what he wanted and he said two things. That I tell my wife, Kathy, that I was having an affair; he didn't care whether I told her it was with a man just so long as she knew I was cheating. And that I give him fifteen thousand dollars for his silence."

Rick felt sick to his stomach. He had grown to admire Rel Jennings in the year that he'd known him. Blackmailing the sheriff didn't seem to be consistent with the man he thought he had known. "Did you do it?"

"Hell yeah," Law said. "I did both in a New York minute." He spat on the ground. "Kathy filed for divorce a month later, which turned out to be a blessing for us both. She remarried a pediatrician in Cullman, and four years after we split I moved here. I live in one of the Gameday condos across the street from Momma Goldberg's, and I practice my other vice discreetly." He paused. "And Rel never said a word. He blackmailed my ass, but he kept his promise. He could have gone straight back to Kathy and blown the whole thing up. But he didn't. Even though I had to pay him, I always thought he'd done me right."

Rick kicked at the sidewalk and walked a few paces away. Law had done a lot of talking, and Rick still didn't have the first clue why the former sheriff had called him. What he had been told was shocking, but not very helpful. He was growing impatient. "Law, why was Rel dogging you these past few months? What was it that he wanted from you, and why did you call me down here? Surely it wasn't to tell me that you're gay and that you had an affair that Rel had outed."

Law Snow's face shined red in the glow from the half-moon above, and Rick knew he'd angered the man. *Good,* he thought. *It's time to quit messing around.*

"Rel knew I had an arrangement with Bully, and he figured I had to know something about Bully's Filipino enforcer."

Rick felt his stomach flutter. *Finally, we're getting somewhere.* "What did he think you knew?"

Law took a step closer to Rick. "He figured I'd seen the two of them together."

Rick tried to keep his breathing steady. "Had you?"

Law nodded. "Of course. Many times in fact." He spat on the grass. "At that cabin I was telling you about, I saw Manny Reyes torture two meth dealers who had double-crossed Bully. She's a hell of a sniper, but the wiry bitch can fight with her hands too. She had both of those bastards crying and begging for a bullet in the head."

Rick's eyes widened. "Are you sure it was Manny Reyes?"

"Five foot three inches tall. A shade over a hundred pounds. Light-brown skin, black hair, and piercing eyes. Speaks fluent Filipino, English, and Spanish."

Rick pulled the lone photograph they had of Manny, taken from the security camera of the Pink Pony Pub, in Gulf Shores, when she'd tried to kill Bocephus Haynes last year. In the photograph, Manny wore a yellow sundress and white baseball cap. "Who is this?" Rick asked, extending the picture.

Law snatched it from his hand and nodded. "Why, that's our girl. Mahalia Blessica Reyes. Hails from Manila in the Philippines. Called Manny by Bully Calhoun in an ode to the great Filipino boxer Manny 'Pacman' Pacquiao."

"How do you know all of this about her?"

Law took another step closer and squinted at Rick. "Lest you forget, boy, I was the sheriff of Walker County for thirty years. I made it my business to know the most dangerous person in town."

"Did you ever see Bully pay Manny Reyes money?"

"Yes," Law said without hesitation.

Rick took in a deep breath. Law had seen money exchange hands, and he'd seen Manny torture two meth dealers at Bully's direction. *If he'll testify to that on the witness stand in Florence, we'll win,* Rick thought, feeling wild exhilaration building within him.

"Law, will you testify to what you just told me on the stand?"

"No, I won't, son."

Rick felt like he'd just been sucker punched in the stomach. "But . . ." Rick couldn't think of anything else to say.

"If I testify that I, as the sheriff of Walker County, Alabama, willingly stood by and watched Manny Reyes torture two drug dealers, who I was knowingly allowing to sell methamphetamine right under my nose to Bully Calhoun, they'll burn me at the stake." He spat. "You think I've lost my mind?"

"So this is all a tease?" Rick asked, his exasperation palpable. "You teased Rel for six months and now, right in the middle of the damn trial, you lured me down here to Auburn only to snatch the treat away?"

"Rel didn't care whether I testified in your trial."

"Bullshit," Rick said. "He was my investigator and he was pursuing an angle here in Auburn. He was chasing information from you that he knew you had to have, and you just gave it to me. Did you ever tell Rel what you just told me about *witnessing* Bully Calhoun paying Manny Reyes to torture someone?"

Law shook his head. "No, I didn't."

"So he never got it from you, but since he's dead you felt guilty enough to invite me down here to the Plains so you could tell me. But then in the next breath you say that you don't have the balls to testify. Is that it, *Law*?" Rick spat the name at him and got within an inch of his face. "Go fuck yourself, *Law*. My partner is dying in Huntsville. My best friend may die in Tuscaloosa. Rel Jennings was shot and killed ten days ago. My friend Bocephus Haynes's wife was gunned down by a sniper ten days ago too." Rick paused to catch at his breath. "All of these deaths or shootings have come at the hands of Manny Reyes or JimBone Wheeler, and you have information that may bring Manny to justice and you're just going to sit on it."

Law kept his mouth shut and his eyes on Rick.

"Say something."

"OK," Law said. "I will. Rel Jennings didn't want me to testify in your case."

Rick wrinkled up his face. "*What?* Why else would he be coming down here?"

A tight smile played on Law's face. "Rel was interested in something more than just winning Alvie's case. He wanted to find Manny Reyes."

Rick flung his hands up in the air and walked away. "Well, so do I. But she's a trained killer and she's been just a little bit difficult to find."

"I know where she is."

The words made the hairs on both of Rick's arms stand on end. "*What?*"

"At least . . . I think I know."

Rick cocked his head at the former sheriff, waiting.

"Remember my cabin? When I told Bully I was going to retire as sheriff, he said he didn't want to lose his safe house for meth deals."

Rick felt a tickle in his brain as the pieces of the puzzle began to fit in their proper places. "So what did you do?"

"I sold it."

"To who?" But Rick thought he already knew.

"Who else? The man who took my place," Law said, spitting tobacco juice on the grass. His mouth curved into a grin, but his eyes remained cold as ice. "Mr. DeWayne Patterson, the high sheriff of Walker County, Alabama."

64

It was all Rick could do not to run back to Law's car, but he forced himself to walk alongside the older man. "Where's the cabin?" Rick asked.

"It's along the Flint River in Maysville, Alabama."

"Where is that?"

"About five miles east of Huntsville. Bully liked the location because it was between Jasper, where he lived, and Sand Mountain, where his primary distributors were."

"Why didn't you say something sooner?"

"Because I didn't want to expose myself. Bully obviously knew that I knew about the cabin. Hell, it was mine."

"Why not say something after Bully was killed?"

"I really wasn't sure Manny would be there. It seemed like a long shot, and I didn't want to open myself up to any kind of investigation of my time as sheriff."

"Why now then?"

Law sighed as they reached his pickup truck. "Because even though the bastard blackmailed me, Rel Jennings was otherwise honest and fair. He came here five times asking for information about Manny Reyes, but he never threatened to tell anyone about my . . . orientation even though I knew he was desperate to find his brother's killer."

"Don't make him out to be a saint," Rick snapped. "You weren't the sheriff anymore. You basically said yourself that no one here cares who you sleep with."

Law shrugged in reluctant agreement.

"Why now, Law?"

"Because of the fugitive," Law finally said, piercing Rick with his gray eyes. "Wheeler would need a safe place to stay if he wasn't fleeing the country. And based on the shootings I've heard about on the news, he appears to be sticking around."

"So you think your old cabin is where they are."

"It's the perfect setup. Central to every place they've hit. Two and a half hours from Tuscaloosa. Two hours from Jasper. Fifteen minutes from downtown Huntsville."

As they climbed in the truck, Rick nodded his agreement, feeling a jolt of adrenaline and fear shoot through his veins. "You really think that's where they are?"

"I'd bet a gold nickel on it," Law said, cranking the ignition.

"Then that would make Sheriff Patterson an accomplice to multiple felonies."

"Yes, it would."

The truck lunged forward onto Magnolia Avenue. "That seems hard to believe."

Lawson Snow laughed. "Not to me."

65

Fifteen minutes later, Rick Drake was on I-85 headed toward Montgomery. When he hit the state capital, he'd take Highway 82 to Tuscaloosa. Though his heart yearned to see his mother and Henshaw was on the way, he knew it was too late and he didn't have time. He needed to see Powell.

He looked at the time on the dash. It was almost midnight. His conversation with Lawson Snow, counting dinner at Momma Goldberg's, had taken almost two hours.

Then he gazed at the folded sheet of paper he'd placed in the passenger seat. Law had given it to him when he'd dropped Rick off at Toomer's Corner. "The address for the cabin," Law said.

"Thank you," Rick said, shaking the man's hand.

"Don't get yourself killed, kid," Law said, and then he pulled away before Rick could answer.

Now, as Rick passed a green sign saying "Montgomery. 30 MILES," he picked up his cell phone and set the piece of paper in his lap, unfolding it so that he could read the listing.

If these were normal times, he'd call Powell or Wade with this news. Powell was a district attorney and Wade was a homicide detective. Either of them could have made some calls and gotten some officers out to DeWayne Patterson's place on the Flint River.

But these aren't normal times. Wade was dead, and Powell was in critical condition at Druid City Hospital. Thinking it through, Rick knew he only had one choice.

And it's probably the best option of all of them. Keeping one eye on the road and the other on his phone, he thumbed through his contacts until he found the number. He looked at the dash. 12:00 a.m. on the dot. Rick clicked on the name that lit up his screen.

His call was answered on the first ring.

"Please tell me you have some good news." The voice was sharp, alert, and on edge.

"General, are you OK? What—?"

Rick heard several short breaths and then Helen Lewis's voice crackled through again. "You don't know?"

"Know what?"

"Tom's grandson, Jackson, was kidnapped tonight at Tommy and Nancy McMurtrie's home in Huntsville. Two of the three security officers guarding the house were shot and killed and the other one died in the fire."

"The fire?"

"Yeah," Helen said. "The bastards burned the house too."

"Oh my God," Rick said, envisioning thirteen-year-old Jackson McMurtrie in his mind.

"Where the hell are you?" Helen asked.

"I've been in Auburn, General. Chasing a lead."

For several seconds, there was silence. Then, in a calmer tone, General Lewis asked, "Well, you called me, Drake. Whatcha got?"

"I know where they are," Rick said. "Wheeler, Manny, Jackson. All of them." He glanced down at the sheet of paper Lawson Snow had given him and read the address to the General. Then, for the next five minutes, he summarized his conversation with the former sheriff of Walker County in the shadow of Jordan-Hare Stadium.

"It's ingenious," Helen finally said after several seconds of silence.

"It's more than that," Rick said, remembering how Law had described the cabin. "It's perfect."

66

When Rick reached the turnoff for Highway 82, he hesitated, but he didn't turn his blinker on. Powell would understand, he knew. *He'd do the same thing,* Rick thought. *Finding the Professor's grandson is the priority now.* Rick doubted he'd get back to Huntsville in time for the raid of the cabin, but he wanted to be there as soon as he could.

Despite the late hour, he decided to call Sandra Conrad to let her know his plans had changed.

Unlike with the General, this time the phone rang seven times before it was answered. Rick was about to hang up when the call was finally picked up.

"Hey, brother." The voice was so weak that Rick could barely hear it.

"Powell?"

"Momma's asleep. So was I, but her damn ringtone is so loud it woke me up."

"Sorry," Rick said. "It's good to hear your voice, man. I thought . . ." Rick's voice began to shake, and the fatigue and emotion took over.

"I know," Powell said. "But I'm on the other side now. They've upgraded me to fair and I should be in a room tomorrow. I'm going to make it."

"Your mom said you needed to see me."

"Yeah," Powell said, and the volume of his voice, if Rick wasn't mistaken, had risen ever so slightly. "Before I was shot, I remember seeing a cop car coming down Eighth Avenue. I figured it was a police escort."

"Makes sense that Wade would line that up."

"It does, but he didn't." Powell coughed, and Rick held the phone away from his ear until the fit ended. "After I was shot, I crawled across the porch and tried to talk to Wade before he died."

Rick again felt heat behind his eyes and could hear the anguish in his friend's weak voice. "What did he say?"

"A lot, but my ears were ringing so bad all I caught were his last two words."

"What were they?"

"Mama tried."

Rick gripped the wheel and thought of his friend Wade Richey, who'd saved his life outside the Boathouse Oyster Bar, in Destin, Florida, during the investigation of Bo's case two years earlier. "Fitting," he managed.

Powell grunted. "I couldn't hear him say anything else, but Wade wrote something in blood on the porch before he died. My brain's been a little scrambled since I've been at the hospital, but earlier this morning I remembered the message."

Rick shivered at the image of the old detective writing something in his own blood just before death took him. "What, Powell?"

"*W . . . C . . . S . . . O.*"

"What?"

"*W . . . C . . . S . . . O*," Powell repeated. "Do you get it?" The question was snapped out in Powell's ultraintense tone, and Rick squeezed the wheel again as the last piece to the puzzle slid into its slot.

"Walker County Sheriff's Office," Rick said, snapping his fingers and knowing Lawson Snow's golden nickel was safe.

"Powell, have you told anyone?"

Coughing on the other end of the line before Powell's voice blared through, seemingly growing stronger with each word. "I told our sheriff about three hours ago."

"And?"

"And he's about to unleash the hounds of hell on DeWayne Patterson."

67

JimBone Wheeler knew something was wrong the second he saw the sheriff's Tahoe pulling up the driveway. It was just past midnight, and JimBone was sitting in the living area that faced the road, thinking through the last piece of his plan to balance the scales, once and for all, with Tom McMurtrie. The kidnapping of the old man's grandson couldn't have gone any better. He now had the bait that would draw them out.

"Manny, is the kid still out?" he asked.

From the back of the cabin, Manny yelled, "Yeah. That Dilaudid shot ought to keep him down for four or five hours." Her tone changed as she entered the small sitting room. "What is he doing here?" she asked, her voice a combination of irritation and surprise.

They watched as the sheriff parked out front and hopped out of the truck, walking toward the house with a lean. He appeared to have something on his face, but JimBone couldn't make it out. Manny got to the door just as DeWayne was about to knock.

"Sheriff," she said, ushering him in with her right hand, "is that a nose guard you're wearing?"

"Where is he?" DeWayne asked, ignoring her question and adjusting the splinted contraption that covered his face. The panic in the man's voice was obvious.

"I'm right here, DeWayne," JimBone said, forming a tent with his hands and swaying back and forth in the rocking chair. He peered at the lawman for a few seconds and then focused his eyes on the window. "You're not supposed to be here."

"I know."

"Then why are you? And why do you look like someone beat the hell out of you?"

DeWayne swallowed. From a foot away, the sheriff's breath and clothes smelled sour, and JimBone wondered how many times DeWayne had vomited and pissed his britches so far that day. "Kathryn Calhoun Willistone broke my nose," DeWayne said, his voice haggard. "She was"—he sighed—"pretty upset that you veered off script and didn't kill Drake and Twitty."

JimBone smirked. "I told you to give her my reasoning."

"I did, but not before she lost her temper," DeWayne said, pointing at the fiberglass contraption that covered his face.

JimBone finally returned his gaze to the sheriff, whose face was a pasty pale underneath the nose guard. "Looks like Kat inherited her father's lack of patience." Then he leaned forward in the rocker. "Why the hell are you here, DeWayne?"

The sheriff sucked in a quick breath. "Because that prosecutor . . . Conrad . . ."

"What about him?"

"He woke up. You shot him four times, but the stubborn fool is still alive."

JimBone shrugged. "So what? So he's alive. I doubt he's going to be turning any cartwheels soon."

"He remembers seeing our police car."

"That's bullshit and you know it." JimBone scowled up at the lawman. "Your cruisers look almost identical to the ones in Tuscaloosa. There's no way." JimBone licked his lips. "Besides, Conrad had his back to us when he walked up the detective's driveway, and he was behind Richey when the bullets started flying."

DeWayne Patterson took a step closer and squatted so that he was eye to eye with JimBone. "It wasn't Conrad who saw. The detective was looking right at us when you shot him." DeWayne exhaled, and the pungent odor of bile wafted into JimBone's nostrils, causing the killer's eyes to water. "He wrote Conrad a message in his own blood before he died."

JimBone's head flew back and he howled in laughter. "That's the most ridiculous thing I've ever heard."

"*W . . . C . . . S . . . O.*"

JimBone squinted at him. "Stop talking in tongues, boy. What are you saying?" But JimBone finally believed he understood. *That tough son of a bitch,* he thought, remembering the dead detective's uncanny resemblance to Sam Elliott.

"Those are the letters on the squad car," DeWayne said, leaning closer. Now the smell of vomit and urine was too much for JimBone to bear. "They stand for—"

JimBone grabbed the sheriff by the throat.

"It . . . wasn't . . . my . . . fault," the sheriff said, speaking with great effort as his throat constricted.

JimBone released his grip and the sheriff fell to the floor, sprawling over on his back and gasping for breath. When he had gathered himself enough to sit up, he gazed at JimBone with terrified eyes.

"How did you learn all of this?" JimBone asked, looking down on DeWayne with disdain. "If true, I would have figured that the police in Tuscaloosa would have wanted to be stealthy about it and not mention anything until they could talk with you." He paused. "And there are a lot of deputies in your department, DeWayne, with the identical cruiser that you drive. If they did come, it seems like you could have deflected them by saying you would investigate the matter yourself."

DeWayne blinked up at him. "I have a mole over in the Tuscaloosa County Sheriff's Office. He called me about three hours ago saying that Sheriff Crowe was headed my way with a posse of patrol cars." He sighed and shook his head. "And my guys were already getting suspicious of me after the shooting on the square last week. That crazy Mexican didn't kill anyone in the basement because Rel Jennings showed up and redirected Drake. But the bastard fired a couple shots at the exit door before the attorney passed through it." DeWayne rubbed his neck, which was red and raw from JimBone choking him. "Let's just say my second-in-command, Roger Hillis, thought it was weird that I would direct Drake and the Jennings family to an exit where someone fired a gun seconds after they should have left the building." He paused and ran a hand over the splint covering his face. "And my broken nose has only cast further doubt on me."

JimBone glared at the weak man. He'd always known that the sheriff's safe house here on the banks of the Flint River, which was less than twenty miles from Tom McMurtrie's farm in Hazel Green, was too good to be true. "So you ran?" JimBone asked.

DeWayne gazed at the hardwood floor. "I didn't think I had a choice, and I wanted to warn you in case someone made the connection about the cabin."

"Bullshit," JimBone said, standing from the rocker and hovering over the other man. "You panicked, DeWayne. You should've stayed put and faced the fire. If you've followed my instructions, there should be nothing that anyone could have on you that would directly link you to me."

"You're staying at my cabin."

JimBone smiled. "It was Lawson Snow's place before yours, and Manny already had a key. You could have talked your way around that and blamed the whole thing on your predecessor." He paused. "If you had one brain cell."

"I had no choice," DeWayne whined.

"Neither do I," JimBone said, reaching down and grabbing the small man and pulling him up by the crotch.

The sheriff squealed in pain and, when JimBone let go, he felt moisture on his fingers. "Do you just have a continual stream of piss flowing down your leg?"

DeWayne didn't answer. "I made a recording," he finally blurted. "The other night, when I spoke with Kat. She was so riled that you didn't kill the people you were supposed to kill." The sheriff paused and reached into his pocket, bringing out a thumb drive. "Here, take a listen. I've got another copy of it saved in a safe place."

JimBone grinned at the lawman, rolling the USB drive between his thumb and index finger but not saying anything.

"I left a note for Sergeant Morris to give to Roger Hillis if I ever turn up dead. It has instructions on where to find the tape." He licked his lips, and JimBone could hear the man's heart thudding.

He's throwing the Hail Mary, JimBone thought, and for just a half of a second, he had a begrudging admiration for DeWayne Patterson. *Dumb as a rock, but not a quitter.*

"So . . . ," JimBone began, pacing the floor of the small parlor. "I guess you've got us over a barrel, DeWayne. We can't rightly kill you and risk our whole plan being blown up."

"Costing us the other half million," Manny chimed in from the foyer. She had remained at the door since the sheriff arrived.

"Exactly," JimBone said, nodding at the woman. "So what do you suggest, DeWayne?"

The sheriff blinked.

"Now that you've flown the coop and left a tape implicating all of us in a bunch of murders, what's next?" JimBone gritted his teeth. "What if the Tuscaloosa County sheriff gets a search warrant for your house and all the property you own and finds this tape you're talking about? Then what?" JimBone snickered. "We all going to share the same cell on death row?"

"I'm not an idiot," DeWayne said, peering up at JimBone with bloodshot eyes. "They won't be able to find the tape with any search warrant."

JimBone's grin widened. "On the contrary, DeWayne. You *are* an idiot. You wouldn't have come racing here in the middle of the night if you weren't a moron." He paused and lowered his voice to just above a whisper. "You think that little recording gives you some leverage against me?"

DeWayne Patterson placed his face in his hands. Seconds later, he began to cry.

JimBone gazed across the parlor to Manny. "Get the kid."

She nodded and the sheriff removed his hands from his face. "What—?"

But he never finished the question as the toe of JimBone Wheeler's size-twelve boot crashed into his nose guard, splattering fiberglass all over the floor of the cabin.

68

At 1:00 a.m., five police vehicles gathered at a gas station two miles from the cabin. All of the cars were from the Madison County Sheriff's Office save one—an unmarked black Crown Victoria with Tennessee plates. Inside the lone outlier, General Helen Lewis sipped coffee from a Styrofoam cup. *Not much stealth about this*, she thought.

Above her, she could hear the rotor blades of a helicopter, and then a voice came through the control speaker in the middle of the dashboard. "Only car at the cabin is a Chevy Tahoe with Walker County plates and 'Walker County Sheriff's Office' written on the sides."

"Patterson," Helen said to herself.

"The lights are off and I don't see any movement," the same voice from the radio added.

Several seconds passed and another officer blared, "Ten-four, Steve. Thank you." Then, five seconds later, "It's go time, folks."

The vehicles pulled out of the gas station, and a mile later the convoy turned right onto County Road 22. Helen grabbed the receiver on her dash and spoke into it. "Do y'all have the river blocked?"

"Affirmative, General Lewis," Steve responded. "A patrol boat is anchored a quarter mile from Patterson's dock and I have the chopper. We'll have the place surrounded by land, air, and water."

Helen sucked in a deep breath as she saw the cabin through the leafless trees. "Please, God, let him be alive," she whispered, thinking about Tom's grandson. When she had come to the farm to tell him the news about Wheeler's escape, Tom had been talking with Jackson on the back porch. *He adores that boy,* Helen thought. No one had told Tom yet about the kidnapping, thinking the stress would be too much, but since learning the location of the cabin from Rick, Helen had been in constant contact with Tommy and Nancy McMurtrie.

"Please let him be alive," the General repeated, her voice rising in the closed confines of the Crown Vic as she followed the SWAT team up the gravel driveway that led to the cabin. *Please.*

69

Helen kept her eyes peeled on the front door of the cabin as the uniformed officers surrounded the structure. Two seconds later, one of the members of the team kicked in the front door while another man slid through a window on the side of the house after jimmying the lock.

Helen opened her door and pulled her weapon. Then she walked toward the house, darting her eyes in all directions and looking for any suspicious movement.

She reached the foot of the steps as lights began popping on inside.

"Oh God!" an officer's voice rang out, and Helen felt her heart catch.

Please, God, don't let the boy be hurt, she prayed again.

Helen trotted up the stairs and slid through the kicked-in door. As she entered the foyer, she saw two rocking chairs in a small parlor to the right. Continuing forward, she passed through a wide opening into a large den, seeing a fireplace and flat-screen television mounted over it. To her left, stairs led to what must have been a loft. To the right was a wet bar with glass cabinets containing various bottles of liquor. The room had tall ceilings and two wooden beams that ran along the middle from the east wall to the west wall for support. Seeing that the SWAT team were all gazing upward, Helen did the same.

Her breath caught in her throat when she saw him. DeWayne Patterson's naked body swung from one of the beams. A noose covered the lawman's neck, and blood ran from his groin down both legs. Helen averted her eyes as she felt her stomach begin to lurch.

Swallowing, Helen gritted her teeth and forced herself to remain under control. She peered at one of the officers. "Did you find the kid?"

He shook his head.

"Anything? Any clues?"

The officer pointed to the coffee table below where DeWayne Patterson's body hung. Helen walked over to it and came to an abrupt stop when she saw the piece of paper. There was something bloody on top of it. "Is that what I think it is?" She glanced at the officer she'd been speaking to seconds earlier, and he nodded.

"Hung his ass and cut his dick off," the man said, walking past her to the table.

"What does the note say?" she asked.

"It's just two words." The deputy frowned and shook his head. "Written in blood."

"What does it say?" she asked, moving her fatigued eyes around the room and looking at each of the officers, whose weapons were all lowered in defeat.

"See for yourself," the officer said, stepping away so that Helen could approach.

She did, and her breath caught in her throat as she read the words aloud.

"Too late."

70

When she was back inside the Crown Vic, Helen's cell phone rang. She glanced at the screen but didn't recognize the number. After waiting for it to ring three times, she clicked the "Answer" button. "This is General Lewis," she said.

"Hello, General. What did you think of the message I left inside the cabin? Did I go too far?"

Helen set her jaw and squeezed the phone tight to her ear. "How did you get this number, Mr. Wheeler?"

"I have my sources," JimBone said. "As you just found out. When your inside man is the sheriff of a county, you have a wide range of access."

"Well, aren't you smart."

"You know that I am."

"What do you want?"

A chortle on the other end of the line. "I like a woman who gets right to it. I bet you would be tough to handle, General. Speaking of, have you and McMurtrie knocked boots yet?"

"Did you want something from me, or did you just call to gloat?"

Silence on the other end of the line, and Helen cursed her lack of subtlety. Finally, the killer's voice, now lower, came through the speaker. "Don't you want to know if the kid is alive or dead?"

Helen closed her eyes and felt her heart rate accelerate into overdrive. "Yes," she said.

More silence.

After a few seconds that felt like an eternity, Helen cleared her throat and spoke into the phone. "Mr. Wheeler, where is the boy? Where is Jackson McMurtrie?" Helen paused. "Is he safe?"

Again, there was no answer, and Helen began to worry that the bastard wasn't going to say any more.

"Mr. Wheeler?" Helen pressed. "Is the boy—?"

"Listen very carefully, General," JimBone interrupted, his voice sharp and matter-of-fact. "I'm only going to deliver this message once, and only to you. If you interrupt me while I'm talking, the boy dies." He paused. "If any part of these instructions is not followed, the boy dies." He again hesitated. "Do you understand?"

"Yes," Helen said, feeling cold sweat on her forehead. She squeezed her hands and noticed they were clammy. She had never been this nervous in her life.

"Good," JimBone said. Then for the next thirty seconds he gave his instructions.

When she clicked off the phone, Helen's entire body was covered in sweat and her hands shook so badly that she had to grip the wheel tightly. She didn't need to write his instructions down due to their chilling brevity.

Simple.

Clear.

And impossible to follow.

In the cab of the Crown Vic, Helen Evangeline Lewis slammed an open palm on the dashboard. *He's going to die,* she thought.

The boy is going to die.

71

Bocephus Haynes sat on the damp grass in front of the headstone. His shotgun rested in his lap, and every so often he checked the weapon to make sure it was loaded. Then he would point it at the name on the grave marker. Grabbing the gun for at least the tenth time since he'd arrived, he again aimed it at the engraved name of a man he had hated his whole life. A man who had once been the imperial wizard of the Ku Klux Klan.

A man who Bo had found out two years ago was his father.

"Andrew Davis Walton." Bo spat the words out loud. Then, tired of playing this charade, he stood and fired the gun. Once, twice, three times. The concrete edifice broke apart in the middle, and the top of the shattered headstone crumbled over the bottom. "How do you like that . . . *Daddy*?" Still gripping tight to the twelve-gauge, he leaned down and retrieved a half-empty bottle of Pappy Van Winkle bourbon. A few years back, a client had rewarded him for winning a case by sending him the fifth, which supposedly was the most expensive bourbon in the world. Bo glared at the brown liquid inside the bottle and took another long pull. The alcohol burned his throat as he swallowed, but it didn't burn near as bad as the one emotion that scalded him inside and out.

Hate.

Hate for the law, which had kept him in a jail cell for ten days when he should have been with T. J. and Lila. The law, which Ezra Henderson was hiding behind to prevent Bo from seeing his children. Bo hadn't been home last night for more than five minutes before a social worker from the Department of Human Resources was knocking on the door. Before he'd be allowed to see his children, he would need to sit for an interview and be evaluated. "Is now a good time to answer some questions?" she had asked.

"No," Bo had said, storming out of the house. He had driven the streets of Huntsville all night before he'd finally ended up at the funeral home early this morning. He'd shown his identification and they'd taken him to the body. Ezra may have banned him from the funeral, but he hadn't told the director Bo couldn't see his wife's body.

For at least an hour, he had stared at her lifeless, cold corpse. After the refrigeration and embalming, the mannequin inside the coffin, while resembling Jazz, simply wasn't her. Jazz was gone. Dead. Taken by an assassin's bullet.

He'd gazed at his wife's body and thought back to when he was a boy. When he'd watched the men wearing the hoods and robes lynch the man who, for forty-five years, Bo thought was his father.

And he'd felt the hate burn within him.

Hate for mankind. For the weakness, the evil, and the utter wretchedness of the human race. Humans had killed Roosevelt Haynes. Another human had murdered his mother. And now, within the past four days, two deranged psychopaths had killed his wife and his good friends Rel Jennings and Wade Richey.

Not to mention Alvie last year, Bo thought, glaring at the ruined headstone of his biological father. In the winter of 1960, Andy Walton had engaged in an extramarital affair with Pearl Haynes, and Bo had been the product of their illicit relationship. Andy's wife, the diabolical Maggie Walton, eventually found out and took her revenge by killing Bo's mother and eventually Andy himself. She would have gotten Bo, too, if not for Professor Tom McMurtrie and General Helen Lewis.

Bo had found a lifeline to sanity when he'd met the Professor in college and a short time later had fallen in love with the former Jasmine Henderson. His love for the two of them was like cold water on a raging fire.

But now Jazz was dead. The Professor was dying. *And Ezra is right. My own kids are better off without me.*

Hate.

Hate for the law. Hate for mankind. And most of all . . .

He gritted his teeth and held the bottle of bourbon to his lips.

Hate for himself.

I hate you, Jazz had told him right before she was shot and killed.

"*I hate you,*" Bo now whispered out loud.

His thoughts flickered with another image of Jazz's corpse, and his heart burned with hate so hot that he had to hold in a scream. He'd left the funeral home on autopilot and driven to his rental house on Holmes. He'd put the bloody shirt and jeans back on and sat in the kitchen of his empty dwelling until the sun went down. Then he'd gotten back in his vehicle. An hour and forty minutes later, he'd been at Maplewood Cemetery in Pulaski.

Sitting at the grave of his father.

Bo took a deep breath and one last sip of bourbon. Then, eyeing the bottle, he poured the alcohol on his head and doused his jeans and shirt with it. When the container was empty, he hurled it at what was left of the headstone, and shattered glass joined broken concrete on the grass below. Bo smirked at the ruined grave marker and pulled a lighter out of his pocket. He took two long strides toward his father's final resting place. *This is where it should end,* he thought. *I should go up in flames with Andy Walton's corpse.*

He flicked on the lighter and then he turned it off. On. Off. On. Off. On . . .

Closing his eyes, Bo began to count, holding on to the images of the people in his life he loved.

"Five." T. J. shooting a basketball from the top of the key and winking at Bo as he ran back down the court.

"Four," Lila, the spitting image of her mother, crawling into his lap on Christmas Eve and asking Bo to read "'Twas the Night Before Christmas" one more time.

"Three." Roosevelt Haynes, the only man he'd ever known as a father, playing catch with five-year-old Bo in in the yard outside the shack they called a home while his mother watched, sitting in a chair in the shade of a cherry tree and peeling green beans.

"Two." Professor Tom McMurtrie hugging Bo on Christmas Day almost a year ago and telling Bo that he loved him.

Tears rolled down Bo's cheeks, and he felt the sting of the flame on his thumbs.

"One." Jazz. In her dorm room in college. Leading Bo to her bedroom the first time they made love.

Bocephus Aurulius Haynes opened his eyes and looked to the heavens above. He let out a scream that began in the pit of his stomach and eventually roared out of his mouth.

Then he glared at the bright-orange fire coming from the portable device. His heartbeat was racing as he moved the lighter closer to his body. Closer . . .

. . . closer.

Tears streamed down his face and he bit down hard on his lip. "*I hate you,*" he cried. Then finally . . .

. . . he released his thumb from the spark wheel, and the flame went out.

For several seconds, Bo stood in front of his father's grave, gazing at the unsparked lighter that just moments earlier might have ended his life. His hands and legs were shaking with equal parts adrenaline and fear. Sucking in a breath, he thought he might vomit. His legs eventually gave out and he dropped to his knees. Squinting at the lighter, he flung the device as far as he could across the cemetery.

Then, as he again felt a wave of nausea, a familiar voice rang out in the darkness.

"Thought I might find you here."

Bo turned his head and saw a silhouetted figure standing ten yards away. "General?"

"You ought to be ashamed of yourself," Helen snapped.

Bo hung his head but didn't say anything.

"Are you really a quitter? You're Tom's best friend. He was your *mentor*, right? What would he think of this?"

"He knows what I've been through."

"And you think he'd be OK with you tucking your tail between your legs and quitting?"

"That's enough, General. Don't talk about things you know nothing about."

"Here's what I know. You didn't post bond on two bullshit criminal charges, so I was forced to do it. And now, when everyone that loves you needs you the most, you're out here getting drunk and drowning your sorrows." She put her hands on her hips and leaned her head toward him. "That about sum it up?"

Not entirely, Bo thought, shivering as he remembered how close he'd brought the flame of the lighter to his alcohol-soaked body. He climbed to his feet, breathing in the bourbon that covered his clothes and skin. "If you're here to arrest me, let's get on with it," Bo said, creasing his eyebrows at her. "I don't want or need a sermon from you." He tried to walk past her, but she stepped in front of him and blocked his path.

"Well, you're in luck, because I don't have time to give you one," Helen said. "And although I should arrest you, I can't fool with that either." She glared at him. "Something's happened . . . and I need your help."

Bo felt another dagger of hate penetrate his chest. "JimBone?"

Helen nodded.

"Did he kill someone else?" Bo asked, gazing down at the grass. "Is it the Professor?" he whispered.

"Tom is alive, but Wheeler did attack tonight," Helen said.

"What happ—?"

"I need you to come with me," Helen interrupted, and the anguish in her voice was now palpable. Her hands were shaking. "Please . . . we must go now."

Bo rubbed his face with his hands, trying to snap out of the drunken rage that had engulfed him. "OK," he said, taking a couple of steps closer to her and gazing into her piercing green eyes. "What do you need me to do?"

Helen bit her lip, and when she spoke again, her voice trembled with fear. "I need you to deliver a message."

72

In his dark room on the fourth floor of Huntsville Hospital, Tom drifted in and out of consciousness. *Something is wrong,* he thought in his rare moments of lucidity before the morphine took him again. He'd seen it in his son's eyes last night. Or was it this morning? Tom had lost track of time, but Tommy's face had been tight and strained. Even doped up on as much pain medication as he was on, Tom could tell that his boy was worried sick and it went beyond worry over Tom. Tom had asked his boy at least twice what was bothering him, but Tommy hadn't replied.

When was that? Tom wondered, trying to remember the last time he'd had a visitor. Over the course of the past few days, it seemed like folks dropped by at least every four to six hours, but it had been longer than that since he'd seen anyone.

Tom envisioned JimBone Wheeler's copper eyes and felt a shiver despite the warm blankets that were piled on top of him. *Has he killed someone else?*

Tom picked up his cell phone and gazed at it. It was four in the morning. He tried to think when he'd had his last conversation with

Tommy. As the thoughts scrambled his brain, he closed his eyes. Seconds later, he was asleep again.

When Tom woke, the room seemed even darker than before. He blinked and realized he was still holding his cell phone. He clicked on it, and the time was now 8:00 a.m. *Four more hours,* he thought. Usually he would have been awakened by a visitor or a nurse checking on him by now.

Tom swallowed and felt something catch in his throat. He rolled to make it easier to cough, but his body still shook with pain as the fit began. He squeezed his eyes tight and prayed that it would be a quick one. It was. After about four hard coughs, his airway relaxed. He opened his eyes and saw a Styrofoam cup being held in front of him.

Tom nodded, and the cup was pressed to his lips. He drank in a tiny sip and then another. The liquid burned going down, but he knew he needed it. As he sucked in a breath of air, Tom smelled a strange odor permeating the room. The scent was out of place for a hospital, but his brain was so muddled that he couldn't quite place it.

"Thank you," Tom managed, laying his head back against the pillow. The effort of coughing and taking two sips of water had drained him of the little energy he'd felt when he opened his eyes.

"You're welcome, dog."

Tom turned his head. He'd assumed the person holding the cup was a nurse, but it wasn't. "Bo?" Tom said, his voice almost gurgling. He'd heard one of the doctors say the phrase "fluid on the lungs," and he figured that was why his vocal cords sounded so weird.

"Yeah, Professor. It's me."

With every ounce of energy he could muster, Tom sat up in the bed and gazed at his friend. Bocephus Haynes wore blue jeans with dark stains down the front and a button-down shirt with several red streaks. His eyes were tinged with red, and his beard, which had been stubble the last time Tom saw him, was now thick and almost full. "You look terrible," Tom finally said.

"Thanks," Bo said.

Tom took in a ragged breath. "What's that smell?"

Bo brought his sleeve to his nose and squinted at Tom. "Bourbon."

Tom cocked his head in confusion.

Bo sighed. "It's a long story."

For a moment, the two friends just gazed at each other. Finally, Tom moved his hand toward Bo, who clasped it in his own.

"Bo, I . . . I'm so . . ." As Tom peered at his friend, whose spirit seemed as broken as his body, emotion got the best of him and he was unable to make his voice work.

"I know," Bo said, nodding at Tom. "*I know.*"

Tom couldn't imagine what Bo had been going through since Jazz's murder and found it hard to look at his best friend without tearing up. Tom bit his lip and squeezed Bo's hand. "*I'm so sorry,*" he finally managed.

"Wasn't your fault, Professor," Bo said, his tone matter-of-fact. "It was mine. I couldn't stop her from going, and I didn't do enough to protect her once she was there."

"You did all you could do."

"No, sir," Bo said, his voice now louder. "I didn't. I let pride and jealousy get in the way." He sighed. "And Jazz is dead because of it."

Tom didn't want to argue with his friend. Still, on this point he couldn't let things be. "Jazz . . . is dead because of a deranged psychopath." He stopped and let out a ragged breath. "And if anyone around here should be blaming himself, it's *me*. I'm the reason he's doing all of this. He wanted to bring a reckoning on me, and by God he's done it."

For several seconds, the only sound in the room was the hum of the heater. Finally, Bo stood from the recliner chair he'd been sitting in and approached the bed. "Professor, there's something I need to tell you."

Tom closed his eyes. *Something is wrong,* he knew. *He's killed someone else.* Gritting his teeth, Tom forced his tired lids open. "What?" Tom asked.

Bocephus Haynes blinked. "Tommy told the General that he didn't want you to know. Said he couldn't bear"—Bo paused, and Tom saw that his friend's lip was quivering—"that he couldn't bear having two funerals in such a short period of time."

"Tell me," Tom said, noticing his pulse rate had shot up to 120 beats a minute on the monitor to the right of his friend.

Bo sat on the side of the bed. "Last night, JimBone attacked your son's house. He killed all of the security officers and set the home on fire." When Tom's eyes widened, Bo held out his palms. "Everyone in the family . . . is alive."

Tom struggled to find his voice. "Are any of them hurt?"

Bo's face hardened and he didn't say anything.

"Spit it out, Bo."

"I . . . I don't know if he's . . . hurt, Professor. It's just . . . it doesn't look good." Bo leaned in close and peered at Tom with eyes that radiated intensity. "And if I can't get you to the farm to answer the telephone at ten o'clock this morning, he'll be dead."

"He?" Tom asked, feeling as if the temperature in the room had dropped below zero. His pulse rate was now 140 on the monitor, but Tom paid it no mind. Instead, he focused all of his attention on the eyes of Bocephus Haynes.

"It's Jackson," Bo finally said, grinding his teeth and trying to keep his voice under control. "The bastard's kidnapped your grandson."

73

There is a reserve tank of energy that every person has.

Incidents have been documented where women who weighed barely over a hundred pounds have lifted objects twice their size in order to save small children. It is not something a person can summon at will, but it almost always involves a love so powerful that the men and women who find themselves possessed with this seemingly superhuman strength many times can't remember what they've done. All they know is that a person they loved so deeply it hurt was in danger, and a switch was flicked.

The tank was activated.

And though love is what triggers the button to be pushed, it is not what fuels the tank. No, the energy producer that fills this reserve pump is another emotion.

Rage.

White-hot rage that burns the heart and soul so badly that a person becomes strong.

Stronger than they thought they were capable of being.

At 8:30 a.m. on December 17, 2013, Thomas Jackson McMurtrie checked himself out of Huntsville Hospital. The nurses on the fourth floor begged him to stay, to no avail. Michael Harper, his night shift nurse, who was pulling double duty that day, would remark that it was the first time he'd seen his patient on his feet other than a few brief trips to the restroom, with which Michael had assisted him. But there he was, standing under his own power next to a huge black man and signing the Patient Leaving Against Medical Advice form.

Minutes later, Tom stood on the sidewalk by the pickup circle of the entrance to the hospital on Gallatin Street. According to his phone, the temperature was forty-eight degrees. Tom wore the same fleece sweat suit he'd worn to Clearview Cancer Institute a week and a half before. He knew he should be cold, but he wasn't. His body was on fire.

"Professor McMurtrie?"

Tom turned and saw Dr. Trey Maples step out of the revolving door at the entrance and approach him. The physician's face was red and he walked with a forward lean. He stopped a foot from Tom. "I haven't discharged you, sir."

"I know," Tom said. "I discharged myself."

Trey's eyes widened and he took a step closer. "Professor, you are not hemodynamically stable enough for discharge. You had a fever this morning, your vital signs are still out of whack, and based on the nurse's notes, you haven't been out of the bed all day and haven't done the laps I ordered."

"I know that, Doc, but something's happened and I have to go."

Trey shook his head. "I know what's going on, Professor McMurtrie, OK? I know about your grandson. I advised Tommy not to tell you because I thought something like this might happen."

"Tommy didn't tell me," Tom said as Bo pulled the white Sequoia to a stop in the circle and hopped out of the car to open the passenger-side door. "My friend did," Tom said, hooking his thumb at Bo.

Dr. Maples laid his hands on Tom's shoulders. "Listen to me, sir. I realize how upset you must be, but you're in no condition to leave this hospital. With your vitals, you could literally die any second."

Tom slapped the doctor on the back. "Thanks for everything you've done for me, Doc." He turned and walked toward the car.

"You'll die," Maples said, his voice cold and authoritarian. The voice of a man who had handed out thousands of death sentences to cancer patients over the years.

Tom stopped and glared at him.

"The stress you're about to put yourself through," Maples continued, giving his head a jerk. "You'll die. Do you really want to do that to your son, especially if your grandson . . . ?" His voice faded away without finishing the rest, but Tom knew the gist.

Tom took two long strides toward Maples and gazed into the physician's brown eyes. "You've already told me I'm going to die. You said it could be a month or two. Remember?"

Trey Maples didn't say anything in response.

Tom squinted at the doctor and felt the rage burn within him. "Well, I think it's time we get on with it."

PART FIVE

74

At 9:00 a.m. on Tuesday, December 17, 2013, Kathryn Calhoun Willistone was forty-five minutes into an hour-long session on her Precor machine. The elliptical trainer was one of several cardiovascular machines in the fitness room of the Calhoun mansion. Sweat glistened off Kat's body, and she watched herself in the glass mirror that covered every square inch of the far wall. When her cell phone rang, she sighed and contemplated not answering it. Had the caller been Virgil Flood or one of her other attorneys, she would have let it ring until she finished her workout.

Unfortunately, after glancing at the screen and seeing the name of the caller, she knew she couldn't ignore this one. She clicked the "Answer" button and decided against formality.

"DeWayne, you better have good news for me."

"The sheriff is . . . hanging out for the moment, sweetie." The voice was cold and did not belong to DeWayne Patterson. Kat slowed her pace on the machine so that she could talk without losing her breath.

"Who is this?"

"This is the guy you hired to do that little job for you."

Kat stopped moving and the elliptical slowly came to a halt. "What do you want?"

"I want you to wire the rest of the money to the Caymans within the next two hours." Pause. "And I need an airplane."

Kat felt equal parts fear and anger, and her pulse quickened. *How dare you?* she thought, wondering how her father would have handled this level of disrespect.

"You haven't finished the job," Kat said, stepping off the machine and sitting down on a utility bench.

"I know that, sweetie, but I still need you to wire the money and get me a plane."

"Oh, well in that case . . . *fuck you*." Kat smiled, feeling adrenaline beat through her. She waited for his response, but instead of the killer's voice, she heard her own on the other end of the line.

"Talk, moron."

Kat felt her stomach turn to acid at the sound of her recorded voice, which was followed by Sheriff Patterson's weak retort. "Mr. Wheeler says that everything is fine and that he is going to fulfill his contract."

"He better," Kat's recorded voice responded. "He was supposed to kill Drake and Twitty. Why did he go cowboy and start killing randoms?"

The voices stopped, as the killer must have either paused or turned off the recording.

"Where's DeWayne?" she asked, hearing and hating the dread in her tone.

"DeWayne has gone far away," JimBone said. Then he whistled. "Mrs. Willistone, if you don't wire that money to the account in the Caymans within two hours and have me an airplane waiting at the Madison County Executive Airport in Meridianville in three, I'm going to send this gem of a recording to the *Daily Mountain Eagle*, to the law offices of McMurtrie & Drake, and to the sheriff's departments in Madison, Walker, and Tuscaloosa Counties." He paused. "Do I make myself clear?"

Kat stood and paced the floor of the fitness room. She looked at herself in the mirror and was startled by the terror she saw in her eyes.

"Do I make myself clear?" JimBone repeated.

"Crystal," Kat said.

75

Thirty minutes after leaving the hospital, Bo pulled up the driveway to the Hazel Green farm. Along the way, Tom had called Bill Davis, who was now home in Tuscaloosa after visiting Tom over the weekend.

"Bill, it's Tom."

"Hey, buck. Have they found Jackson yet?"

Tom had closed his eyes. "No. Listen, Bill, I don't have much time or energy to talk, so I need to make this quick."

"Shoot."

"I need you to come to the farm, and I need you to bring all the steroids you can round up."

"Tom, what's this about? Are you out of the hospital?"

"Checked out against medical advice a few minutes ago. I need you to bring the 'roids . . . and any damn thing else that you think will make me feel good until we can find my grandson."

Five seconds of silence. Then Bill was back on. "It'll take me thirty minutes to get the medicine, so I can be there in three hours. That work?"

"I should be good on adrenaline until then."

"Tom, you know the steroids could give you a heart attack."

Tom couldn't help but laugh. "All you damn doctors are the same. You tell me I'm going to die any day from cancer, but then you sound worried about a heart attack. Bring the 'roids, Billy boy."

"They can also make the visions you've been having worse." Bill paused. "A lot worse."

Tom had blinked as the Sequoia sped through Meridianville and into the long loop at Steger's Curve. "I don't care about that. Just bring what you got."

"Ten-four."

"And, Bill." Tom had rubbed his chin, thinking it through, before making his call. "Stop by your shooting range and bring all the guns and ammo at your disposal."

76

At 10:00 a.m., the telephone in the kitchen of the Hazel Green farmhouse began to ring.

Tom met Helen's eye, who snapped at the officers sitting at the island. "Are we ready?"

"Yes, ma'am," one of the men said, hovering his finger over a recording device.

Then Helen nodded at Tom, who strode over to the landline. On the second ring, he answered.

"Hello."

Static on the other end of the line.

"Hello," Tom repeated.

"Remember what I promised you at the prison?"

Tom nodded at Helen, who waved her arms at the officers.

"It's him," she whispered, slipping on a pair of headphones and slinging two other pairs at Rick, Tommy, and Bo, all of whom were seated around the kitchen table. Tommy put his on, and Bo and Rick shared the other one.

"I remember," Tom said.

"Do you think I've delivered yet?"

Tom paused, knowing he needed to keep the maniac talking. "Do you?" Tom asked.

"Not hardly," JimBone fired back. "Have we talked long enough for the people recording the call to know where I am?"

Tom looked at Helen, who raised her eyebrows. Then he peered at the island, where one of the officers whispered, "Thirty more seconds."

Tom cleared his throat and spoke into the receiver. "Where's my grandson?"

Soft laughter on the other end of the line. "I didn't think you'd answer, old man. Aren't you supposed to be dying?"

"It hasn't taken yet," Tom said.

"I'm glad."

"Why?"

"Because I want to be the one that sees you when death knocks on your door. I want to give you the perfect ending."

"Is my grandson alive?"

JimBone sighed. "Good-looking boy. Must take after his mom's side of the family."

"Is Jackson alive?"

"He was a rambunctious young lad."

"If you harm a hair on his head—"

"You'll what? Beat me up? Kill me? You can barely walk."

Tom glanced at the officers with the recording device. "*We've got him,*" the same officer who had wanted an additional thirty seconds whispered.

"Is he alive?" Tom repeated for the third time.

"I think we've talked long enough now, don't you? One last thing. If anyone besides you comes to where I am right now, the boy dies."

The phone clicked dead before Tom could answer, and everyone in the room looked at the short, squat officer who was now rising from the stool, his eyes wide with excitement. "Griner's Supermarket?"

"Right down the highway. A half mile north." Tom was already heading for the door. When he reached it, he turned to Bo. "Keys?"

Bo reached into his pocket and flipped them to him. "Can you drive?"

"I'll manage," he said, turning the knob and striding toward Bo's car. He could literally hear the thump of his heartbeat.

"Tom, stop!" Helen called after him, but Tom ignored her. When Tom reached the driver's side, Helen grabbed his arm. "I said, stop!"

Tom turned on a dime. "What do you want?"

"Are you just planning to drive down there like a cowboy with pistols firing?" she asked, gritting her teeth. "JimBone Wheeler is a trained killer. An Army Ranger. An assassin. What if he's waiting on the roof and picks you off just like what happened to Jasmine Haynes? What if the pay phone blows up when you get there? What if you find Jackson's body? Tom, Wheeler clearly wanted to be found. He must have another message for us." She paused. "At least let me and the deputies in the squad cars out here follow you."

"And risk my grandson's life? Have you lost your mind, Helen? You heard the man. If anyone comes with me, the boy dies."

"It's a bluff, and even if it's not we can stay far enough back that he won't see us."

"Are you willing to take that risk? I am not."

"He'll kill you," Helen said. "It's a setup and you have to know it. He wanted his location to be found for a reason. Please, Tom, give me thirty minutes so I can get some officers to flank the place and give you some backup." She took a step closer, and when she spoke again, it reminded Tom of a schoolteacher scolding a kid for being too aggressive. "You need to let the law do its job."

"Enough!" Tom said, feeling a coughing fit coming on and swallowing hard to prevent it. "I don't know what I'm going to find, but I'm tired as hell of waiting on *the law.*" He pointed at the five police cars that dotted his driveway. "The law has utterly failed to protect my family. Ironic, isn't it, since I've devoted my whole life to practicing and teaching it?" He leaned close to her. "The law has failed, Helen, and I'm going to do whatever it takes to save my grandson. Either get on the bus or get out of the way."

Helen's eyes flashed fury, but Tom didn't wait around to hear whatever she planned to say next. He climbed behind the wheel and cranked the ignition.

Seconds later, he was on Highway 231 North. In the distance, he saw the sign for Griner's.

77

The General was correct. JimBone Wheeler did leave a message.

Taped to the pay phone outside of Griner's Supermarket was a folded piece of paper. Hesitating only for a second, Tom snatched it and walked back to the SUV. Once inside, he opened the crinkled sheet and read the note. After waiting a couple of seconds to let his eyes rest, he read it again. The adrenaline rush of the past two hours had now passed and his head felt heavy with fatigue. *Come on, Bill,* he thought, hoping Bill Davis would come soon with drugs that would make him strong enough to follow through with the orders on this page.

Tom sighed and put the SUV in reverse. Five minutes later, he pulled into the driveway at the farm as Tommy, Rick, Bo, and the two officers who recorded the earlier call barreled out of the house. He noticed that Helen's black Crown Vic was gone, and he cursed under his breath. "I was too hard on her."

He opened the door and limped toward the carport.

"Professor—" Bo started, but Tom held up his hand.

"I need to sit down." One of the officers opened the door to the house, and Tom made his way to a chair by the kitchen table. Once he was seated, he took in a deep breath and exhaled. The other men gathered around the table, waiting. Finally, Tom handed the note that had been taped to the phone to Bo.

Bo peered down at the Professor, who nodded at him to read the message.

"At 2:00 p.m., walk across the highway toward Trojan Field. When you get inside the gates of the stadium, stay on the sideline closest to the entrance. Bring your cell phone, but do not come armed or I will kill the boy. At 2:15 p.m., I'm going to call you. If you don't answer, the boy dies. If you aren't where I've told you to be, the boy dies. I have the school being watched and if I see any cop activity whatsoever, the boy dies. Bring Drake with you and no one else, and your partner also better be unarmed or the boy dies. If I see your nigger friend Haynes, your son the doctor, or any damn body else, I'll kill the kid. Just you and Drake."

Bo folded the note. "What time is it now?"

"10:25 a.m.," the squat officer answered.

Tom leaned forward and placed his elbows on his knees, trying to get in a position where his back didn't hurt. The morphine had worn off, and his fuel tank of rage was beginning to run low. *Come on, Bill,* he thought again. Then he peered up at the two officers, who had taken up their positions at the island. "I think you fellas need to skin out."

"Professor, we're under strict orders from General Lewis not to leave the premises," one of them said.

Tom let out a ragged breath but kept his eyes fixed on the deputy who had spoken. "You heard what the note from Wheeler said. Any cop activity and my grandson is dead." He rolled his neck to the side, feeling another jolt of pain begin at the base of his skull and run down his right leg. "Now, I'm not asking you, I'm telling you. Get off my farm."

The squat officer blinked away as Tom pierced him with the look he used to give his law students when they hadn't read the assigned cases. "OK," the officer said. "What about the guys out front?"

Tom looked out the bay window at the patrol cars guarding the house. Those cruisers had the crest of the Madison County Sheriff's Department emblazoned on the side of them.

All this law, he thought again, remembering his argument with Helen, *and my grandson is still gone.*

"They need to go too," Tom said.

Ten minutes later, the police presence at the house had vanished and the only people left were Tom, Rick, Bo, and Tommy. Tom gazed at the digital clock on the microwave oven to the left of the island. 10:40. "Gentlemen, we have three hours to figure something out."

"We should let the General know what's going on," Bo said, but Tom waved him off.

"No need for that. I'm sure the two fellows I just booted out are already on the phone with her." He sighed. "Helen doesn't do well when she's not in control of a situation."

"I'd feel better if she were here," Bo said.

"Me too," Rick added.

Tom closed his eyes and opened them.

"Dad, are you OK?" Tommy asked.

"Yeah, son. Just thinking."

"Professor, I'm sure you know this," Bo began, walking slowly around the island, "but if you and my believer follow these instructions to the letter"—he was holding the note in his hand—"then it's possible that JimBone may let your grandson live, but—"

"But he's gonna kill us," Rick interrupted. "And he may kill Jackson too."

Bo nodded at him. "I can't see why he'd set up a drop-off like this without a plan to obtain his ultimate revenge." Bo paused. "His final reckoning."

Tom stood from the chair and placed his hands on the island. He leaned into it, trying to stave off another shimmer of pain.

"What choice do we have?" Tommy asked, not hiding the anguish in his tone. "If Dad and Rick don't follow the instructions, then my son is dead. If they do follow his rules, then everyone may die." He sighed and walked back to the table, sitting down and placing his face in his hands.

"We don't have a choice," Tom finally said, peering at Rick Drake and marveling at how much the kid had aged over the past four years. He looked at the door to the carport, remembering a morning three and a half years earlier when the hotshot young attorney had knocked on that door and asked Tom to come back to the courtroom and try the Willistone case. That kid had been wide eyed and green. Full of piss and vinegar. The man who stood in front of him now wore the worry lines of tragedy in his gaze. He'd lost his father to JimBone Wheeler and Manny Reyes. He'd almost been killed himself a week and a half ago. And if he walked across Highway 231 with Tom in less than four hours, he might die today. "Rick, this is a lot to ask of you. I—"

"I'm in," Rick said. "I wouldn't have a career or a life of any kind . . . if it wasn't for you. I'll call Judge Conner and ask for a recess of the trial this afternoon." He paused, and when he spoke again, his voice was firm and unwavering. "And come two o'clock, I'll be walking across that highway with you."

Tom's eyes stung with tears. All he could manage was a nod. And then the baritone voice of Bocephus Haynes rose to fill the four walls of the kitchen. "'Greater love hath no man than this,'" Bo said, placing a hand on Rick's neck, "'that a man lay down his life for his friends.'" He paused. "John, Chapter 15, Verse 13. I don't remember a lot of Scripture, but I do remember that one."

For several long minutes, the farmhouse was quiet.

Thomas Jackson McMurtrie peered at his son, his best friend, and his partner. They were seated at the kitchen table, each lost in his own thoughts, which Tom suspected were tinged with a number of competing emotions. Regret. Anger. Determination. And most of all, fear. Fear of failure. Fear of the unknown.

Fear of death.

Tom wasn't thinking about death anymore. Nor was he imagining what the afterlife might bring. His mind had been saturated with those concepts for the past fourteen months and he had no use for them now.

There was something else tugging at the corners of his brain. Something he had remembered from long ago. "This is my home," he finally said, startling the others with the intensity in his tone but talking almost as much to himself as the others. "Hazel Green, Alabama, is my home. My father and I built this house with our bare hands." He pointed though the window of the door to the carport. "Those hundred acres out there are McMurtrie land." Tom began to feel the rage burn within him again. "My land." Then he pointed through the bay window. "That school across the street is my school. I was one of the first graduates of Hazel Green High School. I got in my first fistfight on the playground behind the third-grade pod, had my first kiss at the gymnasium, and had my first taste of Jack Daniel's under the bleachers of Trojan Field." Tom gritted his teeth. "The best football player to ever suit up at that stadium over there . . . *was me*."

More silence as the other men watched Tom. Finally, Bo cleared his throat. "Professor, what are you—?"

"I wasn't a saint as a boy," Tom interrupted, still gazing through the glass, paying Bo no mind. "I got in trouble just as much as any other kid. I dipped snuff and chewed tobacco. I smoked my first cigarette when I was sixteen." He paused. "And I played hooky some too." Tom smiled. "I skipped school in the fall to bring in the crop with Daddy." He paused. "And I skipped in the winter and spring because I was up to no good." He chuckled. "Paid for it too. Momma nearly delimbed a whole tree, snapping off switches and tanning my legs and ass up."

"Dad—" Tommy's exasperated voice broke through. Tom silenced his son by looking squarely in his eye before moving his gaze to Rick and then holding it on Bo.

"I know this part of the county like the back of my hand," Tom said, his tone matter-of-fact as he walked over to the sink. "The land . . . the people." He turned on the water and let the liquid run over his fingers. "Even the water." Tom nodded to himself. "Especially the water."

"Professor, where is all of this leading?" Rick asked.

"Have y'all had you a taste from the sink?" Tom asked, ignoring his partner's question and firing off his own.

None of them answered, and Tom smirked. "Fine, I understand. You think I've lost my marbles." He paused. "But do you know where this water comes from? And the water over at the school? And the water down at Griner's? And at all the houses down Charity Lane?"

Again, all he got in response were wide eyes.

"In 1956, me and Daddy built a well out on the southeast corner of that farm out there." Tom paused. "Didn't do it alone. Had help from some of our neighbors, but by the spring of '58, we had water flowing to almost every home in Hazel Green. You see, underneath the well there are pipes that take the water to all of these other places." Tom smiled, spreading his arms out in front of him. "The county helped us with those, and because pipes can sometimes get clogged and need to be inspected, the county forefathers did something else."

"What?" Bo asked, and Tom could see the gleam in his friend's eye.

He's beginning to get it.

"In all of their wisdom, they constructed a tunnel system under the ground." Tom gazed around the room, seeing that he had their full attention now. "Nothing exotic, but tall enough and wide enough that a man could get in there and check things out."

"Could me and Tommy use it to get close to Trojan Field?" Bo asked.

Tom sighed and scratched the back of his neck. "Now that I don't know. I never worked the tunnels." He paused and a wistful grin played on his lips. "But there's somebody who does." He looked at his son and friends. "If he's still alive and we can find him."

"Who is it, Dad?" Tommy asked.

"You remember me telling you stories about Logan Baeder?"

Tommy raised his eyebrows. "The left-handed kid from New Sharon that could throw the ball ninety miles per hour."

Tom nodded at his son. "Would've played in the majors if he hadn't thrown his arm away in middle school." Tom paused. "Logan and his daddy, John Henry, built the tunnel system."

"Professor, if this guy is still alive, how old would he be?" Bo asked.

Tom thought about it, doing the math in his head. "He was four years ahead of me in school, so . . . seventy-seven maybe?"

"Does he still live in . . . what did you call it? New Sharon?"

Tom chuckled. "That was the name of the school. It's long since closed by now, but I suspect Logan hasn't strayed far from home."

"How close?" Rick asked, and Tom could hear the excitement in his partner's voice.

"Just a few miles northwest of here."

"In Hazel Green?" Bo asked, pulling the keys to his Sequoia out of his pocket.

"Technically, yes," Tom said. "But the folks there call it something else."

"What?" Rick asked.

There was a glint in Tom's eyes. "Y'all ever hear of a place called Lick Skillet?"

78

At 10:55 a.m., Kathryn Calhoun Willistone wired half a million dollars from her bank in Jasper to an account she'd opened a month earlier at the International Bank of the Cayman Islands. She'd made it happen with five minutes to spare.

Once she had returned to the limousine, she reached into her purse and popped a Xanax, hoping the drug would chill the anxiety that had enveloped her. As the limo pulled away from the bank, Kat's cell phone rang and her stomach twisted into a knot. This time the number wasn't the sheriff's, but since she didn't recognize the digits, she presumed the worst.

"Did you wire the money?" the voice from this morning asked.

"Yes," Kat said. "Just now. It's done."

"Good. And the plane?"

"Working on it, but I've got to be in Florence at one for that trial that you were supposed to get continued by fulfilling your end of the deal, remember? If I'm going to make it on time, then I need to leave."

"Forget the trial," the killer said. "That's about to be over. The lawyer for the Jennings family is going to be unavoidably detained."

Kat managed a tentative smile. "Good," she said. "But that airfield is small and there's not much space. I'll do the best—"

"You're Bully Calhoun's daughter, for Christ's sake. Make it happen in the next hour or I release the sheriff's tape recording of you. Want to listen to it again?"

Kat's smile faded. "That won't be necessary," she said.

"Get the plane," JimBone Wheeler snarled.

And then the line went dead.

Kat Willistone had always been a practical woman. She grew up with money and power, and so she took it as her birthright and was attracted to those traits like a pig seeks out mud. That was what led her to seduce Jack Willistone, who had been married at the time he first began a relationship with Kat.

Now almost forty years old, Kat knew her childbearing days were almost over and, truth be known, she didn't enjoy living in the Calhoun mansion by herself all that much. When Jack was murdered, she'd scratched and clawed to keep half of his life insurance proceeds. When her father was assassinated, she figured she'd use the eight million in insurance to eventually move away from Jasper. The island of Saint John had always intrigued her.

But then Rick Drake sued her father's estate all over the state of Alabama, and she had to put her plans on hold. *But now . . .*

As the limo pulled up the driveway to the Calhoun mansion, she dialed Virgil Flood's number. He answered on the first ring and sounded out of breath. "Kathryn, I'm glad you called. The trial has been recessed until tomorrow morning. Jennings's lawyer has had an emergency."

Kat felt a sense of warmth spread over her body as she imagined the blue waters of Saint John. "OK, I'll meet you at the courtroom tomorrow in Florence," Kat said.

"Sounds good. Hey, Kathryn," Virgil asked, his tone now inquisitive. "Have you heard about Sheriff Patterson?"

"No, what happened?"

"He was murdered last night," Virgil said. "He was found hanging from a beam at a cabin on the Flint River." Virgil paused, and when he spoke again, his voice was just above a whisper. "A clerk in the courthouse told me that she heard his penis was cut off."

Kat felt a deliciously cold shiver run down her arms. "Damn," she said.

"Damn is right," Virgil said. "Anyway, I'll see you tomorrow."

"See ya," Kat said, and her mouth curved into a grin. *The high sheriff is dead.* Kat could feel some of the chains that bound her to Jasper breaking. She doubted Patterson had anything on her other than the tape recording that JimBone Wheeler had played earlier today. *And that tape implicated DeWayne just as much as it did me.* She doubted the sheriff had anything lying around his house that could hurt her, but even if he did, she didn't plan to wait around to find out.

Kat trotted up the steps to her bedroom and began packing her bags. Once she was done, she called the number for the Walker County Airport.

"Bevill Field," the voice on the other end of the line answered, referring to the airfield by its more commonly used name.

"This is Kathryn Calhoun Willistone. Can my jet be fueled up and ready to fly wheels up in an hour?"

"Well . . . ma'am, I don't know. I'll need to call your pilot."

"Tell Chuck to be there in forty-five minutes ready to roll, or he's fired. I pay him a hundred grand a year to be ready to go at a moment's notice."

"Yes, ma'am. Where will you be heading?"

"Saint John, in the Virgin Islands," Kat said, hooking the phone between her neck and shoulder as she slipped on a pair of flats. "With one stop."

"And where will you be stopping?"

Kat's stomach tensed but she didn't hesitate. "The Madison County Executive Airport. Meridianville, Alabama."

79

The community known as Lick Skillet is located in northwest Hazel Green. The epicenter of the place—or as the locals call it, "downtown Lick Skillet"—sits at the intersection of Charity Lane and Butter And Egg Road. As a boy, Tom had gone to bluegrass concerts with his mom and dad at the four-thousand-square-foot building at the crossroads called the Music Barn.

At 11:15 a.m., Bo, Tom, and Rick pulled into a parking space outside the Music Barn. They saw an old man chewing on a piece of grass, leaning against the structure.

"Well, I'll be dipped in horse manure," Tom said, climbing out of the car on shaky legs. Bill Davis was still thirty minutes out, and Tom was in dire need of a steroid injection. "Logan?"

Logan Nathaniel Baeder pushed himself off the side of the building and approached with a steady gait. He was a shade over six feet tall and had arms that hung to his knees. Logan walked with his chest and elbows stuck out, just as he'd done in high school.

Still the cock of the walk, Tom thought.

"How 'bout it, Tommy Mac?" Logan asked, extending his hand, which Tom shook.

Despite his predicament, Tom couldn't help but smile. He hadn't seen Logan Baeder in over forty years, but the man addressed him the same way he had in school. Shaking Logan's hand was like squeezing hold of a brick. "It's good to see you, Logan," Tom managed.

"You too," Logan said, continuing to chew on the blade of grass. "You sounded pretty shook up on the phone. What can I do for you?"

Tom took a step closer to his old friend, forgoing any pretense. "My grandson has been kidnapped, Logan." He paused and felt heat behind his eyes. "And I think you might be the only person on the face of the earth who can help me."

Logan scratched the back of his neck, and Tom noticed the deep creases in the man's face, proof of a hard life of work and sacrifice. Then, flinging the strand of grass on the ground, he said, "Aiight, then. Tell me the deal."

80

At noon, Kat Willistone sat in a leopard-skin recliner in the cabin of the Gulfstream on the airstrip of Bevill Field. The ground crew was busy fueling the plane up, and Chuck, her pilot, was on his way. They'd be wheels up in less than forty-five minutes.

As she expected, her cell rang at the turn of the hour. Again, the call came from a different number, but Kat knew who it had to be.

"The plane will be in Meridianville by one thirty. Ready and waiting."

Silence on the other end of the line. "Good," JimBone finally said. "Glad to see you have a little of that Bully blood in you."

"You have no idea," Kat said.

"Tell the pilot to be ready for takeoff at two thirty. I have some business to attend to, and then myself and my partner will be on our way."

"The business being the terms of the contract?" Kat asked.

"Yes indeed," JimBone said. "By the time the plane leaves the Meridianville airport, all conditions will be satisfied," he said, and there was a smile in his tone that caused Kat's mouth to curve upward as well. "And then some," JimBone added before ending the call.

81

Dr. Bill Davis arrived in Hazel Green at 12:30 p.m.

"About damn time," Tom said as his fair-skinned friend entered the house, carrying his medicine bag in his right hand. Tom was sprawled out on the couch in the den, covered in blankets. "You bring some guns?"

"Everything I could put in the truck," Bill fired back. Then, looking around the empty house, he asked, "Where the hell is everyone?"

"I'll fill you in on everything, but first I need you to shoot me up." Tom rolled up his right sleeve until the crook of his elbow was showing.

"I'm not going to put it there," Bill said, placing his medicine bag on the coffee table by the couch and unzipping it. Seconds later, he pulled out a needle and a pouch of liquid. "It's a shot, chief, not an IV."

"Where then?" Tom asked.

Bill smiled. "Do you sit heavier on your right cheek or left?"

Tom thought about it. "Right probably."

"Alright, then. Drop your drawers, and I'll make sure I stick this in your left."

Tom smirked at him. "Do you always have this charming a bedside manner?"

"Only in life-or-death situations," Bill said. "Now drop 'em."

Tom did as he was told and, seconds later, felt a hot sensation as the steroids were injected into his body.

"That should give you a pick-me-up in about thirty minutes. And if you're still alive and want another one in an hour, I'll rinse and repeat."

"I'll need another one," Tom said.

"How do you know?"

Tom took the folded piece of paper that set out JimBone Wheeler's instructions and handed it to Bill.

For almost a full minute, Bill squinted down at the note. Then he surprised Tom.

"Drop 'em again," Bill said.

"What? Why?"

"Because I gave you a pussified dose that I thought might give you a little pick-me-up but not run the risk of any damage."

"And now?"

Bill showed Tom a much bigger needle. "Now I'm going to give you the stuff the Oakland Raiders used in the '70s."

Tom grinned and pulled down his pants. "Just win, baby," he said.

Bill Davis said nothing. Instead, he made the sign of the cross over his chest and stuck the needle deep into Tom's left buttock.

82

In the men's locker room of the Hazel Green High School gymnasium, JimBone Wheeler sat across from thirteen-year-old Jackson McMurtrie. The boy's hands and feet were bound together with rope, and his mouth was covered with duct tape.

After offing DeWayne Patterson, JimBone and Manny had put the boy in back of the Tundra and raced away from the cabin, trying to find a suitable hiding place until they could put the final phase of the plan into place. JimBone had chosen the high school gym because of its proximity to the McMurtrie farm and to the football field, where he would give the Professor his reckoning.

Since school had been let out for the Christmas holidays, hiding inside the gym was optimal, and JimBone had incurred no difficulty picking one of the locks and getting inside. For the past ten hours, he and the boy had camped out in the locker room while Manny performed reconnaissance on the outside. She'd parked the Tundra between some bushes on the farm adjacent to Trojan Field, and once McMurtrie, Drake, and the kid were handled, they should have a clean getaway and a five-minute drive to the airport in Meridianville. If Kathryn Calhoun Willistone was to be believed, the plane should be waiting, and JimBone had a feeling she'd be joining them on the trip.

But one challenge remained on the ground, and he'd waited two painfully long years for it. He gazed across the locker room, which reeked of jock odor and urine, and into the eyes of the boy. The kid's eyes had narrowed into slits and he was glaring at JimBone.

"You mad at me, boy?" JimBone asked.

The boy nodded and he tried to murmur something through the tape that JimBone couldn't make out.

"Promise not to yell if I take the tape off?"

The boy moved his head up and down and JimBone walked over to him. "If you're lying, I'm going to do more than spank you, got it?"

The boy's eyes widened and he nodded again.

"Good," JimBone said, and ripped the tape off Jackson's mouth.

The boy yelped but didn't say anything else as JimBone returned to his seat across from him. "So . . . ," the killer said. "How ya doing?"

"I'm hungry," Jackson said.

"Me too," JimBone said. "But that's tough shit for both of us. Unfortunately, the gym here doesn't have a food court."

"There's a McDonald's in Meridianville," Jackson said.

"I'll keep that in mind."

For a few seconds, neither of them spoke. Finally, Jackson gazed down at the tile floor. "You're going to kill me, aren't you?"

JimBone shook his head. "Nope. If I wanted you dead, you'd be dead already."

"You're going to kill my papa."

"He deserves it. He's been a thorn in my side for several years."

The boy's face flushed red. "He was just doing his job."

"And it kept me from doing mine, and I got sent to prison. Now I'm going to give him his."

The boy smirked. "You really think so, don't you?"

Up until that precise second, JimBone Wheeler had been enjoying this interaction. Now he felt a tingle of agitation. "I know so."

"Uh-huh," the boy said, his tone sarcastic. "Just like you got the best of him in Tuscaloosa. Oh, wait, no. My uncle Bo grabbed you by the nuts and you had to jump off a bridge to escape."

JimBone removed a knife and file from his pocket and began to sharpen the blade. "Papa been telling his grandson lots of stories, I see."

Jackson's lip trembled ever so slightly, but his tone stayed the same. "Just like you got the best of him in Pulaski, right? Beat him up pretty good, didn't you? Thought it was over, didn't you?" The boy swallowed. "But it wasn't over. Papa won the case and you went to prison." He glared at JimBone. "Where you belong."

"You sure have a smart mouth, boy," JimBone said, putting the file back in his pocket and standing up. He held the knife by his side and again approached Jackson and sat beside him. He brought the tip of the blade to the boy's neck and pressed forward.

"Oww!" Jackson yelled as the skin broke. JimBone released the pressure and ran his finger along the boy's neck, wiping off the resulting blood and then sticking the finger in his mouth.

Jackson grimaced in horror and JimBone smiled.

"I'm going to taste a lot of McMurtrie blood today, son. Yours and your papa's." He smiled and leaned over to the floor, picking up the tape he'd ripped off earlier. "I think I liked you better when your mouth was closed."

83

In the archives room of the Tillman D. Hill Public Library, Logan Baeder showed Bo, Rick, and Tommy the system of pipes and tunnels that distributed water from the well on the McMurtrie farm to the rest of Hazel Green proper.

"There are three tunnels that sprout from the well," Logan said, pointing at the map with the tip of a number two pencil. "There's this one that runs from the farm all the way to the end of Charity Lane." Logan paused to make sure everyone was following. "And then there's this one here that runs parallel to 231 for about a hundred yards south and then takes a right turn and actually runs under this library building and west another two miles." He stopped again and set the pencil down. Then he tapped his index finger on another set of lines. "And then there's this one here. Because the school uses so much water, the county wanted to make damn sure it could get to those pipes. This tunnel runs east from the farm underneath Highway 231 for about three miles." He licked his lips and looked at each of the other three men. "The tunnel has three exit points, and one of them is right here." Logan held his finger on a box marked on the map.

"I'll be damned," Bo said.

The box had two words written above it in small type to designate the location, and Rick Drake whispered them in awe: "Trojan Field."

84

In his dream, Tom saw the tower and the shadow of the Man. He wasn't wearing his trademark houndstooth hat. The fedora was only for games. On the practice field, the Man wore a baseball cap, stood tall on his tower, and barked instructions from a megaphone. The world knew Paul Bryant as "the Bear." But to his players he was either "Coach Bryant" or "the Man."

"McMurtrie, gotta pick it up, boy. Need you here, Forty-Nine." Tom gritted his teeth and dug his knuckles into the grass. At the sound of the whistle, he launched out of his stance and the pads popped. It was hot. So incredibly hot, and the Man's voice was loud.

"That a baby, Forty-Nine. Here we go. Next play."

"Next play, Tommy," said the voice of Ray Ray Pickalew.

Next play.

Next play.

Tom opened his eyes and felt his heartbeat racing. He sat up from the couch and gazed around the den. Bocephus Haynes sat on the chair next to him. "You ready, dog?"

"What time is it?" Tom asked.

"One forty-five," Bo said.

With all of his strength, Tom rose off the couch. He felt better. Stronger. But strange. His mouth had a funny taste, and he was dizzy. He glanced around the room, seeing Tommy, whose face was tight. Worried. Next to his son was Bill Davis, holding a glass of brown liquid over ice in his hand. Bill was an alcoholic and, to Tom's knowledge, hadn't had a drink in twenty-five years.

"Bill?"

"Don't judge me, you ornery son of a bitch," Bill said, smirking at Tom. "Your body is so full of drugs, Elvis would be jealous." Then, as the grin left the doctor's face, he added, "If I'm going to die in the tunnels below Hazel Green, Alabama, then by God I'm going to die with a bellyful of Dewar's Scotch."

Tom nodded at his friend. "Thank you, Bill." Then, realizing something was wrong, he wrinkled his face and moved his eyes swiftly around the room. "Where's Lee Roy?" he asked, hearing the panic in his voice. With so much going on, he'd completely forgotten about his only housemate. "Where's my dog?"

"He's with us, Dad," Tommy said. "With Nancy and Jenny and Julie. After you were admitted to the hospital, I came and got him."

Tom's heartbeat had gotten out of control. He glared at Bill. "What in the Sam hell did you give me?"

"What you asked for," Bill fired back, taking a long sip of Scotch.

Tom took a deep breath and tried to get himself under control. In the background, he could still hear the voice from the tower. *That a boy now, next play.* He closed his eyes and then opened them, trying to get his bearings.

"It's 1:50 now, Professor," Bo said. "Are you ready?"

Tom looked into the eyes of his best friend. "Bo . . . will you take care of Lee Roy when I die?"

Bo smiled, but his eyes were sad. "Of course, sir. You know I will. Are you OK, Professor?" Then he also fired a glance at Bill Davis. "What did you give him?"

"A boatload of steroids," Bill replied. "In his condition, there was no way he could drive over to that field, much less walk, without them."

Bo held Dr. Davis's gaze, but the physician didn't back off. Bo finally turned back to Tom. "You need your phone."

Tom leaned down and took the device off the coffee table, checking the charge. It had half a bar, which would be enough. "Did Logan show you boys the tunnel?"

Bo nodded. "We're good, dog."

"What about guns?" Tom asked.

Tommy gestured to Dr. Davis. "Doc set us up. We could start a revolution with what we have."

Tom smiled and swayed on his feet, catching his balance after a side step to the left. "I'm OK," he said, still hearing the voice from the tower, but this time closer. In the locker room in Knoxville. *I know it doesn't feel like it, boys, but we got them right where we want them. Now, when we start the second half, the defense is going to go out and stop them. When the offense gets the ball, we're going to score. We got class and we're going to show it.*

Thomas Jackson McMurtrie blinked tears from his eyes and looked around the room. He'd eaten egg custard pie that his mother, Rene, had made in this same room. He'd signed a letter of intent to play football for the University of Alabama at the same kitchen table where Rick Drake had just plopped down, lost in his thoughts. He'd told his momma and daddy that he was going to marry Julie Lynn Rogers at about the same spot in the den he was in right now.

We got class and we're going to show it.

"Thank you, gentlemen, for being with me until the end."

He gave them all embraces, holding his son's a little longer. "I'll bring him back," Tom whispered. "I swear to God I will."

"Yes, sir," Tommy said, wiping hot tears from his eyes. "I know you will."

When he reached the kitchen, he gazed at his partner. "Are you ready to carry out the last act of this law firm?"

Rick nodded. "Yes, sir, I am."

Tom glanced at the clock on the microwave. 1:55 p.m. Then he looked back at his partner. "Let's roll."

Five minutes later, at exactly 2:00 p.m., Tom McMurtrie and Rick Drake walked side by side down the long driveway toward Highway 231. Rick wore the same gray suit he'd worn the past thirty hours, covered with a black overcoat. Tom had changed into loose-fitting khaki cargo pants and a crimson sweater. As the temperature was now hovering in the low forties, he, too, wore his charcoal wool overcoat.

When they reached the highway, Rick gripped Tom by the triceps as they waited for a car to pass by. "You OK, Professor?"

"Never better," Tom said as they crossed to the median and then to the other side.

85

At 2:05 p.m., the Calhoun jet landed at the Madison County Executive Airport, in Meridianville. *Late,* Kat thought, cursing her pilot for tying on a hangover the night before and showing up at Bevill Field thirty minutes late. Once the plane came to a stop on the runway, Chuck's groggy voice blared over the loudspeaker. "We're here, Ms. Willistone. Did you want to get off the plane to stretch your legs?"

"No, Chuck, I'm fine."

"When will our guests arrive?"

"We need to be ready to take off at two thirty."

"Roger that," Chuck said.

Kat undid her seat belt and removed the bottle of champagne she'd had chilling in the plane's minifridge. It wasn't the good stuff, but it would do. Thinking she should probably wait until Mr. Wheeler and Ms. Reyes arrived to let them do the honors, Kat snorted.

"Screw it," she said out loud, popping the cork on the bottle. "I need a drink."

86

They are on their way.

JimBone looked at the text he'd just received from Manny. He'd told her to notify him as soon as she saw McMurtrie and Drake walking down the driveway. From Manny's handpicked perch, she could see a mile in all directions.

JimBone turned and lifted McMurtrie's grandson off the bench and placed him in an equipment bag he'd found in the locker room. As the boy squirmed, trying to get loose, JimBone laughed and zipped the sack closed.

"Go time, kid."

87

Once they'd crossed Highway 231, Tom and Rick had to walk approximately a quarter mile across a long parking lot that serviced both the gymnasium to the right and the football field in front of them. Tom walked as fast as he could, but he knew he was slowing them down.

"Time?" Tom asked.

"2:04," Rick said. "Relax. We're good."

Tom's heart continued to race and the dizziness returned. As did the cacophony of voices, led by the one from the tower.

Football is a game of eyes, movement, and contact.

I want you to be agile, mobile, and hostile.

Tom shook his head, and the dizziness worsened. *Next play, Tommy.* Ray Ray's voice now. Right in his ear. *Next play. Eyes and ears open. Head up.*

"God help me," Tom whispered.

"Professor?" Rick's voice sounded far off and like it was coming through a filter.

"I'm OK, son. These steroids have just got me messed up."

When Gabriel is busy, God sometimes sends Ray Ray.

Tom laughed and caught Rick's concerned glance out of the corner of his eye.

"Almost there," Tom said out loud, trying to talk away the voices.

And that's why I believe that if we come together eleven at a time, why . . . in four years, we'll walk out of here national champions.

Two hundred yards, Tom thought, seeing the stadium where he'd made All-State come into view.

And I'll tell you this. I expect nothing less.

Next play, Tommy.

Agile.

Mobile.

Hostile.

Tom gasped and felt Rick's arm around him. "Time?"

"2:08."

One hundred yards now, Tom thought, forcing his eyes to remain as wide as possible as he saw the red-and-gray-colored Trojan soldier on the side of the stadium.

Eyes.

Movement.

Contact.

Fifty yards. Tom now dragged his feet along. "Time?"

"2:10, Professor. Just a little while longer."

We got class. We're going to show it.

The voice on the tower had faded somewhat, but Ray Ray's was now louder. *Next play, Forty-Nine.*

Then another voice. One Tom hadn't heard in decades. He would never forget Coach Bryant's voice, but how could you with it blaring from the jumbotron at Bryant-Denny Stadium every Saturday? And he'd seen Ray Ray Pickalew just two years earlier. Their voices were distinct and unmistakable.

But so was this one. Quiet. Understated. The voice of a humble man who had raised a son who'd become an Alabama football player, a law professor, and an attorney. Tom's father, Sutton Winslow McMurtrie, whom everyone called Sut.

We can do this.

Tom felt tears sting his eyes as he saw the people he had loved most in his life flash through his mind like a fast-moving projector.

We can do this.

Sut McMurtrie had fought at Bastogne under the worst of conditions. Many of his brothers-in-arms had died, but he had lived to marry the love of his life. Sut and Rene McMurtrie had wanted lots of children, but God had only given them one.

We can do this.

Twenty yards. "Time?" Tom croaked.

"2:12."

We can do this.

Ten yards.

You can do this, son.

Five yards. The voice from the tower was back in his ear. Loud. Like an eighteen-wheeler speeding down a gravel road.

Eyes.

Movement.

Contact.

Tom reached out and put both hands on the side of the stadium and leaned into it, breathing heavily. His eyes blurred with tears and he wiped them clear. He turned to Rick Drake, whose face was tense, his eyes tight. The look reminded Tom of the way quarterback Pat Trammell used to peer at his teammates from inside the huddle.

"Time?" Tom asked.

"2:14," Rick said.

Tom nodded toward a chain-link fence to the right. "There's the gate," he said, wrapping his arm around Rick and letting his partner help him to and through the entrance to Trojan Field.

Tom and Rick walked with purpose toward the sideline nearest them. When they reached it, Tom moved his eyes around the field, seeing nothing. "Time?"

"It's 2:15, Professor."

In his pocket, Tom's phone began to ring.

88

JimBone Wheeler relished the sound of the old man's weak voice.

"Yeah." McMurtrie answered the phone on the first ring.

"Walk out to the middle of the field and stand on the fifty-yard line."

"OK."

When both men began to head that way, JimBone snapped, "Just you, McMurtrie. Drake stays on the sideline."

Fifteen seconds later, the old man reached midfield. "Where's my grandson?" he asked.

JimBone closed his eyes and enjoyed the next few seconds more than any in his life. "Remember what I promised you?"

A ragged breath was the response on the other end of the line, followed by "Where's my grandson?"

"Answer the question, McMurtrie. Do you remember what I promised you?"

"Yes."

"Say it. *Say the word.*"

"A reckoning," McMurtrie finally said, his tone haggard.

"Today's the day," JimBone said as two rifle shots lit up the air.

89

Tom felt the air go out of his chest as the sound of gunfire rang out over the field. Involuntarily, he dropped to his knees. *A trap,* he thought, remembering how Helen had scolded him. *I walked right into it.*

"No!" a kid's voice shouted.

Tom turned to the far sideline and saw his grandson running toward him.

"Papa!"

"Professor!" Rick Drake's voice carried from behind him, followed by three more cracks from a high-powered rifle. Out of the corner of his eyes, he saw his partner fall to the ground.

Tom tried to stand up but couldn't move. He heard his grandson's footfall and he looked up to see number forty-nine heading for him, tears streaming down the teenage boy's face. "Papa!"

Tom reached for him and felt the boy's arms envelop him.

Eyes.

Movement.

Contact.

Next play, Tommy.

Behind Jackson, Tom saw a shadow approaching. He held his grandson tight to his body and watched as the silhouette grew larger and then stood over him.

JimBone Wheeler grinned as he looked down on Tom and Jackson. The killer's copper eyes glowed with equal parts fury and satisfaction as he placed the barrel of a sawed-off shotgun into Tom's forehead. Then, chuckling, he moved the gun to the boy's temple.

"No," Tom gasped.

"Before I finish you off and send you to hell, McMurtrie, you're going to watch your grandson die."

With every bit of strength he had left in his body, Tom lunged for the weapon, catching the barrel with the palm of his hand and pressing up with all of his might.

Then a blast sounded in his ear so loud that the world began to spin. Tom glanced to his right and saw that Jackson was unharmed. The shot had missed.

JimBone Wheeler scowled at Tom and brought the butt of the shotgun down on his forehead.

"You stubborn fool," the killer said. Then, standing, he pointed the gun at Jackson again.

Tom brought up his hands in a feeble attempt to protect the boy. He looked up into JimBone's copper eyes and knew they'd be the last thing he'd see in this world.

But just before JimBone Wheeler could pull the trigger, the killer's chest exploded.

And the sound of gunfire erupted on Trojan Field from every direction.

90

Manny Reyes knew something had gone horribly wrong the second she heard gunshots that didn't come from her rifle. Manny had been firing her sniper's weapon from the press box of the stadium and now saw JimBone dropping his shotgun and keeling over.

Always quick to react, Manny didn't wait around to see whether her partner would recover. She had to get to the truck, which was parked behind the football field a half mile away. Then she'd need to make it to the airfield in Meridianville. Manny glided out the exit to the press box toward the steps that would take her to the bottom. Holding her rifle with both hands, she was halfway down when she saw her path blocked by a sandy-haired man holding a pistol in one hand and a cane in the other. The man's right eye was covered with a black patch.

"You're under arrest, Ms. Reyes," said Ambrose Powell Conrad.

Manny stopped and threw her rifle at the prosecutor, simultaneously reaching into the side of her pants for her Glock. She had grasped her hands around the handle when she felt the impact of a bullet hit her stomach. Manny dropped to her knees but still tried to raise her weapon. Then her shoulder popped as a bullet pierced her humerus. She fell over on her back, still managing to hold her Glock as the prosecutor's heavy feet trudged up the steps. A second later, he was standing over her and pointing his weapon at her nose.

Mahalia Blessica Reyes decided in the next second that she didn't want to go to prison. Looking up at the heavyset prosecutor, whose ruined eye was covered with cloth, she smiled. "You are an ugly man, *señor*," she said, swinging the Glock around toward him.

Powell Conrad fired two bullets into Manny Reyes's forehead before she ever got off a shot. As he watched the life go out of the killer's hollow eyes, he lowered the gun to his side and knelt beside her, glaring at her dead face.

"Mama tried," he whispered.

91

Tom lay on top of Jackson, covering the boy, until the firing stopped. He had closed his eyes but now opened them. Jackson trembled below him and Tom patted his back. "It's OK, son," Tom said. "You're OK." He glanced to his right and saw JimBone Wheeler sprawled out on his back. The madman's chest was covered in blood, but Tom could see that he was still gasping for air.

Sucking in a gust of oxygen, Tom crawled on his hands and knees toward him. When he got within a few inches, Tom saw JimBone's mouth curve into a grin. "At least I got you and Drake, you son of a bitch."

"Wrong, asshole," Rick said, standing above them.

JimBone's eyes darted toward Rick. He opened his mouth but no words came out as Rick unbuttoned his shirt to reveal a bulletproof vest. On the ground below him, Tom did the same.

Bill Davis had brought more than guns and ammo.

"You were wrong about something else, you bastard," Rick said, his voice rising, as he squatted in front of the killer. "You didn't get your reckoning. *I did.*" Rick paused and Tom heard the emotion in the boy's voice. "You killed my father. You hired Manny Reyes to run him off the road." Rick paused and lowered his mouth to JimBone's. "Today is the day that I balance the scales."

For a long moment, the killer gazed wide-eyed at Rick. "Is that what you think, boy?" He glanced at Tom. "Did you tell him that, McMurtrie?"

"It's what you told me at the prison," the Professor said. "That Billy Drake was just an appetizer before the main course."

JimBone blinked his eyes and coughed. Blood began to run out of his mouth and ears, but he was now smiling. Then he laughed long and hard before abruptly stopping and piercing Rick with a glare. "I lied. I don't know who killed your father, Drake. Hell, it could have just been an accident for all I know." He laughed harder. "Even in death the Bone gets the last laugh."

Rick Drake took several steps backward, finally dropping to his knees, as JimBone turned his attention to Tom. "I was just trying to get your attention, old man. And I got it, didn't I?" He licked his lips. "I can't take credit for Billy Drake, but I can for your detective buddy, Wade Richey. And the nigger's wife, Jasmine. And Santonio Jennings. And let's not forget your old friend Ray Ray Pickalew." JimBone laughed again as blood continued to pour out of him.

Next play, Tommy.

Tom heard the voice of his friend in his ear and he glared at the killer. Then, crawling forward until he was an inch from the other man, Tom spoke in a low growl. "You failed. You killed all of those people trying to get to me, and you failed. Cancer . . . might kill me one day," Tom said, speaking through clenched teeth, "but not you."

JimBone Wheeler's laughter eased and his mouth tightened. He reached a hand for Tom, and just as fast it fell limp to the ground. Seconds later, his face went blank as he breathed his last.

92

"Is he dead, Papa?" Jackson asked, walking over to Tom.

Putting his arm around the boy, Tom nodded. "Yeah, son. He is."

"I'm glad."

"Me too."

Jackson looked around Tom to Rick, who was now sitting Indian style on the fifty-yard line. "Is he OK?" the boy asked.

Tom peered at Rick, feeling his heart ache for him. "He's in shock."

Tom heard movement behind his partner. He looked up to see Powell Conrad limping toward him, wearing a black patch over his right eye.

"You're a sight for sore eyes," Tom managed as Powell came within a few feet. "You kinda look like Rooster Cogburn."

"I'll take that as a compliment," Powell said.

"When did you get here?"

"A couple minutes after you and Rick began Pickett's Charge."

"Where is everyone else?"

Powell nodded to the north, where Bocephus Haynes was walking as fast as his limp could take him, with Bill Davis following behind. Out in front of both of them was Tommy, who ran to Jackson and picked him off the ground. Then father and son cried in each other's arms.

When Bo finally arrived, Tom stuck his hand out, and his friend pulled him up and into a bear hug, which caused Tom to yelp in pain.

"Sorry, dog."

"It's OK. Thank you." Tom turned to all of them. Powell, Bo, Dr. Davis, and Tommy. "How'd you do it?"

"The tunnel came out about fifty yards to the north of the stadium," Bo said. "When we climbed out, we first had to deal with a Mexican fella that was apparently a lookout for JimBone and Manny. He was stationed on the roof of the field house with binoculars. Dude was so focused on the highway, he didn't pay enough attention to what was happening right next to him. Tommy snuck up behind him and grabbed his arms, and Powell handcuffed him to the ladder." Bo rubbed his beard and nodded at Tommy McMurtrie, who still had Jackson gripped in a bear hug. "You'd've been proud of your boy, Professor. Once that was done and we saw you, the three of us"—Bo pointed at Tommy, Bill, and himself—"took stances around the north and east sides of the stadium, and Powell covered the west." He paused and glanced at Powell. "Was Manny in the press box like we thought?"

The prosecutor grunted. "Now she's in hell."

Tom let out a ragged breath. "And then the rest of you took down Wheeler?"

Bo shook his head. "No. We didn't have the best view from the north and east. You and Jackson's bodies were in the way. We provided cover . . . but we didn't kill him."

Tom creased his eyebrows. "Who did then?"

"The person covering the south end," Bo said, pointing.

Tom turned and saw a figure leaning against the goalpost. The person wore a black fleece sweat suit and a black cap. It wasn't until she started striding toward him that Tom recognized her.

General Helen Evangeline Lewis walked with a rifle strapped to her shoulder. When she got within a few feet, she removed her hat and gave Tom a wry grin. "I thought it was time the law showed up."

93

On Christmas Day, after the presents had all been opened but while there was still some daylight, Tom asked Jackson if he'd like to take a drive. Though Nancy and Tommy fussed over them, Tom insisted, and five minutes later they were in Tom's Explorer and heading down a dirt road that took them to the north end of the farm. Since the kidnapping and the showdown at Trojan Field a week earlier, Jackson had been pretty quiet, and Tom wanted a few moments alone with him.

When they reached the northern tip, Tom pulled the truck to a stop and looked at his grandson. "Follow me, Forty-Nine."

The boy nodded and hopped out of the vehicle.

The McMurtrie family cemetery was a hundred paces away, but Tom didn't stop. Instead he walked on toward the creek that made up the boundary between Tom's property and the neighbors'. Finding a place on a couple of rocks to sit down, Tom patted a spot next to him, and his grandson did the same.

For several minutes, neither of them said anything and the only sound was the gentle-moving water. For December, the temperature was warm and Tom was grateful for it.

"So, how are you doing?" he asked.

The boy shrugged. "OK, I guess."

"Why so quiet lately?"

Jackson gazed at the creek without looking at him. "I don't know. It's just . . . I've never been that scared before."

"It's OK to be scared," Tom said. "Fear is a natural emotion. I was scared to death."

"You were?"

"You bet I was." He paused. "Anything else wrong?"

The boy shrugged. "I guess I'm just worried."

"About what?"

"Everything," Jackson said, finally looking at Tom with eyes that had seen more than a thirteen-year-old boy should ever see. "I'm worried about Mr. Drake. He was really shaken up after Mr. Wheeler said he didn't kill his dad."

Tom nodded. He, too, was worried about Rick, whom he knew was home today in Henshaw with his mother. *Has he told her the truth yet?* Tom wondered, feeling a wave of guilt pass over him. *If I had just kept my mouth shut, Rick would have never thought that JimBone and Manny were responsible for his father's death.* Tom sighed. At the end of the day, he'd done what he thought was right. *And that's all a person can do.*

"Rick is a strong man," Tom finally said. "He'll recover from the shock of this. I know he will."

"I hope so," Jackson said. "I'm also worried about Mom and Dad. Now that we're living out here while the house is being repaired, they never allow me to go outside by myself." He sighed. "They barely let me out of their sight, and sometimes when I wake up in the middle of the night, Momma is laying in the bed with me. I can hear her crying."

Tom felt heat behind his eyes, but he steadied his voice. "She thought she'd lost you, son. They both did. Give them some time. In a little while, things will get back to normal."

"No, they won't," Jackson said, and now tears had begun to fall down his cheeks. "Things will never be normal again. Things are gonna suck."

"They will, Forty-Nine, I promise you. In a few months—"

"You'll be dead," Jackson cried, turning to Tom with eyes full of anguish. "You're gonna die, Papa, aren't you?"

Now Tom couldn't hold the heat any longer and he felt his own eyes begin to glisten.

"You're gonna die," Jackson repeated, his voice quieter.

"I am," Tom said.

"Soon, right?" Jackson asked as a sob escaped his chest. "A month. Maybe days."

"I don't know, son."

"Well, you see what I mean, then, don't you? Things aren't going to go back to normal. You're gonna die and life is gonna suck."

Tom placed his arm around the boy's shoulder and Jackson leaned into him, finally letting it all go. "I don't want you to die, Papa," he said through his tears. "It's not fair. You're only seventy-three. My friend Todd's grandpa is eighty and his great-grandpa is ninety-nine. They're both still alive."

Tom smiled down at him. "You know, Forty-Nine, someone once told me that it's not about the years." He paused. "It's about the miles. I may only be seventy-three, but there's a lot of miles on this body."

"Are you saying you want to die?" Jackson pulled back from him.

"No, but whether I like it or not, death is going to come anyway. I didn't want your Nana to die . . . but she did."

"That's not fair either."

"I know it isn't. Sometimes this world can be very unfair. But death . . . and sadness are unfortunately a part of life."

"I wish they weren't," the boy sobbed, and Tom pulled him close again, looking out over the creek.

"Me too, son. But there aren't any guarantees. That's why you've got to grab hold of the wheel and live every day to the fullest." He paused. "I am going to die, son, and I wish that weren't the case. But while I'm still here, let's you and I do something, OK?"

The boy pulled back and looked at his grandfather. "What do you want to do?"

"*Live*," Tom whispered. "I want to *live* . . . right up until I'm gone."

Fresh tears filled the boy's eyes, but he finally nodded his agreement. "Yes, sir."

For several minutes, the two McMurtries sat side by side in silence. Finally, Jackson looked up at Tom. "Hey, Papa."

"Yeah, Forty-Nine."

The boy choked back a sob and gritted his teeth, but he managed to get the words out. "Merry Christmas."

"Merry Christmas, son." Tom looked up at the sky, which was beginning to darken. "We best get back to the house before your mom calls the police."

The boy wiped his eyes. "Can we do one more thing first?"

"What?" Tom asked.

"Can you tell me the story about how Darwin Holt broke that player for Georgia Tech's jaw again?"

Thomas Jackson McMurtrie gazed into the courageous eyes of his grandson and smiled. Then, looking out over the creek where he'd fished with his own father as a boy, he spoke in a low voice. "Darwin Holt might have been the hardest-hitting football player I ever saw . . ."

EPILOGUE

Hazel Green, Alabama, four months later

The three men met, as agreed upon, at the northern end of the farm.

Powell Conrad brought a bag of vinegar-and-salt potato chips and a twelve-pack of Miller High Life. Powell still wore a patch over his eye, but his gait had improved and he no longer needed a cane.

Rick Drake brought a pint of Black Label Jack Daniel's, three shot glasses, and the same number of lawn chairs. He had taken the long way to the farm, stopping in Jasper to personally deliver a four-million-dollar settlement check to Mrs. LaShell Jennings. He'd also set a six-pack of Yuengling beer on Alvin Jennings's grave and, next to it, a pint of Bombay gin on Santonio "Rel" Jennings's tombstone. "We cut off the tail of the snake, Rel," he had whispered, kissing his hand and placing it on the concrete marker just as he'd done to Wade Richey's casket 120 days earlier.

Bocephus Haynes arrived last but brought the best tidings of all. As he approached the cemetery, a white-and-brown English bulldog ran out in front of him and greeted Powell and Rick.

All the men petted Lee Roy and scratched behind his ears. Then they sat in the lawn chairs and drank for a while in silence as the crickets chirped in the distance. Finally, Powell leaned forward and peered at Rick. "Was Mrs. Jennings happy with the settlement?"

Rick nodded. "I think she was more relieved than anything, but that money will help her provide for her children for the rest of their lives. It doesn't bring Alvie back, but . . ." He trailed off.

"It was the best we could do," Bo offered.

"I still can't believe we found that thumb drive on Wheeler with the recording of Kat and Sheriff Patterson," Powell said, and the other two nodded their agreement.

"Fitting, isn't it?" Bo asked, taking a long sip of beer. "The St. Clair Correctional Facility is where Jack Willistone spent his eighteen months. Now his widow gets to see what it feels like, but for a lot longer." He looked at Powell. "I wish I could have been there for the arrest."

"It was quite a sight," the prosecutor said, taking a sip of beer. "Sitting in that recliner in Bully Calhoun's jet, drinking champagne out of the bottle." He shook his head at the memory. "She was drunk as a skunk by the time she was cuffed."

"The criminal charges against Kat made everything about the wrongful death case against Bully's estate fall into place," Rick said, reveling in the memory. "A guardian ad litem was appointed to replace Kat as personal representative, and after talking with Lawson Snow down in Auburn, the guardian agreed that the case should be resolved."

"Four million, right?" Powell asked.

Rick nodded and took a pull off his beer bottle. "And though the evidence wasn't as strong in the Zorn case in Gulf Shores, the guardian still agreed to settle that one for a little over two million."

"That's pretty much the whole estate, isn't it?" Powell asked.

"More than half, and Bully had no heirs other than Kat. I guess at her death the state will get the rest."

"That's also fitting justice," Bo said. "Bully Calhoun spent his whole life lining his own pockets and, in turn, hurting the state of Alabama by encouraging the drug trade. Only right that the state eventually reaps the remainder of his fortune."

Rick opened the pint of Jack Daniel's and poured them all a shot. "To justice," he said, holding out his glass, which the other men toasted.

"Justice," Bo said.

"Justice," Powell agreed, his voice the loudest of all.

They turned up their glasses and then Lee Roy let out a low growl. There was a rustling sound coming from the south. "Who goes there?" Powell asked, pulling a pistol out of his pants.

"You boys mind if I crash your sausage fest?"

Powell let the gun drop to his side and smiled. "General?"

Helen Evangeline Lewis strode into the middle of the men. She wore a plaid flannel shirt tucked into tight jeans, and her jet-black hair was tied in a ponytail. "What are we drinking to?" She held out her hand for the pint of whiskey, and Bo passed it over.

"Justice," Powell said.

Helen chuckled and pressed the bottle to her lips, which were painted her customary crimson. "Justice," she said.

"I'm glad you could make it, General," Rick said.

"Well, thanks for inviting me. Seems like you're always inviting me to the party, Drake. If it weren't for your constant texts on the day of the showdown at the football field, I would have never made it to the farm to help out."

"And JimBone Wheeler would have had his reckoning," Powell said.

"Maybe not," Helen said. "But I'm sure glad I didn't miss that event." Then she turned to Bo and said in a teasing voice, "As for tonight, I would have thought that Mr. Haynes over here, him being from Pulaski and all, would have shown me the courtesy."

"I'm sorry, General," Bo said. "I should—"

"Forget it. I'm here now." She paused and, without prompting, took another sip from the bottle and gazed at the biggest tombstone in the cemetery. "I sure wish he was." Her voice cracked ever so slightly, and the men averted their eyes.

"To the Professor," Powell Conrad cried, taking the bottle and pouring himself, Bo, and Rick another shot.

"The Professor," they all said in unison.

"Tom," Helen whispered.

For a few minutes, they all stood around the tombstone. Below them, Lee Roy lay at the foot of the grave.

"So, Mr. Drake," Helen finally said, taking a beer from the cooler Powell had brought. "What's next for you?"

Rick peered down at the ground. "Now that the Jennings and Zorn cases have been settled, I'm going to close the firm."

"Really?" Powell asked, the surprise in his voice palpable. "You're gonna shut down McMurtrie & Drake?"

Rick squinted through the growing darkness at his friend. "It just . . . doesn't feel right there without him. Especially now . . ." He gestured toward the headstone with his beer.

"So what are you going to do?" Helen asked.

"I'm going home to Henshaw," Rick said, nodding to himself as if he'd just decided. "My mom and Keewin need help with the farm, and . . . if it takes the rest of my life, I'm going to find out who killed my father."

Helen took a step closer to Rick. "Let me know if I can ever help you on that score, OK?"

"Will do," Rick said.

Helen took a sip from the beer bottle. "And how about you, Mr. Conrad? You gonna keep putting bad guys away?"

Powell flipped a chip into this mouth. "No, I'm not," Powell said. "Don't get me wrong. I love being a prosecutor, but there's something the Professor told me after the Wilma Newton trial that I keep chewing on."

"What did he tell you?"

"That he thought I'd make a hell of a judge."

Helen smiled and touched Powell's arm. "You would." Then, turning to the last man in the group, she gazed into the haunted eyes of Bocephus Haynes. "And what about you, Bo? What's next?"

Bo sighed and looked at the tombstone. "I don't know, General. Right now I'm fighting for custody of my kids."

"Jazz's father hasn't relented at all?"

Bo shook his head. "If anything, old Ezra is fighting harder than ever."

"Where are you living now?"

Bo smiled. "Now that he and his family are back in their own home, Tommy's gonna let me rent the farmhouse for a while. At least until things settle down." He paused. "I'll probably move in next week."

Helen's eyes misted over as she, too, looked at the grave marker. "He would have loved that."

For a long moment, the voices stopped, each of them lost in their memories of the man they had come to celebrate.

"You've asked all of us, General," Bo finally said, "so it's only fair that you get the question. What's next for you?"

Helen's eyes narrowed and she took a few seconds looking at each of the men before returning her gaze to Bo. "I'm the district attorney general of Giles County, Tennessee." She turned up her bottle of beer. "What can I say? It's all I know." She leaned down and planted a kiss on the concrete headstone. Then she turned and began to walk away.

"General?" Bo said, and she stopped and looked at him over her shoulder.

"Would you mind answering one more question?"

"No."

"Why did you ask me to deliver JimBone's message to the Professor in the hospital?" He paused. "Why didn't you do it?"

Helen peered down at the ground for several seconds. Finally, she raised her head and met his eyes. "Because if Tom didn't make it to the farm, his grandson was going to die. I . . . *knew* you could get him there."

"How did you know that?"

"Because, after his family . . . Tom loved you the most, Bo. He loved you like a son."

Bo started to respond, but the words wouldn't come.

Helen made eye contact with each of them. Though tears now streaked both sides of her cheeks, she made no move to wipe them. "Let me know if I can ever help you gentlemen in Giles County."

As she strode back to her vehicle without waiting for a response, the three men watched her. Finally, Powell Conrad grunted. "That is one *hell* of a woman."

"No, dog," Bo said, regaining his composure and finding his voice. "That's the General."

Thirty minutes later, Rick, Powell, and Bo said their goodbyes at their respective vehicles, which were parked along the dirt road that led to the cemetery. "Now that you're moving back home, do you think you could finally get a decent car?" Bo teased Rick, and they all laughed.

Powell left first, making them both promise to stop in Tuscaloosa for beers and wings at Buffalo Phil's the next time they were in town. Rick and Bo agreed.

Then it was Rick's turn. "You take care of yourself, Bo," he said, climbing into the Saturn. Before leaving the farm, he rolled down the window and gazed up at his friend. "You know the General was right. He did love you like a son," Rick said.

Bo tried to respond but couldn't.

"I know things are hard for us now," Rick said, and his voice shook with emotion. "But if I learned anything from the Professor, it was to never quit." He stuck out his hand, and Bo clasped it. "Don't quit, Bo. Ever."

Bocephus Haynes smiled down at Rick. "Wide ass open."

Ten minutes later, darkness made its final descent on the Hazel Green farm. Bo sat in the lawn chair and drained the remaining shot of whiskey, while Lee Roy still lay at the foot of the grave.

Finally, Bo approached the headstone and put his hand on top of it, forcing himself to lower his eyes. He ran his fingers along the ridges of the name, and then, sucking in a ragged breath, he read the words out loud.

"Thomas Jackson McMurtrie. December 4, 1940, to March 3, 2014."

The cancer had taken him three months after JimBone Wheeler had failed.

Below the grave, Lee Roy whined, and Bo knelt down and rubbed the dog's ears. "I know, boy. God, I know."

And then, bowing his head, Bocephus Aurulius Haynes cried.

AUTHOR'S NOTE

I wrote this story for my father.

You see, Dad loved westerns and war movies. "Shoot-'em-ups," as he liked to call them. In his life, Dad was a banker, a farmer, a builder, and a developer. He lived big and he loved even bigger. He was known as Randy to my mom, his cousins, and his friends; Dad to my brother and I; and Papa to his four grandchildren. He was my hero, and he was larger than life.

He died on March 3, 2017, of lung cancer. At the time of his passing, my wife, Dixie, was also being treated for cancer, and she ended up having surgery to remove most of her right lung exactly a month after Dad died.

Many of you have asked about my courageous bride. Dixie has done well since the operation and has gradually regained her strength. Eighteen months out from the procedure, she is in remission, and we thank God every day for her progress. All that is left from her struggle with the Big C is the residual pain from the surgery, the regular PET and CT scans that she endures to make sure everything is stable, and last but not least, the scars. Physically, she has scarring from her chemo port, now long gone, and the incisions from surgery. Emotionally, she lives with the fear of almost dying and the anxiety of what lies ahead. She does all of this with a brave face and never complains. I am in awe of my wife's strength and grace.

As for me, I struggle with guilt and loss. I liken it to what a plane crash survivor must feel. My family is now almost two years out from the crash, doing well and getting our life back together. But one of us didn't make it.

I miss my dad. As Bocephus Haynes told Tom at the end of *The Last Trial*, Dad was "my guy." He was who I turned to for advice and direction. He was also the reader I most wanted to please with my stories.

So much of the character of Tom McMurtrie was inspired by Dad. Tom's mannerisms, dialogue, love of bulldogs, and yes, his affliction with cancer, were all motivated by my father.

Because of the storm our life had become at the time of his death, I never really had a chance to mourn Dad. I've heard it said that writing can be good therapy. Well, I'm no psychiatrist, but I think I mourned my father by writing *The Final Reckoning*. And now Tom, like Dad, is gone too. But their legacies will hopefully live on.

That is one of the themes of this story. Legacy. Of leaving something behind greater than what you are. My father's legacy was twofold, beginning with his family. He was an only child who married his high school sweetheart, my mother, and they had two sons and four grandchildren. Family was the most precious and sacred thing in his life. The other part of Dad's legacy was his determination to succeed in the face of adversity. As one of the men who gave his eulogy said, and which I borrowed for this story, Randy Bailey stared challenges in the face and always said, "We can do this."

What will be the legacy of Thomas Jackson McMurtrie? Only you can answer that question, and isn't that the joy of reading? A story can mean different things to different people. That is one of the main reasons that I read. It is also why I strive to write.

Thank you for reading this story. And though I don't want to spoil any of the surprises for what the future holds, I'll tell you I'm hard at work on the first book in a new series. One that will have some characters you know, and a few that you don't. A story that I hope will be, in the words of a certain attorney from Pulaski, Tennessee . . .

"*Wide ass open.*"

Robert Bailey
October 14, 2018

ACKNOWLEDGMENTS

My wife, Dixie, has fought her way back to health after surviving lung cancer last year. None of my stories would have ever been published without her encouragement and support. I love her so much and am so grateful for her.

Our children—Jimmy, Bobby, and Allie—continue to inspire me to write, and I'm so proud to be their dad.

My mother, Beth Bailey, is always one of my first readers, and her ideas and support have helped my writing beyond measure. She has been through hell these past couple of years, dealing with Dad's death and helping us with Dixie's fight and recovery. Through it all, she has been the rock and cornerstone of our family. I don't know what we would do without her.

My agent, Liza Fleissig, has been my partner in crime these past six years and has helped me go from wanting to get published to becoming an author. I am forever grateful for her efforts and persistence.

Thank you to Clarence Haynes, my developmental editor, for his expertise and passion. Clarence makes the editing process fun and exciting. I am forever thankful for his guidance, which has improved my stories.

Thanks also to Megha Parekh, my editor with Thomas & Mercer, who has taken my stories to new heights that I couldn't have imagined when I first daydreamed about writing a story about a law professor trying a case.

To Grace Doyle, Kjersti Egerdahl, Sarah Shaw, and my entire editing and marketing team at Thomas & Mercer, whom I am so proud to work with and call my publisher, thank you for your support and for expanding my brand.

My friend and law school classmate Judge Will Powell was also one of my earliest readers, and I admit that many times while I'm writing, I try to gauge what "Powell" will think of the story.

My friend Bill Fowler has been an important sounding board for ideas and has greeted my stories with enthusiasm and excitement. One of my favorite moments in the process is delivering Bill an early draft and waiting to hear his thoughts, which are always insightful.

Thank you to my friends Rick Onkey, Mark Wittschen, and Steve Shames for being early readers and providing me with constant encouragement.

My brother, Bo Bailey, has also been one of my earliest readers and supporters on this writing journey, and I am grateful for his calm and steady presence.

My father-in-law, Dr. Jim Davis, is my proofreader with respect to firearms and has been a consistent source of positive energy throughout my writing journey.

My mother-in-law, Beverly Baca, does so much for our family, and her energy and resilience are an inspiration.

My wonderful friends Joe and Foncie Bullard, from Point Clear, Alabama, were two of the first people in the boat on this writing voyage, and their support has helped me reach many new readers.

A special thanks to everyone at my law firm, Lanier Ford Shaver & Payne PC. I am so grateful for the support of my colleagues.

I also want to thank all of the readers, friends, and colleagues who have reached out to me and provided encouragement during the past two years as my dad and Dixie both battled lung cancer. There aren't adequate words to express how much your support has meant to me and my family.

Finally, though we lost him in March of 2017, I want to thank my father, Randy Bailey. I love and miss you, Dad.

ABOUT THE AUTHOR

Robert Bailey is the bestselling author of the McMurtrie and Drake Legal Thrillers series, which includes *The Final Reckoning*, *The Last Trial*, *Between Black and White*, and *The Professor*. The first two novels in the series were Beverly Hills Book Awards legal thriller of the year winners, and *Between Black and White* was a finalist for the Foreword INDIES Book of the Year. For the past nineteen years, Bailey has been a civil defense trial lawyer in his hometown of Huntsville, Alabama, where he lives with his wife and three children. For more information, please visit www.robertbaileybooks.com.